The Sisters Mortland

The Sisters Mortland

Sally Beauman

HarperCollins*PublishersLtd*

Published by HarperCollins Publishers Ltd.

The author gratefully acknowledges permission to quote from the following: "Time and Again" from *Selected Poems* by Rainer Maria Rilke, translated by J. B. Leishman and published by the Hogarth Press. Used by permission of St. John's College, Oxford, England, and The Random House Group Limited.

Originally published in the United Kingdom as *The Landscape of Love* in 2005 by Little Brown, an imprint of Time Warner Book Group, UK.

First Canadian edition: 2006

HarperCollins books may be purchased for educational, business, or sales promotional use through our Special Markets Department.

HarperCollins Publishers Ltd
2 Bloor Street East, 20th Floor
Toronto, Ontario, Canada

M4W 1A8

www.harpercollins.ca

Library and Archives Canada Cataloguing in Publication

Beauman, Sally
The sisters Mortland : a novel / Sally Beauman. — 1st Canadian ed.
Published in United Kingdom under title: The landscape of love.

Trade Paperback: 0-00-200627-8
Casebound: 0-00-200754-1

I. Title.

PR6052.E31135S58 2006   823'.914   C2005-905456-5

RRD 9 8 7 6 5 4 3 2 1

Printed and bound in the United States
Book design by rlfdesign

[CONTENTS]

Contents

CONTENTS

Time and again, however well we know the landscape of love,
and the little churchyard with lamenting names,
and the frightfully silent ravine wherein all the others
end: time and again we go out two together,
under the old trees, lie down again and again
between the flowers, face to face with the sky.

—"Time and Again," Rainer Maria Rilke,
Selected Poems, translated by J. B. Leishman

When I had finished my prayers and invocations to the communi-
ties of the dead, I took the sheep and cut their throats over the
trench so the dark blood poured in. And now the souls of the dead
came swarming up. . . . From this multitude of souls, as they fluttered to and fro by the trench, there came an eerie clamour. Panic
drained the blood from my cheeks.

—Homer, *The Odyssey, Book XI,* translated by E. V. Rieu

PART I

Five of Cups

WYKENFIELD, SUFFOLK

(*Pop: 102. Industries: agriculture.*) Picturesque and idyllic hamlet, on the south bank of the River Wyke, with a fine thirteenth-century church, dedicated to Saint Etheldreda, foundress of Ely Abbey (*rood screen original; fragments of an early fresco, The Day of Judgment, north wall of nave*). Observe the Tudor and mediaeval cottages (*No. 29 in the Street of especial note*) and the Green Man (*overlooking village green and pond; exuberant half-timbering; the fine pargeting depicts a fox and goose*). The Rectory (*1814, an elegant example of its period*) is adjacent to the village school (*1879, undistinguished*) and the Almshouses (*in the cottage orné style, by a pupil of Nash, endowed by the Mortland family [q.v.]*); all are worthy of inspection.

WYKEN ABBEY *(one and a half miles to the north of the village; extensive grounds)*

The convent was founded in 1257 by Isabella de Morlaix, heiress, cousin, and friend of Winifride of Ely (*q.v.*). To the anger of her powerful family, Isabella rejected marriage and chose the religious life, becoming Wyken's first Abbess in 1258, at the tender age of twenty-two. The Abbey, under the protection of the monastery at Deepden, flourished until the fifteenth century, when its influence began to decline. By the time of the Act of Suppression less than a dozen nuns remained; they finally dispersed in 1538. Their lands were then confiscated by the Crown, passing to Sir Gervase Mortland, a henchman of Henry VIII, in recompense for his role in the vicious suppression of the Pilgrimage of Grace; much of the Abbey was subsequently destroyed. The remaining buildings were occupied by tenant farmers, being finally abandoned in the mid–nineteenth century. In 1919, they were saved from dereliction and restored by Henry Mortland, formerly of Elde Hall (*q.v.*), near Framlingham.

(*Fair state of preservation to some parts of the mediaeval convent structures; extensive demolition, questionable additions, unsympathetic rebuilding, and modern excrescences elsewhere. The cloisters, refectory, and part of the Lady Chapel (thirteenth century) still remain. The moat that surrounded the nunnery enclosure has been drained. The Squint or hagioscope (c. 1450) in the south corridor is quaint, and unique in the county; the reasons for its irreligious placing are unknown. An underground passageway linking the convent to a small edifice in the adjacent Nun Wood is mentioned in diocesan documents of the fifteenth century; it attracted ecclesiastic controversy and was later razed to the ground. The ruins of a stone structure are still detectable, but its original purpose—possibly contemplative—remains obscure.*)

Present owner: Mr. H. G. Mortland. Private house. Not open to visitors.

—K. M. James, *The King's England Guides, Vol. VI: Suffolk* (revised), 1938

God showed me this place. When I first saw it, I knew it to be holy. I was weary from the journey, but I dismounted, and kissed the ground. The masons say they will begin building next Lady Day. I have advanced them a half-year's wages. Tell me, Sister of my heart, was that unwise?

—*The Letters of Isabella de Morlaix to Winifride of Ely, 1257–1301*,
edited and translated from the Latin, V. B. S. Taylor, 1913

ONE

Summer Maisie, 1967

WHEN WE FIRST CAME to the Abbey, it rained for five days. Nonstop. I'd been warned that this could happen in England, in spring and in summer, but I hadn't believed it. Every morning, we'd sit in silence at breakfast. Gramps hid behind his newspaper; my sisters fixed their eyes on their plates; my mother stared at air. I had to be propped up on three cushions to reach the table. Outside the windows was a wet, grieving world.

The laurels by the house hadn't been cut back then, and they dripped dismal black tears. Beyond them, you could see a corner of the old cloister, with a gargoyle spouting rain from mouth and eyes. The lawn had reverted to pasture, and the grasses bowed their heads like a congregation of penitents. The English air was a thick, peculiar mauve. The wind keened: The ground under the beech avenue was littered with broken limbs. I could see a severed arm, a giant's thighbone, and a terrible stump of a head, knotty and twisted round with ivy. It had two huge eyes. I knew they were watching all that grief seeping into the house. They were measuring the damp that fingered the walls and counting the drips from the ceilings—three buckets in that room alone. The wind gusted and moaned in the chimney. The windows rattled. "Well, children," Stella said in a wry way that meant trouble, "there is no possibility of taking a walk today."

She made the same remark, after the same interval of time, every day
for five days. On the sixth day, she took to her bedroom and locked the
door. We tried the usual remedies: flowers, fiction, and food. Julia took
up a tray. Finn took her a bundle of books. I took her a bunch of bluebells (*Hyacinthus nonscriptus*), which Finn helped me pick in Nun
Wood. We made a regular check: Three days later, they were still there
outside the door.

The sun had appeared by then. Stella had refused to sleep in the
large room she'd once shared with Daddy. Instead, she'd selected a
mean little space on the attic floor, where the nuns' dormitories
once were. The long corridors there were hot, dark, and stuffy
smelling. The water in the jam jar had evaporated; the bluebells
had doubled up and died. The packet of cigarettes was unopened,
the emergency tot of Jack Daniel's was untouched, and the tiny
triangular sandwiches had curled. Finn counted and checked the
books. Six in total: *Little Women, Mansfield Park, Jane Eyre, The Secret Garden*, and *Great Expectations* were still there, but the sixth—I
think it was *Kidnapped*—had gone. "Progress," said Finn. She
pressed her ear to the locked door, and we all listened intently. The
air in this house is odd, as you know—it has a weighty, brooding
quality, and we were more aware of it then, when we weren't yet
accustomed to it. So as we listened, it felt as though it listened right
back—and that was weird.

After a while, Finn claimed she could hear the rustle of pages. A
relief. We went off to explore. We investigated the library; it was a
moth-eaten place then—even more so than it is now—and Gramps
said that it used to be the nuns' Lady Chapel. Where the fireplace is
now, there used to be the altar—did you know? We tried the famous
Squint—and found it worked with amazing efficiency. We didn't notice what's so odd about it—not that first time. Then we set off to
map the gardens and the woods and the village and the orchards and
the lake and Black Ditch—

"Did *you* hear the pages rustling?" Lucas asks, interrupting me just as I'm getting going. He looks up from his sketchbook, pencil poised. I steal a quick, squinty look at the page in front of him: twelve inches by fourteen, a satisfying, heavy-woven texture. There's a maze of scribblings, of cross-hatchings, and those shadowings Lucas creates by smudging with his thumb. Out of these blacks and whites, I, Maisie, am being born.

I'm not supposed to look at my portrait while it's in the making; Lucas catches my crafty glance and tilts the sketchbook away out of view. I consider his question. It's hard to remember: It was over ten years ago. I was very little then. It's momentous to lose your father. I didn't truly realize that I had lost him: Every time a door opened, I expected him to walk in.

So in my memory, all the events of that first summer at the Abbey are flurried. They're bright and distinct, like the images on playing cards, but if I try to look at them too closely, it makes me anxious. I feel that some are missing, or the conjuror dealing them has kept certain cards up his sleeve. He shuffles magnificently, the way Dan's grandmother does—but there's sleight of hand involved. Something tricksy is going on.

I concentrate on the locked door and the curling sandwiches. I can smell the musty scent of the Jack Daniel's. Finn and Julia are crouching either side of me. A trapped fly buzzes at a window no one has opened in decades. I think I did hear a rustling sound eventually, and it might have been pages turning. Equally, considering where we were, and the nature of this house, the rustling could have had other origins. The nuns that once inhabited this place inhabit it still, I remind Lucas. They hang out in the upstairs corridors; they congregate on the stairs; their rosary beads clack and their skirts— yes—rustle. When you pass them, the sisters watch you in a pale, patient way, as if they're waiting for you to join them—and they seem certain they won't be waiting too long.

Dead and gone eight hundred years—but that doesn't stop them. Why don't they rest in peace, the way the dead are supposed to? I wonder why they haunt me, when all the people I'd welcome being haunted by—my father, for instance—have never showed up once? "Oh, come on, Maisie," Lucas says. "Stop this. It upsets everyone— and it's tedious. There is no afterlife. No heaven, no hell, no under- world, no God, no devil, no angels, no demons, no ghosts . . . In particular, and for the umpteenth time, there are no spectral nuns. You're a practical child. You know that perfectly well. Stop embroi- dering, and sit still."

Lucas is an unbeliever. Much he knows. He speaks sharply, though, so I realize I've irritated him—Lucas is easily bored. To pla- cate him, I sit as still as a harvest mouse (*Micromys minutus*), and after about fifteen minutes of silent work he relents. I knew he would. Lucas likes my stories. Everyone else at the Abbey is always too busy to listen. Not just now, Maisie, they say, backing away. But Lucas is an addict for information and I'm a good historian, so we make an excellent pair. Unlike Stella, I tell the truth; unlike Gramps, I stick to the point; unlike Finn and Julia, I don't dodge round awkward cor- ners and miss the best bits out. If you want to know about this house and this family—as Lucas certainly does—I'm the one to consult. I reveal secrets—and there are plenty of those. I may be a child, but I'm formidably observant, as Lucas knows. Tell it like it is, Julia says. And I do. I do. I do.

"So when did Stella recover?" Lucas asks in his usual lazy, teasing way. "Was Julia always beautiful? Was Finn always aloof? When did you first meet Dan? Who shot that lion in the library? Do you re- member America? Do you like milk in your coffee or cream?" He yawns, then glances up, eyes narrowed, measuring my face and mak- ing me. Two quick lines, a smudge of the thumb. I like Lucas. He likes me. I think he prefers me to my sisters, though I could be wrong. Anyway, we understand each other, and we both find that restful. He gives one of his small smiles.

"Come on, Maisie," he says in a coaxing way. "I want to know everything. Tell me more."

I like being Lucas's Scheherazade, and of course there's no fear of his executing me when my stories end. There is the danger of boring him, though, and I'm always aware of it. So I'm careful never to give him what he wants. This is a lesson both my sisters ought to learn, and soon. Also, his questions are less innocent than they seem. I sometimes think he's after some specific piece of information, though he'd never admit that. Today, I suspect, it's the lowdown on Dan that he wants. So I decide to give with my right hand and hold back with my left—if you keep Lucas guessing, if you always stay one jump ahead of him, then you don't lose his interest, I've found.

So I pretend to hum and hah, and juggle my memories. Then a memory does pop up, of its own accord, so I say that I'll tell him about Dan's grandmother, alias the wicked witch, alias the Munchkin (Julia's nickname for her; it's cruel, but she is very small).

"I'll tell you about the time she told our fortunes, about the day she read the cards for us," I begin. Then I hesitate. I can feel something cold and hard inside me, as if I've tried to swallow a pebble and it's too big. It's stuck in my throat; it won't come up and it won't go down.

Lucas is watching my face. His expression is kindly, though no one would describe Lucas as a kindly man. Sometimes I think he pities me, and I suppose there could be reasons to do so—stuck in this house with Gramps, who's getting doddery, and Stella, who inhabits a planet far, far from here; plus two sisters who are both legendary creatures of beauty and intellect. People fuss over me, but they won't listen. If the nuns didn't speak to me, I'd be starved of conversation.

I'm the girl in the corner, the one everyone ignores. I do not have breasts yet. Yes, I can see that in the pitying stakes I might score.

"Dan's grandmother—and she told the cards for all three of you? Did you hear what she told Finn and Julia, too?"

"I did."

"Was Dan also present?"

"He was."

"How old would you have been?"

"Let's see. . . ." I pretend to tot it up, though I know the answer perfectly well. I'm the afterthought in my family, the last-ditch attempt at a boy, so there's a long gap between my sisters and me. I was almost seven, Finn almost fourteen, and Julia sixteen. "It was Julia's birthday," I say. "That's why we went to see Dan's grandmother. We were consulting the oracle. Birthdays are a propitious time to do it. There was also a full moon."

"Powerful stuff." Lucas makes another delicate smudge on his page. At this rate, I'll be composed of shadows. *Yea, though I walk through the valley of the shadow of death, I will fear no evil*, says a familiar voice in my ear. *For thou art with me*, I answer silently.

"Sit still, Maisie," says Lucas. "Stop wriggling about." And he frowns.

Beside me, the Reverend Mother smiles. Isabella will be twenty-three in a few weeks: She has glass green eyes and a precious rosary made of jade. Her responsibilities are many, but she always has time for me. Touching my arm, raising a finger to her lips, she glances at Lucas and then steals silently away. Lucas the unbeliever sees nothing. Outside the windows, the sun shines. It hasn't rained in weeks. This is a golden summer, the best summer I've ever known. By the end of it I shall be translated, I feel certain. I'll cease to be a girl and become a woman. I shall emerge from my chrysalis, my wings damp but lustrous, Maisie transformed!

Lucas waits an interval and then says: "Okay—it's high summer.

There's a full moon. You go down to the village, and Ocean's daughter tells the cards. And what did the old witch promise the three sisters, I wonder? A sweetheart? A legacy? A voyage? I bet it was a sweetheart. A tall, dark stranger. Like me."

"None of those things."

"An unusual fortune-teller," he says in his dry way. His manner becomes businesslike, but I know I have his attention. It gives me a small, secret thrill. He angles the sketchbook so there is no possibility of my seeing it and says: "Now, Maisie, you can talk, but don't move your head from that angle. The light's perfect. Turn your face slightly to the left. Undo that top button. . . . Excellent. Clever girl. I'm all ears. Now, go on."

I think, All ears and all eyes, too. Lucas has as many eyes as Argus, and if one of them should briefly close, the other ninety-nine remain alert and watchful. When dealing with Lucas, it's advisable to remember this, so I do.

I try to relax into my pose. I try to concentrate and summon up the past. It's cool here in Lucas's improvised studio, and it is calm. This large room has a stone floor and a vaulted ceiling. It was built by Isabella in the thirteenth century and extended early in the fifteenth, when the Abbey was at the height of its renown. It was once the refectory, linked by passageways to the cloister and the main body of the convent, but those links disappeared at the time of the Reformation, so this part of the building is now islanded. It's quiet and secluded. I can just hear the sound of Julia's gramophone in the distance—she's playing that Jefferson Airplane record again—but that's only because she turns it up full volume. Apart from that alien thump and moan, the only sounds are England: the hum of bees, the rustle of elms, the bleating of this year's lambs. They're almost fattened: off to the abattoir any day now.

The refectory's six tall, arched windows face away from the house, toward the fields, the orchards, and the valley below. In the past, Stella used to closet herself away in this room. She needed to find herself, she said, and this beautiful and tranquil space was just the place to do it. Yes, it was cold in winter, but for someone brought up in Canada, English winters held no fears. They were brief, it rarely snowed—no problem! Then Stella rediscovered English damp, East Anglian damp, which is all-pervasive, which creeps into your bones. Then she discovered just what happens here when the wind swings round to the east, when it howls in from Siberia and sweeps toward the Fens.

The evidence of all Stella's searchings, all her short-lived vocations, is still here. There are the dried-up paints from the watercolorist spring; there's the sewing machine from the dress designer summer; there're the abandoned lenses from the photography period; and there's the clapped-out typewriter from the short-story-writer phase. That was the longest of the vocations and the last. Maybe Stella has finally found herself (I wonder how you do that?). Maybe she's given up looking. Either way, she avoids the refectory now.

Lucas has taken it over. He and Dan have just come down from Cambridge for the last time. They survived finals and arrived here, hideously hung over, the day after the Trinity May Ball. "It's the last long vac," Dan declared, "so let's make it a memorable one." Dan often stays at the Abbey now—he could stay with his father and grandmother in the village, but he prefers it here. He's encamped in his usual room in the main house and will stay till the end of the holidays. Lucas has visited before, but never for long—he never stays anywhere long—so this protracted visit is surprising. I don't think anyone exactly invited him, though I suppose Finn might have done. He's here for an indeterminate period. It could be the remainder of the summer, it could be less, it could be more. Lucas never makes plans—or if he does, he refuses to communicate them: He simply arrives when he feels like it and departs without warning or farewell.

I can accept this, because Lucas and I understand each other; but for Finn and Julia, it's hard.

He's not interested in creature comforts. He sleeps under an old army blanket, on a lumpy couch in the corner. He brews coffee on a paraffin stove. When he wants a bath, he swims in the river. When he wants food, which isn't often, he comes up to the house, charms Stella, and raids the larder. Stella is a fine cook, and she thinks Lucas is a genius—an impression Lucas does nothing to discourage, I've observed. On the table over there, under a muslin fly protector, I can see her latest offerings to the artist-in-residence: a slice of Madeira cake and a lopsided, golden pork pie.

It's had a bite or two taken out of it. Next to it, propped up on an easel, turned to face the wall, and hidden behind screens, is the portrait Lucas is supposed to be painting—his recompense for living here all summer scot-free. It's a gigantic picture of Julia, Finn, and me, and Dan says it's going to be Lucas's magnum opus—for this year, anyway. It's to be called *The Sisters Mortland,* which I consider a dull, stupid title. Lucas doesn't seem to work on it very often—though he may work on it at night.

I'm not sleeping too well at night. Sometimes the nuns disturb me; sometimes it's my dreams. And once or twice, when I couldn't sleep, I've crept out of bed and come down to the garden, and I've seen the lights in here, blazing away. Lucas closes the interior shutters, but there are six bright slits striping the ground outside, like golden bars. It could be that these sketches of me are preparatory work for the portrait, or they may be unimportant, something he does to pass the time. I'd like to ask Lucas if they matter and why they might matter—but I know he won't answer: He's a secretive man. . . . It takes one to know one, as Bella likes to say: I'm a secretive girl.

I think they must be important, because Lucas says he plans to complete four drawings of me this year. I'm sure that's an honor. It must mean that something about me interests him. The first drawing, *Spring Maisie,* was finished in the Easter vacation. *Summer Maisie* is the one he's working on now; *Autumn Maisie* and *Winter Maisie* will follow in due course. I'm not allowed to see them until all four seasons are finished. I'm not allowed to inspect *The Sisters Mortland* portrait, either—and neither is Julia or Finn. I've tried several times to sneak a look, but I've always been thwarted. When he's out, Lucas locks the windows and the door. He bought a new padlock for the purpose. "How paranoid can you get?" Julia says. Julia's just returned from a year's postgraduate study at Berkeley, California. It's affected her clothes and vocabulary. "Paranoid" is now a favorite word.

"Come on, Maisie, you're daydreaming," Lucas prompts. "Talk to me. Your face is getting set and fixed. This won't work if you look sulky. It's all wrong."

"I don't sulk," I reply. But I've heard the warning note of irritation, so I concentrate again. I'm beginning to wish I'd selected a different event to describe, but there's no getting out of it now. That round, cold pebble is still stuck in my throat. I frown, Lucas waits, the pencil hovers, and—obedient to him as always—I walk back into the past.

I watch the three of us set off, that afternoon, for the village. We take the path through the woods, something we rarely do. Julia is wearing a new white dress; it has paper nylon Bardot petticoats that make the skirt stiff and bell shaped. It has *broderie anglaise* around the neck. She's turned into a woman overnight, and she's so blazingly beautiful that it hurts my eyes. My sister Finn is wearing old clothes as usual: ancient slacks, a crumpled blouse, and sandals. She's slender and straight as a willow wand. I can tell what Julia's thinking—she's usually thinking about herself, so it isn't too hard—but with Finn, I can't. She's intricate, like a knot I can't undo.

My sisters stride ahead, arguing. I bring up the rear. I'm wearing brown linen shorts, chestnut brown Clarks sandals, and a white Aertex shirt that Finn's long outgrown. I've been reading the "Famous Five" books in secret (they're top of Stella's list of forbidden literature) and, like the immortal George of Kirrin Island, I want to be a boy. I whistle to the dog only I can see—we were between dogs that summer, just as we are now. I put my hands in my pockets and scuff my shoes. I count the trees and name them as I pass. I think I am happy; happiness is catching. After a while, Finn and Julia stop arguing, and Finn—who has a very sweet voice—begins to sing, first a madrigal, then, jiving about and laughing, Elvis's "Blue Suede Shoes."

We come out of the wood, and the heat of the sun hits us. The valley below us is burning gold. The hedgerows are thick with elderberries; thirty elms march in a long line down the lane. The apples in the orchards are ripening; the wheat ripples. God has arranged forty-one cows in perfect formation in Acre Field. There are larks overhead, so high that I can't see them, but I can hear them, piping alarm, filling the sky with nervous song. I breathe in the air of England; it's buoyant in the lungs and lifts my heart. Finn takes my hand; even Julia is elated. We start dancing, running, and jumping down the hill.

At the bottom, as arranged, Dan is waiting for us. He's grown tall since I last saw him—and that's over a year ago, I realize. He used to come to the Abbey every day, but now he seems to avoid the place—if there's a reason for this, I, as usual, have not been told. Even so, he and Finn remain close. She's been to Dan's house before, many times, but for Julia and me, this will be unknown territory—we've never got past the gate; Dan has always forestalled us and barred the way. We walk through the village. It's silent in the afternoon heat. Thirteen hens peck on the verge.

Nothing's changed here for centuries; I like that. Julia claims it's a bore. The ancient crooked cottage in which Dan lives is the last house on the left, facing south, exactly four hundred paces beyond the duck pond. The front entrance is never used, so we troop round to the back, where it's shady and the door stands open.

It's an old, low doorway. Dan, Finn, and Julia have to bow their heads as they enter. I follow, and after the dazzle of the daylight, I'm blinded, in the dark.

TWO

The Boy in the Glass

THIS COTTAGE HAS FOUR ROOMS—Finn's told me that much. Downstairs, the front room has to be kept spick-and-span because it's used for wakes. Dan's mother, Dorrie, was laid out in that room, wearing her white satin wedding dress and holding her white prayer book. The telegram of condolence Daddy sent is still kept there, Finn says. Dan's grandmother framed it, and it hangs in state over a fireplace that's never used.

That terrible death—Dorrie was only nineteen—occurred at the end of the war. Fourteen years seems a long time to leave a room unused, especially in a house as cramped as this one, but Finn says it's the custom, and besides, Dan's grandmother can be superstitious and pessimistic and always believes another death might be imminent, so it's as well to be prepared. I'd have liked to inspect this funereal front parlor, and Daddy's telegram, but that door is closed.

We are in the kitchen at the back, where the family cooks, washes, eats, and lives. Narrow stairs lead up to the two bedrooms above—they have to accommodate Dan's father, grandmother, and Dan. Before we came, I asked Finn where they all slept in that case, and Finn said Dan slept in his father's room, where else? When I pressed the point, she became flushed and angry. She said I was a nosy brat, that it was none of my business; that not everyone racketed around in a great barn of a place with twenty bedrooms. Twenty bedrooms most of which are unfurnished, mouse infested, and unusable, I could have replied. But I didn't. I saw my questions could be hurtful to Dan and that Finn was protecting him. Even so, I'm curious. Dan is tall, and his father is a giant, though a gentle one. Do they sleep in the same bed, I wonder—the marital bed, where poor Dorrie once lay—and, if so, do they sleep side by side or head to toe?

I'm also curious about washing facilities—basically, apart from the kitchen sink, there aren't any—and I'm very curious about lavatories. Finn says there's an outdoor WC in the garden, beyond the pigsty, and it's perfectly serviceable. Every estate cottage in the village has this arrangement—I do know that much—but I've never been in any of the cottages: The village women don't like us; they whisper behind their hands when we pass; they call us the "weird sisters," which is rude. So I've never experienced the joys of peeing in a little stone shed. I've been planning to visit Dan's on this occasion, but Finn's read my mind and she's already intervened. I'm not to pee during this visit. I'm not to want to pee or even consider peeing. The privy is off-limits. A visit there would be humiliating for Dan and perilous for me; it would incur punishment. I know Finn's punishments. They're implacable, immediate, and painful. So I'm not going to risk it.

"I've made tea," says Dan's grandmother when we've been in the room ten seconds.

I can feel Finn's eyes on my face. "Maisie won't have tea, just a small glass of water," she says hastily.

"Yes, please, water, Mrs. Nunn," I say, well drilled. Tea makes me pee.

We all stand around the table, waiting politely for Bella Nunn to sit down first. My eyes are beginning to adjust to the lack of light now, and the room is taking shape before me. It is every bit as strange and marvelous as Finn promised, and it's spectacularly dirty. But then

Dan's grandmother "does" for us at the Abbey and I've seen her cleaning methods, so this is no surprise. There are rolls of sluts' dust on the cracked linoleum, the sink is full of unwashed dishes, and the table feels greasy. Julia's worrying about her white frock, I can see that; her face is rigid with disdain. She hesitates before sitting down—the chairs are sticky—and with one slow, appalled glance takes in the spread on the table. There's a plate of fatty ham, sliced thickly and attracting bluebottles; there's lettuce, already doused with salad cream. There's a dish of beetroot and a slice of pie I recognize—purloined from Stella's larder and one week old. Slabs of bread and marge, a dry-looking, unnaturally yellow cake, and a slippery heap of hard-boiled eggs decorated with sprigs of wilting parsley. In the center is a pink blancmange in the shape of a castle, surrounded by a moat of tinned tangerines. It's three in the afternoon.

"Oh, Mrs. Nunn, you've gone to so much trouble," Julia says in a faint voice. "You really shouldn't have bothered. We've only just had lunch."

"Rubbish, I'm starving. This looks delicious," says Finn with a glare.

My eyes flick up to the doorway, where Dan is still standing. I catch on his face an expression of misery and shame so acute that I'm shocked to the heart. He turns away and examines the yard outside with studious interest, as if he's never seen it before. I notice for the first time that although it's the holidays, he's wearing his best suit, the one bought when he won a place at the grammar school. He's long grown out of it. A good two inches of shirt cuff are visible. The shirt, a white nylon one, is freshly washed. His lace-up shoes are brilliantly polished. He's been shorn. Last time I saw him he had a Brylcreemed teddy-boy forelock; but I think his school objected. Now there's been a violent haircut, a short back and sides that make him look like a Borstal boy. There's a rash on his neck. Finn says he's begun shaving, but if so, the process has gone awry.

"Gran made the cake specially. Won't you sit down, ladies?" he says, turning back to us but not looking at us—and I realize it's the first time he's spoken since we met in the lane. His voice has altered as cruelly as his appearance: Its pitch is uncertain, and his vowels have been ironed. I think he's practiced this terrible remark and the wooden gesture that accompanies it. He's tried to scrape Suffolk out of his voice; he's killed off that odd, graceful Romany lilt that he learned from Ocean as a child, a lilt you could hear when he was excited or pleased. What is left is a sad amalgam: his grandmother's odd Cockneyish intonation mixed with grammar school genteel. I think maybe he's trying to imitate his village friend Nicholas Marlow (now at Winchester) or possibly Nick's mother, she who occupies the Old Rectory, she who runs the Women's Institute, she who could patronize God, Julia claims.

Bella Nunn places a large brown teapot on the table. She sits. We all sit. I accept huge helpings of hard-boiled eggs, pie, ham, Heinz-smothered lettuce, and beetroot, all foods I loathe. It pains me to eat animals. The beetroot bleeds. I fix my eyes on my bleeding plate, which is a Queen Elizabeth II coronation plate—Bella is a staunch monarchist and very keen on the royals. It's heraldic, gilded, and chipped.

I think: Oh, Dan, what has happened to you?

It was I who saw Dan first. No one in my family will ever accept that. They say I was far too young to remember. They say it's just another of my tedious tales. Finn, who's very jealous of her bond with Dan, is especially caustic about my claims. Julia, who can't stand him and never could—or so she likes to pretend, anyway—says, "God, Maisie, you're such a little fantasist, you know. Who gives a toss who saw him first anyway? He's the Munchkin's apprentice. He's her familiar. He comes with the Abbey, the same as she does. He's always been around."

This isn't true. I saw Daniel on the day of Daddy's funeral—and that isn't something I'd forget, is it? Am I likely to be confused?

It wasn't a funeral as such, of course—though I didn't understand that then. My father was a hero. At nineteen, he was flying Spitfires. He survived the Battle of Britain but later died in New Mexico, United States of America, where we'd gone, at Stella's insistence, to cure his lungs. He came back with us on the boat to England, packed in a small urn that was inside a reinforced box labeled NOT WANTED ON VOYAGE in Stella's hand. When we arrived at the Abbey, or "the ancestral dump," as Gramps dolefully calls it, the urn lived on the chest of drawers in Stella's room; it stayed there for months. There was a great to-do about the urn, and where it should be put, and what ceremony was appropriate. First it was to go in a niche in the church, next to umpteen other illustrious Mortlands. A stone was to be carved by one of Stella's artist friends (almost all Stella's friends are artists of a kind).

Then, no, a memorial window would be more in keeping, a window that would match the one opposite it, erected to the memory of a great-great Mortland uncle who died valiantly in some distant, forgotten war. Then it was to be the churchyard; then a special enclosure in Acre Field—a place Daddy always loved as a boy. Then it was the bluebell wood, because Stella claimed that his eyes, which we've all inherited, were precisely that shade of blue. And finally, when Gramps kicked up a fuss and said no son of his was going to end up where the blasted dogs got buried, it was the church again, but the budget had shrunk, so the stone shrank, too, and the great carved baroque statement of Stella's imagination became a small, neat, rectangular pigeonhole. It reads: GUY MORTLAND, DSO, DFC. 1920–1955.

On the great day when the urn would be put in its final resting place, we processed to the church: first Gramps and Stella, then Julia and Finn, then Bella Nunn and me. Bella, caretaker of the Abbey in our absence abroad, had been promoted. She was now housekeeper, cleaner, confidante, and nursery nurse. Bella had been devoted to my father, so she was there to pay her respects—also to be my warder, to make sure I didn't ruin the ceremony by fidgeting or sniffling or shaming the family in any way, however small.

In the church, we sang Daddy's favorite hymn: "We plow the fields and scatter the good seed on the land . . ." Then came some prayers from the rector and a very long poem, read by Stella, composed by Stella, and "polished" by some distinguished literary man, another of Stella's friends. The man of literature had promised to be there, but unavoidable business detained him in London. The villagers had been invited, but Gramps was so upset, he wrote the wrong date on the black-bordered cards; besides, it was harvesting time, so everyone was working and no one came. The church was empty, echoey, and cold; the pews were very uncomfortable. I was a chubby sort of toddler, and my legs were too short to reach the hassock, let alone the floor. Bella smelled of mothballs and kept my hand imprisoned tight in hers. I sat beside her tiny person and tried to remember Daddy, as Gramps said I should. But the memories would slip and muddle, and I could snatch only glimpses: arms held out, the smell of his skin, the time he coughed blood into his handkerchief and Stella cried. I may have imagined the last incident. I may have imagined all of it. I was only one and a bit when he died.

After a while I grew bored. I stared at Bella's curious shoes—stout and black, with scarlet laces. I stared at Bella's coat, trimmed with some dead animal fur that was rufous and snarled. I stared at her rings—numerous—and her jet necklaces—several strands. I stared at her wonder of a hat, which had the eye of a peacock's tail feather stuck in its black band. I fiddled with my prayer book and stretched and wriggled, until Bella, losing patience, gave me a sharp pinch on the hand. I fell still and silent; I lifted my eyes and looked round the church. I examined the Day of Judgment painting, in which jeering devils pitchfork a crowd of naked people over a precipice into the red fires of hell. I examined the marble Mortland Crusader, asleep on his tomb, and the brass plaque commemorating a Tudor wife: It had been polished so often, her head was erased. I inspected the memorial window to the great-great-uncle of the unknown war, then looked at the window nearest to me, the one that would have been Daddy's memorial window, had not money become tight in recent years.

It was made of clear leaded glass, set in panes. In the pane nearest to me, I saw a marvelous boy. He had wild black hair, black eyes, a straight nose, a wide mouth, and white, white teeth. He was wearing a small gold earring. His expression was one of ferocity and accusation. He was disembodied, without neck, trunk, or limbs. Having appeared, etched on the glass, he disappeared. He manifested, at intervals, three times. "I'll kill that boy when I get him home," Bella muttered as we were leaving. We were in the churchyard, and the boy, still ferocious but now with a body, neck, arms, and legs, had just reappeared from behind a gravestone. "I'll tan his hide," she said when she spotted him in the lane, dangling from the branches of an elm. He made a final manifestation when we were back at the Abbey. Suddenly there his face was, pressed to the library window, staring fiercely through the glass. Stella was handing round tiny sandwiches, Gramps was pouring sherry, Julia and Finn were playing on the lionskin rug, Bella was making up the fire. Only I saw him. The library is on the first floor; there is a thirty-foot drop from the window to the flagstones. The boy and I stared at each other for several minutes. Something was troubling him. He lifted a grubby hand and rubbed his eyes. Then I blinked, and he was gone.

That was Dan. I now know that he must have climbed a drainpipe to reach that window, though Dan claims he flew. And I've recently discovered why he was troubled—though he insists I imagined the tears. But such details don't matter. My view of Dan was fixed from that day onward. He's the boy in the glass. And although he's now greatly changed in most respects, to my eyes he is still the wild boy for whom I felt an instant affinity—the boy who's forever on the outside, looking in. Whenever I meet him, I want to say: Admit him now! Open the window! Unlock the door!

THREE

Ocean's Daughter Tells the Cards

"M ORE BLANCMANGE, MISS JULIA? I know you're partial to it," Bella says, heaping a great spoonful on her plate before Julia can say a word. Julia, whose loathing of blancmange is well known by all present, including Bella, can barely suppress a shudder. Bella, not without malice by any means, gives her a merry glance. Her small black eyes flash with amusement. "Swallow down that tea, girls," she says. "And Maisie, you'll have to have a sip. I'm starting with the leaves."

"Can't we have the crystal ball, Mrs. Nunn?" I say—I've been eyeing the ball longingly all through tea. It's on the dresser, veiled in a white silk handkerchief.

"No, we can't. Not first, anyways," Bella replies. "There's a right order and a wrong order. First it's the leaves, *then* it's the crystal, *then* the cards."

There's no arguing with Bella, who is both bossy and stubborn. Also short-tempered: If we rub her the wrong way, there'll be no fortune-telling at all—and we want Bella to tell our fortunes passionately, even Julia, who pretends it's all hokum. Bella has the Gift; she's told us this so often, and Dan has told us this so often, that we all believe it. The Gift comes down from Bella's Romany ancestors. "Some people inherit a house, or a hunchback," Bella will say to me. "Some people inherit a dukedom, or that himofilia, like them Russian princes. I inherited the Gift. How many children did Ocean have?"

"Fourteen," I'll answer. I'm well rehearsed.

"And how many got the Gift?"

"Only you. You were the one."

"I was the one," Bella will say beadily. "So watch out, Maisie. You can't pull the wool over my eyes. I see through walls and doors."

Now, she pours an inch of black tea into a cup and passes it to me. It's thick with leaves. I sip it carefully, under Finn's watchful gaze. I've promised Stella and Gramps that I'll describe the witch's den in great detail, so while Julia chokes down her blancmange, and we all wait for her to finish, I survey the room.

I already love it. I love its darkness and glitter. I admire the scarlet roses Bella has painted on the beams. I admire the mirrors framed in shiny tin that hang in the deep window recesses, hinting at and distorting the outside world. I like the many knickknacks, and the spangled ribbons strung from the dresser hooks, and the shiny brass pots, and the cushions on the bench by the black-leaded stove. They're covered in flowers and stripes and spots, scarlet and yellow, sunflower orange, leaf green and raspberry pink; there's one that I especially covet, sewn with tinsely stars. Best of all, and right next to me so I can inspect it closely, I like the ancestral wall.

It's set up like a small altar, with a shelf trimmed in scarlet flannel and a night-light candle glimmering away beneath the photographs, so the people come alive. There in the center, in pride of place, is Bella's mother, Dan's great-grandmother, the fabulous Ocean Jones. She's sitting on the sepia steps of a wooden caravan—the kind of caravan I've never actually seen but aspire to live in. It has a curved roof, huge wheels, a stovepipe chimney, and painted shafts for the shaggy piebald pony that's grazing nearby. In the doorway, in full Romany fig, is Ocean herself. No question about it: She's superb. First, she's fat; second, she's craggy; third, she has dark, dark eyes that are fixed on the beyond. She's wearing long embroidered skirts, several layers of them, a waistcoat, a billowing blouse, umpteen necklaces (*that's* where Bella gets it from), and a head scarf trimmed with coins, fixed low upon her brow. Her white hair—which she never cut, just as Bella claims never to have cut hers; it is very bad luck— is worn in a plait as thick as a horse's tail. It hangs over her shoulder all the way to her waist. She's wearing a man's boots and holding a man's pipe—and there are men in the photograph, standing either side at the foot of the steps, but they're dwarfed by Ocean's presence. There's no doubt who rules this clan, I think. It's the first time I've understood the word Finn's used of Ocean: matriarch.

Ocean died in 1949, when Dan was four—I know that, Bella's told me often enough. She foretold her own death and prepared for it with care. In those days, the Gypsies still came to this part of Suffolk every year, often at harvesttime, when there was casual work to be had. They made their encampment in bender tents down by Black Ditch and sometimes remained there through the winter. Then they moved on. North, south, east, west: England was theirs. They'd visit cities—they'd always done stints in cities, Bella says— but they preferred to sleep in fields, under stars. They went as far north as Yorkshire, where people were *tight*, and as far south as Dorset, where they had a more liberal hand. They attended fairs the length and breadth of the country. They made pegs and patchwork, tools and ornaments, which they sold. They picked hops in Kent, dug potatoes in Lincolnshire, collected scrap iron everywhere, and had an annual pitch in London's East End. Bella nearly married a pearly king, she says, a king so charming, so gifted with the gab, that he could wind her around his little finger. She met him at Epsom, on Derby Day. He had thirty thousand pearl buttons on his king's suit. The Eye of God was emblazoned on the back of his jacket; there was a sun and moon on his lapels. Bella took one look and *fell*. But Ocean didn't like the cut of his jib, so in the end Bella saw sense and married Dan's grandfather instead. Dan's grandfather was a *steady* man, just as Dan's father is—and, Bella says, a *steady* man is what a woman needs.

It had been Ocean's wish that she might die here, down in the fields by Black Ditch. She was particularly devoted to Wykenfield and had many friends here, not to mention a daughter, namely Bella, who'd married out but of whom Ocean remained fond. It wasn't to be. She gathered the ninety-six members of her immediate family around her and died, on the stroke of midnight, near Scunthorpe (a location that could be improved on, I feel). According to Roma custom, the caravan was burned only when the male head of the family died, but in Ocean's case—in view of the Gift, her willpower, and the force of her personality—an exception was made. This very caravan, torched within hours of Ocean's death, was, in a sense, her funeral pyre.

There is no photograph of that great event, alas. I have to make do with pictures of Ernest Jones, Ocean's husband, one of the legendary Gypsy Joneses and therefore distinct from more common or garden people who bore that name, Bella's explained. I peer at clusters of Oceanic daughters, trying to pick out Bella among her swarming sisters. And I stare at Ocean's wild boy-children, with their bare feet, ragged clothes, and swaggering princely good looks. I can't really believe they belong in this century, but then all these pictures were taken before the war, and—Gramps says—prewar is another world. Where are these princes now? I wonder. Are they still alive? Are they still Romany? Are they still traveling? I hope so. I look at their unshorn curls, thin limbs, and black-eyed gaze: Any one of them could be the Daniel I thought I knew, the Daniel I mourn.

I'm wondering where the photographs are of Bella's Suffolk

family—it's tribal, too. There are still four Nunns, vaguely related, in the next village; there are fifteen (Finn and Dan counted once) in the churchyard here. But there's no image of that steady man Bartholomew Nunn, Bella's late husband, or of poor Dorrie, her only child. There's no picture of Joe Nunn, Dan's father, either. (Dorrie married a cousin; as Gramps says darkly, there's a lot of interbreeding around here.) In fact, I realize, there's virtually no evidence of Dan's father in this room at all; it's Bella's domain. True, there is a framed certificate that states Joseph John Nunn won the East of England Annual Suffolk Horse Ploughing Match eight years running—I know this is a great achievement: Dan's told me so. And there is a shotgun on a rack on the far wall, and that's probably his or Dan's—but it could be Bella's. I know she both shot and snared rabbits as a girl, and unlike me, she has no respect for animals; they're walking food, that's all. If a chicken gets old or broody, she dispatches it with an ax: Chip-chop and into the pot, she cries. I once saw Bella decapitate one of Stella's chickens, and I can't forget it. Blood spouted from the severed neck; the headless chicken flapped round the yard for two long minutes. Her name was Miranda. She ate corn from my hand.

Dan clears his throat. "Better get a move on, Gran," he says in his awful new voice. And with an air of great ceremony, he produces a packet of cigarettes and hands it round. He's blushed scarlet, and his hand is trembling slightly. I wonder who the Woodbines are supposed to impress—Finn, presumably?

Julia gives them a look of immeasurable pity. "No, thank you, we don't smoke," she says in her prissiest voice.

"Oh tosh," says Finn, taking one.

Leaning across the table, Dan strikes a match and holds it out to her. For a second I see it flare in Finn's astonishing eyes. She and Dan exchange a look. It is like a knife, that look. It cuts them off from the rest of us; it hacks out a huge space in which they're completely alone. I feel shocked, though I don't exactly know why. I feel as if I've peeped through a keyhole, opened a locked door, and spied on the forbidden. It's the way you feel when you look down the Squint—and I don't like it. It makes me nervous, so I start to think about peeing, which I mustn't do. I think Julia notices the power of that glance, too, but Bella is the only one to react. She gives one of her small, tight, malicious smiles.

Bluish smoke curls in the air about the table, so it seems to shimmer. The stove is well stoked. The fug in the hot room intensifies. I'm beginning to feel a little faint and breathless—I expect it's the excitement. After rising to her feet, every inch Ocean's daughter now, Bella fetches the crystal and the cards.

Bella likes ceremony, and now that I'm older I can see that there was some theater, some fairground razzamatazz, involved. There needed to be a degree of buildup, so she played with us to begin with, examining our palms, tracing the lines on them, shaking her head, muttering, and giving enigmatic frowns.

"Now, *here's* a husband and a half," she says, turning Julia's palm this way and that. "Well, who'd have thought it! You're a dark one, and no mistake," she cries, examining Finn's. "Roses all the way for you, my darling," she says quickly, clasping mine. "See that cross on the palm? Pure luck, that is. All your life through." Neither Julia nor Finn has a palm cross. I feel proud. I crease up my hand so the cross mark deepens. No doubt about it, the lucky mark is there!

Next it's the tea leaves. We each have to swirl our cup around, then tip the liquid dregs into a special white china bowl. We pass the cups to Bella for her inspection. Again, she makes a great palaver of it, turning them this way and that—and it's then, or so I decide afterward, that something starts to go wrong. Either Bella can't read the leaves or she dislikes what she sees in them. She keeps picking up the cups and putting them down, and comparing them, and then comparing them again, until I think I'll die of suspense. "Unclear," she says finally. "They won't speak. They're resisting me. We'll try the crystal. Where's the birthday princess? You're first, Miss Julia. Come up here."

She and Julia go into a huddle at the end of the table. I'm beginning to feel hot and sick from all the horrible food. I can still taste sulfurous eggs and beetroot and blancmange. I want some fresh air. If I were less in fear of Finn's wrath, I might suggest a visit to the stone shed in the garden, but I don't dare. I try to fix my eyes on the Ocean photographs and the altar to the dead, but the images are starting to swim about and merge. The back door is still wide open, but no air seems to be entering. Bella is muttering and sighing; Dan has lit another cigarette, and the acrid smoke drifts across the table. It's aiming itself at me, and I can't understand why it does that, because the atmosphere is still and clammy and there isn't the least draft.

"Well, miss, you'll get everything your heart desires," I hear, and Julia, looking flushed and triumphant, returns to her chair.

Next it's Finn's turn. She bends over the crystal, and her hair falls forward like a veil. It's very frustrating: All I can see is Finn's thin brown arm and her mane of corn gold hair—unlike Julia's, it could do with a comb. I fidget about, but no matter how I try, Finn's been positioned so the crystal is invisible. I can't even see Bella's face, though I can hear her in an indistinct way. She's been muttering and murmuring for an age, and she seems to be getting agitated. Something is happening, certainly. The room feels darker and hotter, and there's a vibration, a perturbation, in the air. It's like the plucking of a string, like the reverberations afterward. It's the way the nuns announce their presence in the corridors—and I know I'm not imagining it because when I look at Dan, I can tell he's sensed it, too: He's paled.

"I see a sacrifice," Bella says, the words suddenly clear in the midst of the mumbo-jumbo. She sounds bewildered, or possibly afraid. She murmurs something indistinguishable—I think she's lapsing into Romany; then she makes an odd humming sound. It's like listening when Gramps tunes the wireless, half a sentence, two notes of music, snatches of song—all those voices concealed in the airwaves! But Bella is homing in on one particular station, I can sense it, and suddenly it comes through, loud and clear. "The second shall be first," Bella pronounces in anguished tones. Then she loses the wavelength, or maybe there's interference, for she pushes Finn away and covers her ears. Finn looks at her uncertainly—I don't think she's enjoying this—and Bella rallies. "And a great deal of travel," she says in a hollow voice. "I see a journeying. Many seas to cross, but safe harbor in the end."

"Book your passage *now*," Julia whispers as Finn sits down. Julia smiles—she's always envious of Finn, and I know she's delighted that Finn's future sounds less promising than her own. Finn ignores her. Her face is set. Did she even hear Julia? Did she see anything in the magic crystal? I long to know, but I can't ask: It's my turn.

"Now you, my little darling," Bella says, and I stand up. The sickly feeling at once intensifies. I position myself by Bella's chair. It all feels dreamlike. Bella makes me lean across the table so the crystal is hidden from Finn and Julia and only we can see it. She wipes it with the white silk handkerchief—very thoroughly, as if she's polishing a doorknob—then flicks the silk away. I look at her face, which seems odd, not like Bella's usual face at all. Her eyes are half-closed and rolled back so the whites are showing. She keeps cocking her head, as if someone's whispering in her ear. I look at the crystal. "Deep, deep," Bella murmurs. "Look deep into it, Maisie, right into its heart."

I look and I look. I'm expecting to see a scene from my future, very small, but like a film. The crystal is going to show me a story—or perhaps a face. Maybe I'll see the man I'm going to marry, I think, because when I stop being a boy I suppose I will marry—what else is there to do? Maybe it will show me my future children. I'd like to see them. I'd like lots, like Ocean. If I've got to have them, I want a tribe.

I start wondering if my children will inherit my eyes, as Dan inherited Ocean's. I start hoping they will, because then Daddy will live on forever. But although I'm looking closely, and concentrating hard, all I can see is my own reflection, a wavering Maisie. Around me, inside me, there's glass, clear glass, with a curious flaw deep in my crystal heart. This flaw is tear shaped. It's large. I find it has a hypnotic effect, that flaw. I stare, and I discover it can alter shape and formation like a cloud. I watch, and I see that it's swelling, gathering up other clouds and absorbing them. It's getting larger and thicker. The whole crystal is beginning to mist over and cloud up, until all I can see is one whirling white spherical swirl.

Finn stands up. I think it's Finn. I hear her chair scrape back. She says: *Maisie, what's wrong? Dan, stop this. Maisie isn't well.* I hear this distinctly, and at that point—though I know it's forbidden—I reach out to touch the crystal. It flies up to meet my grasp; then it plummets. I can hear the distant sound of smashing glass.

Before I know it, I start falling, too. I fall a very long way and land outside, in the small dark yard at the back of the cottage. I've landed in a curious position, with my head between my knees. Julia and Finn are fussing about somewhere, and Dan's brought me a glass of water. I drink it down thirstily in one great, reviving swallow. My stomach gives a heave and up it comes, all that bleeding beetroot and fleshy pink blancmange.

I feel restored immediately. It's shaming to be sick in public, but I don't care—I feel cleansed. Julia's moaning in disgust, of course, and worrying about her new white dress; she keeps a safe distance, but Finn and Dan are more practical. Finn fetches a bowl of water and a cloth, and Dan cleans me up. "There you are, Maisie," he says. "Clean as a whistle. And your color's coming back. Always better out than in." I'm grateful to him for being so cheerful and businesslike, but I'm worrying about the crystal. I know I smashed it. "Don't you fret about that," Dan whispers. "Accidents happen. Plenty more where that came from. There's another nine in the kitchen cupboard. Gran likes to keep a good supply."

His old voice has returned. He gives me a hug, and I find that comforting—but I'm not certain I believe him. However many replacements Bella may have, I'm sure it's bad luck for everyone present when a crystal gets smashed. Dan lifts me up and carries me into the kitchen to say good-bye to Bella. He's reassuring and hearty—but he can't meet my eyes.

"Better call it a day, I think, Gran," he says as we reenter, with Finn and Julia crowding in behind us. But it's too late. There are shards of glass all over the linoleum, the teapot's upset and smashed, but Bella is still seated at the table, and she's spread out the tarot cards. She doesn't look up when we enter, she's so concentrated. She's moving them this way and that, feverishly fast, picking them up, slapping them down, altering the arrangement. The cards are very powerful—even more powerful than the crystal: Bella's explained this many times. I stare down at the table from my vantage point against Dan's strong, broad shoulder. I love these cards, with their beautiful enigmatic pictures, but you have to be skilled and wise to read them. What they seem to say and what they're *actually* saying can be opposite things.

Bella's using the Rider-Waite deck, her favorite. She's using the Celtic Cross spread. I can see some of the Major Arcana: I see the Lovers, I see the Tower (a dangerous card). I see the Hanged Man— I'm sure it was those cards, though I was looking at them upside down. The Empress is reversed; the Tower is reinforced by—oh, calamity!—the Five of Cups. Then Bella brings her fist down, smack, on the table. She spreads her fingers, gathers up the cards, then sweeps them on the floor, all seventy-eight of them. They tumble down in a flurry of colors, spinning this way and that. When they land, they all land facedown. All of them, every single card in the pack, facedown—except for one.

We stare at that one card in silence. I can sense that Finn and Julia are spooked. I can feel the tension in Dan. I feel odd and light and unworried. I listen to the world outside. I can hear a tractor in the distance. A child cries for its mother. My hearing's so acute. I can hear the elms growing. I can hear the larks singing half a mile away in Acre Field.

Finn bends down and, before Bella can stop her, reaches out to the one card that's facing upward. "Don't touch it—oh, Finn, don't," Julia whispers, but Finn ignores her. She flips the card over, so we can't see that frightening picture anymore. Then she rises, turns back to Dan—and that look happens again. For one second, I think he'll have to kiss her; but he doesn't.

Finn takes me in her arms. "Come on, Maisie," she says gently. "You're tired. It's time to leave."

At that point, Bella recovers. I can see her making a huge effort. She cranks herself up. She becomes brisk and rings down the curtain. She stops being Ocean's daughter. She reverts to Dan's gran, chief meddler and general factotum at the Abbey. She says it's time for Dan to get cracking with the brush and dustpan. She says she could do with forty winks. She says we've worn her out; she says that's more than enough jiggery-pokery for today and more than enough hocus-pocus. . . .

"I blame that pie," she says, regarding me sidelong. "I had my doubts about the pie from the start." She gives my arm a sharp pinch. And sends us home.

There, the nuns are waiting for me: I see them clearly for the first time. Welcome, Sister, says Isabella, and she lets me hold her rosary. Five decades of jade beads, single silvers for the Paternoster, mined in the Orient and powerful with prayers.

Made for my hand: Each bead fits snugly in that cross on my palm.

FOUR

Mixed Doubles

M Y HOUR IS UP.

"Well, well, well," Lucas says, putting down his pencil. Lucas has been listening intently to this episode in our history, but I'm not sure he's understood it—or enjoyed it. This may be because, being an unbeliever, he doesn't take such events seriously—a mistake, in my view. But I suspect he disliked one aspect of it. It was unwise to have mentioned that look, I feel. Sometimes I think that Lucas, for all his gifts and alleged genius, is jealous of Dan. They're friends, but there's an edge to that friendship that I don't understand.

They met up in their first Michaelmas term at Cambridge, when they had rooms on the same staircase at Trinity, and they've been like brothers ever since. Julia moved on the fringes of their set while she was at Newnham, but she was a year ahead of them and never as close a friend as Finn has become. Lucas and Dan adopted Finn the second she arrived at Girton. They became famous as the "gang of three," as the "Unholy Trinity"; they became inseparable. So Lucas must be envious of Dan rather than jealous, I decide. He's certainly envious of Dan's glorious ancestors, and who wouldn't be? I am.

"Just one card remained face-up?" he says, closing the sketchbook before I can sneak a look at it. "I think I can guess which card that was."

"I'm sure you can," I reply with irony. I dislike it when people underestimate my stories—it's presumptuous, precipitate, and irritating. So I tell him that, true to the card's prediction, my pet hamster died the following day. In fact it was two weeks later, but the cards can see a long way—years—into the future, and I feel a little adjustment is perfectly fair. In any case, as I know but suspect Lucas doesn't, the Death card doesn't indicate a death—or not of the obvious kind. That would be a very crude, immature, foolish reading, Finn says. The point is, we experience deaths all the time. There's the death of love, for instance; the death of hope or innocence—and the death of the heart. It can be these kinds of death that the card indicates. Shall I tell Lucas that? I decide I won't. Stories require symmetry and a good firm ending. "His name was Hamish, and he died in agony," I add. (Not strictly true, either. He just keeled over. Hamsters do.)

Lucas says that is truly extraordinary, that he has a new respect for Bella and her powers, etc., etc., but I can tell he's only humoring me. People are always humoring me; it's very tiresome indeed. "That's enough for now," he adds, glancing at his watch. "I'm going for a swim. This time tomorrow, okay?"

"I can't come tomorrow," I remind him. "We're all going to Elde. We're going to see the Viper. It's the annual visit. I told you. We'll be out all day."

Lucas gives a shrug. He's preoccupied by something, and besides, he's not interested in the Viper or our family crises—money means nothing to him. "The day after, then," he says indifferently. "Run along now, Maisie, there's a good girl."

I'm told to "run along" a dozen times a day. "That's fascinating, Maisie," Gramps said this morning when I was explaining prime numbers to him. "Tell me later, darling. The test match will be on in a minute. Run along now—I expect Stella could do with some help in the kitchen, don't you?"

And he was right: Stella did need my help. Stella values my assistance; she likes to know where I am; she likes me by her side. I skinned the tomatoes for her—dip them in boiling water and watch their skins shrivel, watch them curl. I skinned eighty-seven expertly and told Stella the story of Marsyas, who was flayed alive by Apollo. Stella had a headache; she seemed anxious and tired.

"That's such a cruel story, Maisie," she said, looking at her watch. "I'll finish those, darling. It's time you went down to the refectory. You mustn't keep Lucas waiting. Run along."

Now, Lucas stands in the refectory doorway, watching me leave. I'm supposed to go straight back to the house; that is the rule. But I told Stella that Lucas would be drawing me for two hours, not one—so I have sixty minutes of freedom. Three thousand six hundred seconds—the nuns don't approve. They shake their heads; they make tut-tutting sounds. Little girls shouldn't lie—and to lie to their mothers . . . Is there no end to this rebelliousness, this wicked guile?

I creep past them, averting my eyes. I make for the house, and then, when I'm past the cloister wall, so I'm sure Lucas can't see me, I double back. I have a plan. This house and this garden are so ancient, they have centuries of secret routes—and that knowledge is useful on occasions like this. There is only one path to his studio, as far as Lucas knows. It is flanked either side with huge, impenetrable walls of yew, and it's made of gravel. It leads directly from the cloister to the refectory, where it opens out into a small courtyard, also graveled. It then continues on, through the old convent gateway to the fields outside the nunnery's enclosure. It crosses a deep ditch, where the moat once was, and descends to the valley and village below. So anyone approaching his hideout from either direction will be seen or heard—or so Lucas believes. He always keeps one ear cocked for the telltale crunch of footsteps on gravel. Well, he won't hear them today.

The sisters who founded this convent were devout—so devout that they chose to renounce all contact with the outside world. But I'm not the only rebellious one. Some of their number must have rebelled, too, or been less devout than they appeared, because the nuns constructed secret entrances to their enclave—and two of those entrances, or perhaps exits, still remain. One is in the corner of the Lady Chapel, now the library, built into the paneling and leading to a flight of hidden stairs. The other is in the far corner of the cloister—and it's this one I make for now.

I pause, just to check no one's looking for me or watching, though it's only midday, so I'm sure I'm safe from alarm for a while. Stella will be in the kitchen, making lunch for the tribe. Gramps will be in the library, listening to the test match. Bella will have finished making beds and brushing dust under the carpets; she'll be on her way back to the village by now. I climb up onto one of the buttresses, which gives me a view of the whole house and the gardens below. This south front of the convent is three stories high; it has twenty-one windows, twenty-one eyes. They sparkle darkly. Those in the library, where I saw Dan materialize that day, are wide open. I can just hear that measured male voice that punctuates English summers: "And D'Oliveira steps up to the crease," it says. That's Gramps taken care of. No sign of Stella, and little danger from that quarter until the clock strikes one. Stella's making tagliatelle for lunch today. She'll be fully engaged ironing out sheets of pasta and feeding them through her latest acquisition, a fiend of a machine. Or she'll be reading at the kitchen table, as she likes to do while pots simmer. It's Jane Austen at the moment: *Mansfield Park* for the twenty-fourth time.

I look down at the gardens: I have plans for these gardens. Apart from the vegetable and soft-fruit section—looked after by Stella and Joe Nunn and flourishing—they're in a state of disgraceful neglect. In my mind, there's a pergola—I've already selected the roses to climb on it; there are wildflower meadows, an arboretum, and a parterre. I'm going to be a Horticulturist—and for that you need vision. A kind of double vision, perhaps. When other people look at the Abbey gardens, all they see is untamed nature, roses reverting to briars, bridal swathes of bindweed, seedlings in the paving, and so on.

My eyes are more clear-sighted: I see an orderly Eden. I shall start to create it this summer—next week, maybe. Soon.

Meanwhile: Where are Julia and Finn? Answer: Safely occupied on the old rutted grass tennis court, below me. They're playing a game of mixed doubles with Dan and his friend Nicholas Marlow. Nick is a junior doctor at a London hospital now. He has a week's leave and is staying at the Old Rectory with his parents, but he spends most of his free time here. He is partnering Julia. Dan is partnering Finn.

The match shouldn't take long in that case, and its outcome is inevitable, I decide. I assess the players: Nick plays a strong, reliable club game. Julia has a vicious serve and a mean backhand; she is fiercely competitive. Dan has moments of erratic brilliance but, unlike the others, has never had tuition—and it shows. Finn can run like Atalanta; she's extremely agile and graceful, so I love to watch her, but her motivation is nonexistent. It's just a game, she says haughtily: Who cares who wins?

Julia cares, for one. As I watch, she powers down one of her unkind topspin serves, aimed at Finn's unreliable backhand. To my surprise—I can scarcely see the ball, and on this court the bounce is always unpredictable—Finn gets her racket to it. She hits a lob—probably by accident, but it could be intentional, with Finn you never know—and it's a stroke of great delicacy. The ball sails upward in a slow, high, lovely curve. It sails over Nick at the net and over Julia, who stretches for it but misses. It's bound to go out, I think, but it doesn't. At the very last moment it appears to hesitate, to redirect. It lands on the newly painted baseline with a puff of white. "Love–fifteen," shouts Dan.

"Good shot, Finn," calls tall, dark–haired Nick Marlow. He's wearing traditional whites; he's more sporting a partner than Julia prefers. Julia scowls at the sun and says nothing. She's readying herself to serve again, this time to Dan.

I look at Dan, who stands on the baseline waiting to receive. His manner is nonchalant. Dan has been transformed by Cambridge, where he had a brilliant, much envied career. He plans to become a great film director. He no longer looks awkward or gauche, and he's handsome again—oh, that Romany rock-star look, Julia says in a cold, dismissive way, but I don't care what Julia thinks or pretends to think. To my eyes, Dan is one of Ocean's princelings again. He has grown his black hair long, so its Gypsy unruly locks touch his collar. He's playing tennis in a white cotton shirt and torn blue jeans. He's tall, tanned, muscular, and strong. He's not wearing sneakers, and his brown feet are bare. He looks at ease, capable of anything—and his voice has changed again, too. The Suffolk has disappeared totally, but the vowels are no longer painfully ironed. It's now impossible to place him. You can't put him in one of those English pigeonholes of region or education or class, as some people (the Viper, for instance) like to do. If you didn't know about his Roma ancestry, you might guess he'd been born Irish and blessed with Irish charm. If you did, Dan would never reveal that you were wrong.

Julia scowls at him, raises a golden arm, tosses the ball high, and smashes it down the center line. Dan doesn't move his racket. "Foot fault, I think, Julia," he calls in a lazy, provocative tone. Julia proceeds to double-fault twice. When she loses her temper, her game becomes more aggressive and her aim less accurate. Things aren't always the way I imagine they are, I remind myself, and—occasionally, not often—I read situations wrongly. Maybe this match will take longer than I'd anticipated—and maybe its outcome isn't so certain after all.

I watch my long-limbed sisters for a few seconds more, then remember my plan. I have fifty minutes of freedom left: I mustn't waste time. I jump down from the buttress and wriggle under a great tangled arch of brambles in the corner below it. I've hollowed out a little crawl space here, and it's not too prickly. Only one scratch: I lick the beading blood on my hand. Six feet in, I reach the part of the cloister wall that's now crumbling, where the door and the secret stairs must once have been. A wicked part of the Abbey: I hang by my hands over a steep drop, where the moat was. Then I let go. I fall ten feet, land on soggy ground, and roll over like a parachutist—no harm done. I creep along the length of the old moat, a deep ditch that follows the outer line of the cloister walls. I've made a good, well-trodden path here, concealed by long grass, elder bushes, and a tangle of hawthorn. Finally, I reach my perfect espionage point, a huge black yew (*Taxus baccata*) planted by my father as a boy. No one's clipped it since he died.

It's a good twelve feet thick and fifteen high. When I lie down under its black branches, I'm invisible—and I have an uninterrupted view of the refectory, its windows, and its door. I lie there, in heat and darkness. The scent of the yew is pungent. Yews grow well in graveyards, Bella says. They like the rich graveyard food. In the distance, a shotgun fires. Someone's after rabbits or pigeons; someone's on the hunt, on the prowl.

When I was little, Stella taught me that poems could cure nervousness. It's the concentration that's involved. *The boy stood on the burning deck, / Whence all but he had fled,* I chant. I move on to the intricacies of *Hiawatha.* I begin my favorite section, "The Ghosts." Its rhythms soothe:

> *Then the shadows ceased from weeping,*
> *Ceased from sobbing and lamenting,*
> *And they said, with gentle voices:*
> *"We are ghosts of the departed,*
> *Souls of those who once were with you.*
> *From the realms of Chibiabos*

Hither have we come to try you,
Hither have we come to warn you . . ."

Lucas emerges at last. He has a rolled-up towel under his arm—
so it was true, he did intend swimming. He steps out onto the gravel
and lifts his face to the sun. I think how thin and sharp and hungry
he looks, with his unkempt hair and his narrow, alert face. His odd
tawny eyes are set too close together; he resembles a hawk or a
kestrel—and, as they are, he's solitary. Lucas avoids the others. He
likes to be alone. He likes to hunt alone, too—or so I think. I'd like
to know *what* he hunts and why.

He closes the heavy refectory door, and—yes—padlocks it. He
puts the key in the pocket of his old, paint-stained trousers and
turns down the path to the valley below. He passes under the huge
arch where the nunnery gates once stood. The high boundary
walls that once supported this arch have crumbled away, and there's
now only a plank over the moat ditch. Lucas strolls across it and
disappears out of sight. I wait exactly five minutes and twenty-
eight lines more.

Then, when I know it's safe, I scramble out from the yew and
make for the windows at speed. I can't believe that Lucas would
close and lock all of them, not on a day as hot as this one, surely? All
I need is a tiny gap, just one of six left unsecured. I can be in and out
in an instant—and I'll see what Lucas has drawn in his sketchbook.
I'll see the Maisie that he sees. I want that so much, it's making me
breathless. I'll see his version of me—and I'll see his version of the
sisters Mortland as well.

The sun beats down on my head. A jet from the American air base
at Deepden screams past, low in the sky. It's hot. The plane's thunder makes the air reverberate, lightning flashes on its wing. I check
each tall window in turn. Every one of them is forbiddingly fas-

tened. He's closed the interior shutters as well. I inch along the window wall, craning my neck, pulling, and pushing—and then feel anxious. What if Lucas comes back? Suppose he left something behind and returned to get it? Better make sure.

I run across to the entrance arch. My gaze angles down the lane, across Acre Field. There are fewer hedgerows now. Mr. McIver, to whom Gramps sold the tenant farms and almost all of our land, has embarked on what he calls "rationalization." Acre Field is unaltered, and it's still pasture, but the five fields beyond it—they have gone. Nuns' Field, Grandage, Pickstone, Wellhead, Holyspring: I recite their names under my breath. Boundaries unchanged for centuries, and in one year efficient Angus McIver has obliterated them. He's created one vast, unhedged fifty-acre wheat prairie. The wild orchids in Wellhead will never bloom again.

I can see farther, though, now that the hedgerows have gone. To my right, I can see Nun Wood, which lies between the cloister ruins and Holyspring—it's overgrown now, but the path to the sinister building the nuns made there can just be glimpsed. To my left, I can see the river winding along the valley—and there's no sign of Lucas. Where has he gone?

I narrow my eyes and scan. The roofs of the cottages; the three new bungalows on the village outskirts; the Pines, where Colonel Edwardes rears his Heavy Hogs; the Old Rectory gardens; the Doggett brothers' apple orchards; Angus McIver's barns; the road . . . No Lucas anywhere. Then I spy him. He's chosen to swim in Black Ditch, perhaps because it's less polluted than the river. The river water used to run cool and clear, but it's now sluggish and patched with scum. Lucas isn't wearing a bathing suit—that could be another reason. Black Ditch is less visited than the river, where a few optimistic fools still fish from time to time.

I see a distant, white naked shape raise its arms, leap, and plunge. The water in Black Ditch is icy—and I'm safe. I run back to the windows, and what do I find? I find that Lucas has made an error. The third window on the left is closed, but its shutter is ajar. There's a dark, narrow gap, and if I climb on the sill and press against the glass, I can make out a pale shape propped against the largest of the easels. It's the portrait. It must be the portrait. Lucas must have been working on it. The screens have been removed.

I press my face tight against the glass. It burns my cheek. A blue-bottle buzzes by my ear. A freckled spider, spinning a trap between the astragals, retreats to the corner of its web. It watches me with re-fracting, jeweled eyes. Almost, almost: If I can refine my angle of vision just a little more. I edge along the sill and try again. My eyes are adjusting to the interior darkness now. I raise my hands to shade out the sun. I teeter on the sill, which is so narrow that it's hard to bal-ance. I'm now at the perfect angle. I stare.

Propped against the easel, angled with care, in such a way that Lucas must have calculated it would be readable, is a large white piece of cardboard with a message on it. It reads: "MAISIE, GO AWAY."

I drop to the ground. I'm saddened. I'm giddy. That shotgun fires again. In the distance, I can hear Stella calling my name. This is a be-trayal. Lucas has betrayed me. I'm seasick with dismay.

My Mother Superior comes to me then, as she always does in times of trouble. Light of foot, silent on the gravel, green-eyed Isa-bella flies to my side. She takes my hot hand in her cool one and gently wipes my eyes. We pace back and forth, side by side. We walk up and down until I am calm again. I shall repay Lucas for this, I de-cide. He'll prize no more secrets out of me. And he'll be the loser—now I shall never tell him my greatest secret, the secret I've kept safe for seven years.

I almost told him this morning—because sometimes it weighs on me, and I long to unburden myself to someone. But I'm glad I kept silent. Serve him right, with his "Run along, Maisie," and his padlock, and his insolent message. He isn't worthy of the truth; I see that now. So I shall never tell him what I saw in Bella's crystal—and I shall never tell him why the crystal shattered. My secret will remain eternally inviolable: That is my resolve.

Isabella inclines her head in quiet approval. Maisie, where are you? Stella calls, closer now. I can hear her anxious footsteps on the path.

One o'clock. We're here. I'm here, I reply.

PART II

The Lovers

I am returned now, Winifride, from the visit to my brother's manor at Elde. He still believes he can persuade me to renounce my vows and marry, so the usual brotherly threats passed the days. I had hoped to find a letter from you on my return: I looked forward to it as a starving man would bread and wine. When I found nothing, I felt afraid.

You will chide me for this and ask what practical progress I have made. Well, Sister, I will answer that I have dismissed the first rascally team of masons, that their replacements are industrious, that I learn from my mistakes, and that the buildings we planned together begin to grow at last. I will answer that I work ceaselessly.

And I will confess that I am lonely, Winifride. There are good women among the sisters here, but not one to whom I can open my heart. This enforced silence weighs on me.

Write, I beg you—and, as you love me, Sister, do so soon.

—*The Letters of Isabella de Morlaix to Winifride of Ely, 1257–1301,*
edited and translated from the Latin, V. B. S. Taylor, 1913

My darling Stella, It's done! I've fixed it with the CO, & the chaplain & Pa. And, guess what, darling? We won't have to wait weeks while they fiddle-faddle around with banns, we can do it by special licence, this Friday in the chapel here at the base. It's not the most romantic place, darling, but we don't care about that, do we? I'd marry you on a rock in the Pacific—I'd *swim* the Pacific to get to you, if need be. Oh darling—I hope this makes you as happy as it makes me. The squadron's been up twice already today—two of the new boys bought it, one was only 18, with 9 hours' training. I took out a 109—the pilot bailed out, but he got his chute tangled & I'm not sure if he made it. I managed 30 minutes' shut-eye, & now I'm fine. I feel immortal this morning, thanks to you, my darling one. All I can think about is our future, & what we'll do at the Abbey after the war. Let's have lots of babies—how about six girls who're nearly as beautiful as you, darling, & a couple of boys like me? Sweetheart—we're being scrambled—love you with all my heart—Guy.

—Daddy's forty-second letter to Stella, dated from the postmark, July 30, 1940.
Assembled and arranged for posterity, in a new leather album, 1962, by
M. Mortland, his third daughter, aged 9.

FIVE

Vigils

N O O N E I N O U R F A M I L Y looks forward to the visits to Elde.
Stella, who knows that, always tries to compensate and to cheer
us the night before. And so tonight she's made a special dinner and, as
it's such a warm, still, perfect summer's evening, we eat it outdoors.

Nicholas Marlow and Dan set up a long trestle table in the cloister courtyard, Stella swathes it in one of the starched damask cloths
that usually appear only at Christmas, and I decorate it with a line
of candles in glass shields. Finn arranges pyramids of fruit on vine
leaves, Gramps descends to the cellars with Dan, and—after a long
search—they return with armfuls of bottles. Gramps says that one of
them—it had been hiding itself away for just such an occasion—
contains a legendary, magical wine. We fetch the good glasses in its
honor. In the kitchen, Stella and Julia are decorating a rabbit terrine
with bay leaves; Dan shot these rabbits, three of them, yesterday. A
chicken and a guinea fowl are roasting—Celia and Rosalind are
roasting. They've been basted with butter and sprinkled with thyme,
and they smell tempting, but I won't be eating them. I am now a
vegetarian: Someone has to make a stand. In the slow oven, there's
a great earthenware dish; peppers and aubergines, tomatoes and
courgettes, all from our greenhouse, are simmering away. The air is
fragrant and festive—and perhaps the smell of good food reaches as

far as the refectory, for just as everything is ready, Lucas appears. Another chair is fetched, we run relays back and forth to the kitchen; at eight, when the sky is still warm, when the first stars can be glimpsed, and the shadows are mauve, we sit down.

I'm on one side of the table, between Gramps and Stella, the customary place for the invisible girl. Dan and Nick Marlow have taken the two ends, and opposite me, Lucas sits in the center, with my sisters flanking him.

"I trust you enjoyed your swim, Lucas," I say at the first opportunity. I'm careful to give no hint of the true situation: Let Lucas remain in a state of uncertainty. I can see him thinking, Did Maisie read my notice or didn't she?

Julia lights the candles. I watch them gutter, then flame. And I watch something else ignite, too, something fueled by the twilight, by the wine, by the still, sweet evening air. It passes from face to face, from hand to hand, around the table. It is a flickering, insubstantial thing. I think it might be contentment; it could be something fragile, like hope or joy; it might be something dangerous, like rivalry. I can feel it brush past me, a ghost in the air. I can see it in my sisters' faces and in the faces of the three young men. Nick is the gravest, the quietest, and the most contained. Lucas watches, watches, with his Argus eyes. Dan—who is a little drunk—is the wildest of the three, talking, arguing, flirting, teasing—it's a fireworks display.

And it's laid on for Finn's benefit. He rests a hand on hers for emphasis, Finn meets his eyes, and—in the flicker of the candles—I see that *look* happen again. It's very brief, and it seems to make Finn self-conscious. She moves her hand and turns away. I watch the swallows hunt the skies. When the fruit and the cheese are brought out, Gramps rises and pours the special wine into the tall, slender glasses—even I am given some. It's a historic wine, gathered the summer before the war.

"It's delicious, sir," Nick Marlow says. "Nineteen thirty-eight. That's the year my parents first came to Wykenfield."

"Remember it well!" Gramps says, raising his glass.

Nick has excellent manners and always knows how to draw Gramps out. This is kind; on occasions like this, he does tend to get ignored. "What do you remember of that year, sir?" Nick continues.

"Well, to tell you the truth, not much, I'm afraid," Gramps replies. "It's all a bit of a blur. I think I spent most of it listening to the wireless—I knew another war was coming, and I was waiting for those politician johnnies to wake up, I suppose. I was worrying about Guy—I knew he'd join up the instant war was declared. But"—he raises a finger and wags it—"the very same question you've just asked occurred to me earlier, when Dan and I found the wine. So I hunted out my old diary—always keep them, you know—and here it is! Nineteen thirty-eight. So let's see what I was up to. . . ."

He's produced a small red leather booklet. Julia sighs and rolls her eyes. Gramps thumbs the pages. I can see that they're all blank—unlike me, Gramps is not a keeper of records, and if he notes down appointments at all, he'll write on the back of an envelope or some other scrap of paper that he can be sure to misplace very soon. Blank page, blank page—and then, at last, an entry. I crane my neck and read. It says, "GUY'S BIRTHDAY!!!" My father would have been eighteen. Gramps closes the little book at once and puts it away.

"Well, it was a good harvest that year," he says quickly. "I can certainly remember that. McIver had been my tenant for about five years, and he'd made a lot of improvements. Drainage and so on. So we had a bumper harvest. The milk yields improved. I was thinking of going into pigs, Tamworths, just in a small way, pigs are interesting animals, highly intelligent—but McIver was against it. Still, never mind that, too long ago, very boring for you youngsters. You're not interested in the past, too busy thinking about the future, and so you should be, only natural—love, life, marriage, careers—"

"Exactly," Lucas says, making me jump. "We're on the edge of a new era. We are poised on the brink of life," he goes on. "The question is—shall we swim upriver or down-? Finn, Julia, what do you think? Shall we head for the ocean or the source? Dan, which do you favor? Nick, which will it be, the shallows or the rapids?" He frowns. "No, don't answer. You don't need to—I can predict. I know what each of you will choose."

I do, too, I decide—and I'll be more accurate than Lucas, who is, I suspect, no more sober than Dan. I give him a cold look. I don't like the tone he's used, and I don't like the way he interrupted Gramps. I don't like the way he's excluded the three people on my side of the table, either. Don't we have futures? Don't we have a choice? Upriver or down-?

"I doubt it's that simple, Lucas," Nick Marlow replies. "Some rivers are subject to tides. They all have currents. You might choose to swim upriver and get swept out to sea. You shouldn't forget that. Build it into your calculations before you predict, maybe."

The remarks are made quietly, but they're corrective; Lucas frowns. He doesn't like to be challenged—and I suspect he doesn't like Nick, either. I can't be sure. "How very wise you're getting, Nick," he says. "I blame medicine. It must be all those hours you spend with the dead, the diseased, and the demented. Stop being boring and rational. It's not a question of currents and tides. It's a question of willpower."

"Oh, give it a rest, Lucas. Retract your claws," says Finn.

"Finn's right. Don't spoil things. And don't *start*," says Dan. Julia smiles. She enjoys nothing so much as contention.

"To all your futures," Gramps says in a firm tone—he may be ineffectual at times, but dissension at table is one thing he will not tolerate. I can tell that he's time traveling: He's thinking of the past, and my father, and other celebrations held here—celebrations that looked to a future very different from the one that lay in store.

I sip the wine, which tastes green and fresh, gold and warm. The shallows or the rapids? I think. The source or the ocean? Which will I choose when the moment comes? I watch the sky, which is fading from silver to gray to black. The swallows and the swifts have disappeared, and the tiny pipistrelle bats (*Pipistrellus pipistrellus)* that nest in the Abbey's roof are now hunting in their place. They flicker overhead and swoop low by the cloister walls. Soon it will be night. An owl shrieks in the beech avenue, and my nuns, who returned to their cells after Compline, murmur and meditate. Eventually, Stella notices how quiet I am and touches my arm. Time for bed, darling, she says. You're worn out. You're half-asleep.

And I'm spirited away. I climb the stairs to my room and open the window—it's such a hot night. Below me, in the cloister courtyard, the candles on the table still glimmer. I can see the firefly lights of cigarettes. Dan is opening more wine, and Lucas is pouring it. Gramps has withdrawn—he'll be on his way to the library to get drunk. He always hits the bottle once a year, the night before we go to Elde. Now they're free—these five are free—from restraint. Julia slips inside and puts on a record—not too loud, but loud enough. She dances back to the twilight, raises her slender arms, moves to an irresistible beat. *Talkin' 'bout my g-g-generation*, stammers an angry, famous voice. Stella comes into my room with a glass of warm milk.

She draws the curtains and settles me in bed. I lie back in my white nightdress, on my white pillow, under white sheets. Outside, it's still light. Stella settles herself in her old place, in the chair by my bed. She knows I dislike going to Elde as much as she does, so tonight she'll tell me a story the way she did when I was younger. She leans her head back and closes her eyes. There are tired lines around her eyes and threads of gray in her fine, short, dark hair. I know she's fretting about a thousand things—she always is. "Tell me how you met Daddy," I say. "But you have to begin at the beginning, and leave nothing out."

And so Stella does. She tells me how she was born in Edinburgh, how her father took his family to Canada when she was six months old, and how she grew up on a farm in Ontario, dreaming of a Scotland and an England she'd never seen. She tells me what a bookworm she was as a child; how she devoured books, how books were her sustenance, just as they are Finn's. "Mine too," I say, but Stella doesn't like the books I like, and as usual she isn't listening. She presses on.

"No reading at the table, Stella," her father used to say when she smuggled a book into meals. So she'd put it away—*Kidnapped,* or *Jane Eyre,* or *Great Expectations*—and then continue in the yard and (with a torch) under the sheets half the night. Except she wasn't in the yard or in bed, of course, she was in that other world. She was trapped in a treacherous tower; she was watching mad Mrs. Rochester rend Jane's wedding veil; she was staring at Miss Havisham's spider-infested bride cake.

"Those books still color my life," she says now, sighing. "Maisie, when will I learn? Books, books—an addiction to stories. No one should live like that. I do *know* that—but I can't cure myself."

I don't want Stella to be cured—besides, if it hadn't been for the books, she might never have come to England, never have met my father. Think of the consequences: I wouldn't have been born. I wouldn't *exist*. Luckily, Stella was not cured of the book addiction. When she was eighteen and left school, her parents gave her a special present, the one gift for which she'd yearned. They gave her a year in England. She would travel to England, and—staying with a network of aunts, cousins, and parental friends—she would finally visit the places she'd dreamed of so long. She crossed the sea on a huge liner, traveling steerage. She arrived in Liverpool and at once took a train to her native Edinburgh. It was the autumn of 1938:

That weakling fool Chamberlain was promising peace for our time.

Stella spent a week with two maiden aunts in Morningside, and then the great journey began. I love the details of this pilgrimage and the way it winds me into sleep. Using a complicated network of trains, buses, and charabancs, Stella worked her way southward; she went to Walter Scott (the Borders), then Wordsworth and Coleridge (the Lakes) . . . During the winter of that year, she walked the moors at Haworth with the three Brontë sisters, strange companions and unsettling ones; but Stella, who knew their work by heart, was well prepared for this. She visited Lawrence in Nottingham and Tennyson in Lincolnshire. Arm in arm with Dickens, she explored the streets of London, then she sped northwest to Shakespeare, the forest of Arden, and Warwickshire. There she stayed with yet another spinster aunt—for some considerable time. After that it was Thomas Hardy and Dorset; then—it was late summer—Jane Austen in Bath. Stella pursued her beloved Austen to Lyme Regis and finally to Hampshire. That September, she was in Winchester Cathedral paying homage at Austen's grave when she became aware of a stir among the other visitors. She closed her copy of *Mansfield Park* (then being read for the fifth time). She was puzzled by whispers in the nave and by a discernible outbreak of excitement—or was it fear? She left the cathedral and approached the knots of people gathered outside. She asked what had happened. They told her war had been declared.

Stella's mind had been so deeply lodged in Austen's world that for one moment she failed to understand them. But she adjusted swiftly. When, the same day, her parents wired her from Canada and begged her to return, she refused. By then, Canada did not feel like home anymore, and she was determined to help the war effort. Luckily, the Shakespeare maiden aunt was happy to accommodate her—so she remained. Of course she remained, I think, closing my eyes: Stella had to stay, because the cards were going to deal her a husband, and he was then only a few heartbeats, the next hand, away.

There was a dull interim period, it's true, in which Stella undertook various kinds of war work in London and elsewhere. I don't really listen to that section of the story—I'm still mapping the route of that book pilgrimage, and I'm noticing for the first time what an unnatural number of maiden aunts Stella possessed. How odd that not one of these women survived long enough to feature in our lives—they've never visited, they've never written, they've just disappeared. Maybe they're all dead and gone, I think. Maybe the war wiped out all these spinsters. . . . I'm beginning to drift off on an eddy of maiden aunts, but I'm fighting sleep, determined to stay awake. For at last the dull interim period is over, and Stella, a farmer's daughter, has found her wartime métier. She's become a land girl, first on a farm in Warwickshire (Shakespeare *again*), then briefly in Norfolk, and finally on a tenant farm in Suffolk, run by a Mr. Angus McIver and situated in the village of Wykenfield.

"And there," Stella says, "on a beautiful June evening—it was quite late, and I'd been working since five—I walked up from the valley to Holyspring. I sat there, below Nun Wood, for a while. It was such a calm place—so quiet I could hear the river below. I lay back on the grass and watched the swallows. I remember listening to the bomber planes, setting off from the base at Deepden. You'd hear them leave every evening, and every morning you'd hear them return—"

"What were you wearing?" I ask, though I know, but even on the edge of sleep I want it confirmed.

"Well, nothing very alluring, I'm afraid," Stella says in a dreamy way. "I was still wearing my work clothes—boots, dungarees, an old checked shirt. I was sweaty and dirty—I probably had hay in my hair, because I'd been working with the horses that day. . . . Anyway, there I was, in the fields just below the Abbey. And for some reason, I decided to walk back that way. The house was closed up then, it was too run-down and not really big enough to be requisitioned. Gramps was in London . . . well, I didn't think of him as Gramps, of course. I just knew the house belonged to a Mr. Mortland—and that there was a son, a son who was a fighter pilot, stationed in Sussex somewhere. . . ."

"And Sussex was a long way away."

"So it never occurred to me that I'd meet anyone that night. I walked up past the woods to the lane. And I stopped by the old nunnery gates, just below the refectory. The light was beginning to fail. It was so peaceful that it could be hard to remember the war, though I always tried to, because . . . well, those planes would go over, and the next day not all of them returned—"

"And then you heard footsteps."

"And then I heard footsteps, coming down the path from the house. I turned round, and I saw a young man. He was standing by the refectory door, looking up at the sky. He was very tall, with fair hair. He didn't realize I was there at first—I think I startled him. Then he turned toward me, and I saw he had the most astonishing eyes—the darkest blue eyes I'd ever seen. We looked at each other, and—"

"It was love at first sight."

"Something like that," Stella says, and I can hear the sound of a smile in her voice as sleep gathers me up. "Something marvelous and strange, certainly. Something I'd never experienced before—though the books had prepared me, of course. . . . Are you awake, Maisie?"

I'm sure I hear the question, but I don't seem to be able to answer it. I drift in a tide, and while I float there I hear the door shut softly. I dream myself back into a wartime summer's night. I'm listening to the sound of Daddy's footsteps on gravel, and I dream his approach so well that I rise up from my bed to greet him. I tiptoe to the windows, and once there, knowing he's close, I ease the curtains aside and wait.

But then that dream eddies away as it so often does, and, hearing music, I begin dreaming my sisters. They and three young men are still awake on this long summer's night. I dream cigarette fireflies and the pouring of wine. I dream my sister Finn reciting a charm. She says, The brink of life, the brink of life. Then someone—is it Dan?—hears the charm and stands up. He begins to dance, and gradually the others rise to their feet. I dream them moving to the music in the moonlight, the three men threading my sisters between them, so their dresses look like bright silks woven through a dark tapestry. I curl up by the window. Music billows the curtains; moonlight glitters like a knife.

At three-thirty exactly, I wake. The air is cool, the floor is cold, and the room is full of shadows. The cloister is deserted and the music has ended; I stretch out my limbs, which feel stiff and antique. The shadows in the room are very deep, and I could be afraid of them. I decide I'll go to Finn, who will always take me in and protect me at night. The Abbey sighs, but I tell myself that there are advantages to sleeplessness. The whole house is in darkness. The whole house is mine. Now it's the hour for Vigils: I can go anywhere and see everything. Why should I fear ghosts, when I can be a ghost myself?

I step out onto the landing. This house has seven staircases, one for each day of the week. Below me, nuns pray; a clock ticks.

I visit Julia first. She, Finn, and I all have rooms on the same corridor. I creep along the passage. No mouse could be quieter; not a single board squeaks. I ease open Julia's door—what a catastrophe of a room this is! Moonlight shines in—Julia never draws the curtains. She never hangs her clothes away, either. There they are, all her flower-child dresses, drenched in moonlight, silky skins she's sloughed off. I can smell her favorite scent, L'Heure Bleue, but there's something else, too, something that smells like incense. It's a secret scent, the scent of something she smokes, of a substance she brought back from California. This substance, which she's concealing from Stella and will not explain to me, has magic powers. It can transport you, my sister says.

I creep across to her dressing table. Its looking glass shows me Maisie. I startle myself. On the wide, tumbled bed behind me, Julia stirs.

I turn to look at her. She is naked. She has kicked the sheets aside. The moonlight makes her limbs marble. I look at her round, sculpted breasts, at the long curve of hips and thighs. The moon is bleaching her amber hair to palest gold. One lock is twined about her throat, the rest tumbles across the pillow—her hair is so thick, so long. Her face is calm with sleep, heavy with sleep. I would give almost anything to look like Julia and to know what I know Julia knows.

I creep back to the dressing table and check the right-hand drawer. I ease it out silently. Lacy stockings, gossamer underwear— who pays for these things she's recently acquired? White lace, black lace—and underneath, just as they were the last time I looked, her contraceptive pills. There's also the white plastic scallop-shaped box with her Dutch cap, acquired from a special clinic in London, because our doctor—Dr. Marlow, Nick's father—will not prescribe contraceptives to unmarried women. Julia boasted about this device when she was up at Cambridge, but she doesn't need it now. I count the little pill capsules: Monday, Tuesday, Wednesday, or Moanday, Tearsday, Wailsday, as Julia calls them, quoting someone. Yes, she's up-to-date, as I knew she would be. Julia takes care of herself. Julia is a goddess—"*Vénus toute entière*," Dan says of her, and I don't think it's a compliment—but the goddess is a sensible girl.

It's Finn who's the rash one in this family—though most people would never suspect that, for Finn is covert and quiet. I creep along the passageway to Finn's room now and open the door carefully—Finn, unlike Julia, is a light sleeper. Even when she dreams, Finn remains wary and alert for the least sound.

This room, striped with moonlight, is in perfect order. It's very plain: My nuns approve. There's a drugget mat on the floor; the walls are lined with bookshelves; the looking glass is tiny; the dressing table's bare. This room smells of air. The window is wide open; the curtains move like phantoms in the breeze. The narrow white bed is neatly made, and it's unoccupied. At four in the morning, it seems, my sister Finn is—where?

"Where?" I say the word aloud, and it startles me. Where, where—I have to find her. I creep along to the end of the corridor, go down one flight of stairs, up another, through an anteroom, and out again. What a warren Gramps created when he restored this house. Cross a landing, and you cross centuries. I'm in the Middle Ages; I'm in the modern world. The water pipes clank, the nuns pad past me silently. In her cell, my Reverend Mother falls to her knees. Where is she, Maisie? Where is your sister? she asks. I fetch a stool, because I know I'll need it—I'm not tall enough yet to spy unaided. I open a door—it looks like a cupboard door but isn't—and step into the concealed corridor, the Abbey's secret world.

I position the stool, climb up, and apply my eye to the small, square, ancient aperture. It's very cunning, this Squint. It's an architectural, ecclesiastical mystery. Other squints exist—they're not that rare in churches, but they're usually placed in the transept and angled to give a view of the altar in the nave. But in a nunnery, and angled *away* from the altar? That seems strange. All I know is that in the mid–fifteenth century, when the nunnery was already over two hundred years old, this device was inserted—and Isabella says it breaks her heart. For reasons unknown, someone liked to watch the nuns at their orisons. Whoever watched them was tall. The aperture is set six feet two inches from the floor—I've measured, so I'm sure.

I approach it cautiously. I look down into the dark. My gaze angles down a tiny tunnel, through four-foot walls to the Lady Chapel below. It's the library now—and my nuns have absented themselves. I can see the lamp on the Indian table and the snarl of the lionskin rug. Propped up on the sofa cushions is my grandfather, deeply asleep. There's a half-empty whiskey bottle next to him—the prospect of visiting his childhood home has taken its usual toll. I had thought my sister might be here, talking to Gramps and trying to cheer him. . . . I'm wrong. I look and I look and I look, but there's no Finn here.

Finn isn't in the kitchen, either. She's not in the drawing room or the dining room or the scullery or the pantry or the hall. I scurry up the back stairs to the corridor where Dan has his usual room. I daren't open that door, but I press my ear to its panels. What a little spy you are, Maisie, Dan has said when he's caught me meddling. I don't deign to answer. I'm the girl in the corner, the girl everyone fusses over, the girl everyone ignores. No one ever tells me anything. If I didn't spy, I'd be in the dark eternally. I live in a maze of un-knowing—Maisie's maze—and I hate it. I need to be informed.

Dan is asleep. I listen closely. I listen lovingly. Alone and asleep—I'm certain of that. I press my ear to the door panels. I can hear a man's deep, regular breathing. No Finn there.

I run back downstairs and creep outside to the cool of the gar-den. I try the cloister and the beech avenue. I creep down past the yews to the refectory, but Lucas can't be working tonight: There's not a chink of light from between the shutters and no sound. I edge back toward the house along the yew path. The moon has passed be-hind a cloud, and the darkness alarms.

All the shadows are filled with desolation. I can see shapes that seem to beckon: Over here, they whisper. Look, Maisie, over here. The flagstones in the cloister are cold under my bare feet, and they make me think about the dead, all those dead—generations of nuns, those tenant farmers who once lived here, fathers and daughters, mothers and sons—all those dead who have to lie for an eternity underground.

This way, Maisie, they whisper, holding out their arms. But I won't lie down with them. It must be so cold. And so dark. Never to see the sun again, never to breathe air. Or to be dust, like Daddy. It fills me up with fear.

I hasten back to the house and wait where I feel safer, in the shelter of its walls. Isabella joins me there. She wraps me in her cloak and warms my hands in hers. *Benedicite,* she begins, and her blessing unfurls. Before five, the sky begins to warm and the birds begin to sing. There's a nightingale in Nun Wood, and it pours out its heart to the dawn. The scents of the roses intensify, and color steals into their petals. A fox barks. When the sun is stronger, the buds will unfurl.

At six, it's the hour for Lauds, and the nuns commence their morning prayers. *Quicumque vult salvus esse,* they whisper with me. At six-fifteen, just as they're readying themselves for Eucharist, I hear quiet footsteps, stealthy footsteps, on the refectory path. I shrink back, and a pale shape steals toward me. I've seen them before, these transgressives, these shadows, creeping back to morning prayers. This phantom doesn't see me; she hesitates in the cloister and scans the house, with its twenty-one watchful eyes. She's barefoot. She's carrying her shoes. She glances over her shoulder, hesitates, paces back and forth in the shadows, and then—as if suddenly resolved—runs inside. I follow and confront her in the hall. I see that this ghost is my sister. It's Finn, and I've startled her. She cries out, "Who's there?"

She's afraid. She swings round and stares at me. I stare at her. I have a sentence prepared, and it's accusatory—but when I see her close up, it won't be spoken. Her face silences me. She looks so blinded, so stupefied. She's very pale, and her breath is coming fast. Her white dress is patterned with delicate scarlet flowers, and in this light it looks unearthly, as if she's bleeding from every vein. The fine cotton is crumpled, and the skirt is torn. Her lovely hair is disheveled, and there is a mark on her neck, a dark purplish plum-size, thumb-size bruise. We look at each other in silence, my sister and I. All the questions I want to ask won't be said. What's the point in asking? I know part of the answer, anyway: I can read it in her eyes. She's been with Lucas—and he hasn't been painting her. Lucas is a strange man and is capable of many things, but even Lucas can't paint portraits in the dark.

I know that much—and it tells me nothing. Something has happened here, and it's something from which I'm barred. Finn could tell me, but words wouldn't get me there. She's in a remote country, and I don't speak its language, I don't know its tongues.

"Oh, Finn, what if Dan finds out?" Out the sentence spills. I wait for retribution, for Finn's inevitable rage. Finn hates to be spied on. She hates to be interrogated. She'll never forgive me for this. I take a step backward, but to my astonishment, there's no anger, no reprimand. Finn gives a strange sigh and falls to her knees. She clasps me around the waist and hugs me to her tightly. When she lifts her white face, it's transfigured. "Oh, Maisie, I'm so happy," she whispers. "I'm so miserable. And so afraid."

I look at her doubtfully. I know there's no point in asking her to translate: I wouldn't understand. She scrambles to her feet and grabs my arm. "Promise you won't tell," she whispers. "Promise me, Maisie. Give me your hand." We clasp hands, and I promise. I would never betray Finn, and she knows that. I swear eternal silence, even so.

Finn hugs me tight and kisses me. She's trembling. I realize that under her thin dress, she's naked. Her face is alight, yet her eyes brim with tears. She rocks me in her arms, the way she did when we first came here, when I missed Daddy and the nightmares were so bad.

Then, abruptly, she releases me. I'm waiting for her to comfort me, to take me back to bed—but tonight she's distracted, and she forgets me. I don't exist for my sister: I'm a solitary child. Finn watches some airy gesture, some lingering touch invisible to me, and her face contracts. Then, fleet of foot, silent as a ghost, she turns and runs up the stairs.

I remain in the hall. It has a floor like a chessboard. It has a grandfather clock with a weight and a pendulum. I know something huge has happened. The clock ticks away the minutes and chimes away the quarters. In another five hours, we'll be leaving for Elde.

SIX

Ancestral Voices

Before we leave for the annual visit, we assemble at the dining room table: It's the annual council of war. I have an ache low down in my stomach—it started before breakfast, and although I ate nothing, it won't go away. At first I felt hope—I thought it might be significant. But it isn't. I've gone back to my bedroom three times to check. Clean underwear. Not the smallest speck of blood. Something is wrong with me. What is wrong with me? Who can I ask?

My nuns are agitated. They're worried about Finn; they're worried about Elde—someone's soul is on the slide; there's a scorch of sin in the air. It's nine when I go back downstairs, so it's Terce, third hour of prayer for the day. Psalms sing in my ears. Psalms pursue me down the stairs—even Julia can't drown them out, though she seems to try hard. She's only just got up—hours after everyone else. She plays the Grateful Dead and runs a bath. "Close the door on that infernal racket, for God's sake, Maisie," Gramps cries as I reenter the dining room. He has the annual hangover. He is at the head of the table, Stella opposite him. She's decided to wear the blue dress my father bought her just before he died. It's twelve years old. "That dress becomes you, Stella," Gramps always says when she wears it. And I suppose it does. It brings out the gentle prettiness of Stella's face. It magics away my mother. In her place, I see a sweet-faced, blithe, confident girl.

I take my seat at the table, to the left of Gramps and opposite Finn. Finn's lovely eyes are fixed on air. She hates this annual ritual, and she's already tuning out. I try to tune out, too. *Sink me the ship, Master Gunner,* I declaim. *Sink her, split her in twain! Fall into the hands of God, not into the hands of Spain!* . . . It's a rousing poem, but it's not effective today. I try other devices. I try imagining how this convent must have been when it was first built, when Isabella watched her masons at work, when prayer retained its power. I try unstringing the centuries of change; I try to understand why Gramps restored this house in such an inept, haywire way. What possessed him to create this dining room by these means? He carved out the room by dividing the double-height Lady Chapel in half horizontally, thus ruining a sacred space; one that was perfectly proportioned became two whose proportions are deformed. Above my head is a gimcrack false ceiling. It has fake beams and bosses carved with the Mortland family arms. The whole room is hideous. Even the windows, lucent, original, one of the Lady Chapel's glories, have been despoiled. The inserted ceiling chops them in half. There's a gushing of plumbing—Julia has finished her bath. Water gurgles along the ancient network of lead pipes, reaches the crack it's made in the far corner of the plaster, and drips into the bucket placed below.

Gramps gives a groan. "You see?" he says. "You see? If the plumbing isn't fixed, if I don't get the roof seen to soon, you know what will happen? We'll have the whole place down about our ears. Dry rot— death-watch beetle, who *knows* what's up there? I'm going to make it very clear to Humphrey. And Violet. Things are reaching crisis point. I'm not going to mince my words. All I'm asking for is justice. I mean, three minutes. Three minutes! I ask you, is it fair?"

· · ·

And so it begins. This annual council of war has two stages. There's the reciting of the ancient grievances. When we've been through these hallowed refrains, and only then, we move on to this year's tactics and campaign. Gramps's grievances go back a long way. All the way back to the day of his birth, in fact, which event occurred, in the Blue Bedroom at Elde, on July 24, 1892. It was an easy delivery, lasting only a few hours. At twelve noon on the dot, a fine lusty male child was born. At two minutes *past* twelve, just as the midwife was wrapping the son and heir in his shawl, his mother experienced a new and curious pain. She clutched her stomach and moaned. Consternation! The newborn was hastily bundled into the arms of a maid; the midwife bent over the bed and gave a cry of surprise. One minute later, at precisely three minutes past twelve, baby number two popped out into the world. (Can midwifery really have been that primitive then? I wonder, when Gramps gets to this part of his refrain. Who were the incompetent doctors involved? How come that in nine months' pregnancy, no one had noticed there were *two* babies? As Julia says, don't ask.)

This male child, also fine and lusty, was my grandfather. Identical twins. Like as two proverbial peas in a pod—with just one tiny difference between them, a difference imperceptible to the eye. The noon child, christened Humphrey (all male Mortlands have names that begin with "H," "G," or "E"), would inherit Elde and the considerable loot that came with it. The three-minutes-later twin, christened Henry, faced the more uncertain future of the English younger son.

Henry, alias Gramps, accepted this. Gramps always emphasizes how fond he was of three-minutes-older Humphrey and how he never felt the least resentment as child or man. He always devotes several passionate verses to this section of the ballad, and I believe all he says. My grandfather is not materialistic or worldly. He's benevolent. He finds it hard to think badly of anyone, though he makes an exception in the case of Humphrey's wife, Lady Violet—or the Viper, as she's known.

In 1914, when they were twenty-two, both brothers volunteered within days of war being declared. They were commissioned in the same regiment. Humphrey, showing an instinct for self-preservation he's always retained, became an adjutant and was attached to the general staff. He never saw the front line. Gramps did. His first posting was Ypres. His next was the Somme. I'm familiar with the details of the battles there, but I don't know what happened to Gramps, for he refuses to be drawn out. All I know is that in 1918 he returned from France an altered man. He returned to Elde—and his first action was to burn his uniforms. This ceremonial burning was a public affair.

Gramps made a tall wooden pyre in the middle of Elde's great central lawn. Every uniform he possessed went onto it, doused liberally with paraffin; it burned for hours. The family could be relied upon to ignore this eccentricity, but if word had spread to the village or beyond, it might have been misinterpreted, so the servants were bribed to hold their tongues. His parents became alarmed, and after a few tense months his father began to see that this younger son might have difficulty making his way in the world. None of the traditional avenues seemed open to him. The church was out—Gramps was refusing to attend morning prayers in the family chapel, and he went on as he began: Apart from marriages and funerals, he hasn't set foot in a church since 1918. The army was clearly not on the cards, and the civil service, the Foreign Office, the colonial service—even the most far-flung branches of it—weren't looking too promising, either. Gramps wasn't anxious to serve king and country in any capacity, and there was another problem, too. "No brains, you see," Gramps always announces at this point. "Humphrey got the lot. No brains, can't remember a damned thing, and hopeless at exams."

Luckily, there was a solution: *land*. In addition to Elde, the family had several minor East Anglian estates, all with pleasant houses suitable for a man of his status. The suggestion was made, and Gramps took to it. He liked the idea of being a gentleman farmer. He began reading up on it and became interested in eighteenth-century crop rotation methods, abstruse vegetables, rare breeds of chickens, and Jersey cows.

But the estates suggested didn't appeal. What he wanted, he told his astonished father and relieved brother, was the Abbey at Wykenfield. It came with only four hundred acres and only two tenant farms, and the house was a semiruin—but it was just what he desired. It was a place of great beauty, a place where he could hear the beat of England's heart. The land was heavy Suffolk boulder clay, but, properly tilled, properly husbanded, Gramps knew he could make it fruitful. As for the nunnery buildings—and at this point in his story, Gramps always looks up at his fake-beamed ceiling with pride—he could see the possibilities there, even if the rest of his family was blind.

Besides, he'd always felt an affinity for this place, ever since he'd cycled here, one prewar summer, as a boy. He liked the fact that its connections with his family went back so far. Although the links between the Mortland family and Isabella, foundress of the Abbey, are subject to debate, and the corruption of her surname, "de Morlaix," to "Mortland" has never been entirely explained, Gramps has always believed that Isabella was his ancestress. Not his direct ancestress, obviously, given her vocation, but a close one, through one of her several brothers, maybe. And whether she was or not, she spoke to him. Gramps heard her voice when he came to inspect the house in the spring of 1919.

"And I wasn't having one of my turns, either," he will say when he reaches this dramatic point. "Admittedly, I did have them now and then—a lot of men did, I wasn't alone. But this was completely different. I was standing in Holyspring, looking down at the valley, and I heard Isabella's voice. Heard it distinctly—and a most beautiful voice it was, too."

"What did she say, Gramps?" I always used to prompt at this point.

"She said, Henry Mortland, this is the place. It is destined for you . . . something along those lines. I can't remember the exact words, but that was the gist—"

"But how did you know it was Isabella? Did she tell you? Did you see her?"

"Well, not as such . . . not exactly. I just sort of sensed her. You can't be too literal about that kind of thing, Maisie, you know."

"What was she wearing? Was she in her nun's habit? Did she have a veil? Were you afraid?"

"Certainly not. I remained calm and compos mentis throughout. And, oddly enough, I don't think she *was* wearing her habit. I'm pretty damn certain she was dressed in blue."

Gramps has reached this part of the family ballad now. He pauses and looks hopefully at me. He's waiting for me to prompt, to ask the old ritual childish questions that he always enjoyed. I don't want to disappoint him—it hurts to disappoint him—but I can't make myself ask about Isabella or the voice or the strange incident in Holyspring. I can't, because I don't believe in it anymore. I don't think it ever happened. Isabella speaks to me, but I don't believe she ever addressed Gramps. I don't believe in the incompetent midwife, and if smooth Humphrey hadn't confirmed it, I wouldn't believe in the fatal three-minute gap between the twins. It's all rigmarole. It's all embroidery. I'm not the only storyteller in my family—they're all at it. Nothing but stories, night and day.

And, unlike my stories, these are so much eyewash. They're designed to cover up the truth—not reveal it, the way I do. The rest of my family papers over the cracks—and they don't even do it well. Look at the wasted opportunities here. When I tell Lucas about the voice in Holyspring—which I shall do soon, I decide—I'll really make something of it. I know exactly how Isabella sounds and what she wears. And the timing can be improved: The scene won't take place on a spring afternoon. Moonlight would be much better. Or perhaps a summer's dawn.

Poor Gramps. Poor Stella, whose turn is coming next—Stella is an even worse storyteller than my grandfather. Long practice has made her bedtime stories smooth and enchanting to me, but I've had to train and pester her to achieve that. At other times she muddles dates, she gets bogged down in detail, she hares off on diversions; unless you prompt her, she never tells you what people looked like— or what they were wearing, which is always of prime importance, I believe. Hopeless, both of them. Anyway, you can summarize the Mortland decline in three sentences, the three truthful sentences that are too painful to be spoken, that are therefore always hidden within this great family web of words.

First: Gramps, though kind and good, is—financially speaking—a babe in arms. What he failed to lose installing fake ceilings and leaky plumbing, he lost on the farms and the stock market with astonishing speed—his American investments were especially unwise. Second: My father, who would certainly have turned things round and made a go of it, never had a chance to do so, thanks to the war and the TB, which did not respond to the New Mexico climate or the latest miracle drug, streptomycin, in which the sanatorium, and Stella, believed. Third: Stella, the brave widow with three children to support, has even less of a clue about money than Gramps, and she's a poor judge of character, too. Despite years of evidence to the contrary, she still believes that Humphrey is fundamentally decent; she still believes that Humphrey will take pity on our impoverished state and assist us—he is, after all, a very rich man. I look up; Stella is stating this view now.

Oh, give me a break, Julia mutters as, finally, she makes her appearance, wafting in on a cloud of scent. *Dream on,* she murmurs as Stella continues to speak, and Julia sits next to silent, preoccupied Finn. And Julia is right. Any family feeling, fundamental decency, or instinct toward charity Humphrey ever had was knocked out of him by his wife, Lady Violet, years ago. Humphrey has a well-trained memory. He's forgotten that at the time of my father's death, he swore to take care of Stella, Julia, Finn, and me. He's forgotten that it was always his father's intention to make further provision for Gramps. The steady drip, drip, drip of the Viper's contempt for us has washed away such considerations. Humphrey's attitude now is— why throw good money after bad?

"I can't understand why you should expect Humphrey to cough up," Violet said—is reported to have said—last year. The Viper is a plain-speaking woman. "Why the devil should he? Sell that damn house, Henry. God knows why you're so obsessed with it, anyway. It's wasted a prodigious amount of money, and it's been an albatross around your neck from the start. And Stella, forgive me—but be practical for once. Go and get a job—surely even you can get a job of some sort? Obviously there are certain difficulties, with which I sympathize . . . but they're not going to disappear overnight, that much is obvious, and meanwhile one can't just sit around on one's backside, you know, waiting for money to fall from trees."

I stare at the table, this oft quoted speech going round and round in my head. I can't decide: Was the Viper right—or wrong? And which difficulties did she mean?

The remark was made at three-thirty in the afternoon, and it brought matters to a swift conclusion. Gramps rose to his feet and said: "Violet, I sold half the Abbey lands to pay my son's medical bills. I sold the remainder to educate Finn and Julia—and to make provision for Maisie, of course. All that's left is the house and the gardens. If I sold them tomorrow, what would I get? Enough for a pittance of an annuity, that's all. I shall not do that. My son loved the house, and his children will inherit it—it's the only thing I have to give them, and give it to them I shall. Furthermore"—Gramps was getting worked up—"furthermore, your remark to Stella should shame even you. Stella has raised three girls in circumstances of great hardship. She has given them her love, her time, her unremitting devotion—she's sacrificed her life to the girls! She's had to scrimp and save; she's worked her fingers to the bone. She never stops working! This morning, before we left for Elde, Stella was up at six. She tidied the house. She cooked breakfast and washed up the dishes afterwards. She gave Maisie an English lesson. She cleaned out the henhouse, fed the hens, dug up the vegetables she'd grown, and prepared a nourishing supper, which we will eat on our return. . . ." Gramps fixed the Viper with a wrathful eye. The Viper sighed.

"What did you do this morning, Violet?" Gramps concluded, his tone scathing. He was scenting triumph, I suppose.

"I had breakfast in bed, as usual, then a leisurely bath," Violet replied without batting an eyelid—as Julia remarked afterward, she does have matchless nerve. "Then I discussed the details of lunch with my cook and the greenfly on the roses with one of my gardeners—we do not, of course, employ unpaid drudges at Elde. After that, I went for a gentle stroll by the lake with my charming grandson. Innocuous activities, I feel. So if you're accusing me of something, Henry, have the courage to say so. But first, take a close look at your own circumstances. As Humphrey and I have warned you, time and again, your refusal to face painful facts will end in tragedy one of these days."

"I knew what she was getting at," Gramps says now, turning red and staring hard at the table. "And I damn well wasn't having it. So I gave her a look of scorn, a look that would have withered most women . . . and I said: 'Violet, I cannot think why Humphrey married you. I will listen to no more of these wicked insults and innuendos. You are a viper, Violet. And you have poisoned this family's heart.' "

"Grandson? I didn't know there was a grandson," says a voice from the door. It breaks the awkward eddying silence that has followed Gramps's last words. I turn around to see that Dan has entered. He's carrying a notebook. He greets everyone present, with the exception of Finn. He compliments Julia on her dress—she's wearing one of her antique caftans today; her wrists are heavy with slave bracelets that jingle whenever she moves. He bestows on her a lingering glance of naked admiration—which is odd, since he loathes Julia—and slides into the chair next to me, directly opposite Finn. His manner is charming—Dan is always charming these days—but I can scent his anger from two feet away. Finn does not look up but keeps her eyes bent upon the table. I think: He can't know where Finn was last night, surely he can't know?

"I asked Dan if he'd join us," Stella begins hastily to explain. "I have one or two suggestions to make, and I just thought—every year we go round in circles, we make plans, and they're never effective. Dan is almost part of the family, he's known us so long. He's our honorary son, in a way," she continues, smiling at him, "and I'm sure it will help to have his viewpoint. He can look at all this from a fresh angle, and—"

"Tell me about the grandson," says the honorary son, flicking open his notebook. He doodles a few lines and then draws a small rabbit being produced from a hat. "I'm familiar with the rest of the cast. I know about Humphrey and the Viper, of course. I know about their son—he died young, didn't he? But the grandson—I must have forgotten there was a grandson. Now, he does sound promising. Age?"

"Twenty-seven." It's Julia who answers. "And before you ask, Dan—yes, he's unmarried. His name is Edmund. Violet and Humphrey brought him up. But don't imagine some Mr. Darcy.

Imagine a fat oaf with three brain cells—you won't be far wrong."

"Julia, please," Gramps interjects. "He's Eton, Christ Church, and the Royal Agricultural College. 'Oaf' is hardly the correct term."

"Okay, 'creep,' then," says Julia. "A creep who slunk into Oxford after every conceivable string had been pulled; a creep who just scraped a third. A creep who came into his trust fund two years ago. A creep with an unearned income of two hundred thousand a year. The apple of Violet's eye and earmarked to inherit Elde, obviously. It breaks your heart, doesn't it? But if you're imagining . . . What are you imagining, Dan?"

"Let's ask Finn," he replies dangerously. "Finn, what am I imagining? You usually know."

"Not on this occasion," Finn answers in an equally dangerous way, looking up for the first time. She gives Dan a long, still, combative look, but he avoids her eyes.

"I think I was imagining that an appeal to the grandson might succeed, where all other appeals have failed," Dan continues. "Why not? He's young; he's male. And if the appeal were made in the right way, by the right person . . . what man could resist Julia? I guess that's what I'm saying. Julia, looking the way she does today."

His eyes linger upon my elder sister. I see color rise in her cheeks, and I can't believe she's going to fall for such mockery, not from Dan, surely, when she must know how much he dislikes her and when she claims to detest him. But Julia is vain, and Dan is handsome, and his preference for Finn has always galled her. I can see she's tempted, though still cautious, because she knows Dan and knows he might be setting her up—he's devious that way.

"I wouldn't bet on my chances," she replies with a frown. "I'd be delighted to rid him of some of his surplus cash—and we could certainly use it. But Edmund isn't a soft touch."

I stand up. I mumble some excuse—no one takes any notice, no one cares whether I'm present or not, no one would dream of asking my views. Invisible to everyone, I push back my chair and cross to the door.

I hear Stella say: "I think Dan may have a point. In fact, it's a clever idea. It's so hopeless trying to explain things to Humphrey—Violet will always intervene. But if Julia could talk to Edmund, just take him aside for a few minutes and explain. We wouldn't be asking for very much, and this time it's a business proposition. . . . Now, here's my idea: I really believe it could succeed. Cooking schools are all the rage these days—have you noticed? I suddenly thought how much nicer it would be, learning to cook here at the Abbey rather than in some London basement. Just imagine it! Lovely gardens, fresh produce, eggs from my hens . . . We'd need to improve some of the bedrooms, perhaps, because it would have to be residential, but I'm sure that wouldn't cost very much. . . . I've drawn up, well, I've drawn up a scheme. And I think we could get it started very quickly—but we would need some capital, just to get us going. Dan's been over the figures with me, and we think that one thousand—Dan thinks two, because he says we'd have to advertise . . . but I'm sure we could do it for less. Let's say fifteen hundred at the very most. And it would be a loan, obviously—you'd have to make that clear to Edmund, Julia. It's a loan that would be repaid, with interest. Once the profits start coming in."

"Stella, that is the best idea you've ever had," Gramps says quickly with a glance in my direction. "You're a superlative cook. This could solve—well, it could be the answer to everything! Where are you off to, Maisie dear?"

"The kitchen," I reply. "I'm hungry."

"Oh good," says Stella, who always likes to feed me up. "There's lots of fruit, darling, and a fresh loaf I've made. . . . Don't wander off, will you? We'll be leaving soon."

Silence falls. Everyone around the table stares at me expectantly. "This is such a fine idea, Stella," Gramps says after a pause. "Why didn't you mention it before?"

Stella hesitates, looks at him uncertainly. I know why she didn't mention it, to Gramps or any of us: because she knows in her heart that this scheme, like its many predecessors, is going to fail. Even Stella can't go on being optimistic forever. She is a good cook—but she could no more run a business than our cats could.

I close the door.

SEVEN

Starling

I RETREAT TO THE HALL. I move across the black and white flags like a chess piece: Sometimes I choose to move indirectly, like a knight; sometimes I swoop on the diagonal like a bishop; but today I inch one single square at a time, like a pawn. I listen to my nuns, who are now at work in the gardens, and to Bella, who's Hoovering upstairs. I listen to the buzz of words in the dining room. I look at the prospect of Elde.

I know how each second there will pass. On the way, Gramps and Stella will argue themselves into optimism. This time it will be different, they'll say. But that optimism will start ebbing the second we pass through those tall iron gates and enter the drive. There the house will be, in all its cold gray magnificence. Stella will point out the lake, the familiar temples and obelisks, as we pass. She'll exclaim at the foresight of Capability Brown, who laid out the park and planted that great avenue of oaks when the trees were only a few feet tall. No one will remind her that she says this every year, on the same bend of the drive. Our spirits will be sinking too rapidly for comment—and when we enter the house, they'll plummet. Elde strikes a chill to the heart.

Humphrey will be affable; the Viper will be wearing her famous pearls. We'll be allotted twenty minutes for sherry and one hour for lunch, and then we'll be shepherded back to the glacial drawing room, impatient Violet snapping at our heels. There, Finn will be silently scornful—which is how she hides pain. Julia will be as defiant as she dares, and I . . . well, what will I do?

The rest of the family will settle down for the post-lunch strife, the period when twelve months of wary truce collapses and hostilities break out anew. The Viper will be timing them. She'll allow an hour and a half of hand-to-hand fighting; then, when she judges our side is sufficiently demoralized, weaponless, wounded, and in retreat yet again, she'll dictate the terms of the treaty. They're straightforward. Abject surrender. That sums it up, I feel. I don't want to watch this humiliating process—and I'm not allowed to do so anyway. I'm too young for family warfare. Not too young to be told all the details on the way home, or too young to have them repeated indignantly for months afterward, but too young actually to witness them—Gramps has decreed.

So I'll be sent outside. I'll exit the marble halls of Elde. I'll walk in the gardens (huge; full-time staff of nine). I'll walk for ninety minutes. Sometimes I'm escorted.

Usually I'm escorted.

Once or twice, I've escaped and walked alone.

I inch my way across the chessboard floor, but I can hear the agitated voices from the dining room, so there's no solace there. I retreat to the kitchen. Once I've closed the door, the council-of-war arguments are inaudible. Gramps, with his usual gift for planning, placed the kitchen several hundred yards away from the dining room, just as it is at Elde.

The terrible disorder that affects the rest of the house doesn't penetrate here. Everywhere else, there's a fatal accretion of *stuff*, and no matter how much Stella tries to control it, it creeps back within a day. Letters, newspapers, magazines, discarded sweaters, Wellington boots, tennis shoes, Gramps's pipes, Julia's clothes, Finn's books, coffee mugs, glasses, gardening gloves, secateurs—they're all on the march, and the second Stella cleans and tidies a room, chaos returns and the random reinvades.

But here, everything is in its right place. The kitchen is scrupulously clean, despite Bella's best efforts to dirty it—Stella keeps it that way. The flagstones have been scrubbed, and they shine from centuries of feet. The copper saucepans have always been there, on the rack over the range, and they gleam. The pewter dishes on the great black dresser have always been ranked in that orderly way, and there isn't a speck of dust on them. The old wireless sits in the right place—it was there when Daddy was a boy. On the kitchen table there's a pile of bills in brown envelopes, but it's always been there, and no matter how often Gramps gets out the checkbook, the pile remains the same size. I find that comforting. This room always calms me: I like order; I dislike change. On the table, there's a bunch of marigolds in a blue mug, Stella's "things to do" notebook, her copy of *Mansfield Park*, a garden trug, and a trowel. I flick open the Austen. Stella has reached chapter 10.

I can't hear my nuns in this room. I sit down at the table. I'm not hungry, I never feel hunger, but perhaps I should eat something— maybe that would make the pain in my stomach go away. If I tell Stella about the pain, will I be allowed to stay here and not go to Elde? No, she'll refuse: I've tried before and never succeeded. Stella says I'm too young to remain on my own. I borrow a page from Stella's notebook and start drawing the pergola I'm planning. I begin writing the list of roses I've selected to climb on it. I've never actually seen any of these roses, but I've read about them, and their scents, their colors, and the formation of their petals are clear to me. I write down: "The Bride, Wedding Day." Then I scrunch up the piece of paper; I tear it into confetti. I'm not in the mood. Unlike Lucas, I can't draw very well. My pergola looks peculiar. It looks childish. There's something strangely wrong with the perspective. The perspective is skewed.

I examine Stella's notebook closely, but there's nothing of interest. It's filled with pages of arithmetic, with the computations for her cookery school. When the sums don't balance, they're in her writing; when they do, they're in Dan's. I look at her list of things to do—twenty tasks and only three of them crossed out—and decide I'll relieve her of some of them. I can't bear sitting here anymore. How much longer can this council of war continue? What are they talking about in there? Another hour before we leave for Elde. I pick up the trug and the trowel, find the egg basket, and go out to the kitchen garden. Dan's father, Joe Nunn, who keeps any produce he needs in return for his work, is hoeing the long lines of peas and beans. I feel hot and cross, but Joe pretends not to see. He helps me dig up some new potatoes—sweet and fragrant, with the thinnest of skins. We pick some broad beans, too, and I slit open one fat pod with my fingernail: baby beans, so tender you can eat them un-cooked, embryo beans, in a white velvet womb.

I taste one, but it's bitter. As soon as Joe Nunn has his back to me, I spit it out on the ground. "There's another gleanie gone," Joe says. "Mister Fox is back, and he finally found a way in. Mind you tell your mother, Maisie. I've dug out the old wire and replaced it. Goes down two feet now, so he won't be digging under that in a hurry. Those gleanies are stupid birds, though. I warned your mother many a time—worse than chickens, they are."

I leave Joe and walk past the wigwams of runner beans and sweet peas. There's a frantic fledgling, a starling (*Sturnus vulgaris*), trapped inside the fruit netting, beating its wings against the roof of the cage. I release it. It flies off and escapes to the trees. I walk on.

In the orchard, I collect the eggs from the henhouse. Joe doesn't say "warned," he says "warnt." "Fox" sounds more like "folks" when he says it. He has soft consonants and long, slow vowels. I can imitate him—but never very successfully. I wish I could speak as he does, as Dan used to do. *Warnt*, I say under my breath, *warnt*. It sounds more powerful than "warned." Stella's hens are Rhode Island reds: I've found eight eggs, eight dark brown, softly freckled eggs. They're still warm in my hands. I give the hens and the guinea fowl some scoops of corn. I can see where Joe's replaced the wire round the run, and I can see the evidence of a violent death—it's Jessica that's gone. The grass is bloodstained, her feathers are everywhere. I stoop to pick them up, beautiful dappled feathers, ebony and ivory and gray—but Joe is right, gleanies are unintelligent. They have the wit to roost in the trees at night, but they don't check what's hiding in the long grass when dawn comes and they fly down.

I pick up the egg basket, and the trug, and turn back to the kitchen. Bees hum on the lavender (*Lavandula angustifolia* 'Munstead', a dwarf lavender, but the best sort). The council of war must be over now, I think, and I begin on some poetry as I walk. "Now sleeps the crimson petal, now the white," I say aloud. I've reached the third stanza, "Now lies the Earth all Danaë to the stars, / And all thy heart lies open unto me," when something catches my eye, a movement at the very edge of my vision. It's Lucas, walking up the back drive. He's pushing a bicycle. He has a small duffel bag, his equivalent of a suitcase, slung over his shoulder, and something furtive about his movements suggests he doesn't want to be seen. He glances back toward the house. I step out from behind a large bush, startling him. He hesitates, then—there's nothing much else he can do, I'm barring his way—he stops. I think he is not pleased to see me. He doesn't greet me. He doesn't smile.

"That's Julia's bicycle," I say.

"Is it? I just borrowed the first one I found."

"Where are you going?" I look at the bag slung over his shoulder. "You can't be leaving?"

"Such a face, Maisie! Why not? It's a fine day. I thought I'd go for a ride."

"I don't believe you. You *are* leaving. You're taking off again. That's why you're creeping up the back drive like a thief. Where are you going? Does . . ." I stop.

"Does what?"

"Does Finn know? Did you tell her?"

Lucas gives me a measuring look. "Does Finn know?" he repeats in the most irritating way. "Possibly not—almost certainly not, since I only decided ten minutes ago. I don't see why it should matter. But as you've spied me out, Maisie, you can tell her, can't you? Is something wrong? Is there some problem I'm missing here?"

I do not reply. "You can tell her," he continues after a pause, "that I'm cycling to the station. From the station, I'm getting a train to Cambridge. In Cambridge, I'll be staying with a friend. Not a friend Finn knows. Can you remember all that?"

"A woman friend?"

"How fierce you look, Maisie," he says with great politeness. "I'm afraid I have to tell you that's none of your bloody business. Or Finn's."

"When are you coming back? Tomorrow? You can't leave like this, not after . . ." I swallow down Finn's name. I swallow down the memory of her face last night and that blind, bewildered look in her eyes. Lucas waits; he's possibly amused. "After—after you made an appointment with me," I continue with guile. "You said you were going to draw me again tomorrow."

"Did I? Well, I'm sorry, but we'll have to rearrange that. We'll do it another time."

"What about the portrait? You haven't finished painting the portrait."

"It will wait." Lucas's manner has been growing increasingly cold.

"I may abandon it altogether, who knows? The atmosphere here . . ." He glances back at the house and frowns. "It's not right yet. You and your sisters aren't right yet, either. Something needs to happen, maybe I need to rethink . . . I'm sure the problems will be resolved, and I'll find a way through. I usually do. Good-bye, Maisie. Enjoy your time at Elde."

He mounts the bicycle and pedals off. Why does no one ever tell me the truth? Lucas was lying about the bicycle, that's for sure. All the other bikes are stowed away in an old shed, and indeed he could have taken any of them. But not Julia's; her bike was put away when she went to California. It was chained up, it hasn't been used since, and the key to the padlock was lying on Julia's dressing table when I crept into her room last night at four. How could she have given it to Lucas in the hours since then? She's been asleep, she's been lying in a bath of scented water for half the morning, she's been at the council of war.

Maybe Lucas stole the key from her bedroom, I think. Maybe he won't return—and if he doesn't, he'll never finish *Summer Maisie*. There'll never be an autumn or a winter Maisie, either—and that possibility frightens me. I run back to the house, very fast.

I get as far as the door of the dining room. I find it's ajar. I'm about to push it back when I realize the family conference is over and everyone has dispersed—everyone except Dan and Finn, who are still there and alone.

"That was unforgivable . . . ," Finn is saying in a low, angry voice. "How could you encourage Stella like that? Why build up her hopes? You know what will happen. This scheme will fail, the way the others all failed. Flirt with Julia if you must, I'm past caring— but don't you dare play games with Stella and Gramps. You know how desperate they are. And to do it in front of Maisie—it's cruel and underhand. Why do you deliberately set out to hurt me?"

"Because you hurt me," Dan replies, and his voice shocks me. "You hurt *me*. Week by week, day by day—you're doing it *hourly*. Why shouldn't I retaliate? Learn what it feels like, Finn. And don't imagine I'm going to stop. This is just the beginning. I'm going to put you through hell. Every time you betray me, I'll betray you. You want to break my heart? That's easy enough. But I'll smash yours—"

"Don't say that. Don't use words like that." I can hear tears in Finn's voice, and that confuses me: Finn never cries. "Why can't you understand? Why are you so jealous? You know there's no need. If you'd only listen—I've tried to explain—"

"He's my *friend*—try explaining *that*, Finn. There was a time when we didn't need explanations, you and I. Christ, I hate your explanations and your lies, and I hate the fucking expression on your face right now. Just don't fucking touch me—"

I hear the rustle of sudden movement, then some inarticulate sound from Finn. It sounds as if she's choking, and I think, Maybe Dan is choking her, maybe he has his hands around her throat—he sounded furious enough, he sounded insane.

I'm afraid. My hands are starting to shake. The air has that scorched smell again. I'm still holding the baskets of eggs and vegetables. I can't breathe. I don't know what to do: Should I go in or fetch Stella? Beyond the door there's now silence, but the silence is full of hot, urgent noise. I ease the door back and peep round it. Dan has Finn up against the table. His leg is between Finn's legs, and he's bending her backward. Her blue dress has ridden up over her thighs, and she's holding him, clutching on to him as if she's drowning, her hands locked around his neck and waist. He has his hand on her breast. He's cradling her head. Her hair flows back, cascades back, ripples beneath his fingers. Their eyes are closed; their mouths are open; their mouths are joined.

What is he doing to her? What is happening in this house? I don't understand.

．　　　．　　　．

I walk away from the door silently. It's half an hour before we're due to leave, and for fifteen minutes I walk the corridors. I patrol the house of despair. Gramps is slumped in the library. Stella is sitting at the kitchen table, staring at the sums in her notebook; I watch her sink her head in her hands. I listen to the house; I hear its timbers shift and settle, groaning with age. Mice scuttle behind the wainscot. My nuns are out in force: all the pale sisters, down on their knees. They know there's a crisis: I can hear them chanting psalms, I can hear them rattling beads.

I look for Isabella, but she won't be found, so I return to my bedroom and change my clothes. I choose my outfit with care. I know what costume I need. I tie a ribbon in my hair. I put a small white handkerchief in the pocket of my dress. It is eleven a.m. on July 21, 1967. By the time Stella calls me, I've made my plans.

PART III

The Tower

What can I say of Elde? The present house occupies the same site as the Tudor manor built by my husband's ancestor Sir Gervase Mortland. Of that earlier building, and its mediaeval core, no trace, alas, remains. Gervase, a fine man of considerable bravery, had served King Henry VIII with unswerving loyalty, but once his king was dead, his position was undermined by envy and intrigue. During the reign of that Papist bigot Mary Tudor, he was arrested on trumped-up charges relating to the Pilgrimage of Grace insurrection of some years before; imprisoned in the Tower, he was executed there in 1554. With his death, the fortunes of the Mortland family declined: its modest but ancient title was forfeited; the manor house at Elde fell into disrepair.

Blood will out, however. By dint of loyal service to their monarch, the rightful prestige of this ancient family was eventually restored. Two Mortland sons died defending the Royalist cause against Cromwell. Others would fight valiantly against rebellion in Ireland and Scotland, Guy (1650–1691) at the Boyne and Edmund (1670–1735) at Glencoe. Edmund later married the fifth daughter of the Duke of Suffolk, in 1710. It was he who first planned the great rebuilding of Elde. This project, delayed by his invalid wife's lingering death, was finally realized by his son, Henry (1712–1802).

The present magnificent house was completed in 1770. It is an adaptation, by Wyatt, of a design by Palladio. It is not without its critics. One has even found it 'vainglorious'; others have claimed it can look 'alien' or 'mournful' under grey English skies. I have no patience with such views. Elde's exterior, with its twenty-five bays and those soaring Corinthian columns, will always signify all that is England to me.

My husband first brought me here on the day he proposed. I looked from the man to the house, from the house to the man, and I weighed their history. With that decisiveness for which I am known, I said to myself: 'Violet, this will suit you admirably.' I have never changed my mind.

—Violet Mortland, *A Very English Upbringing: A Memoir,* 1955

EIGHT

At Elde

M AISIE, how perfectly charming you look, my dear," says Lady Violet. She bends down and gives me a flickering viper kiss by my ear. "Doesn't she look charming, Humphrey, Edmund? Such a pretty frock. So refreshing to see someone appropriately dressed for her age. Modern girls will grow up far too soon."

We're at Elde; the annual humiliation is under way. Violet prefers the double-barreled technique: two birds with one salvo. Having wounded me and at least winged Finn and Julia, she advances on Gramps. He and his twin, Humphrey, are standing in front of the marble fireplace. Even now—both will be seventy-five in three days' time—it's hard to tell them apart. On the wall nearby is a portrait of them as children: two identical blond boys, staring out of the frame with unconscious arrogance. They have matching black Labradors. The chilling symmetry of Elde can be glimpsed behind them; they're seated in its park. I dislike this portrait. I dislike all portraits. Portraits mislead.

"Now, which is Henry and which is my husband?" Violet says with a smile. She always goes through this ritual. She finds it vastly amusing. She kisses Humphrey, then, pretending to realize her mistake, Gramps. She knows which twin is which, obviously. No one would be in any doubt, really, despite their uncanny similarity of stature and features. Humphrey radiates complacency; Gramps has been to the Slough of Despond and back—and that journey shows in his eyes.

Certain aspects of Elde never alter. One is the nature of the food—the Viper has a horror of waste, so the portions are always mean; the other is the nature of the drinks. Humphrey advances now to a huge silver tray engraved with the family arms. On it is a battalion of bottles and decanters. But don't get your hopes up, Julia likes to say. Some warmish sherry is produced, and five glasses are poured. These glasses, famous for their dimensions, are then handed around. They are small.

No, they are minute. They are infinitesimal. They are Thumbelina glasses, so teensy that it's almost impossible to drink from them. Perhaps that's the idea. Without consultation or discussion, Finn and Julia are handed flat lemonade. So am I. Cousin Edmund brings it over to me and inspects the dress Violet admired. It's a blue cotton Liberty print. It has a sash, smocking, and puff sleeves. It was a present from Gramps for my eleventh birthday, and I'm thin, so it still fits. The skirt is too short for me and ought to be let down. Despite the heat, Edmund is wearing yellow corduroy trousers, a checked shirt, and a bristly jacket. His tie matches the shirt checks. As he's in the country, he's wearing conspicuous brogues.

"Very pretty, Maisie," he says. "And how is life treating you?"

"It's treating me particularly well," I answer politely. "This is a golden summer. It's the best summer I've ever known."

Edmund looks nonplussed. "Good show," he remarks. "No more trouble with the nuns, then?"

I wish Julia had never told him about my nuns. She mentioned it years ago, and Edmund's never forgotten it. He beams down at me, eyes twinkling in an avuncular way. Across the room, Stella has launched herself on the genius of Elizabeth David, and Gramps is detailing the Abbey's roof problems: Cassoulet, nail fatigue, I hear. I inform Edmund that the nuns have been quiet lately, which seems to disappoint him. A silence falls. At Elde, you get exactly twenty minutes to drink your four drops of sherry—and ten of those minutes have already passed. Julia, who knows this, makes her move.

She executes a superb maneuver around two huge chintz-covered sofas, past an exquisite bonheur du jour. The Viper tries to head her off, but it's difficult to do that in a room the size of two tennis courts, and Julia is swift. She's clearly taken Dan's suggestion to heart. "Edmund," she cries, drawing him away from me, "it's such ages since I've seen you. How marvelously well you're looking. Love the tie." If Julia were greeting any other man, her approach would be cooler—and subtler—but arrogant Julia regards Edmund as excessively stupid, so she's prepared to lay it on with a trowel.

Two golden arms encircle Edmund's neck. Two sapphire eyes sparkle with delight. Two rosy lips are pressed to his cheek. Edmund recoils.

"I think we should go in, Humphrey," the Viper pronounces at once. "Ring the bell, would you? Stella, my dear—I'm afraid you'll find this a very dull lunch. But Humphrey does not like foreign food. And neither do I."

"Oh dear, I've just remembered something," Stella says. "I'm so sorry, Violet—I should have warned you when I telephoned. Maisie is a vegetarian now."

"Is she? How extraordinary. Well, we're having cold consommé and poached salmon, so that's slightly a problem, but I'm sure Mrs. Hunt can rustle something up. Even at such short notice. I'll send word. Tell me, Maisie my dear—do you wear leather shoes? I see you do. I feel you should be consistent. . . ." All this as we trek to the dining room. "Now, Henry, I've put you next to me, of course. And Stella, next to Humphrey—so you can have your annual heart-to-heart. Finn, over here, and Julia—no, not that side, my dear, I've put you next to your sister. How tremendously fashionable you both look. Is that one of those miniskirts I keep reading about, Finn? Most original. And you belong in a harem, Julia. Now, Maisie, sit there next to Edmund—yes, yes, that chair, dear. . . ."

And there we are, as always, at the long, long table. The crystal glitters. The sharp knives shine. A shadowy servant pads back and forth. Like all servants at Elde, he's made himself deaf, dumb, and blind. I stare at the famous Adam plasterwork. The walls are arsenic green. There's a cornucopia of anemic fruits over the carved door cases. I can see a white pineapple, a white apple, white grapes, white pears. Over the chimneypiece is a huge gilded looking glass—it's by Adam, too. It's tilted at a curious, disturbing angle, as if it might fall and smash at any second. I can see all of us in it, frozen in time, arranged at Violet's behest, with the dangerous daughters as far away as possible from the beloved grandson and heir.

I watch small Maisie, in her Alice-in-Wonderland outfit. She eats the special offering that eventually appears—well, she eats some of it: two thin slices of cheese and a lettuce leaf. She chews and chews. Everyone else eats jellied bones and dead fish. Maisie eats one spoonful of the bread-and-butter pudding and, when no one is looking, spits the fat sultanas into her spoon. Humphrey likes nursery puddings, and so does Edmund, it seems. Edmund has two helpings and pats his expanding waistline fondly. "We can't tempt you, darling?" his grandmother asks, and—when he shakes his head regretfully—the Viper smiles. Julia has been discussing her time in California, and her attempts to engage Edmund in conversation across several yards of polished mahogany have been noted. Now she's to be rewarded for her pains.

"The summer of love?" Violet says, eyebrows raised. "How interesting, Julia. You make it sound so very different from the newspaper reports. Quite fascinating, to hear of these developments at first hand. Why just the summer, I wonder? If these changes are as radical as you say, one might have hoped they'd endure rather longer. . . . What will happen come the autumn, my dear? Still, never mind that, and since we're on the subject of love . . . Edmund has some wonderful news for us—haven't you, Edmund dear?"

Edmund glances at me; he does not seem eager to impart this news. It's a reluctance Violet does not share. "Edmund is engaged to be married," she continues. "He's finally found the most charming, delightful girl. Lettice Rutland's granddaughter. Lettice and I came out the same year, of course, and we'd always quietly hoped . . . indeed, once or twice we put our heads together. Young men will be dilatory, and Edmund has always refused to be rushed. But of course, that was only sensible in the circumstances. Luckily, he's always been able to spot the wrong girls and their ruses a mile away. . . ."

She allows the sentence to drift. Silence falls. Julia has flushed with irritation. Finn is on another planet: She's on Venus or Mars. She's staring out through the windows at the great lawn where in 1918 Gramps burned his uniforms. She's tried to cover that plum-size, thumb-size bruise on her throat with a scarf. She's remained pale and incommunicative throughout lunch. "I think I might go for a walk," she says when we're back in the drawing room and the coffee is being poured.

She doesn't wait for Violet's permission. One minute she's with us, the next she's gone. I edge toward the French windows. I can see her walking at great speed, head bent, along the Viper's famous herbaceous borders. She looks neither to right nor left. I watch her disappear beyond the tight-clipped yew hedges. "What is your wife-to-be called?" I ask Edmund, who is standing next to me, making conversation in a desultory way.

"Veronica," he answers. The name is pronounced dully, without discernible joy. A pause follows. "Maybe you'd like a walk, Maisie," he adds. "You like gardens, I recall."

"I'm going to be a Horticulturist," I reply. And Violet, seeing an opportunity to separate her grandson from predatory Julia, endorses this plan with warmth—just as she does each year. We step out of the cold room into the heat of the sun and walk between the borders. Halfway along, Edmund takes my hand.

We spend half an hour on the borders. We play a game. Edmund says he'll give me a shilling for every plant I identify correctly. I select *Lavandula spica; Geranium endressii;* Delphinium 'Black Knight'; *Aconitum napellus* (which is poisonous); *Lilium regale;* and three blighted hybrid tea roses, all named for queens. The lilies are actually Madonna lilies, not *regale,* but I know Edmund can't tell the difference, and by then I'm bored.

"Two more, and I'll give you a ten-bob note," Edmund says, more cheerful now. I look at him in silent scorn. These borders, though pretty, are predictable. I learn the Latin names of five plants, birds, and mammals every day, and I've been doing this for years. So I could name every plant in these borders, and there must be three hundred varieties or more. I identify two obscure clematis, and Edmund is impressed. He says I'm a very bright girl—how on earth do I remember all that stuff?

"I write it down. I collate it," I reply, staring at the ground. A folded brown note is handed over. Edmund paces up and down.

He inquires how my lessons are going. I tell him that the rector still comes on Thursdays, and we're studying Hume. I tell him Mrs. Marlow still comes twice a week for history and geography. I tell him how many aristocrats had their heads chopped off in the first weeks of the French Revolution; I tell him the exact length of the longest river in the world. It is the Nile, and it's 4,160 miles from its source in Lake Victoria, to the point where its delta meets the sea. I do not tell him about Isabella and my nuns and the lessons they impart. But I do tell him I'm still learning three poems a week and at present am working on Milton, cross-referencing to the Bible, an interesting task. It's pleasant to have a listener, and I find I want to reward him. I tell him of my new interest in Greek myth and astronomy: I give him presents. I give him Iphigenia at Aulis, and the astonishing Pleiades, star by shining star.

Edmund backs away and inspects the horizon: "Off to school in September, maybe?" he asks.

I do not reply. A silence falls. He essays a few more stock questions. I confirm Finn has another year at Cambridge and that she's reading English literature. I confirm she has not yet decided on a career. Edmund regards careers for women as eccentric; he frowns. I tell him that Julia will be going to London in September to work on a newspaper. "A journalist?" Edmund says. He inspects the wide blue sky. "What's she going to write about? Dresses? All that fashion nonsense? Can't quite see her as a lobby correspondent, not in the clothes she wears."

This seems to be a joke. He laughs in an uneasy way. He paces a while longer, breaks off the heads of some lavender, rubs it between his palms. He examines a small, fluffy, motionless cloud. Finally he says, "Right, Maisie. Where now?"

"We could go to the Wilderness again."

"We could." He looks intently at his watch. "It's quite a way. Is there time?"

Eventually he decides that there is. We set off at a brisk pace, along the Lime Walk, through the Rose Garden, and past the herb parterre. The heat bounces off the gravel; the air is scented with marjoram and thyme. I can hear the voices of gardeners in the distance, and so can Edmund. "Let's cut through here, it's quicker," he says. "And it's cooler. It must be eighty degrees out here."

We turn aside, into the birch grove. The shade brings my arms out in goose bumps. I shiver. To enter the Wilderness, we have to go through a tall wrought-iron gateway emblazoned with the Mortland family arms. It's locked—but Edmund has brought a key. We pass through the gate, which he relocks behind us. We are now in Elde's secret world. The grass here is left uncut; it brushes my thighs, and the scent of it in the sun is heady. "Did I tell you I like your dress?" Edmund asks as we walk toward the lake. There is a bench there, by the waterside.

There is also a temple, on a small knoll behind us. It's dedicated to the goddess Artemis, and one year he took me there. Today, it's the lake. We sit on the bench, side by side. It's made of iron, and its slats cut into me. I can't describe it as comfortable, but the view is tranquil—and it's a hidden place, a private place, as well. When we've been sitting on the bench for a few minutes, Edmund mops his brow. Then he slips his left hand under my skirt. He rests his damp palm on my knee, then my thigh. I sit absolutely still as he moves it cautiously upward. He's looking at me in a beseeching way, so after a while I recite the sentences he's taught me. "I put on clean knickers this morning," I say. "White knickers. I like to wear white underclothes. I like to be clean."

I ignore him as I say this. I look at the lake, and the plants at its border, and the birds. There are irises, and there's a huge clump of *Gunnera manicata*. Its leaves are the size of an umbrella—larger. Its thick stalks bristle with crimson hairs.

Edmund is now motionless. I can feel the heat of his palm. I wonder if he wants me to protest, as I did the first time, but it appears not. I watch as a moorhen moves fussily across the still, dark water. It has a flotilla of chicks. I begin to count them silently: one, two, five, nine. Edmund stands up abruptly. He moves behind the bench. I know I mustn't look around until he tells me, so I continue to watch the lake. There's the moorhen, nine chicks, two ducks, and a drake. In the distance, gliding toward me, is a swan.

I can hear sounds behind me now, and they remind me of the sounds I heard this morning behind the dining room door. There's urgency to them, perhaps desperation. "Look at me," Edmund says in a choked voice. "Look at me. Turn round."

I turn round. He's right behind me, not two feet away. His face is crimson. His mouth is slack; his eyes are wide. He's holding that thing in his hand. It looks like a fat stick of rhubarb, only livelier. He rubs it and shakes it at me. I pretend to watch for a minute or two; then I take the small white handkerchief from my pocket and hand it to him. I've never done that before. For a moment his rhythm falters, then it speeds up again, even faster than before. I'd hoped that might be the effect, as I'm anxious to truncate matters. Last year it went on for three minutes ten seconds, and Edmund wanted me to touch it. I wouldn't. I dislike slimy things.

There's a blur of white, and red, and white. As I'd hoped, it doesn't take long. He gives a shudder and then doubles up, as if he's been winded, and groans. Buttons are fastened; I rise. We walk back through the long grass at a smart pace. When we're in the lovely shade of the birch grove again, I hesitate. I had intended to explain our current situation, and Stella's plans, but suddenly I can't be bothered. So I come to a halt, and I say: "Edmund, that will be two thousand pounds."

At first, he thinks he's misheard. Then he imagines I'm teasing. He stares at me in a wounded way and then tries to plead and cajole. When he realizes that's ineffective, he loses his temper. He starts to insult my family and me; he calls me names. He asks who is going to believe me, for he'll simply deny it all. . . . I will record his remarks.

"My word against yours," he says. "Not much of a contest, is it? Everyone else thinks you're mad, not right in the head—little Maisie, who walks in her sleep and talks to dead nuns—the girl who won't eat, the girl who doesn't grow, the girl with no friends, the girl they daren't send away to school. Are you still taking the medication, Maisie? Is it working at last? Humphrey says you're dopey with drugs—and that's why you walk round in a trance half the time. Violet doesn't agree, but then Violet thinks you're retarded, of course.

Even your mother knows there's something terribly wrong. They're all scared witless you'll turn out like that father of yours. Don't you realize the reason they're so obsessed about money is you? Who's going to take care of Maisie, what's going to happen to Maisie—that's what they're discussing in there right now. Christ! If only they knew. You may not talk like a normal person, or think like one, but you're cunning, even so—I see that now. You're a liar—a filthy little liar, Maisie. And luckily for me, everyone knows that. So who's going to believe you?"

"I don't foresee a problem," I reply politely, and I pull the wet scrunched-up handkerchief out of my pocket. It smells sour. I toss it up in the air and catch it. He gives a great bellow of anger and tries to grab it, but I'm too fast for him. I snatch it away, and then I run.

There's no way he can catch me; he's far too slow and heavy. He lumbers behind, and I stop only when I reach the Madonna lilies, thirty feet from the Viper's French doors: I know I'm safe there. When Edmund finally catches up with me, I'm cool and collected; I'm staring at air.

"Please, Maisie," Edmund says, his chest heaving, trying to catch his breath. "Listen to me. I thought—I thought we were friends. Forgive me, I didn't mean what I just said—I lost my temper, that's all. You can't help the way you are. It isn't your fault. You're clever in many ways, quick off the mark, original. I like talking to you—I always have done, and you know that full well. You know what it's like for me, being here, putting up with Violet, being told who to marry and who I am. I don't have any choice—can't you understand that? I'm fond of you, Maisie, deeply fond. I never intended any harm. If I had my way—I always planned . . ."

A bead of sweat drips from his brow. He sounds as if he's being strangled. I really can't bear to listen; it's so pathetic, so predictable. In another universe, I could be merciful to Edmund, because I understand misfits. But I'm not in that universe now. "Make the check out to Stella, please. And give it to me before we leave," I tell him. "If it bounces, you know what I'll do."

And, to my surprise, for I wasn't sure my plan would succeed, he obeys me. As we're climbing into Gramps's Wolseley for the return journey, Edmund sidles up. He presses a folded envelope into my hand. I see the fear flare in his eyes. I nod, so he knows he's safe and I'll keep my side of the bargain, then I climb into the car.

It's a long drive back. I fall asleep, and I dream. I dream all's well that ends well: The roof is mended; Stella's cookery school is prospering; Finn and Dan are reunited. Strangers never look at me oddly; they don't whisper behind my back anymore. In my dream, Lucas has finished his portrait. I take my father to admire *The Sisters Mortland*—this is a good dream, and Daddy's come home. We're together at last.

We inspect the portrait for a long time, hand in hand, in the quiet of the refectory. I think Daddy must have come straight from that wartime airfield in Sussex, because he's wearing his leather flying jacket, and he looks very young: younger than my sisters, younger than Dan. His eyes are such an extraordinary blue—he looks fearless. I ask him what Edmund meant—why should my resembling Daddy make people afraid?

I ask him how many sorties he flew and how many enemy planes he shot down today. *Never in the history of human conflict has so much been owed by so many to so few*, I say to him. I'm sure this must reach him, but my words echo around the refectory. I'm not sure Daddy can hear me. He doesn't reply.

It's a perfect summer's evening. There's the smell of new-mown hay; swallows dart through English skies. My hearing is acute again, the way it was that day at Bella's. I listen to the wheat ripening. We gaze at *The Sisters Mortland* for a long time, my father and I.

I think Daddy is impressed by Lucas's work, and I think it moves him. He gives a sigh. *My beloved girls*, he says, his voice so low that even I can scarcely hear him. The portrait is very true, very like, and it brings tears to his eyes.

Finally, I show him Lucas's four drawings of me. There I am in spring, summer, autumn, and winter—Maisie transformed. I look grown-up in the portraits, tall and elegant, not abnormal, not peculiar at all. Daddy reads the pictures with close attention, then gathers me tight in his arms. *Ah, Maisie*, he says. *Don't cry. I understand. I understand.*

PART IV

Retrospective

[NINE]

Correspondence

August 5, 1989, 2:15 a.m. Fax from Daniel Nunn, the Oriental Hotel, Bangkok, to Jonathan Aske, the Royal Academy, London.

Jonathan—Indeed I remember you from Cambridge. Who could forget? It's twenty-plus years, but the memory's indelible. Sorry you've had to write four times, and at such length—I'm permanently on the move, working on umpteen campaigns back to back. I know you need a reply quickly, so I'm faxing this.

To answer at least some of your questions: Yes, Lucas told me about the retrospective, but I didn't know you were organizing it. And I didn't realize it would include so much of his early work. Obviously, *The Sisters Mortland* has to be there. It's been the subject of so much controversy, rumour, and surmise that you could hardly leave it out. But I can't believe Lucas has agreed to include the 1967 drawings of Maisie, Julia, & Finn. Is this definite? He's never allowed those drawings to be exhibited before.

You say you regard this as a "coup." I don't see it that way. That summer at the Abbey ended badly, and I prefer not to dwell on it. I don't want to intrude on the Mortlands' grief, or compound it, and it makes no difference whether it all happened twenty-two years ago or two hundred. So I can't help with background, and I won't answer the questions you raise. If Lucas intends showing those drawings, I want nothing to do with it.

As for *Trinity Daniel*: Yes, it's pencil and chalk, three linked portraits of me, a kind of triptych—or so Lucas used to say. He drew it just after Finals, in 1967, the day before we left for the Abbey—he dashed it off in a couple of hours. We were in my rooms at Whewell's Court, Trinity—and the location is the sole reason Lucas gave it that title. There's no other reason I'm aware of—who suggested there was? Why should there be?

And, yes, I do own it: Lucas gave it to me. But I'm moving house, so at present it's in storage. And likely to remain there—God knows when I'll get around to moving in. I'm not sure I'd want to lend it for the exhibition, anyway.

I move on from Thailand tomorrow, so it's no good trying to reach me here—or anywhere else. I won't be back in England for months.

I'd reconsider the inclusion of those drawings, if I were you.

Daniel Nunn

August 5, 1989. Letter from Daniel Nunn, the Oriental Hotel, Bangkok, to Lucas Feld, Notting Hill, London.

Dear Lucas,

You bastard—what's all this about a retrospective? You never said a word to me. Some curator called Jonathan Aske, or Arse, is hounding me—did you put him on to me? He says he was at Cambridge with us. I don't damn well remember him, and he's a total shit, a bloodsucker and a pompous *evil* man. He's written six letters. I lost the first two and ignored the next four, but he won't take a hint. He phoned my PA in London eight times last week. He's now got this hotel number, and he's already called twice—I was out at the shoot both days, so luckily I missed him. I've just sent him a Get Lost fax.

He was writing to ask if I'd lend *Trinity Daniel* for the exhibition—at least, that was his excuse. Once he'd buttered me up with that enquiry, he went on to ask a hundred questions about that summer at the Abbey—all hypersensitively worded in view of what he calls the "tragic events." I didn't answer them. I can't bear to think back to that time. It was such an extraordinary summer: everything seemed possible; we had the future in our grasp, and then, suddenly—it was like that scene in *Love's Labours Lost*: Enter Mercade, the messenger of death. I didn't see that coming, and I should have done. Maybe you did.

Sorry, Lucas: it's three in the morning, and I can't sleep. It's one of those nights when the past pursues you. I had to make the weekly call to Dad—who hasn't been well—and that's always difficult. Then I had to get Aske off my back. I know it's no good phoning you—I'll just get that damn machine. So I'm writing instead. I wish I could talk to you: Aske says you've agreed to show the drawings of Finn, Maisie, and Julia—I cannot believe you'd do that.

Christ, I'm depressed. I hate Bangkok—it's a fucking miserable place, crawling with fat pedophile sex-tourists. It's ninety degrees outside, and the humidity's 100%. I'm burning those anti-mosquito smoke things, and they're useless—I can't breathe, and I'm covered in bites. I've got veins full of venom, and I've done six fifteen-hour days on the trot. This new hotshot director is a pain in the ass, we're going over budget—the whole commercial is spinning out of control, and I can't seem to stop it—it's like the worst kind of trip. Tomorrow, there's a cast of thousands, but today we had a simple setup, one establishing shot of the TAA plane on the tarmac. Wunderkind pissed about for the entire morning, altering the lighting, rejigging the camera angles. In the end, we got a shot that should have taken one hour maximum. It took Ingmar thirty-five takes.

Twenty years ago, I'd have sold my soul to get a campaign as big as this: twenty years ago, I probably did. Now too many people are chasing me. I'm suffering from a surfeit of planes, hotel rooms, rampant egos, and sheer mind-numbing fucking *idiocy*: you can imagine the effect. A surfeit of brandy, too, probably. Thai brandy, tastes foul, but to begin with, it helped me sleep.

Send me one of your cards, Lucas—it would cheer me up. Send it to the Lutetia in Paris—I'll be working in Paris next week. Tell me this retrospective isn't going to happen. Tell me you're going to keep those drawings at home, hanging where they always did. I can't stand them being exposed to the hordes and their greasy curiosity. Tell me—oh, I don't know—that there was nothing we could have done, that we couldn't have foreseen, that it wasn't our fault.

Tell me you're alive—it might remind me that I am.

Dan

10.8.1989. Card from Lucas Feld, London, to Daniel Nunn, Hotel Lutetia, Paris.

Now, dear Dan, what's the matter with you?

1. You remember Jonathan Aske perfectly well. He played Laertes in that Brechtian *Hamlet* you directed at the Cambridge ADC. I don't know whether he's a bloodsucker, nor do I care. He's useful. That's that.

2. The retrospective has my blessing. I'm lending *The Sisters Mortland* and all the finished drawings of Maisie, Julia, and Finn. I want *Trinity Daniel* alongside them, so stop being difficult.

3. What happened that summer is now irrelevant. My work ain't.

4. I didn't see it coming, any more than you did. How could we? If we could foresee accidents, they wouldn't be accidental, *n'est-ce pas?*

5. I am alive—very much so. So are you. You just need a different job. How can advertising agencies use the term "creatives" and keep a straight face? It's a blasphemy. And I did warn you.

Lucas

August 12, 1989. Postcard from Daniel Nunn, Paris, to Lucas Feld, London.

Sorry, Lucas. Don't worry—I was waving, not drowning. If I can dig out *Trinity Daniel*, I'll think about lending it. Just tell Aske to bugger off. I'm in New York tomorrow, then LA, then Tokyo. Will get in touch when I'm back. That "irrelevant" was monstrous—but I guess you knew that.

Dan

December 27, 1989. Card from Lucas Feld to Daniel Nunn, Highbury Fields, London N5.

Dan—Where are you? No one's heard from you for months. Surely those TAA commercials must be in the can by now? I've been trying you at home, without luck. I met someone at a party the other week, and she said you were in Tokyo; someone else said New York. I finally called your agency, but they're being tight-lipped and won't give a forwarding address. Listen, now Christfest is over, why don't you come and drink a toast to the

New Year & the new decade with me? If you're in London, give
me a call. On our own—no ex-wives, I promise.
Lucas

P.S.: You're not angry with me, are you? Don't be. We've been
friends too long for that.

*January 1, 1990. Letter from Joe Nunn, 29, the Street, Wykenfield,
Suffolk, to Daniel Nunn, Highbury Fields, London N5.*

Dear Son,
It did my heart good to talk to you last night. I was glad to know
youd be home soon and that youd been thinking about your old
Dad on New Years Eve. You must'nt worry on my account, as I'm
feeling fit as a fiddle. I'm sitting by the fire in my new Xmas slippers. They fit a treat. Hector McIver came in this afternoon he
gets more like his father Angus by the day and he's a dab hand
with the electrics, so the long and short of it is that the new telly is
all set up. Hector said he's never seen a screen that big—its caused
a stir in the village I can tell you. How you managed to get it sent
and the slippers to, when your the other side of the globe, I'll
never know. And to hear you last night clear as a bell, you might of
been next door instead of a hotel in Tokyo Japan, I could'nt get
over it. I wish your Gran was here to see it.

I have your Xmas gift all wrapped up and ready Hector advised
not to post it. I was getting in a bit of a fret about that, but as he
says your moving about and so best keep it here till you are next
in Wykenfield, which I hope will be soon Danny. It is always a red
letter day for me when I see my dear boy, you know that.

I dont have much news to report. Things are quiet here as
usual—All Quiet on the Eastern Front as you used to say, I expect you remember. Hector thinks of oil seed rape in Acre Field

which will be the last of the pasture gone if so, but has not yet
decided. That rumour about the Abbey being let has come to
nothing. The house is still all shut up and I hear is going to rack
and ruin with my old veg garden nothing but docks and nettles.
I have not been out and about as the weather is bad and snow
is threatening. Not much to add except I am ticking over and
cant complain and am as pleased as punch with the new telly. I
watched out for that advert you wrote, as per instructions. It
came on after the news finally. That is a bit late for me but it
was worth the wait and gave me a hearty laugh. You could always tell a joke well and it made me very proud of my son. As
your Gran used to say I do not know where you get all your
cleverness from, Danny.

My prayer is this will be a joyful new year for you, bringing
you all you hope for. A new decade to and soon it will be a new
century and a new milenium which is a thought and a half isnt
it. Give my best to your old friend Nick Marlow when you see
him. He sent an Xmas card. I often think of him he was always
a good pal to you.

Sending all my love to my dear son. Let me know if your
going to be able to get down here but dont fret as I know how
busy they keep you. Best be off to bed now I will post this in
the morning.

Your ever loving Dad

*May 30, 1990. Letter from Jonathan Aske, the Royal Academy, London, to
Daniel Nunn, Highbury Fields, London N5.*

Dear Daniel,
A parcel was delivered to me yesterday, and—to my utter
surprise—I found it contained Lucas's 1967 triptych drawing of
you at Trinity. There was no covering letter—perhaps you mis-

placed it—but I assume it came from you. May I also assume that means we have your permission to hang it in the retrospective? It would be marvellous if that were so, but I do need formal written consent. I know you hate red tape, so to make things easier, I'm enclosing the necessary forms. I'll need you to return them as soon as possible. The exhibition is still some months away, but we have to work so far in advance—the penalties of bureaucracy, alas!

I do hope you'll give your permission: it's one of Lucas's best early drawings and an intriguing companion piece to the Mortland sisters' works. It's fascinating to see how he's captured different aspects of your personality, and, of course, he is a consummate draughtsman. For me, it brought back 1960s Cambridge with a startling immediacy. What a handsome firebrand you were—the iconoclast of the ADC and the Film Society! Those anti–Vietnam War demonstrations you organized—what a heady time that was!

But 1967 was also a tragic year for you, as I appreciate. Without wishing in any way to pry, it would help to know more about the circumstances at the Abbey that summer—I think I mentioned this when I first wrote. I'm now finalizing my biographical and critical introduction for the exhibition catalogue, and I'm only too aware of the gaps. Lucas has never given interviews, or discussed his work, as you'll know. His past is a closed book—and of course I fully respect that. He has not barred me from further investigation and interviews, however, and I have managed to obtain a good deal of new, and, I feel, illuminating information relating to the post-1970 period. Two of his ex-wives—somewhat to my surprise—gave me invaluable help regarding their portraits.

But when it comes to background information relating to *The Sisters Mortland,* I continue to draw a blank. This is deeply frustrating. The painting is of key importance: it was Lucas's breakthrough work and has exercised an extraordinary hold on people's imaginations ever since first exhibited. As you may know, it's been the subject of intense academic scrutiny. It has been interpreted in many different ways—none of which, I believe, explains the painting's peculiar power or its unsettling effect. It has also attracted speculation of the most vulgar sort. Given the circumstances, gossipy speculation was perhaps inevitable. Needless to say, I will not be pandering to such curiosity and will ignore such trivia in anything I write.

I have approached the other people who were living or staying at the Abbey that summer (with Lucas's knowledge, I must stress). The grandfather is no longer with us—a pity, as he sounds a delightful old buffer, if not the sharpest of intellects. Stella Mortland would have liked to assist me but feels the events are too painful to discuss. I did meet her briefly and found her difficult to pin down, a strange, nebulous, haunted person—she has suffered a blow from which she will never recover, I suspect. It was somewhat irritating to drive all the way to Cornwall (she's now living with some painter near St Ives) to be gently rebuffed. She could have made the situation clear on the telephone, and I certainly feel she might have spared me her inamorata's truly hideous daubs, but never mind that. She seemed touchingly anxious to display them and I fear thought I might be able "to do something for him." As you may imagine, I fled.

I've also approached Nicholas Marlow. As a doctor, his professional take on that summer's events would have been invaluable to me. He feels the episode is best left closed, however, and unfortunately, due to his pressure of work, I've been unable to see him. Julia Mortland (what a force de nature that woman is!) has been of help, though I'm not entirely sure how reliable Julia is. Her sister—well, let's just say her sister has not been cooperative.

That leaves you. You were in a unique position. You'd known all three sisters since childhood. You were close to Lucas. At the Abbey, you were both an insider and an outsider, involved, yet able to be objective. So I have always felt that your recollections would be of greater assistance than anyone else's. If we could discuss this—perhaps you would let me take you to lunch or dinner?—I know it would be of help. And you could rest assured that I would disclose nothing of a sensitive nature. I'd be guided by you as to what information should be revealed—or concealed. My one concern is to provide a background that may illuminate these extraordinary drawings and *The Sisters Mortland*—which I believe to be one of Lucas's greatest paintings, a seminal work.

I have no wish to resurrect the arguments as to whether the fall was accidental or suicidal. I certainly do not wish to raise the spectre of love affairs. There's been quite enough speculation of that sort. Obviously, in view of what transpired, people have an unholy fascination with the relationship between Lucas and the sisters: to which I say—It is none of your business. (Though I must confess, I can't help being intrigued—they are extraordinary creatures, are they not?)

No, what I need are your impressions—of the Abbey, of Lucas's working practices, of the Mortland family, and so on. If you could give me an insight into what I like to call the "interpersonal dynamics," it would be hugely valuable. Finally, a clearer sense of the chronology of that summer's events would help. As I understand it, Lucas began on the drawings of the sisters and the portrait in mid-June, when you first arrived with him at the Abbey. He completed the drawings in July and then left on the 21st to spend a few days in Cambridge. On his return, he concentrated entirely on the portrait. He finished it at the beginning of August and showed it to the family, one week before the tragedy.

That timing has given ammunition to critics of the feminist persuasion: frankly, these women are pests. There have been accusations that the portrait acted as a catalyst, provoking the sad events of that summer—these allegations emanating, needless to say, from the wilder fringes of the sisterhood. I have no patience with such foolish, irresponsible arguments. In my view, phrases such as the "male gaze" are so much cant. Nevertheless, this exhibition may revive such controversy, so I'd welcome the opportunity to refute such suggestions once and for all. A clearer understanding of the sequence of events that summer would help me do that.

Lucas, when pressed as to exact dates, is evasive—as is his wont. So any confirmation or elucidation you might provide would be invaluable. I wonder, did you by any chance keep a diary? Did anyone keep a diary, that you know of?

Forgive all these questions. I'll take up no more of your time. But the arrival of Lucas's drawing of you has excited me and made me more determined than ever to pursue answers to these puzzles.

Do get in touch. It's now ten months since I last heard from you, and it's proving singularly difficult to track you down. I trust you are well,

Kind regards,

Jonathan

December 3, 1990. Letter from Nicholas Marlow, Duncan Terrace, London N1, to Daniel Nunn, 29, the Street, Wykenfield, Suffolk.

Dear Dan,

I've just heard the news of your father's death—it was a great shock and it's left me deeply saddened. He was the kindest, gentlest of men, a pillar of my childhood—I always felt the deepest respect and affection for him. I didn't even know he was ill. I heard from him last Christmas—we always sent cards—and I went to see him the last time I was in Suffolk, but that was years ago. I find it hard to go back there—too many memories. Now I wish I had. He was so proud of you, Dan, such a link with our past, such a fine, good man. I can't imagine Wykenfield without him.

This is how I heard: my parents sold the Old Rectory when my father retired, do you remember? They're still living in that house they bought in Ireland, but my mother stays in touch with some of the old friends in Wykenfield (many of whom have died or left—I hear the village is greatly changed). She heard of your father's death from Angus McIver's widow, Flora, and called me at once. She said you'd been in Wykenfield since last May and that for the past six months you've been caring for your father.

Dan, I wish you had let me know—why didn't you? Lucas and I, all your friends in London, have been concerned for a year now. One minute you were in Tokyo, the next you just disappeared off the face of the earth. Now I find that you weren't abroad, as everyone believed: you were in Wykenfield—the last place I'd have expected.

I know how hard these last months must have been. Flora McIver said it was cancer, apparently—I know no more than that. Why didn't you contact me, Dan? You know that's my field—even if the disease had gone beyond treatment, I could have helped—and I would have done, at once, surely you can't have doubted that? I would have wanted to be at the funeral, too. I regret not being there more than I can say—and so does Finn. She happened to call today, so I told her. I thought she'd know—I was sure you'd have contacted her, but I suppose she is difficult to reach, always travelling. She was very upset and sends her love. Like me, she was devoted to Joe and hates to think of you going through all this alone and unaided.

Dan, something is very wrong, isn't it? And has been for some time—from before the onset of your father's illness? I hear various rumours—Julia brings them back from the TV studios. People say there's been some kind of putsch at the agency. People say you've been ill or had some kind of breakdown. They talk a lot of nonsense—and I ignore it. You are my oldest and closest friend. I want you to tell me what's happened, and tell me how I can help, if help is needed.

Lucas claims the trouble began when the issue of this damned retrospective came up. He thinks it brought back memories of that summer at the Abbey, he thinks you still blame yourself for what happened to Maisie. I don't know how you can possibly feel that. You weren't to blame in any way: none of us was—except that we were blind to distress.

Well, I don't intend to be blind to it a second time. You have three days to answer this letter. If you don't reply, I shall come to Wykenfield in search of you.

One final thought—I must catch the post. The last time I saw you, you were taking pills to wake you up and pills to make you sleep. I warned you about them then. If you're still using them—get rid of them. And anything else you may be supplementing them with.

If you can't do it, I'll help you.

Nick

December 5, 1990. Letter from Daniel Nunn, 29, the Street, Wykenfield, to Nicholas Marlow, London N1.

That was a good letter, Nick, and I shall cherish it. I used to despise that word "cherish"—sounds like a brand of fabric conditioner, yes? But I've been discovering what it means in recent months. Now I cherish everything—and it's too fucking late. I used to ring my father up every Sunday night, from wherever I was in the world. I'd ask him how he was, and he'd always say: "Can't complain." He never did complain, not about anything, not about losing my mother, or looking after Bella for five years of Alzheimer's, or working day and night for a pittance, or living all his life in a shitty dump of a tied cottage he didn't even own after paying rent on it for fifty years. He didn't complain about a son who was ashamed of him and couldn't wait to get the hell out. And he didn't complain about dying.

He just got on with it. That really breaks me up. Everything breaks me up. I can't stop crying at peculiar moments. I didn't shed a tear at the funeral, but wept over cornflake packets in a Deepden supermarket next day—why is that? It's difficult to analyse, but I'm weeping for Joe. I'm weeping for my mistakes. And—yes, you're right—I'm mourning Maisie as well. I don't even know why—it's just one long fucking awful retrospective. All futile, I know—but I'm not good company at present, so I'm going to ask you not to come and see me just yet.

I need to be alone for a while. Please allow me that. The McIvers—Flora and her eldest son, Hector, you'll remember him—were very good to Dad, and they've been extraordinarily kind to me. They say I don't need to sort the place out yet, and I can stay on here for a bit if I choose. At the moment, I can't face going through all Dad's stuff and all Bella's stuff. I tried and tried to get him to move—I wanted to buy a cottage in the village for him, and one came up for sale a couple of years ago—but he wouldn't hear of it. So nothing's altered here, everything is still as you'll remember it: the pictures of Ocean, the Tarot cards, Joe's ploughing certificates—there are still nine crystal balls in the kitchen cupboards. I look at them, and I don't know whether to laugh or weep. Much good so-called clairvoyance ever did me: I've been fucking *blind* for most of my life. And it's hard being here with all this stuff: it's just bits and bobs, bric-a-brac, without meaning or value—except to me, of course.

So I may stay here and tackle it, or come back to London for a while and then return to sort things out—I haven't decided. Meanwhile, as per your instructions, I've chucked all the mother's little helpers. I give you my word—I've just done it, tipped the whole lot down the sink—and it wasn't hard, not really, because I'd been weaning myself off them for months.

I'll come to see you soon. I'll get in touch. I'm sorry I didn't contact you before, but there was nothing you could have done. There was nothing anyone could do—it was too far advanced. It was mainly a question of pain management—you'll be familiar with that term, but I was not.

It would be good to see you, Nick. And good to talk the way we once did. I'd like to talk about Dad—I'd like to talk about Maisie, how it happened, why she did what she did. I'd like to talk about the summer it all went wrong. I feel there's a truth there somewhere, something we've all missed. And you might help me find it, perhaps.

Do you remember the day we made ourselves blood brothers? I was about six, and you must have been eight or nine, and we'd been fishing in the lake at the Abbey. You were after perch—there were plenty of perch. I was hoping to catch a shark. *Plus ça change* . . . I sometimes think.

Give Finn my love if she calls again, will you? Greetings to your family, to Fanny, who must be quite grown up now, and to little Tom—does he still remember me? I often think of them, and you.

Blood-brotherly love to you, Nick, and true gratitude,
Dan

PART V

The Hanged Man

This week *Hotline* puts top creative Dan Nunn in the hot seat. He's just off Concorde & could do with a shave, but that's life in the ad-world fast track.

HL: *So what's the secret of sublime copywriting, Dan?*

DN: Brevity. 10 words max. Oh, & artwork that features tits.

HL: *Hey, no satire! How d'you connect with your target audience?*

DN: Think biblical. Invoke lust, gluttony, envy, or fear. Always works.

HL: *Heav-y! What gives you the biggest satisfaction in your work?*

DN: You can't qualify satisfaction. Either you're satisfied—or not.

HL: *Tch, tch, pedantic—lighten up! What's the bottom line, Dan?*

DN: Capitalism. However clever the ad, if you don't increase sales, forget it.

HL: *Classic. Future plans?*

DN: Sleep. I haven't slept in four days. So yeah, some sleep would be good.

—*Hotline*, "Media Today," Metro Radio, May 1988

News in that creative supremo and sixties trailblazer Dan Nunn has parted company with Nunn Loewe Ridley Fletcher Wally, the agency he set up in 1986. Rumours of boardroom spats have been circulating for months. Nunn, winner of a record number of D&AD awards, is the stellar creative behind such industry highpoints as the Nicey-Spicey TV campaign that boosted sales 250 percent in six months and swung the massive GFT £80m integrated account. He penned the notorious "That Way/This Way" ads and the lacerating "Handful of Dust" TV/Cinema/Poster onslaught that won him the D&AD President's Award in 1988. No comment from Nunn, said to be in Tokyo finalizing the £10.5m TAA campaign. "This parting is amicable," claims anon. at Loewe Ridley Fletcher Wally. Watch this space!

—*Campaign*, "Inside Track," May 1, 1990

DEATHS:

On 19th November 1990, JOSEPH JOHN NUNN, of Wykenfield, Suffolk. At home, after a long illness stoically borne. Funeral: St Etheldreda's, Wykenfield, 23rd November at 11 a.m. Flowers care of Messrs Paternoster & Gladhall, Undertakers, 5, the Street, Deepden. Donations to Cancer Research.

—*West Suffolk Clarion*, November 20, 1990

TEN

Trinity Daniel

I<small>T'S</small> F<small>RIDAY</small>—or Frightday, as Julia used to say. What's worse, it's Frightday the 13th.

Gran could have told me, and would have told me, that on such days of ill omen it's wiser to stay at home. But I'm back in London, and I, Daniel Nunn, have turned over, yes, a new leaf, I'm keeping a record of my days, and so far this week, it reads:

M<small>ONDAY</small>: Nothing happened.

T<small>UESDAY</small>: Don't think anything happened: spent most of it asleep.

W<small>EDNESDAY</small>: Galvanic activity. Phoned fifteen people.

T<small>HURSDAY</small>: Fourteen people didn't call back. The bank did.

I feel I can improve on this. So, with a little chemical assistance (apologies, Nick, but I regressed, so I didn't tip all those mother's little helpers down the sink), out I ventured. And where did I come, this Frightday? I came to the worst possible place. To a corner office on the twenty-fifth floor of a glinting glass building. It's the office of a man I detest, as I've just remembered—and it's too late to escape. This office has a biblical view; it gives you dominion over London. I can see spires, domes, congestion, and a curious haze. The haze may be something to do with the vision problems I've been experiencing lately or the chemical assistance; on the whole, I blame traffic fumes.

I've been in the office a while, and it's just occurred to me that I've been examining this view for too long, or with too fixed an attention, so I jerk my head round to the aircraft carrier deck that comprises the loathsome man's desk. It's then I notice the date, which I can see printed out on the day's schedule in front of him. I can read upside down with exceptional speed, and I've observed that next to the name "D. Nunn" and the time of the appointment, 4:15 p.m., it says "15 minutes." It's underlined and in bold. This doesn't bode well. Better be quick.

Not an enormously long time to plead my case, I'm thinking, especially as at least five minutes have already been used up in fake bonhomie and loathsome yelps of "Where have you been hiding yourself, Dan?" and "Seriously great to see you" and so on. Another two—I'm having problems tracking time—wasted themselves on the astonishing fact that the man I've come to see is wearing one of his signature bow ties, and it's a lime green one. Which gives me, by my unreliable estimate, about another eight in which to make my pitch. No problem. *No hay problema.* I'm the pitch king, and famous for it. I used to clinch it inside two.

I approach the desk, put down my briefcase, and sit. I think: Engage turbodrive. I'm about to accelerate away when I realize the loathsome one is holding something. He's holding a magazine, one of those newspaper color supplements, and he wants me to look at it. I deduce this with Sherlockian speed, because he's waving it under my nose and jabbing a finger at the front cover. He says, "You've been out of the loop, but you've seen this, I expect?"

It's *The Sisters Mortland*. It's an article about Lucas's retrospective. And no, I haven't seen it. That is quite an achievement; that took dedication and skill on my part, because there's been a deluge of publicity. Now I can't avoid it. There it is, famous Lucas's most famous portrait. It's the Abbey, it's the last summer at the Abbey. It's Julia and Finn and poor broken Maisie. It's my twenty-three years ago and my yesterday. It's everything I see in the dark when I can't sleep at night.

There's more to come. A hand is flicking the pages, a voice is saying, "Hang on a nanosecond, I know I saw it somewhere. . . . Ah, here we are. Now, Danny boy—is that you, or is that you, or is that you? Only joking, no offense."

Truly Wildean: And what's more, Oscar actually remembers how much I detest that sobriquet. I follow his pudgy finger, stare, and there I am, in triplicate. *Trinity Daniel.* I'm chalk and pencil. I'm in my rooms at Whewell's Court, Trinity College; it's the day after the last part II finals exam. The sun's shining, the sky's cloudless: All is right with the world. I'm twenty-two, ambitious, careless, insecure, and talented. Sometimes I'm confident, and sometimes I'm obnoxious, but if others have noticed that, I haven't—as yet. Give me time.

Yes, I'm at Whewell's, next to the rooms Wittgenstein once had, and in a few months, once the long summer vac is over, I'm going to start revolutionizing world cinema—watch out, Truffaut; watch out, Godard. I plan to get into movies via advertising. One week I direct a commercial, next week Hollywood's at my feet. . . . That's roughly the scheme, and, aged twenty-two, I can't see any flaws in it. Meanwhile I'm sprawling on a rug surrounded by lecture notes, and as soon as Lucas finishes scratching away at his sketchbook, we're going to meet Finn. The three of us—inseparable, the Unholy Trinity, Varsity has nicknamed us—are going to punt upriver. We're going to get drunk, sublimely post-exam drunk. And once Lucas, sketchbook in hand, has wandered off, I'm going to hold Finn in my arms. We'll lie there by the Cam in the cool green shade of the willow trees, and . . .

And the page is being turned. I look away fast, but not before I've glimpsed one of the other drawings they've reproduced: *Summer Maisie, 1967.* That drawing was to have been one of four. Now there'll never be an *Autumn Maisie,* or a winter one. Now I'll never direct a movie. Time moves on.

"Sad," remarks the man I've come to see, tossing aside the magazine. He knows the story, of course. Everyone knows the story, up to a point, because Lucas is now internationally celebrated and *The Sisters Mortland* is a painting people get obsessed with. It's the one you see reproduced everywhere, the one students buy prints of and pin up on their walls. "The Meltdown Sisters," the man opposite continues, and laughs. "Wasn't that their nickname at Cambridge? One can see why. Julia still has that effect. But it's the middle sister that intrigues me. Something about her face—I never met her, more's the pity, just point me in the right direction, woof, woof. The one with the weird name, what was her name?"

"Finisterre," I reply.

And I want to add so much, I can feel it welling up, a great spillage of detail. That she was called that because when Stella was pregnant with her second child, she was staying in Scotland, near yet another of the sanatoriums that were attempting to cure her husband. Her waters broke one evening when she was alone and listening to the shipping forecast. That Stella, being Stella, saw nothing outlandish in this name, because "Finisterre" was a wild, beautiful place, so what the word signified was immaterial. That no one ever spelled the abbreviation correctly; that no one called Finn by her full name anyway—except me. I used to use it, stroking her hair, lying together in yesteryear's fields. *Ou sont les neiges d'antan,* Danny boy? Long melted. Long gone.

The man opposite is still yakking; the word *retrospective* is being used. When he starts saying how he must catch it, it has only two more days to run, I reenter the atmosphere and understand. He glances at his watch, frowns, and then—he looks at me, actually *looks,* for the first time since I slid into his office. And what's happening behind that bland face with its modish spectacles? Well, there's a wee tussle going on. On the one hand, my stock may have risen—it's something to be Lucas's friend, there are definitely a few Brownie points in having been drawn by him, especially when the drawing concerned is now in a, Jesus-wept, "must see" retrospective. On the other hand, he'll have heard the rumors; there are enough of them eddying around.

I wonder distantly which stories he's heard—the ones put about by my enemies or the ones whose source is my friends? Not that they differ much, and not that I have many friends left in the advertising industry. So which is it—the gifted but insecure+bereavement+ overwork+breakdown+all very sad version? Or the arrogant prick+ substance abuse+total burnout+always had it coming to him variation? Almost certainly the second—which is the one I prefer, anyway. I wonder if he's factoring in past favors—in a moment of myopic mania, I gave this man his first job. . . . Always be nice to people on the way up, because sure as hell you'll meet them on the way down.

Was I nice to him? It's hard to recall, but I think I might have fired him, in which case the prospects of my getting the Wunderbar campaign aren't looking too good. It's only up for grabs because, at the last minute, the creative who *was* handling it suffered some mishap, some unforeseen mishap. Like flu or shingles or terrorist attack or ME or PMT or TATT or death by firing squad or . . . I stop myself. It took half my diminishing stash of coke, two tabs of amphetamine, four Anadin, a couple of Peptos, half a bottle of cough mixture, a gargle of vodka, and four espressos to get me to this office, and the effect on my brain isn't *quite* what I'd hoped—instead of sharpening my wits, it appears to be juicing them: They're deliquescing. I'm experiencing slippage. Now that I look at the Widmerpool opposite, I'm none too sure it *is* the Wunderbar campaign that I'm here to discuss. It could be something completely different. I search the smooth face for clues: Skoda? Life insurance? The Labour Party? Tampax? That new fizzy orange drink?

No, right first time, it's Wunderbar. Crap chocolate, crap ads. But Widmerpool doesn't see it that way, it seems. His instinct is, the product needs repositioning . . . and the person to do that repositioning, he begins to explain, is not me, despite my track record, my undoubted talents, my numerous industry awards, despite the undying respect and the undiminished admiration this man feels for me. . . . Translation: This bastard has dragged me all the way down here to kiss me off. Will he admit that? He will not.

He has, it seems, gone out on a limb. He's discussed it in-house. He's twisted arms, pushed the envelope, called in favors, bent over backward, and done his damnedest to make the Wunderbar boys see things his way—but they won't. I know what they're like, he tells me: They're born-again conservative, narrow-minded, tightfisted, and allergic to risk. *And, Dan*, he says, dropping his voice an octave, *let's face facts—at this moment in time, you* are *a risk. Would you bring it in on budget? Would you make waves? Would you even turn up? Hand on heart, Dan—and it hurts me to say this—I can't truthfully be sure you would. Frankly, Danny, you've always been a bit of a prima donna, and when you were delivering, that was fair enough. But now? You might go on a week's bender. You might shove a kilo of coke up your snout. You might freak out totally, the way I hear you did in Tokyo. You might get the next plane to Honolulu two days into the shoot. Frankly, from what I hear, you're capable of anything these days, and . . .*

A *kilo* of coke? I wish. Shall I tell him these scenarios aren't too likely because I haven't worked in a year and, frankly, I'm broke? Shall I tell him that if I weren't broke, broken, chewed up, and spat out, I wouldn't be here now, talking to him, let alone talking about the crappy Wunderbar account? Shall I tell him that, okay, I've been slow, but now I understand: This is his revenge, he never intended to consider me for this job, and he lured me here for the sole purpose of shafting me? Shall I show him how desperate I am? Break down or offer to crawl? I can see that's what he's waiting for. I can see that would make his month.

No way, frankly. He is—and always was—a poisonous pompous power-crazed prat. Let's be clear: He's unforgivably thick. He's a lazy subliterate snot rag, a reactionary and an arse licker, a tuft-hunting, vindictive, talent-bypassed, five-star pain up the butt. He's a Thatcherite, a sneak, and a shit stirrer, he's a twit and a twat. He's an Olympic gold medal asshole. He's an epiphyte, a pudding puller, and a zit. He's the human equivalent of a bum boil; he's a vasectomy, a weasel, a wank merchant, an intolerable whoreson zed. He's one fucking unnecessary letter. . . . And he wouldn't know a good ad from a fart in the face.

Which was precisely why I fired him, I now recall. That and the bow ties. I stand up.

For one swooping second I experience the joy, the ecstasy, the Joycean epiphany, there would be in telling him this. The lovely words are there on my lips. But I never speak them. I never speak them, because I've glanced down at that expensive expanse of desk, and the magazine cover has arrested me. I've looked at *The Sisters Mortland,* and they've looked back at me, and suddenly I've understood: I don't need to be here. I need to be back there, at the Abbey, in the eternal summers at the Abbey, and I need to be there at once.

I'm out of there in a blink. Hoist the briefcase and run. Down in the express lift. Out onto the pavement, into a taxi. I direct the driver to Piccadilly. Once I get to the gallery, once I'm in front of that painting, my whole life is going to make sense. I close my eyes. The traffic is snarled. Winter in London. It's already dark on the streets.

These amphetamines do the weirdest things to one's heartbeat. First fast, then slow, a buzzy percussive effect. Finisterre, Finisterre, Finisterre. It's a pretty fine mantra. All the way to the academy, I repeat it under my breath.

ELEVEN

Squint

OUTSIDE THE GALLERY, something strange happens. I'm standing there on the pavement opposite, all revved up—and suddenly, no warning, I'm irresolute. A Hamlet moment. A bipolar moment. I blame the cough cure: God knows what's in that.

Shall I negotiate the pedestrian crossings or just throw myself under the next bus? Should I return home, where I could end things less messily? The temptation to end things has been strengthening recently. I've been stockpiling old-fashioned razors—now extraordinarily hard to obtain; I've had to trek round umpteen shops. But I can't decide: throat—fast and fatal, but requiring a certain dexterity; or wrists—slow and stoic, the noble Roman touch? I have several useful lengths of stout Manila rope, strong enough to take my weight. I've cornered the market in sleeping pills, and have a stash of pretty major painkillers, so if I'm feeling squeamish, there's always the coward's way out. Admittedly, I've been too cowardly to take even this route so far, though late at night the temptation is sometimes great. So concentrate, Daniel: To cross or not to cross?

Over the road, huge banners advertising the retrospective bulge and flutter in the back draft of a bus. Lucas's familiar hawky features ripple, then coalesce. It's starting to rain; people are putting up umbrellas; all around me there's that late afternoon, ending-of-the-office-day mania and crush. My eyes are on the opposite pavement, where a thousand strangers parade, pass, pause, and push. I'm watching them with the dreamy, glassy detachment that now afflicts me, which may be a by-product of my exiled, jobless state, or the Peptos, or just life, when suddenly one of the figures detaches and becomes recognizable. It's Nicholas Marlow. It's my oldest friend, the man I promised to contact six weeks ago, the man I've almost telephoned a hundred times but never have.

He's wearing a dark overcoat and walking at speed. He seems oblivious to the rain, the traffic, and the crush. Will he turn in to the gallery? Surely he can't be going there, too? He is. I watch him go under the archway, mount the steps. He doesn't hesitate or look at the placards; he makes straight for the entrance. And that's it: The black prince is cured of irresolution at once. The red DON'T CROSS man is showing, a cab screeches to a halt; I heft my briefcase under my arm, duck and weave between the cars, under the dark arch, up the steps, marble underfoot, parquet underfoot. I know which gallery I'll find Nick in—and sure enough, after a few hundred anterooms, a few thousand passageways, there he is. He's sitting on a bench in front of *The Sisters Mortland*. He has his black-coated back to me. He doesn't look around; he's completely absorbed—and even in my jittery state I wonder: What does he see here? Does he see what I see—or something else? How does he read these figures, these colors, these codes, these women, these shapes?

Slowly, reluctantly, I raise my eyes to the portrait. I know it so well, yet every time I look at it, it morphs. It will not remain stable; it retains a nasty capacity to alarm, puzzle, perturb, delight, arouse, blind, and illuminate. It's very large; the figures are almost life-size. Three sisters, two still living, one long lost. The gas-jet blue gaze of three young girls meets mine, and it's—fearsome. I close my eyes to shut it out. Some afterburn of their stare scorches my retina. *Finisterre*, I say to myself under my breath, and when the buzzy panic in the hushed room subsides, I cross to my friend and touch his arm. "Nick," I say. "It's me. I'm back."

He swings round, and for a moment I catch on his face an expression I've never seen before. I don't know where he is—in some Timbuktu of the mind—but it's a place that's left him solitary and bereft. It takes an effort for him to escape that region, wherever it is; then he rises, his countenance relaxes, his eyes warm, and he grasps my hand. It's so long since anyone's been remotely pleased to see me that I can't deal with it—kindness and friendliness undo me in a way antagonism never would. The air blurs; the room tilts.

Nick puts his arm around my shoulder. He draws me down on the bench beside him. "Let's just sit here for a while," he says eventually. No doubt he's made some quick and immediate medical assessment—I think it's pretty evident I'm not in too good a state. But then—to judge from the expression I glimpsed on his face— neither is he. And that's strange, because Nick has it all: honorable profession, well-merited esteem, home, children, and wife. Whereas I have—what? No job, no parents, no children, no wife, negative equity, a reputation that's shot—and all too few compensating factors. These days, even sex is . . . well, let's not get started on *that*.

Those differences fall away as I sit beside him. None of them matters, not one jot. Nick has always possessed this gift. He quietens clamor; his friendship is so sure that he gives me back myself, and the fragmentation, while I'm with him, blessedly stops. We sit there side by side in a silence that starts to feel companionable. I turn my eyes back to Lucas's painting. I look at the three sisters: one I disliked, one I liked, and one I loved. Lucas has given them a stillness that's charged—as if they're about to step out of the canvas and speak. I look at Valkyrie Julia, at Finn, and at Maisie. In the portrait, she is tiny, dwarfed by her elder sisters—but then she was small for her age, a thin, grave, disconcerting child. My grandmother told her fortune once. "What did you see in the crystal,

Maisie?" I asked her. I knew she'd seen something—the crystal had smashed.

"That is a secret I will never divulge," she replied—she talked in that stilted way, like a small ticking time bomb of an automaton. And she was true to her word. She never told anyone—not even Finn, and I know that because I asked, after the accident.

What was your secret, Maisie? I think, looking at Lucas's painted child. She's holding a tiny pair of scissors in her hand—I've never noticed that detail before. A minute pair of scissors and, behind her, light, from an unidentifiable source. In this spilled eerie light, I can see a shape—some creature, perhaps. Lucas's shapes are infinitely suggestible, fluid, and ambiguous. But I reckon it's a bird. I'm almost certain it's a swallow. Scissors, and a maybe-swallow, in a maybe-English, maybe-stormy, maybe-sky behind Maisie's head.

When did I last see a swallow? I think. And, thanks to the quiet of the gallery, or the reassurance of Nick's proximity, or the unpredictable pills, or the unnerving blue burn of three pairs of eyes, I'm released. I'm not even aware it's happening, the swoop is so fast. One minute I'm most definitely there, on the bench. The next I'm in my English childhood's infinite space. I'm sitting by Black Ditch with Nick; I'm building a den with him, in Nun Wood; I'm watching my father plow a field, and Bella is saying, That's artistry, that is. Then Bella has grasped my hand, and she's leading me through the Abbey, on and on, through a maze of passageways, until we open a door— it looks like a cupboard door, but it isn't—and there the stepladder is, in readiness. Up you go, Bella whispers. Didn't I promise I'd show you? And she helps me up the steps, and there, right in front of my eyes, is a small, square aperture. It's a marvel, Bella says.

I look at it doubtfully. The marvel is ancient, the stone and mortar around it is crumbling; spiders lurk in its crevices, I'm certain of that—and I have a terror of spiders. Furry spiders, black ones, small ones with sacs of venom under their eight little legs. Spiders can move fast; some spiders can jump. What if there's a whole nest of them eyeing my approaching eye? Nip, nip, do spiders have teeth? I can sense those tiny hungry mouths, just waiting to suck all the jelly from my eyeball. I imagine being blind, being eyeless . . . "Get on with it. I haven't got all day," Bella says. "It's only a room," she says, and I can sense scorn, gathering impatience. "Born in that room, you were—right by the middle window. I told you that story often enough. I thought you was a boy then—but I must've been wrong. It must've been a girl I was holding, some little scaredy-cat girl. . . ." And, to reinforce this insult, she gives me a pinch.

That does it. I apply my six-year-old eye to Bella's marvel. The marvel has a name. It's a Squint.

I'm very afraid I'm going to see nuns. Skeletal nuns, maybe—nuns with a nasty vitality, though they're umpteen centuries dead. Last year, on my fifth birthday, a team of archeologists turned up at the Abbey. They had written permission from the Mortlands, then in New Mexico, for a dig. They dug in the cloister, finding not very much. They dug in the moat—and found bugger-all, as Bella had predicted they would. They turned their attentions to Nun Wood. There they exposed the foundations of a small round building, finding evidence of a fireplace, of clay pots and some domestic use—but no altar or signs of worship, which, as the head archeologist said, was odd, since—according to documents—this structure, beyond the nunnery confines and dating from the mid–fifteenth century, had been used by the order as a place of meditation, prayer, and retreat.

Nick and I were already losing interest. We'd had hopes of this archeology—it was a novelty, at least, and in Wykenfield anything remotely new and different was a treat. But it took an age, digging trenches, sieving earth, brushing dry clay off terra-cotta fragments of nothing much. We'd been hanging around, hoping for something *really* grisly, and bits of what looked like old flowerpots weren't it. Then, their last week in Nun Wood, the team dug one final trench, at right angles to the building's foundations. Two feet down, they hit stone. And under the flagstones—there were three flagstones, and they were smooth edged, small, and lozenge shaped—they found . . .

They found what I'm very afraid I'm going to see now. Three skeletal babies. Three ancient skeletal babies with rosaries in their bony little hands and with thick, well-preserved leather thongs around their bony little necks. Nick and I were there, avid and appalled, as the team took their soft brushes and eased earth from the eye sockets. One baby had a nest of worms in its ribs. The head archeologist swore; his female second-in-command said, *I don't believe this, surely the nuns couldn't have—Dear God, look how tiny they are, they're newborn, they can't have strangled them, surely?* And then there was a kerfuffle and a whispered conference, and Nick and I were turfed out. All of which was twelve months ago, and I still don't understand, because while I may not know much about nuns, I know one thing: They're not like other women, and they can't have babies.

So whose babies were these? Who killed them, and why? I've asked everyone—and I'm none the wiser. I think Nick, who is three years older than me (and the son of a doctor), may know the answer. I'm certain Bella does, and my father—but they aren't telling. I wish they would. If they would, this trio of nun-babies might disappear from my dreams instead of dangling there, like charms on an evil bracelet, the minute I close my eyes at night. I'm going to see them now, in the Squint, I'm certain of it. Those little white faces, with loose jaws and blind eyes, with their tiny fishy spines and broken, bead-clutching hands—that's what I'm going to see at the bottom of this dark tunnel. Given my surname, I think of them as brothers and sisters: I can smell them, and their sour infant malevolence, wafting up. My eyes are still tight shut (Bella can't see that), and I don't intend opening them without protection of some sort. A prayer might do it, but I haven't got a whole lot of faith in prayers—they've never brought back my mother, Dorrie, and I've prayed for that often enough. So I try a charm instead. It's a Romany charm, one Ocean taught me. It's sibylline and sibilant, a snaky whisper of words that I only half know, only half understand: I say it under my breath, three times, one for each murdered baby, then I open my eyes.

And it's worked. No nuns. No babies. My astonished gaze angles down a tunnel that works a bit like a periscope in reverse. I see an unastonishing room, the Mortlands' library. Its every detail is familiar to me, not surprising in view of the fact that I'd been there ten minutes earlier with Gran, helping her dust the disused tables, shake out the white sheets on the fat armchairs, and rearrange the white paper pleats in the sooty fireplace. Bella's spat on the silver photo frames, then polished them on the sleeve of her jumper. It didn't get the tarnish off, and even I can see Gran's getting slipshod—but does it matter? The Mortlands are absentees. They left Suffolk toward the end of the war, when Guy Mortland was invalided out of the Royal Air Force, and they've been on the move ever since, grandfather, son, wife, and—as of now, according to Bella—two daughters who are called Julia and Finn. They've been in the Isle of Wight, Scotland, Switzerland, and—latterly—Canada and America. None of these places has cured Guy Mortland, who has something wrong with his lungs—and other problems besides, Gran says, tight-lipped. Who knows when, if ever, this family will come back?

So what can I see of the Mortlands now? I can see a dead lioness rug with a broken-toothed snarl. I can see a stuffed cobra rearing up to support a brass tray, on which Grandfather Mortland liked to place his evening glass of whiskey. I can see huge hulking pieces of furniture that came from Elde Hall, the grandfather's childhood home; these are known as the "good pieces," and Bella's supposed to wax them. I can just see paneling (one panel slides back to reveal a staircase, but it's disappointing and leads nowhere much) and regiments of books whose leather covers smell moldy—I'm allowed to flick them with the feather duster occasionally, but not to read them yet. The Squint has an angle, so I can't see the best part of the room: I can't see the marble fireplace that's been inserted on the east wall—where the nuns once had their altar, Bella says. And I can't see my favorite objects, the ones I lust after, which rest on the mantelpiece.

These are three hollow carved ivory spheres, made by some Chinese magician-craftsman; they're peopled with coolies and dragons and junks, and each has seven, eight, nine smaller spheres inside the others. All of them, even the innermost—and that's tiny, the size of a pea—are carved with these hieroglyph creatures, and all of them can rotate. How did their creator contrive that, when each sphere was carved from a single tusk, when there's no way in the world of opening them and never was?

I try repositioning myself, squinting this way and that, but no matter how I try, I cannot see that part of the room. So I inspect the evidence of the Mortlands instead—I like doing that, because this family's story is so richly familiar. I've been hearing snatches of it for as long as I can remember; I like to put their history and their possessions together and see how they match. At home, we have bits of England, acquired when Gran was a girl and still traveling; we have scraps of Ocean; we have Dad's plowing certificates, precious to me because they remind me his artistry is inherited—Joe's grandfather worked these fields, and his grandfather before him. With luck, I'll inherit it, too; meanwhile, I can go and talk to these quiet men, who are lying in the churchyard. But here . . . well, the whole world's in this room. It's like looking at the big map on the wall at the village school and seeing a pink empire, a pink India, a pink Africa. There's the lioness some uncle shot in Botswana, and the cobra table another uncle admired in some Calcutta bazaar, and the magical spheres that a trading great-great-something brought back from the Opium Wars—whatever they were. All this, plus those hulking "good pieces" waxed by decades, centuries of Gran-equivalents . . . I can see it makes our cottage, even with the tarot and the plowing certificates, a bit limited.

Meanwhile, looking down at the room from this angle is giving it new interest. It's like a dolls' house, and I can arrange the Mortland dolls where I decide they fit. The grandfather—who Angus McIver says knows less about farming than his arse—fits on the sofa, drinking a whiskey eternally. The father, Guy, now ill but once a white hope, fits with the collection of miniature signed cricket bats. The elder girl, Julia, who's as pretty as a picture and a right little madam, Bella says, fits by the looking glass on the far wall. She has golden hair and is dreaming of a prince—possibly me, I feel—who will one day come and rescue her. The younger girl, Finn, is a bookworm. That's all I know about her. I put her by the bookshelves. The mother, Stella, doesn't seem to fit in this room, but Bella says she's a good cook, so I whisk her off to the kitchen. Which leaves—the son. There isn't a son yet, but they're trying for one.

And—thinking of the son who's being attempted, what will he look like; will this family ever come home, so I can actually make friends with them (I'm short of friends apart from Nick; at school they pull my hair and call me a pikey, a dirty Gyp)—I turn my eyes at last to the windows. These windows have been cut in half by the floor Grandfather Mortland installed, but they're still huge, three, four times my height and more, soaring up to pointed peaks and crowned with motherly angels. The clear panes are set in lead, and they've been altered, so they open. On the smooth stone of their sills and on the smooth stones each side of them, stones that are called quoins, I can see, yes, I can just see the familiar bullet grooves.

And it's with these grooves, which I love to touch, which I like to rub superstitiously and fit my fingers in, that I enter this room. I enter it with a flourish, via a tragedy. Aged six, I've already given this drama a fine name: It's called Danny in the Lion's Den.

These bullet grooves, four in the sill, five in the quoins, were spat out from a Messerschmitt's guns. It was spring, it was wartime. One minute all was somnolent English calm, with Gran and her daughter, Dorrie, dusting away in the Mortlands' library. The next, there was the drone of a fighter plane's engine. An insect-size speck of silver glinted in the sky, the far side of the valley—and my father, who was in the cloister below, rested on his spade. He squinted, trying to identify the plane. *Not a Spitfire*, he thought, and bent to pick up the packet of Cotter's Early Giant carrot seeds that he, an essential worker, was about to plant in the trench he'd just dug. *Not one of ours*, he realized, straightening up, watching the insect become a bird, climb, and approach closer.

Then he glimpsed the wasp yellow nose cone, the blunt-edged wings in profile. *Messerschmitt*, he thought, or shouted, as the plane commenced a fabulous dive, out of the sun, over the orchards; but if he did shout, the whine of the engine drowned his voice, and he could do nothing, just stand, silent and disbelieving, watching the plane open fire, watching it aim its guns straight at the Abbey, straight at its many-windowed south face and straight at the heavily pregnant figure of my mother, Dorrie, who—at that moment, at that exact, ill-fated moment—had put down her duster, turned away, and leaned out of one of those wide-open windows, perhaps to call to him.

With my six-year-old eyes, I squint at that moment of destiny and catastrophe. I know what happened next. A miracle happened next. The bullets missed Dorrie. They missed me, curled up snugly in her womb, lazing away the last amniotic fortnight of a trouble-free pregnancy. The German pilot of the plane, a plane Gran persists in calling a Mister Smid, was less lucky. He banked, turned, attempted to regain height, failed, and, having misjudged the speed and angle of his dive, or perhaps blacking out from the G-force, plunged into a herd of Friesians in Acre Field. There he incinerated himself and four cows in a conflagration that burned for two days, a conflagration watched on and off by the entire village, with the exception of Dr. Marlow, his wife, and his infant son, Nicholas, all of whom, according to Gran, disapproved of this sport—but then what could you expect, they were from Cambridge; they were stuck-up, they were newcomers.

That verdict seems a bit hard to me. Consider the consequences of that gunfire. For what happened next? Dorrie went into labor, that's what happened next—brought on two weeks early by sheer fear, and her waters broke there, right there, between the lionskin rug and the middle window. I watch the familiar scene: There's my unknown mother, collapsing; there're the shouts and cries and my father running for help. There's Bella, kneeling grimly and professionally between her daughter's spread legs—and all ought to be well, because Bella is one of fourteen children, she's assisted at no fewer than six of her mother Ocean's confinements, and childbirth holds no mysteries for her. But this birth doesn't obey the rules; it starts breaking them. For although this is Dorrie's first child and she's a slender creature, little more than a girl, so Bella's been expecting a long labor, this baby doesn't intend to hang around, and inside of fifteen minutes, less, when there's blood leaking everywhere, I'm crowning. Then *whoosh,* out I come: Exit one tiny alien from the escape hatch.

One little pointy-headed Martian, slithering into Bella's hands. The alien's slippery, I'm slippery, and by then—there's a great wash of blood—Bella's frightened. She drops me, and I land on the lionskin. A fearsome sight, infant Daniel, apparently: black Gypsy hair, muscled arms, a fierce face, clenched with pain and indignation; my bloodied hands are gripping the thick purple cord of the umbilical.

I'm performing a version of the Indian rope trick. I'm climbing back up the umbilical into the womb—and when I fail, I announce my frustration in a way Bella won't let me forget. First, I open my eyes, click, like the shutter of a camera. Then I open my mouth, wide, pink gummed, and tragic. No need for a shake or a slap on the back: I open my mouth, and I give one anguished, epic yell—only one cry. Bella's never heard the like of it. It echoes around that huge room in that huge religious house, and it chills Bella's blood. Supernatural powers, she senses it at once. The Gift, passed down the female line from Ocean to me. This Roma newborn knows that his mother, slumped back on the parquet, is busy dying. This cry is prescient. He knows he's killed her.

At which point, fetched as quickly as possible, but too late, enter that village newcomer, Dr. Marlow. He arrives in his Ford motorcar, my white-faced father beside him. He races up the stairs to the library-cum–Lady Chapel. He cuts the umbilical. He wraps me in Bella's petticoat, and he tries to stanch the hemorrhaging. He doesn't succeed. My silent mother dies—and I still don't know where. I didn't know when I was looking down that Squint with my six-year-old eyes, and I still don't know, several centuries later—several millennia, is what it feels like—sitting on this bench beside Dr. Marlow's son, in a London gallery.

Did Dorrie bleed to death on the parquet or on the way to the Deepden cottage hospital or in a ward at that hospital some hours later? I know I killed her, but I want to know where. It might help, somehow. Bella used to say: *In the hospital, silly. She was holding that little white prayer book I give her, the one with the leatherette cover, she would have it. And when she was gone, Joe and I dressed her in her wedding gown, which was hard for him, I hate to see a grown man weep, childhood sweethearts they were, and that dress wasn't a year old, ten yards of slipper satin, it used up all our coupons. And then we laid her out in the front room, and the whole village come to pay their respects, and when the Mortlands heard—*

Joe wrote and told them—they sent a telegram, and there it is, on the wall, I framed it—poor Dorrie, she thought the world of them, always looked up to them, she'd have wanted it to be there.

But did I believe that? Do I believe that? I used to hunt for Dorrie in her white slipper-satin dress. I used to think that if I crept and peeped and spied, I'd find her, and she'd tell me what really happened. She'd tell me she forgave me. She'd explain why she abandoned me. She never did—and the facts weren't much help. I was born on V-E Day—no argument about that, it's there on the birth certificate. And my mother, Dorrie, died on V-E Day—as attested to by my best friend's father, who signed the death certificate. So, a historic day—and a historic birth: A war-and-peace birthday, Gran used to say when trying to comfort me. It was the Messerschmitt's fault, not mine, I must always remember that. If it hadn't been for the plane, it would have been a normal birth and Dorrie would still be here to care for me. *Stop that sniveling*, Gran would say, giving me a pinch. *Think, Danny, just think—how many babies get to be born on a lionskin?*

A fine tale. Better ignore the more pedantic queries, perhaps, such as, What was some rogue German fighter plane doing circling Suffolk fields that particular May? Why was Gran's helmeted Hun hellbent on eliminating one nineteen-year-old pregnant Englishwoman, fondly watching her husband planting carrots? (Cotter's Early Giant—there was always too much detail here; it was the excessive detail that first made me suspicious.) What was this belated kamikaze mission? The war in Europe was over. Besides, this story was always subject to slippage—like most stories, Bella told me. When she'd been at the Mackesons', that Mister Smid could transmute; one time it was a Dornier.

"I did check," I say now in the somnolence of the gallery. At least, I think I say the words aloud, but maybe I don't, because Nick doesn't react, and neither does the elderly custodian who's sitting at the entrance to this room—there's no one else here; it's close to closing time.

And check I finally did, when I was fifteen and at the grammar school. I went to the archives of the local newspaper and sat in a sweat over ancient, browning musty volumes. Result: confirmation of all my suspicions. There was an incident with a Messerschmitt, and it did unloose a hail of bullets at the Abbey. No one knows why. There was speculation it had been heading for the bomber base at Deepden and peppered the Abbey out of pure devilry. Not too likely, I'd have said. Maybe this German, separated from his squadron, was in extremis, in which case, he has my sympathy. He did die, and horribly, when his plane plowed into Acre Field—but this all happened four years before V-E Day, two years before my parents married, and forty-eight months before I hit the lionskin.

"I want the truth," I said to Bella when I got home from the archive. Bella gave me one of her Ocean looks—ancient Roma wisdom, eyes fixed on the far beyond, etc. I wasn't having it. "Come on, Gran, what happened?" I said. And I got chapter and verse: Yes, it was all true, location, sudden onset of labor, window, Cotter's Giants, lionskin. The only embellishment was the Messerschmitt: Gran had added that in when I was small, when I would pester her with questions, and—in a way—it could have been true, because when my mother was standing at that window in the Lady Chapel, she saw something.

As to what she saw, Gran could not, in the circumstances, be certain. It might have been the fatal plane, doing a spooky repeat flypast four years later. It might have been something else, but whatever it was, Dorrie, who had never manifested the Gift before, had seen something uncanny, something to which even gifted Gran was blind and something that was terrifying. So terrifying that she went straight into labor.

I stand up. The gallery's gone very quiet. Nick isn't breathing. I'm not breathing. I'm thinking about my past, I'm thinking about my culpability. I had difficulties with the story of my birth as a child; later, I grew a skin. I found you could make those background shames and their attendant pain disappear if you emphasized them. So, at Cambridge (where there was the odd snob, just the odd thousand), I dined out on Roma ancestry, on Ocean and Bella and a plowman for a father. Okay, I was a pikey, but I wasn't stupid: I knew there was no point in trying to pass, and it was the sixties, when to be a working-class exotic was not necessarily a disadvantage. Handled right, it was the strongest of trump cards.

Once started, I couldn't stop. I glorified and embellished, and by the summer at the Abbey, when Lucas painted this portrait, I had the bloody story of my birth really well honed. I regaled people with it—and one of the people I regaled, one twilight evening, was Maisie. It was a few days before the annual visit to Elde; we were all in the library. I took Maisie across to the window and showed her the marks where Dorrie's lifeblood, and my birth, stained the parquet.

"She saw something terrible?" Maisie said, frowning. "Was it the nuns? Or those three dead babies?" Because, yes, so help me, I'd told her about them, too.

"Terrifying," I corrected. I'd had too much wine. "She saw something terrifying."

"You're sure it was the middle window?"

"Definitely. The middle window."

"It's the window I saw *you* in," she said in that odd fixed way of hers. "I was the first of my family to see you. It was the day of Daddy's funeral, though it wasn't a funeral as such, of course. That is why we are friends."

"Yeah," I said. "Right." And I drifted away to join Nick, Finn, and Julia.

Three weeks later, Maisie went up to the library when no one was there, opened that same window, stood on the sill, and jumped. Thirty feet down, onto the cloister flagstones. There's a school of thought (it's Stella's) that she didn't jump, that she stood in the window and then slipped.

I don't hold with it.

I found her.

I can't stand thinking about it.

"Back in two seconds," I say to Nick, moving off fast. "I just have to . . . I won't be a . . ." Speedy. I'm out of that room, I'm three miles down the corridors before he can speak.

"*Help*," I say to the first uniform I encounter. It wouldn't surprise me if he took me into custody, but no, he's a kindly soul, this cicerone of the gallery. He takes my arm, indicates some stairs, and— sure enough—when I've circled the inferno a few more times, I find the right door. There I am, blessedly alone, my reflections and me, Daniel in triplicate in the gentlemen's lavatory.

TWELVE

Look Closely

I'D LIKE TO BE CLEAR: I blame everything that's happened subsequently—everything—on the two minutes and twenty seconds I then spent in that cool, quiet, white-tiled space. Opening the door, closing it behind me, glimpsing the ghastly spectacle of myself mirrored back at me, I'm clear what I have to do. I have to sober up, get clean and stay clean. I have to junk the dwindling stash of stuff I told Nick I'd junked six weeks ago.

I have to get a grip. I have to reform. I must start now. At once.

If I've made mistakes in the past, I won't waste my energy on them. What's done cannot be undone, so there is no point in castigating, or cracking up, or rushing around hardware shops and chemists, stocking up on Stanley knives and acetaminophen and geriatric Gillette razor blades. Who does that help? It doesn't help anyone, and it certainly doesn't help me. So I will not think of Finn, or Maisie, or lost loves, or past guilts, or failed careers, or wasted talents, or betrayed fathers. It's all too damn biblical: I will leave such melodrama behind me. I will, magisterially, move *on*. I'll do what every sensible person does: I'll settle for second best, good works, and nonentity.

How do I see myself in, say, five years? The word *burgher* springs to mind. Yes, a good burgher of Islington, a paterfamilias, perhaps, unless they're extinct. I can see it now: the modest London house, the modest country cottage, *The Guardian* on the breakfast table, the eco-aware car, and the compost heap. The donations to Oxfam, the 2.4 children, the sensible wife, the pension plan; the brisk walking weekends, the three-weeks-in-a-charming-*gîte* holidays; the odor of sanctity, the consolations of principle, the sure and certain hope of the resurrection . . . Oh, the blamelessness of it: I can't wait.

I approach the washbasins. My mind is resolved—I'm so damn re-solved, I'm positively godly. And then . . .

And then, something goes wrong. The tap won't turn on, and when it does finally turn on, it won't fucking well turn off. One minute it's a dribble, the next we're talking Niagara. The lights be-come excessively bright, then excessively dim, and before I can do a thing it's back, the wastage of years is back, filling the room, rever-berating around the room, howling in my ears, thumbing its nose at me.

So I do what I suppose I knew I'd do all along. It's the joylessness I can't stand. The diurnal joylessness: No one warned me about that. In the acres of print I've read this past year on such hitherto unex-plored and derided subjects as male midlife crisis, bereavement guilt, and depression, not one guru, medic, crank, or charlatan has men-tioned joylessness. They didn't describe its serpentine approach—the decades it takes to slither up on you, so you never even notice it's there until too late, until it's got you in its anaconda grip, and it's crushing the life out of you. And they didn't suggest a cure, either—but that doesn't matter, because right here in my pockets I have one.

I have several, in fact. And just to be on the safe side, I select three. It's ignominious, it's undignified, and my hands are twitching so much that I nearly spill half the cure down the Niagara Falls, but I get there in the end. I cut a precious penultimate line of best Boli-vian and Hoover it up an eager nostril. I crunch two amphetamine tabs, then gulp them down. I light a Marlboro and blow gusts of hot heretic smoke at the ceiling sensor systems. I wait for a response: red lights, alarms, sprinkler activations, uniformed intervention at the very least, and—what do you know?—nothing happens. Nothing at all. The errant tap continues to gush. The world turns. My reflections splinter and refract. And then there's the rush of relief, the return of conviction, the sure and certain hope only chemicals can give you. *Hieronymo's mad againe.* With one bound I'm free, I'm out of there—and I'm back in the gallery.

Nick hasn't moved. He doesn't seem to react when I return—which is odd considering the light-years that have passed, the galaxies I've been visiting. Never mind, there's a lot to look at in here, there's a lot to *learn* in here, and—thanks to my enhanced chemistry, my rebooted synapses—I can see it with new eyes. I start prowling about. I prowl busily, first this wall of portraits, then that one.

On the wall behind Nick are some of Lucas's later works. His notorious later works. I don't like them. The light is remorseless, and so is his eye. Two of the wives, several of the mistresses. All his subjects look bleached or drained, as if Transylvanian Lucas applied his mouth to their jugular, sucked out all their blood, and then—when there was just a faint heartbeat still remaining—picked up his brush and painted their last agonies.

They're pitifully calm. You can tell that death has just interrupted them. There they were, reading a book, cradling a child, drinking a glass of wine, making love, smoking a ciggie—and suddenly there was a soft tap at the door. All aboard, a voice said to them, and the journey they're about to make is there in their eyes, their pale zombie eyes, which are filled with living-dead resignation. There's a glitter to their eyes, too, a certain gloating malevolence, as if they'd like us, their watchers, to know that we'll be joining the same train, that we'll be packed in the very same boxcars. What's more—and this I particularly dislike—there's a clear intimation that this journey's going to be brief. Hades, only one stop: We're all disembarking at the very next station.

Well, thanks, Lucas, but I think I'll skip this ride. I don't want to look at these stripped, naked women—Lucas nearly always paints women. I don't want to look at those drawings of Maisie, either: the drawings on the next wall, the drawings that make Maisie look deformed and desperate. I look at the early drawings of Finn instead. *Orchard Finn*, a lovely girl, book in hand, sprawled beneath a tree, abundant apples scattered in the grass beside her. *Finn at Black Ditch*, a nymph-girl standing next to a dark stripe, a Styx of ominous water. *Finn by Nun Wood*, *The Dormition of Finn* (her eyes are closed), *Dreaming Finn* (her eyes are open). Finn, again and again Finn—there must be ten, twelve, fifteen drawings here, I realize, more drawings than I've ever seen before, more than I knew Lucas made, more—far more—than he's ever shown me.

A multiplicity of black-and-white Finns—and they're starting to dazzle me. I think, When did he do these drawings? How did he have time, that summer, to do so many drawings? Where was I when he worked on them, when she posed for them? Surely I was with her almost every hour of every day that summer?

But, of course, I wasn't. That was the summer Finn slipped away from me, the summer I lost her. I think: He's my friend, try explaining *that*, Finn. And it seems to be a sentence I might once have said, but I can't remember if I merely thought it or actually articulated it and, if so, where or under what circumstances—except that I was jealous, obviously, just as I'm jealous again now, jealous and bereft, standing here watching a multiplicity of Finns I never knew, Finns I never suspected, dancing down some tunnel of the past and—as ever—eluding me.

In the last of the drawings, a tight close-up of her face—it's called *Final Finn*—she is screening her eyes with her hands, and she's wearing a wedding ring. Lucas's wedding ring—since Finn was, disastrously, the first of Lucas's several wives. The drawing's undated; it's another I've never seen. I stare at it hard, too hard, until its sense starts crumbling, until it's a mess of lines and scrawls and smudges, until it's random and means nothing. When did Lucas draw that? When the brief marriage came to its unlovely end or afterward? Or on their wedding day, perhaps? Half an hour after they left the register office in Cambridge—that would be my guess. *Final Finn*: Yes, I can imagine that. It might interest Lucas to combine hail and farewell. But then Lucas is a gifted artist, very possibly a great one, and great artists are odd. The havoc Lucas causes is the lifeblood of his paintings, but Lucas never notices the havoc—he's blind in that respect.

He discarded Finn; he's discarded Julia—several times, if you can believe the gossip; but their affairs are always brief, or so people say, occurring and recurring only at times when they'll cause maximum damage. So: Two out of three of the sisters Mortland is Lucas's score, and no doubt, if circumstances had been different, he'd have moved on to Maisie eventually. Given a few more years, he'd have gone for the hat trick. And for once might have met his match, I think, turning round to face the portrait and remembering the Maisie I knew, the Maisie who can't be explained by "freakiness," or a form of autism, or by being "touched," as they used to say in the village, but the Maisie who was like a land mine, some lethal discard on a battlefield, antique mechanism in full working order: the Maisie I thought was innocent and dangerous.

A child's inscrutable blue gaze meets mine. We stare at each other, across the gallery, across the decades. And at that point, precisely at that point (Nick will later claim it's when the dope really kicks in), I understand that this small, lost child is trying to escape from the frame in which Lucas has imprisoned her, and *she wants to tell me something.*

I start moving toward the picture fast, dimly aware that somewhere to my right Nick is rising to his feet and suggesting something—that we leave, probably. But I can't pause to listen to him, or even glance at him, or at the custodian, who was seated at the entrance, who is also rising to his feet. No, I have to concentrate exclusively on Maisie, on what she is saying and trying to show me. *Look closely*, says a small, familiar voice—and no, I'm not imagining it, I'm not having some kind of trip; this bears no resemblance to those moments I've experienced recently, when alcohol, dope, and misery make me see the invisible. *Look closely*, says the voice, *look closely*.

And I do. I look at Maisie in her blue dress, holding her pair of tiny, half-hidden scissors. She, in the center, is the source of the painting's charge: You can feel the high-voltage flow between her and her sisters. Finn is gripping her hand, Julia clasps her shoulder; the sky behind them is irradiated. All three, linked by some unseen galvanic force, send out a current that sparks off the canvas. It's fluorescent—I can feel it light me up. It's disturbing; it's modern and ancient. I can try to distance myself from this; I can make myself note the painterly references all the academics hymn, *Les Demoiselles d' Avignon*, *The Opening of the Fifth Seal of the Apocalypse*. Yes, looking with their critical eyes, I can see those echoes and mockeries; I can see that the sisters' pose is like, and unlike, that of Botticelli's Graces—but that tells me nothing. Three Graces, three fates, three sibyls, three witches: I look at the strange way in which all three sisters' faces seem turned toward the spectator yet are discernibly tilted, as if they're looking up at something unseen. I look at the disconcerting perspective this gives the painting—so its effect is El Greco vertiginous. I look at the background—insofar as there is one—which could, I suppose, be a room, but which I've always assumed to be a postmodern nowhere-everywhere, a terrifying distillation of that wasteland, the twentieth century.

I see an abstract of floaty jagged misaligned shapes that resist interpretation, but I can't see beyond them. All I can see, all I can really see, is the riddling danger of Lucas's creation. I try to decode this weird perspective, this unnatural realism, this last-days' iridescence. Something huge is about to happen here—it screams out of the paint—but I can't tell whether it's joyful or appalling. What are these three sisters looking at? Are they watching a resurrection or some final catastrophe?

Look closely, says that small voice one final time, and although I can sense movement and stir behind me, I do. I get right up close, so close that I can see veins beneath the painted skin and the air's very brushstrokes. And when I do, there's—revelation. Those floaty mis-aligned shapes suddenly cease to be random or imagined: They become recognizable. That dark leonine smudge of color in the left foreground, for instance—isn't that familiar? That threatening snaky shape, which uncoils in the shadows behind Finn, that serpentine *thing* that has so puzzled critics—don't I know that? And above the sisters' heads, those three indistinct spheres that seem to float in the indeterminacy of the background, spheres that some commentators have claimed are moons, a little constellation held in the sisters' galaxy, forever fixed by their triple-force gravity—why, they're not moons at all, they're nothing so fanciful. What I'm looking at is a place—one I could recognize blindfolded. That leonine smudge is a lionskin. That snaky *thing* is a vulgar table, brought back from a Calcutta bazaar by one of many colonialist Mortland uncles. Those three moons are the ivory spheres that used to fascinate me so, the ones I lusted after, in my childhood.

Look closely, and we're in the library at the Abbey. We're in the Lady Chapel. Or, to be more precise, we're looking down at that space from the vantage point of Bella's marvel, the irreligious Squint, that medieval aperture set at man-height in a building occupied exclusively by women.

By holy women. Which is surprising. It may explain why the sisters' faces appear to look up and why the painting induces this celebrated sense of imbalance or vertigo or, as others have suggested, voyeurism—yet as far as I know, Lucas never knew of the Squint's existence. He rarely spent any time inside the Abbey itself. He had no interest whatsoever in its history or its architecture. I cannot remember him ever sketching there—he always worked outdoors or in the refectory. And when we finally trooped down to the refectory, on the memorable day when he unveiled the picture, no mention was made of library, Lady Chapel, or Squint—I'm absolutely certain of that. Am I certain of that?

"Where have you *put* us? Where are we?" Maisie said after a long, silent interval—she was the first to speak. The room stank of turpentine.

"In my imagination," Lucas replied kindly. "And there you will stay," he added.

Someone must have shown him the Squint, I think. Who showed him the Squint—where, and why, and under what circumstances? And then, *pace* Nick, all the chemicals do kick in, and it's like mainlining rocket fuel. My mind is off and away. Boy, it's fast. It's like a greyhound, like a bloodhound. It's following the scent of those summer weeks; it's loping up stairs, nosing along corridors, through anterooms. It's rewriting the maze of the Abbey's interior, it's reexamining the placing—the very precise placing—of the three sisters inside this frame, and it's noticing for the first time that the unearthly light falling across the sisters' hair comes from a source I recognize. It comes from one of the Lady Chapel's windows. The middle window, to be exact: the window next to which I was born. The window where—if you can trust Bella, which you probably can't—my mother looked out at the world for the last time and saw something terrifying. The window where Maisie jumped, or slipped—or, I suppose it's feasible, was pushed—and fell thirty feet onto the flagstones.

"*What happened?* I have to know what happened," I say out loud. At least, I think I say those words, but maybe I don't, because suddenly, without warning, all the air molecules decide to disobey the laws of physics, and they start rushing about, so the gallery atmosphere begins whirling and gusting. I'm getting a private view of chaos theory: I'm watching all those strings of the universe unraveling. *Don't touch the canvas. Move back,* says a voice, and I swing round to see the uniformed guardian of the gallery approaching fast, and he's definitely not pleased, he's definitely agitated. He's red and irascible, but—curious, this—the faster this troglodyte runs at me, the less progress he makes, so instead of advancing, he begins to recede farther and farther away into some dim and tunnelly distance. I watch him vanish at giddying speed, and then, just as I realize that this room is insufferably hot, hellishly hot, and I'm about to tumble out of the heat into some cool, dark, welcoming emptiness, I feel Nicholas Marlow, doctor son to a doctor father, grasp my arm and retrieve me.

Some while later: I discover I'm outside, in an unstable city, on a wavering pavement. I'm sucking in great gulps of megalopolis carbon monoxide. I'm sitting on steps, with my head between my knees; Nick is holding my briefcase and bending over me. I straighten up: I can't wait to explain, to spell it out to him. The words refuse to be said in the right order, so no doubt I sound a bit emotional, a tad irrational, but I'm pretty sure I manage "Squint" and "Lady Chapel." I stumble on "perspective," but I manage "suicide."

And then I stop: Nick's expression, faintly embarrassed, concerned, anxious yet irritated, has finally registered. "Breathe in— slowly," he says. "Are you okay now? Dear God, what the hell are you *on*, Dan? When did you last sleep? When did you last eat?"

"Can't remember."

"Think."

"I recall a kebab. With chilies. With onions."

"A recent kebab?"

"Fairly. Five days ago? Six? Who cares? Nick, listen, this is important. . . ."

Nick refuses to listen, though I grab his lapels and gibber furiously. He spends a couple of years inspecting my eyes, checking the pupil dilation, no doubt—and his readings don't appear to please him. He raises an arm, and next minute we're in the back of a taxi. I weep for a while—this happens, I'm used to it, nothing to worry about. I trance out and surface around Euston Road. I demand to know where we're going.

"I'm taking you home with me," Nick replies. "I'm going to feed you and try to talk some sense into you."

"Home?" This is alarming. I'm already reaching for the door handle. "Home with you? No way. You've got to be joking. Let me out of here."

Nick sighs. "It's okay," he says, sounding infinitely tired. "Julia's out."

"You swear?"

"I swear. She won't be back before midnight at the earliest. She's at some awards thing."

THIRTEEN

At the Palazzo Julia

THE LIGHTS ARE ON UPSTAIRS; gold spills from the fan-light; the front door's been repainted a glossy black; there's a gleaming brass dolphin door knocker, and—can this be true? Yes, it is—there are window boxes. So there've been some changes since I was last here—not surprising given the fact that I'm banned and haven't set foot inside this house for—how long? Nine years. For once, I can be exact. I was last here nine years ago, the occasion being the christening party for Nick and Julia's second child, Tom. I was Tom's godfather (a brave choice on Nick's part, ferocious opposition on Julia's). Finn was his godmother. Nine years ago. Finn went to work abroad immediately afterward, and I haven't seen her since. She sends a card at Christmas. The last one had a robin on it.

I stand on the front steps while Nick pays off the taxi. Its engine chugs, a curious blurry mist is drifting around this now desirable area of Islington: *du côté de chez Nick*. Welcome to the Palazzo Julia.

When Nick unlocks the door, I can hear a violin being practiced upstairs, up and down the scales. A dog, also upstairs, woofs a greeting but doesn't appear. I last saw Tom when he was five—Nick contrived that meeting, as he'd contrived all the others; we took Tom to the zoo. We had to pretend that we'd bumped into each other, in case interrogator Julia discovered who had bought her son an ice cream, who had watched the penguins with him and his daddy. I haven't seen my godson since, though I'm very fond of Tom, a melancholy little boy: a world expert on dinosaurs—I used to ply him with plastic dinosaurs; I raided London for new dinosaurs.

Four years since I've seen him, and I'm not to see him now. He's upstairs with the nanny, and it's nearly his bedtime. Nick will just pop up to say good night, then he'll join me downstairs in the kitchen. He's ashamed to meet my eyes when he says this. We stand awkwardly in the hall. I feel sorry for Nick—and I don't blame him. I don't want to cause trouble, and if Julia finds out I've been here, there'll be fission. Besides, I can imagine what I look like—some vagrant, some crazy person. . . . I'd only frighten Tom. No, better absent myself.

I scuttle downstairs. There have been changes here, too—this kitchen, this temple, now takes up the entire basement floor. It's the size of . . . well, a modest ballroom. Limestone underfoot, lighting so complex that you could play with it for hours. I twiddle a few halogens and dimmers. No doubt about it, I'm in la Julia's domain: It's horribly sumptuous.

Nick doesn't keep me waiting long. He's soon back: overcoat off, jacket off, tie removed, sleeves rolled up. Now he looks less like the distinguished oncologist he is and more like my friend of yesteryear, the one I used to share a flat with when I first came to London. Nick has always been everything I'm not—disciplined, principled, reserved, for example. He's always been practical, too—it helps being married to la Julia, I guess. So the promised meal's under way at once: I'm seated at a huge table, with a glass of Delphic Spring, the best-tasting mineral water I've ever had, and Nick is preparing food for the prodigal.

He's opening a fridge—it's magnificent, it's morgue sized. He's extracting a megaefficient plastic container; it has a handwritten label. Julia's homemade soup, and what a treat *that* will be. He's putting the nourishing soup in a kryptonite saucepan on the gargantuan Aga (of course there's an Aga, there had to be). There are—can I believe this?—*three* kinds of bread: something round and Italian, spiked with rosemary and garlic; something homely and lumpy that looks vaguely Irish; and—the *pièce de résistance*—a huge, yeasty-smelling, crusty brown loaf. A nutritious trinity that Julia presumably knocked up in between being a perfect wife and mother, running her empire, and accepting her latest award as TV's ultimate alpha female.

Nick can sense my eye on that loaf. He may suspect satire, or he may simply have remembered that my bread of choice is springy snow white Eternaloaf—a wonder that doesn't develop mold for a month, even in *my* kitchen. "Wholemeal," he says on a faint note of apology. "Julia's special. It'll do you good. Organic. Stone-ground, I expect."

Oh, I expect so, too, Nick. I know where the wheat for this bread came from: from Arcadia, from the fields of our Suffolk childhood, that's where. The rain that watered it was acid-free, and the ground that nourished it was manured, not doused with chemicals. It was sheltered from the wind by ancient hedgerows that provided havens for little birds, beasties, and butterflies. It was harvested by hand, not some monster gas-guzzling combine. It stood in gold stooks, where it was dried by God's own sun, and my dad, granddad, and great-granddad—they were responsible for its threshing and winnowing. My gran gleaned the stubble, singing a Wordsworthian song, and I'd lay money she sewed the sacks at the mill where some Chaucerian type ensured it was ground to the correct nutty consistency. This bread is *England*. It is my past—and Nick and I are the last generation for whom that's true. As small children, we watched the ending of Arcadia. It's now vanished forever.

A depressing thought. Still, the young'uns can always catch up, I remind myself. They can always read Thomas Hardy, or—if that's too much of a strain, which these days it probably is—there's always la Julia's TV cookery programs.

What must it be like, I think, watching Nick whisk eggs—what must it be like to live with such perfection? What would he think if I brought him back to my place, that other London that's only a mile or so away: two-week-old doner kebabs and chicken tikka masalas and Big Boy burger takeaways festering in the unemptied kitchen bin; a sink full of unwashed dishes, because the dishwasher had a seizure several aeons ago? What would he make of sour milk, green bread (yes, even Eternaloaf sprouts mold eventually)? What would he say to cupboards groaning with Nicey-Spicey sauces—I did their campaigns, and the punishment was several centuries of the stuff— and a million dusty jars of prehistoric Herby Toppings, all heavy on the monosodium glutamate and additives? Would he decide I was well past my use-by date, like them? Or would he throw himself down in a sagging armchair, accept a stiff drink, eat cod and chips out of newspaper, smile that old wondrous smile—and talk: talk for hours, until midnight, two, three in the morning, both of us as happy as kings, the way we once were, pre-Julia?

I watch him narrowly. He's pouring that nourishing soup into two elegant bowls, and the soup smells good. He's putting plates of good things on the table—salmon that has never seen a fish farm, salmon that's never been fed pink dye, salmon that's swum gloriously free in unpolluted oceans. The eggs are from happy hens—Stella's happy hens, I feel, the ones Finn and I used to feed for her. The cheese is from Flora McIver's dairy, my dad grew the lettuces, and the ham came from some orchard-rooting, mud-wallowing porcine prince- ling—one of those 260-pound Heavy Hogs that Colonel Edwardes (formerly Indian army, now retired) used to breed in that land of lost content, aka my childhood.

It's a feast. It's kind. It's magnificent—and it's tragic. Because watching Nick make these preparations so deftly, efficiently, and quietly, I've seen the expression in his eyes, and—he can't disguise it from me, I know him too well—I've seen that he too is afflicted with *joylessness*. He's a fellow sufferer—it shocks and pains me to realize that. When did that happen? I think. When did Nick change; when did the optimism of our youth get wiped from his face, like an equation wiped from a blackboard?

Obvious, really. If I hadn't been running so fast for two decades, I'd have seen it long ago: about ten minutes after his marriage to la Julia.

"Are you happy, Nick?" I ask him somewhere midfeast. I don't know why that question suddenly pops out. I'd been meaning to ask him about Finn, I was working my way around to Finn—I know she stays in touch with him and sister Julia. What a foolish question to ask: Are you happy? Who's ever going to answer that one honestly?

"Intermittently," he replies—which I think *is* pretty honest and certainly more truthful than I'd have been. If he'd asked me, I'd have said, *Sure, had the odd setback recently—but I'm over that now, and things are on the up. . . .* Or something similarly fatuous. But I have a compulsion to lie about my own well-being. No one will ever get me to admit to feeling low, let alone anything worse or more permanent. Depression, deep-seated gloom, black misery, loss of all self-confidence, inability to sleep, alcohol dependency, a burning knowledge of my own failures and stupidities, a dragging sense of the world's essential pointlessness, a weird preoccupation with dope, rope, razors, and barbiturates? Not me, squire. As one door closes, another opens—that's my motto.

"When were you *sure* of being happy, truly happy, Nick?" I ask, and to my surprise, because I'm expecting him to change the subject, Nick actually gives the matter some thought—as if the issue's been on his mind lately. He sits opposite me: late forties, dark haired, handsome, grave, measured, considerate, and innately well mannered. He's graying at the temples, and that enhances his good looks. The good man, the good doctor: I can imagine how relieved his patients must feel the first time they set eyes on him. The women would be attracted to him; women invariably are. And no matter how ill you were, he'd inspire hope. Even if a cure eluded him, you'd know the care would be exemplary, right to the end—an end he'd ensure was both gentle and dignified.

Nick frowns. "Well," he begins, "we were both happy as children, obviously."

I let the "obviously" go. Nick grew up in a large Georgian house, with devoted, cultured parents. He took a scholarship to an illustrious school where he excelled. He took another scholarship to Imperial College, London, where he gained the top first of his year in medicine. He always had clean clothes, clean hair. His father healed the sick. His mother ran the Women's Institute, the local Tory Party, and the parish. They listened to concerts on the wireless. They possessed books. They knew the difference between right and wrong. Mrs. Marlow, for example, knew that it was *wrong* for a lovesick fourteen-year-old boy to buy a bottle of Woolworth's scent as a birthday gift for Finn Mortland. No, he must make the *right* choice. It must be something impersonal and appropriate. I took that advice. I bought a book token. Thirty years later, I still regret it.

Dr. and Mrs. Marlow didn't drink, other than a glass of sherry or wine on high days and holidays. Unlike Gran, they didn't overdo the Mackeson's, and unlike Gran, they didn't believe in corporal punishment—so demeaning. High-minded and superb: no five bob a week put aside for a decent funeral, no blowing half Joe's weekly wage on a flutter on the horses. No ducking or diving or buying on tick; no filching, nicking, scrimping, and saving. No tiny, pinching, wheedling, tyrannous Gran; no sad, mourning, isolated father. No nits, no ringworm, no agony over the accent, the clothes, the table manners . . . Shall I remind Nick that our childhoods, however golden in retrospect, were somewhat dissimilar? I stay silent. Nick is dear to me. He is loyal and always has been. I think of sitting by that lake at the Abbey, Nick fishing for perch, me fishing for shark. Yes, Nick, we were happy then. We *were*. Definitely.

"You were 'happy' at Cambridge. I was, at Imperial. It's a devalued word, anyway." Nick is still working his way through the waste of decades. His frown deepens. "And after that, when we shared a flat. At work . . . well, at work, I've always been . . ."

"Dedicated" is the word he's looking for. He doesn't use it. Instead, with customary modesty, he gives a shrug. "Work helps," he continues awkwardly (Nick doesn't like talking about himself and must be out of practice, living with Julia). "I can make a difference to people's lives, at least sometimes I can. When I'm working, I'm absorbed, I have to be—so happiness or unhappiness are irrelevant, really."

I can't bear to look at his face. I stare at the table. Have I made a difference to people's lives? Well now, I've written words that are lodged in people's brains, words they'll never get rid of. Yes, I'm there, in the lumber rooms of people's minds, muddled up with snatches of Shakespeare, dirty songs, comedy catchphrases, Wordsworth's daffodils, and football scores; huddled up with Elvis and the Fab Four and that obscenity "My Way." I'm there in the rubble, along with movie clips, wise saws, quips, quotes, politicians' lies, porno pix, and royal scandals. Sorry, but no one who's heard it will ever forget the Nicey-Spicey jingle, however devoutly he or she may wish to—and guess who wrote those immortal lyrics? You're never alone with a Strand; naughty but nice; *Vorsprung durch Technik,* as they say in Germany. You've been Tango'd; That way/This way; Labour isn't working; go to work on an egg; shall I show you fear in a handful of dust?

Yes, along with my peers, I've contributed to the collective cultural soup. Oh, and shifted a lot of *product,* kept the global economy ticking over, obviously. Who put the consumer in the consumerist society? Who helps you shop till you drop? Who reignites your desires when they're in danger of dying? I do. Or I used to do, until I just couldn't fucking well go on, because it was such shite and so shaming.

"And apart from work?" I prompt, because it's necessary to keep Nick talking. If he stops, he might start questioning me, we might get round to the subject of me—and that's the last thing I want.

"When I married," he says, rising to fetch some fruit and turning away so I can't see his face, can't read his eyes. "When my children were born . . ."

His sits down again. There's a silence. Nick's two children are separated by a gap of years that may or may not be significant. His daughter, Fanny, was born seven months after his wedding and must now be about twenty. There were some problems with Fanny, though I'm vague as to the details. She dropped out after a year at Oxford, went abroad, found herself again while in Sudan or Yucatán—this seems to be the modern way—and then returned to university. Yes, she's now at one of those universities women like Julia consider safe substitutes for Oxbridge, universities such as Durham or Edinburgh. Then there's nine-year-old Tom. So, does Nick's remark mean that he was last happy nine years ago—or does it mean nothing? I notice he skipped past his marriage pretty fast—and that doesn't surprise me. No doubt he had good reasons for marrying Julia, but I'm certain—I've always been certain—that they didn't include being in love with her.

I take an apple from the bowl in front of me. I take a bite from it. A surfers' wave of melancholy crashes over me. The apple smells sweet; it's a Maxton, an old variety—I'm one of the few people left who'd recognize it instantly. Nothing much to look at, but it smells and tastes like the apples I used to pick in the Doggett brothers' orchards. I liked those bachelor brothers, who've been dead twenty years. All the trees they planted, fed, pruned, nursed, cosseted, and fussed over have gone. The trees were too large, too slow to pick, uneconomic; besides, there's no money in fruit now—or so I hear. Not much by way of subsidy, insufficient demand; everyone except Julia buys imported. It took a day—it took a man and a digger one day—to uproot the lot and burn them.

I used to do piecework for the brothers, who were always kind to me. I'd help with the tar spraying in the winter, help pick in the summer, help store on the slatted shelves in the sheds, where the apple scent was intense, so powerful, I can still smell it now, at this table. Finn used to help me. In the spring, when the blossom was out, there was a certain tree she and I used to climb. *Orchard Finn*: Christ, memory's unbearable.

"There's a right way to pick an apple and a wrong way," I say now in a dead voice, in the dead brothers' accents, the accents I once shared. "Remember, Nick?"

"I remember." He reaches across the table and rests his hand on my arm, a gesture of solidarity, of comfort. And I suddenly feel tired, extraordinarily tired, so fucking exhausted that I couldn't put one foot in front of the other.

"Sorry," I say. "I'm okay. Really, I'll be fine in a minute. I'm just— weary. I think it's all this food. I'm not used to such good food, and it's meeting you. Meeting you unexpectedly. Looking at the portrait . . ."

I hesitate. I'd still like to tell him about Maisie's voice. I still want to explain the discovery I made. But that discovery is losing its incandescence. It's getting imprecise, blurry, and drab. So Lucas might have used elements of the library in his painting's background? So what? So I'm being stupid and literal. So I thought I heard Maisie's voice? Put it down to cocaine rush; call it tripping. Nick might call it hallucinating. Nick is a doctor, and—not that I'm in the least paranoid—doctors can have you sectioned. Do I want to end up in rehab, in a fashionable retreat, on some twelve-step program? Nick paying the bills—he'd certainly do that—and me taking my turn in the daily circus alongside the anorexic models, the alcoholic soap stars, the sad comedians?

My name is Daniel, and I am a . . .

I don't think so. Change the subject. "Why were you at the gallery, Nick?" I ask. "Why were you there in front of that particular painting?"

"No reason." He glances away. "The exhibition will be coming off in a couple of days. I'd been meaning to go, but I've been too busy. I missed the opening night party—Julia went, but I couldn't. An impulse, I suppose—I was just passing."

No, you weren't, I think. "You sat in front of that one painting for hours, Nick. You didn't look at any of the others. Is that usually what you do at exhibitions?"

"Probably not. But your sense of time isn't reliable, Dan. I sat there for ten minutes—fifteen at the most. And that painting's worth fifteen minutes of anyone's life."

"I left the room, went to the john, then came back—and you didn't even notice."

"I was concentrating. I was thinking about the past. There was something you wrote in your last letter to me—'the summer it all went wrong.' I was thinking about that. The two of us, finding Maisie that day, on the flagstones. What happened afterwards—everything that happened afterwards. The tricks life plays."

There's a silence. Should I correct him? It was I who found Maisie. Nick reached my side a minute or so later, a minute that in retrospect looks like a lifetime. I say nothing—what's the point? Besides, I've just noticed something. Nick is hesitating. His eyes meet mine, and out of nowhere I sense need—not something I'd ever expect from Nick. I can scarcely believe it, but, yes, my radar's certainly picking it up: I can sense revelation. Nick is about to tell me something, I realize—*needs* to tell me something. It's a strange sensation:

Suddenly the man opposite me is my double. He isn't the controlled, calm friend I thought I knew; he's like me—dancing on the end of a rope, looking down at a precipice.

I feel a rush of concern, pride, and bewilderment. I may not be an obvious candidate to help anyone out of a fix—but I won't let Nick down; I'll repay his years of loyalty. Whatever he needs—advice, sympathy, consolation, assistance—I'll be there for him. But what's wrong? What could possibly be wrong? I look closely at his face; he doesn't say a word, and suddenly I know what this unspoken, and to Nick unspeakable, problem is. Infidelity. That is the only possible explanation for his hesitancy, for the shame and pain that are shadowing his eyes: I think, *Dear God, at last, he's met someone else at last. He's seen the light, and it's call-the-lawyers time, thanks for the memories, and ciao, Julia.*

Good-bye and good riddance, as far as I'm concerned. I'm not Julia's number one fan, and I've never understood how she got her claws into him. Nick deserved someone so much better—and there were umpteen candidates, as I vaguely recall: intelligent women, beautiful women (well, Julia's both those things, I admit); women who were kindhearted, warm, loyal, faithful, and principled (not her most notable characteristics).

Of course, once Fanny was born, Nick was trapped. He was doubly trapped when Tom arrived. No way would Nick abandon his children. So he's soldiered on, lived with anomie for two decades, and those two decades have cost him—I can compute the cost in his eyes now. Being married to a woman you can't respect is expensive.

But Tom is still only nine—so what kind of woman could possibly have made Nick change his mind? She'd have to be a woman of worth, someone extraordinary. When and how did he meet her? Could it be someone at the National Health Service hospitals where he works? Nick does some private practice as well, so perhaps it's someone who, like him, has rooms in Harley Street. A female consultant? A heart surgeon? Who is this paragon?

I can't wait for him to tell me. I'm feeling a burst of sympathy and affection—though it's not as pure as I'd like, it's not unalloyed; I admit that. There's a certain mean triumphalism: *Screw you, and about time, Julia.* There's also a gossipy curiosity, which I despise and regret, but there you go—sainthood eludes me. Perhaps those ignoble emotions are visible in my face, and perhaps Nick sees them, for the expected confession never comes. He's about to speak—and at the last moment does not speak. That habitual mask of reticence covers his face again—and I know I've failed him.

Instead, he begins to talk about me, to ask about me. What am I *on*? What exactly am I taking, and how long have I been taking it? Am I working? Have I finished clearing up my father's belongings, or will I be returning to Suffolk to complete that difficult task? What's happening to my London house? Is it still on the market? Am I short of money? Am I still harking back to Maisie's accident? Has any type of antidepressant been prescribed? Have I tried to get professional help? Have I considered counseling?

"Dan, I was shocked when I saw you," he says with great gentleness and his customary courtesy. "I blame myself. I should have come to Wykenfield six weeks ago. I shouldn't have waited. I waited because you asked me to—and that was wrong. You can't continue like this. Can't you talk to me? Won't you talk to me?"

And, given another minute, I would have done. Out it would all have spilled, because there comes a point when loneliness is killing and confession is irrepressible. And how I'd have regretted it, one hour, two hours later. I don't like opening up. When pride is all you have left, intimacy's inadvisable.

I'm saved by an interruption. I'm saved by the nanny. She calls down to Nick from the head of the stairs at the crucial moment.

Tom has had a nightmare, a really scary one; he's woken up, and she can't get him settled. If Nick could come and talk to him . . . Nick rises. I can see anxiety and guilt in his face. "Tom isn't sleeping well," he says. "It's just a phase; he's worrying about school, I think. And Julia's out a lot, my working hours are very long. That doesn't always help. . . . Would you mind, Dan? It shouldn't take long, then I'll make us some coffee."

"That's fine. Really. Coffee would be great. Give him my love."

Nick moves toward the stairs, hesitates, then mounts them and disappears from sight. I'm impressed. Across the room there's a table weighted down with bottles: vodka, gin, whiskey, and wine. He didn't warn me away from those bottles, he didn't even glance in their direction, though during the course of the evening, I have: several times.

I'm not used to such trust. I feel stronger immediately. I glance at my watch. It's nine-thirty, and no danger of la Julia before midnight. We can talk for at least another hour.

I wonder, a little sadly, who'll crack first, who'll confess first—me or Nicholas?

FOURTEEN

Reflections

So Nick has found love, I think. Well, I'm glad someone has. But I'm not going to think about love or its evil twin sex, because if I get started on that, I'll empty the vodka bottle.

No, more immediate matters require attention. Nick was "shocked" by my appearance. Now that I'm fortified by food, nourished by pure water, it's time to find out why. A mirror—I need a mirror. I investigate and discover that there's a sumptuous cloakroom off the sumptuous kitchen. I enter and, steeling myself, risk my reflection. When did I last face a mirror? Clearly some time ago, because there's now a stranger in it. This specter hasn't shaved today. He has dead eyes, wild tangled hair, and London pallor. He's anorexic thin, clad in a crumpled black suit—why am I wearing a *suit*?

The white shirt's grimy, the fingernails are filthy. Worst of all, most distressing of all, this haunted apparition is wearing a gold earring. Where the hell did that come from? Wasn't I good-looking once? Reasonably so, anyway. Not as handsome as Nick, but okay. I look at myself and I think, *Christ, I'm reverting*. I've turned back into a Gyp. I belong in a bender tent, my Roma genes are resurfacing.

I take action fast. I comb the Gypsy hair, scrub the fingernails, lather the face with scalding water and soap; a vestige of color returns. I remove the offending earring. And I go through my pockets: no half measures, this time, I'm going to do it. Out go the last of the coke and the last of the speed; out go some squished white powdery things that may or may not be aspirin. Farewell two blues (unidentifiable, possibly Es), a couple of reds (maybe vitamins, maybe temazepam), and out goes—what is *this?*—an amyl-nitrate capsule. The girl who gave me that—which girl? some girl in a club, at a party a hundred years ago—this girl promised that, if broken and sniffed at the crucial moment, it would prolong and intensify orgasm to an unbelievable degree. So it seems a shame to miss out on *that.* Maybe I could . . . perhaps I should . . . after all, you never know when such things might come in useful. . . . No: This time I'm going to be thorough. The whole lot, every last one of them, goes down the lavatory.

I flush it, and—can you believe this—the pharmacopoeia won't dissolve. I flush again. It *still* won't dissolve. The malignancy of inanimate objects is fucking unreal. I drape a few yards of white Andrex over the pan, flush once more for luck, and flee from the ignominy.

Still no sign of Nick. Back in the kitchen, I start prowling about. I'm getting twitchy, and to divert me from all those bottles of alcohol, I start opening la Julia's kitchen cupboards: anything to distract me. No additives here, you can be sure of that. Five kinds of balsamic vinegar; eight virgin varieties of olive oil. Jars of salted anchovies; tins of line-caught tuna; sixteen different pasta shapes; nine different kinds of dried beans and lentils, all with their glass jars, Jesus-wept, dated. Smoked paprika, laksa paste, Madagascan vanilla beans, dried fungi, mulberry jam, capers, cods' eyes, sharks' scrotums, pickled hedgehog brains—if it was very, very expensive or very, very arcane or very, very fashionable, la Julia had it. But then she probably made it fashionable in the first place.

I did a campaign with la Julia once, back in the unimaginable past when she was still speaking to me. It was called "That Way/This Way."

It was a classic "before" and "after," but with a knowing post-modern irony built in (or so we said; that argument could extricate you from anything). In the "before," some young slattern tipped something generic, tinned, gloopy, and disgusting into an evil saucepan. Think Hell's kitchen: dirty Formica, screaming kids, fat hubby smoking a fag and reading a red top. This woman, she's a crap wife, a crap mother: Husband's in line for a heart attack, kids are destined to start shooting up and nicking cars any second—and all because Mum won't make an effort, won't spend those few extra pennies.

In the "after," enter the Valkyrie: beautiful Julia, radiant and calm, Rhinegold hair snaking over her glorious shoulders. Stainless-steel über-kitchen; husband with a three-piece suit and a six-figure salary; two polite, school-uniformed, atypical clone-children; and on the stove a Le Pentole pan into which Julia is decanting the product. The product came in biodegradable eco-aware cartons. It was allegedly organic. In fact, Julia had pronounced it muck, and it had taken a hell of a lot of naughts on the end of her already massive fee to get her to sign—thus proving, as I'd always hoped, that la Julia was venal.

You could do it that way, purred Julia's famous voice over the shots of the soon-to-be-widowed slattern with generic tinned gloop. *Or you can do it this way,* she continued over shots of ticks-all-the-yuppie-boxes kitchen. *Make the choice,* she murmured as husband sniffed the product appreciatively, then curled an arm around her slender waist and kissed la Julia's superb neck, while Julia—who had perfected the art of ironic flirt to camera lens—gave us all a deeply knowing, languorous *oeillade,* making it very clear that handsome husband would be getting more than an instant supper that evening.

Julia played both parts—herself and the slattern. The prosthetics, wigs, and makeup teams did a brilliant job. Even people who knew Julia well didn't recognize her in slut guise until the third or fourth viewing. And people loved that; it generated a thousand articles, acres of free publicity—how, *how*, had we contrived the disguise?

Sales soared. We'd pressed all the holy buttons: sex, snobbery, satire, and domestic guilt, a four-cherries lineup that's by no means easy to achieve, whatever people tell you. That ad made Julia a star. Prior to that, her TV appearances had brought her recognition, and given her beauty, there'd always been interest from *Vogue*-y mags and so on. But she'd always come across as too elitist and, to be honest, too damn upper-class really to register on the popularity Richter scale. Now everyone adored her; they couldn't get enough of her. True, her detractors got a lot of mileage out of "That Way/This Way" and just what that might imply in a Julia context. None of that did her the least harm. Scandal and gossip ensure wall-to-wall coverage; without scandal, these days, it's hard to become an icon. In public, Julia was smart enough to take such jokes in good part. *Look*, people said, *isn't she great?* She's stunning, and she can laugh at herself.

In private, Julia was *not* laughing. She was incandescent with rage—and I know, because I was on the receiving end of it. Somehow she came to the conclusion that "That Way/This Way" was designed to ridicule her. Somehow she decided that it was I who started the round of blue jokes, I who fed those rumors about her past and her proclivities. Possibly guilty on the first charge, definitely not guilty on the second—I have too much affection for Nick to spread rumors about Julia. But guilty or innocent, it made no difference: Julia was gunning for me. And, oddly enough, those ads marked a watershed, I see in retrospect. From then on, I was banned from this house and my friend. I lost faith, and success tasted sour to me; Julia, meanwhile, flourished.

Julia was never going to be content as a celeb cook, along with all the other Antonias, Nigels, and Olivias; she'd fallen into that world via journalism and virtually by accident. Years of dinner parties for well-placed friends, a TV pilot, a trial-run first series, and she was launched. The moment advertising fame gave her a secure power base, she diversified. It was Julia who had first uttered the word *lifestyle* in my presence. She didn't blush. And it was that slippery world that she then conquered. Now, if you have a couple of hundred thousand spare change, you can hire one of Julia's several companies to do up your house. If you're not quite in that league, no problem: You can buy Julia textiles or tableware. There's a Julia Mortland *batterie de cuisine,* and if you're really hard up, you can settle for JM paint: seventy-five shades of off white. It's appalling.

I stare at Julia's walls. Julia is now an arbiter. Endorsement from her is worth thousands. She's worth millions. All her paints have clever names. They're called things like Thrush's Throat and Heron's Wing. Unless I'm much mistaken, this is Skylark.

How many skylarks were there in the fields of my childhood? Thick as the autumnal leaves in Vallombrosa, as I recall. Now they seem to be extinct. They've gone the way of the dodo: I didn't see one, not one, in all the months I spent nursing my father in Wykenfield. Loss of habitat? Too many toxins? I know the feeling. Last summer, Hector McIver sprayed his crops with pesticides five times during their growing cycle. . . . On the other hand, toxins have their uses. I pat my pockets. I stare at the fruit bowl. Do I dare to eat a peach? Do I dare to smoke a cigarette? Even on Julia's premises, I feel I do. I'm circling the room now, I'm getting frayed, and I need to bypass those bottles. Out come the Marlboros. Thank God I didn't get rid of them. Inhale deeply: Feel better at once. I prowl around a bit more, and I discover—a treasure trove.

Next to a gleaming utility room, I find, Julia keeps a quaint notice board. Attached to it are umpteen Post-it reminders, all arranged neatly under the heading "ACTION." I read: "Perpetua—take Tom Maths coaching." "Juanita: Floor polishing! Dry cleaning! Laundry! Call Vet! Call Window-cleaner!" "Perpetua—please declutter Tom's cupboards!" I add a Post-it of my own. I write: "Julia, beware! Your husband's thinking of leaving you."

I put it at the top, marked "Immediate Action," then have second thoughts and scrunch it up. How to get rid of this incriminating evidence? Eat it, perhaps? No, I bury it deep under eggshells in the sweetly clean bin, inside a deodorized rubbish bag. Then I'm back at that notice board fast, because pinned to that board there are photographs. I inspect them closely: There are several of Nick and Tom, and they don't look recent. There are several of daughter Fanny, and they can't be recent, because she looks much as she did when I last saw her nine years ago—clever, bespectacled, and censorious.

"Hi, Fanny, how's life treating you?" I asked, drifting across the room at that christening party, blind to forty other guests, aware only of dazzling Finn, who was nearby, talking to Nick and her ex-husband, Lucas.

"Better than it's treating you," Fanny replied. "That's your fifth glass of wine in half an hour. I counted."

Just what I need, I thought: an observant eleven-year-old. I said: "Fanny, you're right. But I'm nervous."

"You're always nervous. Don't be. Stop obsessing about Finn and talk to me. I liked that Nicey-Spicey ad, especially the dancing clove. It was truly excellent."

"Thank you, Fanny. 'Obsess' cannot be an active verb. How's school going?"

"God, I hate you," she replied. "You are a total tosser."

Exit Fanny. Puberty really does do the strangest things to people. I stare glassily at the notice board. Umpteen pictures of Julia, including one of her with Lucas at the opening party for his retrospective . . . and then, at last, the grail I've been searching for. It's in the corner, almost hidden behind that flurry of Post-its: a photograph of Finn.

I knew there had to be one—she and Julia *are* sisters. I look at the woman Finn's become. She's cut her beautiful hair—that's the first shock. Her hair is cropped as short as a boy's; it's tousled and bleached by the African sun. She's wearing loose khaki shorts and a T-shirt; her long bare legs are tanned; she's thinner than I remember, and Finn was always slender. Does she look older? I can't tell, she's wearing dark glasses.

She's with a group of black children; their liquid gaze is fixed anxiously on the camera lens—who took this picture? They're in a somewhere-nowhere, a patch of scrub—in Botswana or Mozambique or Ethiopia or wherever it is that Finn is currently stationed. Finn abandoned her Cambridge literature course when she married Lucas. After the loss of their child and the divorce, she returned to education. She took a degree, then a doctorate in, of all punishing subjects, agricultural economics. Since she left England nine years ago, she's been working for an acronym—and I can never remember which, I've got a block on it. Could it be WHO?

She's an expert in subjects I don't understand, such as irrigation, water purification, bilharzia, immunization programs, UN grant aid, and third-world crop policies. She does good. She works in places I've never been, has never remarried, and sends me cards with robins at Christmas. I don't know where she is, and I don't know *who* she is, not anymore—and that enforced ignorance (it's not my fault, she doesn't answer my letters) really hurts, it actually hurts. My chest aches. Examining that picture, I'm finding it hard to breathe. Love and loss hit you in the heart region, I discover. They constrict the aorta: I must remember that when next conversing with cynics.

My Finn has gone—the photograph finally makes me understand that. When I think of Finn, when I dream of Finn, when I wake up sometimes from hot dreams and kind imaginings and believe for a blessed moment in the dark that she's there, that I can touch her, I'm communing with ghosts. For I imagine Finn, see Finn, as she was twenty years ago or more, a golden girl who dared anything. Now she's a woman, with a doctorate, cropped hair, and a different ID. She has moved on; I've regressed. No wonder she doesn't answer my letters, carefully worded and appropriate though they are. Why bother answering pleas from a middle-aged fourteen-year-old?

I nick the picture. I can't believe it will be missed, and I don't care if it is. I need it more than Julia. I pocket the picture, flee back to the kitchen, and—still no sign of Nick, what on earth is he doing?—I decide *I'll* make the coffee.

There's nothing as delightful as instant: none of my beloved and sustaining Nescafé. There is an espresso machine, however. I'm a technophobe: I approach it warily. It has more twiddly knobs, valves, and levers than a life-support machine. It has international diagrammatic instructions designed for three-year-olds. It would be easier deciphering Linear B or the Enigma code, but eventually I get the hang of it. I insert water in one promising orifice and Organic Free Trade Handpicked-at-Dawn in another. I press a few buttons, and things start happening. *Houston, we have ignition.* Substances suck, gurgle, and burp in a promising way—and then, behind those noises, I hear others. I hear a chugging sound, and then, *shit*, there's a rattle as the front door opens.

Nick has also heard the taxi draw up, that's obvious. He's down two flights of stairs and back in the kitchen before Julia's got her key out of the lock. Home early. Caught red-handed. We don't need to say anything—we're both aware of our predicament. "Julia starts the new series tomorrow—it's on location, she'll be picked up at six," Nick says in a low voice as I drop into the SAS crouch and move fast toward the stairs. "I'll call you then. I leave for the hospital about six-thirty. That's not too early?

"No more pills, Dan," he continues as we scale the basement stairs. "No dope, no alcohol, no nothing—then first thing tomorrow we'll sort something out. Give me your word?"

"I promise. Absolutely. I swear. I haven't got any stuff left, anyway."

Nick and I, a two-man team on a dangerous mission. Should have maintained radio silence, I think. Will Julia have caught the sound of our lowered voices? You bet she will. She's a one-woman AWACS.

The encounter occurs in the hall. It's brief. There's just time for Julia to give an annihilating smile and kiss my cheek. "Dan—what a lovely surprise," she cries. "You're not leaving, are you?" Perfect aim: a full burst of ammo straight in the face. Five seconds—and I'm outside on the doorstep. She didn't miss a beat.

The door closes, and I walk away, eyeing the other houses in this prosperous terrace. It was a decaying slum of rooming houses when Nick and I shared a flat nearby; now every fanlight signals gentrification aggressively. I get halfway along the mournful street—and then I remember my briefcase.

Did I leave it in the hall or the kitchen? I slink back to Nick's house. I hesitate on the steps. I spend a lifetime gazing sourly at the two lollipop bay trees in pots—slipping a bit there, Julia. I'm about to knock on the door of doom when, in the front basement area directly below me, a sash window is thrown open and, on a blast of warm air and nicotine fumes, Julia's voice floats up.

"You left him *alone*?" she demands. "Are you out of your mind? I can't breathe in here. The whole house stinks of cigarettes—I smelled it the second I walked in. Well, thanks, Nick—he's been snooping around, opening my cupboards, moving all the stuff on my notice board. How could you bring that man to my house? Tell me you kept him away from Tom, at least."

"He didn't even *see* Tom. I was talking to Tom, that's why I left Dan alone. Tom had a nightmare again, and I was upstairs ten minutes at most. Calm down—this is ridiculous."

"Where did you meet him? I don't bloody believe this. Did you *arrange* to meet him?"

"No. I bumped into him in Piccadilly. I'd just left the hospital, and I was on my way to Hatchards. There's a book I needed."

Interesting, I think, leaning over the railings, eavesdropping avidly: So Nick can lie. And lie well—a nice veering from the truth, uttered without the least hesitation. Why didn't he want Julia to know he'd been at Lucas's retrospective? Why was the deception so smooth? Surely honorable Nick did not make a practice of lying to Julia? But then Nick had lied about the gallery visit to me, too, I realize.

"But why bring him here? Nick, how could you? You know what he's like. He smashes things and trashes things and contaminates everything. . . ."

"Julia, he's down on his luck, he's out of work, his father's recently died, and he isn't well. He hadn't eaten in days, or slept, by the look of it. What am I supposed to do?"

"Oh, for Christ's sake—I wouldn't be well if I was coked up to the eyeballs. I'm sure he fed you some sob story—he's very good at those. Why can't you see through it? He was always a two-faced shit. He's a horrible man, and he was a horrible boy, too—following Finn around like a cringing puppy, sucking up to Gramps and Stella, living in that disgusting dump with that old witch of a grandmother. Always on the cadge, both of them. She nicked stuff—food, clothes, writing paper, you name it. She was bloody brazen. She had a thing about books—I caught her once, in the library, with an armful of them—and you know what she had the nerve to say? She said

Gramps had given her the loan of them. Christ, the bloody woman couldn't even *speak* English, let alone read it."

"It's called being poor, Julia. You can hardly blame Dan for his grandmother's failings."

"Yeah, yeah—check the silver, that's all. Check you've still got any alcohol left. You can be certain he won't have left empty-handed. He'll have nicked something, I know it. Oh, I see you've fed him. Great. That's just great. Have his table manners improved? Or does he still hold his knife like a pen and talk with his mouth full?"

"For Christ's sake, keep your voice down. You'll wake Tom again."

"I'm upset, fuck it. I hate to think of him here. I warn you: The next time you want to play the Good Samaritan, think again. Just don't let Dan into your life, because everywhere he goes he creates mayhem and misery. Always has done, always will. Ask Finn. Remember Maisie. If Maisie had spent less time talking to him, if he hadn't filled her head with all his crappy stories, that accident would never have happened."

"That's ridiculous. Whatever was wrong with Maisie—and there were a lot of things wrong—it had nothing to do with Dan. Maisie was *ill*. Face facts, Julia."

"I suppose it doesn't matter what he did to me, either? What about that ad campaign? That was a perfect example of dear Dan's technique. That bastard set me up. I was a laughingstock for months. And he spread rumors about me—horrible, vile rumors."

"There were rumors about you before then. Let's at least try to be accurate."

"Then be accurate about him, for once, because if you weren't so bloody blind, you'd see him for what he is. He's a devious, silver-tongued *arriviste*—a common little *toad*. He's a troublemaker. He's on drugs. And I will not allow him near my son. That's final."

"He's Tom's godfather. And he's my friend. My oldest friend."

"So drop your precious friend. Everyone else has."

"Maybe I prefer not to follow the herd. Let's leave it there, shall we?" Nick replies. His tone is cold.

There is a fraught silence. "Christ, you can be a sanctimonious pain in the arse," Julia snaps, then, "What's that noise?" she says on a new note of panic and suspicion.

And there is indeed a background noise, I realize—a rattling, fizzing, whistling noise that has been brewing under and behind the marital argument. Now it's too loud to ignore. Sounds of movement and consternation float up from the basement. There is, suddenly, a powerful whiff of molten coffee beans. Julia gives a cry of alarm. A Vesuvian grumbling and rumbling can be detected. *Houston, we have a problem. . . .*

The espresso machine erupts. It actually *blows up*. The explosion is loud. I wait there on the steps until I'm certain there's no injury to life or limb, then I creep mournfully away.

It doesn't matter about the briefcase, I decide. It was only a prop—and it was empty anyway.

FIFTEEN

The Love/Sex Quandary

I CREEP HOME. I creep all the way along Upper Street, mourning Gran, who nicked food for me, who nicked books for me. We had one book in our cottage, the Bible. In the library at the Abbey, there were two thousand—Maisie and I once counted them. I finger the photograph of Finn in my pocket. I creep across the road at the Highbury and Islington roundabout—now *there's* a place to go under the wheels of a ten-ton truck: It's quite difficult not to.

I commence the weary trek across Highbury Fields, which do not resemble the fields of my childhood. These onetime pastures have shrunk over the centuries. Now they're reduced to a small, ill-lit urban park intersected with erupting tarmac paths; the grass is covered in dog shit. There are notices every two yards telling people not to do things: not to skateboard or cycle or let their dogs off the lead or allow their dogs to foul the environment. Do not murder, mug, or molest—they'll be adding those any day now.

On the corner below my house is a small lawless group of youths in hooded tracksuits. These hoodies are always there; they ebb and flow, their numbers fluctuate, but basically they're always there. It's difficult to say what they're up to—and I've spent a disproportionate amount of time watching them these last few weeks, since, apart from making calls no one returns, or contemplating razor blades, or rewriting my CV, I've got bugger-all else to do. They're possibly dealing; maybe they're just hanging out. One of them—I think he's the boss man, the ringleader, and I think he's called Malc—has recently acquired a flash mobile, the kind all those yuppie bankers use. It's the size of a brick, and it's kept permanently plugged to his ear. Who's he *talking* to?

I'm making progress with Malc. My street cred's improving. He used to give me the glare, but now he just looks. This afternoon, in an optimistic mood, on my way to the Wunderbar fiasco, I raised a hand as I passed and said, "Hi, Malc." Whereupon he lifted a fist and said, "Yo, man." It was the first time he'd acknowledged my existence. He was the first person to address me in five days. I was grateful.

I'm a fast learner. "Yo, Malc," I croak now, approaching crabwise in the sepulchral light, wondering if Malc & Co. are going to render the rope and the razor blades superfluous. Malc makes an animal sound, and his hooded friends—just think of them as *monks*, I tell myself—his hooded friends all crack up. They start slapping one another's palms and making ribald gestures and laughing. Malc has said, "Gorra vizier," which takes a while to translate. But eventually I work it out. I have a visitor.

Very funny, Malc. Luckily, although I'm constantly in demand—life's one long party, what with the milkman calling once a week and the refuse men always knocking on my door—I'm not in the mood for late night callers anyway. What I'm really in the mood for is putting my head in the gas oven. Julia affects me like that. It's not too cheering to eavesdrop, hear no good of myself, and be reminded of how uncouth I was, how leprous I am. I want to go back and knock on her door and say, *I've changed, Julia.* Unwise. I walk on. I have that now familiar ache in my chest cavity.

I walk on the few yards to my house. My very large house, bought in a moment of speed-induced insanity; my dilapidated house that I paid too much for eight seconds before the housing market began to crash; my unrenovated house that was the height of desirability two years ago. My house—a five-story reproach for hubris. A mortgage the size of the third world debt; soaring interest rates, behind on the repayments . . . repossession is threatened, which will at least ensure that I get rid of it. I'm facing bankruptcy, but that's okay. I've been bankrupt in more important ways. I can deal with it.

Next to the gate is the latest FOR SALE sign. One of the many neighborhood maniacs has a grudge against such signs. He's mounting a crusade against them. As soon as they're erected, their posts get the chop. This one had lasted twenty-four hours—a record. Now it's been axed; it's propped against the garden wall, and—what is this? I really do have a visitor. I stop and stare in disbelief. Sitting on the wall, unfazed by late night London hazards such as Malc and crew, is a young woman. A girl, a pretty and attractive *girl*, insofar as I can tell by streetlight. She's dressed like an exotic urban warrior. Her demeanor seems chaste and thoughtful.

"At last," she says, rising from the wall. "I've been waiting over an hour, Dan."

She sounds faintly aggrieved. I have never set eyes on this girl. Did I make an appointment with her? Not possible. Apart from doctors, funerals, and Wunderbar, my life has been an appointment-free zone for a year now. She's mounting the front steps behind me; she's somehow insinuated herself through the front door. I close it on the jeers and cheers erupting from Malc and crew, switch on the hall light, and examine her.

She returns my gaze steadily in a myopic way. She shows no inclination to help me out; but eventually, slowly, and with a wincing reluctance, a memory does begin to filter through. It's vague—it's vaguely worrying. Last encountered at a club or a party at least a hundred years previously. There were epilepsy-inducing flashing lights and booze and coke by the bucketload. There was trance, house, and techno. I've a nasty feeling there was dancing—I've an even nastier feeling that I danced. Then she was dressed like a nymph; tonight it's an erotic kickboxer. Even so, yes, I recognize her. *It's the amyl-nitrate girl.*

Does she have a name, this enchantress, this Circe who gave me the magic means to enhanced orgasm? I think she does, a boyish, honest sort of name—and suddenly I've got it. "Frankie," I say, hurrying after her. This girl doesn't hang around; she's already sashayed through to my sitting room, she's already examining the private objects on my mantelpiece. "Frankie," I say, "this really isn't a good time. . . ."

Well, I say something like that. The exact words don't matter, because the amyl-nitrate nymph isn't listening. She's examining those mantelpiece *objets:* a Chinese ivory sphere and an ancient book token next to it. She picks them up; she looks at them carefully; she looks searchingly at me. Eventually, after a spacey pause, my words appear to penetrate. "*Wrong,*" she replies. "It's the right time, Dan. I read the tarot tonight and the cards were, like, unambiguous?"

She's committed two sins in one sentence. There are two modern tics I cannot tolerate. One is the moronic Oz/U.S.A. interrogative, in which statements are habitually pronounced on a rising inflection as if they were questions. The other is using the word *like* as punctuation. I know it's pedantic, I know it's old fart and uptight and sad—but fuck it, I do write, or I used to. I do work with words, and I care about them. So the pedant in me should show this girl the door, like, now. On the other hand, she's suppressing a smile, and there's a certain amusement in her eyes, so those tics could be deliberate, she could be reminding me of something, or teasing, sending me up; in which case she must know about my pedantic quirks . . . *and I must have told her.*

Suddenly I'm really worried. What else did I tell her? What else did I *do*? My memory's saying our meeting was brief, confined to that club

and that dance floor. But my memory isn't reliable and can be merciful; it has a tendency to edit things out. So maybe the meeting, the encounter, was of slightly longer duration. Maybe this girl and I went on
somewhere, and in that place, wherever it was, certain intimacies occurred . . . like confessing my conversational prejudices, for instance, or
banging on about a dead grandmother and tarot cards.

I don't like the look of this. How did we get from tics and tarot
to amyl nitrate? That's quite a conversational jump. Why would the
subject of orgasm have come up? Surely we didn't . . . no way could
I have . . . why, this girl's *young*, it's difficult to say how young, but
young enough to be well out of bounds for a man like me. She has
a Lolita-ish look, and I'm no Humbert Humbert. Late teens, mid-
teens? I'm in a low state, and my synapses are shorting—I'm having
problems processing this. I'm not helped by the fact that she's wearing a ton of makeup, but I think she's easily young enough to be my
daughter, and even pre-Thailand, pre-Tokyo, when this encounter
must have happened, even then, when I was ricocheting around like
a pinball, even then I had standards. Or did I?

The room is starting to mist up. Time is slowing the way it does
in a car crash. I try to examine her face. Her face is distracting me.
Her face and her figure. She has an arresting figure and an intelligent
face, and what's more, her unusual appraising eyes are sending me a
message. I seem to be receiving a burst of Morse from those greenish eyes—an exciting burst of semiotics.

You don't mean what I think you mean, do you? I Morse back. *Oh yes,
I do*, comes the answer.

I stare at the girl for a few centuries. I stare at the objects in her
hands. Her expression is eloquent; she's holding my past in her
palms, and it's crying out to me. I've been here before, I realize. I've
been in similar fixes before. Two years ago I could deal with it, and
now I can't. Two years ago, I'd wake at four a.m. in a stranger's room;
I'd retrieve my scattered clothes, tiptoe out of the stranger's door, and

leave her sleeping. No note, no follow-up calls, and no repercussions beyond a new understanding of pointlessness, some shame, and a certain indefinable but dragging acquaintance with misery.

Yes, it's a bleak place, this love/sex quandary. Been there, seen that, got the Expense-of-Spirit T-shirts—and nothing on God's earth will persuade me back there.

No way, sorry, I Morse, and something dies in the girl's eyes. Gently, I take the two objects out of her hands. I replace them on the mantelpiece. The girl, the young woman, says nothing. She moves away from me.

I replace the book token. It's creased and faded, but the handwriting inside is still clear. I examine the message a boy wrote all those years ago: "Wishing you a Happy 14th Birthday, Finn! Please use this to buy a really great book! Yours sincerely, Daniel Nunn."

The boy's writing is round and unformed. I still made elaborate loops on the tails of letters, as I'd been taught to do at the village primary. What possessed me to write "Yours sincerely"? Why sign myself "Daniel"—and add my surname? *What do you want for your birthday, Finn?* I'd asked her weeks earlier. *What I want most of all is a bottle of scent*, she replied. *It's called Taboo, Dan, and they sell it in Woolworth's.*

Was Finn being kind, because she knew I had very little money, though I'd been saving for months? Possibly; but I think she really did want it—Taboo was cheap; it smelled powerful, sexual, and adult. But I didn't buy it. Nick's mother talked me out of it. And that was easy enough: I lived in perpetual, cringing terror of doing the wrong thing, of saying the wrong thing, of being exposed as a . . . well, as a *common little toad*, I suppose. So I listened to Mrs. Marlow and bought this "impersonal and appropriate" present. I couldn't bring myself to give it to Finn; it felt like a betrayal.

I lean the book token against the mantelpiece wall. I place the carved ivory Chinese sphere next to it, secured by a blob of Blu-Tack adhesive. Its internal hemispheres rotate as I lift it. Something else Gran nicked from the Abbey. She gave it to me when I was seven, a few weeks before the Mortlands left New Mexico and came home. *Who's going to miss it, Danny? If they ask, I'll just say it got broke. You mind you keep it safe now.*

And keep it safe I did. To this day no one knows I have it, not even Finn, not Julia, not Nick—and not Lucas. Lucas may have incorporated elements of the Lady Chapel library in the background of his *Sisters Mortland* painting, but he could never have seen three ivory spheres on the altar-wall mantelpiece. By that summer, there were only two; the third was secreted away, as it had been for years. It was part of a cache of sacred Finn relics under a floorboard in the room I shared with my father, at the Nunn family's ancient crooked tip of a tied cottage.

So much for my theories, I think; so much for drug-induced insomnia-fueled insights. I turn round, wondering if the amyl-nitrate girl is similarly insubstantial. But no, I haven't imagined her. She's real, and she's still here. She's wandered down to the other end of this long room—it runs front to back; the bay at that end overlooks Malc & Co., or it does when the shutters aren't closed; the bay this end overlooks a back garden jungle. Yes, she's wandered down there, is meandering around on the bare boards, is examining the boxes and crates I've never unpacked, and is inspecting the only piece of furniture in the room. It's a large, cutting-edge-fashionable sofa, bought in Milan two years ago when I was between planes. I had it shipped over; that was the sort of thing I did then. I can't remember why I bought it, except I was in the store, and I saw it, and in a blink I'd imagined a future for it. On that sofa, I was going to sit with a wife and children: a happy family engaged on a familial task. What task? I think we were unpacking decorations. Yes, it's true: We were about to decorate a Christmas tree.

Christ, what were we going to do next, sing carols? I stare at the sofa. It's white, it's minimalist, and it's not child-friendly. I don't understand why that other Daniel ever liked it—though Frankie seems interested in it. She's inspecting it; she's weaving her way toward it— she seems a little unsteady on her feet, I notice. She's now sitting down.

"So you're still camping out?" she remarks. "You still haven't unpacked?"

That "still" is alarming. She can't have been here before, surely? If we did go on somewhere after that club—and I'm almost certain we didn't—surely I couldn't have brought her here? *Tell me I didn't do that....* Then I know I didn't do that; it's not possible. On paper I owned the house then, but I didn't move in until months later, after I'd finally returned from the collapse, the freak-out in Tokyo. The day I moved in, I received the McIvers' telephone call. I left at once for my father's bedside at Wykenfield.

" 'Still'? What d'you mean, 'still'?" I say, moving toward her. Who is she? Why is she here? She is pretty, this punky Circe. She has thick glossy hair, dyed a defiant, unnatural red gold. It's twisted and spikily gelled and pinned with a glitter of ties and jeweled clips; she has several silver rings in her ears and a small sparkling stud in her left nostril. She has Nefertiti eyes, a green gaze, too much blusher, and freckles. She's wearing umpteen silver bracelets; they chime when she moves. Her fingernails, painted purple, are bitten. Her long, slender legs are embellished with spray-on jeans and kickboxer boots. She appears to be wearing an Edwardian corselet-type thing under a softly luxurious leather jacket. I can't place her accent, which is standard young-speak and estuarine, with a faint drawl on the vowels that suggests the estuarine is adopted, not natural. Did she work in PR? I think she might have done. That party might have been for the latest guns'n rape rap group, and she might have represented them in some junior capacity. Yes, the rap group that did the backing track for one of my ads. *Shall I show you fear in a handful of dust?* No, not that ad, some other.

"You said you were moving," she replies. "When we met at that party—and that was like fifteen months ago? Plenty of time to unpack." She frowns. "What's that rope for? Why have you got all that rope coiled up over there? Is that some kind of artwork?"

"No, it's to mend the sash cords. All the sash cords are frayed. They have to be replaced, and for that you need Manila rope. . . ." I come to a halt: *Cotter's Early Giant.* When one is lying, too much detail is a giveaway. "Frankie," I continue, "I'm not sure why you're here, or how you know where I live, but it's late, and I've had a lousy day, and irrespective of what your tarot cards may have told you, I feel you should leave now."

"You don't know why I'm here?" Her expression, wounded and affronted, becomes dismaying. "Oh, great, thanks a lot, Dan. Now I feel *really* welcome. Okay: I'm here because you told me to come. You said, 'Frankie, I have to catch a plane to Bangkok in three hours' time, and that is a bitch. Now I've found you, I don't want to leave you. I'm away for months, but I won't forget tonight. I won't forget you. The second I'm home, we have to meet and talk again,' you said. Then you gave me this."

She delves into her jacket pocket. She retrieves a card, and I inspect it: incontestably my handwriting, incontestably my address—and incontestably, no matter how fried my brain, I would never, *never* have made the speech she's just quoted. I look at her uncertainly. Despite Nick's good food and all that purifying water, I'm still not sure she's here. I'm still hoping she may be some trippy aftereffect. Then I see she isn't. My hallucinations are painfully plausible, but this hallucinatory girl is now reacting in an implausible way. Her eyes have filled with tears, and she's begun crying.

"You don't remember," she says. "That's how much it meant to you. You remember my name—and that's it. You don't remember how we talked. I've never talked to anyone that way before—I can't believe you'd forget that. All those things I told you—all those things you told *me*. About how you grew up in Suffolk, right, and your mum was dead, and your grandmother was Romany, and she had second sight—it was called the Gift—you see how well I remember every detail? But then I would, I've had over a year to think about it. I've thought about it every day, I've thought about *you* every day. How amazing you look. How totally sexy you are. How sad you seem. How funny you can be. I mean, like *seriously* funny. Why hide it, right? I love you."

The tears are now spilling down her cheeks. Her hands, with their touching bitten nails, are shaking. I can see that she means what she says—or believes that she does, which amounts to the same thing. I can see that she is indeed young, too young to have grown those necessary protective skins, young enough to risk being absurd. I can also see, and should have noticed earlier, that she's not sober. Either it's taken Dutch courage to make this speech, the words of which are occasionally slurred, or she's well and truly stoned. I stare at her, uncertain what to do. I didn't think there were any more guilts to discover, and now, out of the blue yonder, here's another.

"Frankie," I begin, trying to make it gentle, "I'm sorry—but I don't remember any of this. There are reasons for that. I wasn't in a good state then, and I'm not in a good state now."

"You think I don't *know* that?" She rises alarmingly to her feet. "You think I can't *see* that? That's why I'm here. I can help. I can cure you. Okay, it doesn't have to be love, you may not be ready for that, that's cool—I understand. We can just *make* love, right? Where's that amyl nitrate I gave you? You promised to keep it for—you know . . ."

And before my startled gaze, she peels off the leather jacket and begins to unhook that witchy black corselet thing. It unhooks down the front. She has beautiful shoulders; she has amazing breasts; her bracelets chime . . . I recoil sharply. "Frankie," I say in a firm voice, "do that up now. Put that jacket back on immediately. Sit down on that sofa and pull yourself together. I'm going to make you some coffee. When you've drunk that, you'll feel better. We'll sit here for a while and have a sensible conversation, then I'll call you a cab, and you can go home and get some sleep and forget this ever happened. Believe me, and I speak from bitter experience, that is by far the best course of action."

Well, I make a speech along those lines. It's not as fluent as that, and it's less trite, but that's the gist. When it produces no discernible change, I repeat it, with variations. Eventually it has the desired effect, in that Frankie calms down and the corselet thing gets refastened. There are still a few residual problems, however. I discover I've aged a few more millennia. I discover she's tenacious and obstinate, this amyl-nitrate girl.

"Go home?" she says, eyeing me sadly. "I so don't have a home. I've been sleeping on this guy's floor, but we had a fight, and he threw me out. If I can't stay here, I've got nowhere to go. I'll just end up walking the streets. Oh, Dan, it's really weird—I'm so miserable. My life is one big miserable mess. D'you have any food—I'm like, really starving?"

Through a mist of fatigue, I hear alarums. I begin to see Frankie might be manipulative. But I'm tired, I'm exhausted, I'm running on empty here. I suspect this is 90 percent garbage, 10 percent genuinely troubled, but can I be sure? Supposing I'm wrong, what then? I can't abandon a stoned girl to the tender mercies of Malc Inc. Besides, troubled girls have been on my mind recently, and this difficult girl is reminding me of someone I once knew . . . I'm certain, almost certain, it's Maisie. I have no idea why; there is no physical resemblance, the speech patterns couldn't be more different. But I can sense some ghostly shadowing, some echoing imbalance. I don't want to cause any more harm, even inadvertently. *We were blind to distress*, Nick wrote to me.

And so, in the end, after more crying jags and pleading, I give
way. It's agreed that Frankie can spend this night, and this night
only, on my Milanese sofa. Apart from that small concession, I'm
firm. It's astonishing, I can't believe it: I feel quite fatherly. Yes, I'm
turning into that paterfamilias I imagined earlier. It is a far, far better thing that I do than I have ever done, I tell myself as I make
comforting Nescafé and root around for some not too stale gin-
gersnaps; as I trudge upstairs and downstairs fetching blankets and
cushions. I get Frankie settled on the sofa. I turn out the light. I
tell her to get some sleep, and with a distant sense of progress
made, and heroism imminent, I move quietly toward the door. By
now the fatigue is intense: I've stepped through a mirror; I'm wad-
ing through unreality. The long day has caught up with me. I've
been pushing a boulder up a mountain all day long, and I can't,
won't, push it one inch farther.

"You were in love with her, weren't you, that book-token girl?"
Frankie says in a wan, sniffly, muffled voice. "I could tell from your
face. Are you still in love with her?"

"Go to sleep, Frankie," I reply. I'm not really listening. I'm standing in the doorway, looking at the shadows in the hall. I feel old, in-
credibly old: I'm Tiresias. Outside, a helicopter is circling, and it will
be a police helicopter, searching the London streets, on the lookout
for muggers, molesters, murderers—all the usual suspects.

"Finn. That's an odd name. Who was she, this Finn?"

"Someone I used to know," I reply, realizing that is the truth. "We
lived in the same village when I was a child. She was one of three
sisters."

"Why do you sound so sad? Did she die? Did you lose her?"

"No, she didn't die," I answer. I'm looking at the dark, listening to
that helicopter; it's lower now and still circling. "But there was an accident, a terrible accident."

"Finn had an accident?"

"No, the youngest sister. Her name was Maisie. She fell from a high window."

"Was she killed?"

"No. She wasn't killed. If she had been, it might have been more merciful. But she survived. She's still alive—after a fashion."

"That's terrible. Is she . . . in a home?"

"Yes, a very good one. It's run by nuns; nuns look after her."

"That's really sad. Do you go and see her?"

"No, I don't. Not any more. Go to sleep now, Frankie."

"Won't you tell me what happened?"

"Sleep well," I reply, and close the door.

I mount the stairs to my room. I lock the door. I don't trust Frankie, and I don't want visitations. Through the thin curtains, the street-lamps stripe the walls with prison patterns. I lie down on the bed, too tired to undress. The past day moves in my mind like the sea, and I wait patiently for the moment when the waves will quieten. Slack water: The helicopter continues to circle.

On the chest of drawers opposite the bed is a sealed wooden box some eight inches square; it contains Joe's ashes. Joe was six feet three: When I collected it, its size cut me to the heart, and its weight, its weightiness, appalled me. I must take those ashes back to Wyken-field. I'll do what I should have done weeks ago, and I'll do it soon, I promise myself. A son's last task: I'll bury them in the fields or the woods he loved, or perhaps the gardens at the Abbey where he tended the vegetables. *Docks and nettles*—those gardens had reverted to docks and nettles; he mentioned that in one of his letters to me, the letters I used to skim, the letters I now know by heart—too late, of course.

I close my eyes, and at last alone, at last quiet, I watch the last day of that last summer at the Abbey. I'm still not *clean*, but I'm cleaner than I've been in weeks. My mind feels washed and translucid. I've nearly reached the white place that's the other side of exhaustion.

Frankie's final question circles in my mind; the helicopter circles overhead. Memory is random, cruel, slippery, and deceitful.

I stand and move across to the desk in the window. I take a blank sheet of paper and pick up a pen. I think: *What did happen that last day, Dan?* Were there no clues? What happened? Tell me what happened.

PART VI

The Empress, Reversed

Wyken Abbey, home to our School of Cookery, is situated in one of the most beautiful, tranquil, and unspoilt areas of Suffolk. It is surrounded by apple orchards, ancient woodland, and a field system little changed since the Middle Ages. Although the nearby village of Wykenfield is small and may appear remote on maps, communications can be surprisingly good. There is a reliable train service from London to Ipswich and a branch line to Deepden; from there, a twice weekly bus serves our village.

Most of the produce for the Abbey School of Cookery will be provided by our own beautiful gardens, which are extensive. We insist on the highest standards: all our vegetables, herbs, and fruit are grown organically, without artificial fertilizers or pesticides. All eggs and poultry will come from our own hens; meat will be supplied by local farmers, who rear their animals humanely.

Wyken Abbey is a Grade II* listed building, associated with our family since the founding of the convent in 1257 by Isabella de Morlaix. It has had a colourful history and retains that atmosphere of calm recorded by the nuns who lived, prayed, and worked here for three centuries. The mediaeval refectory, cloisters, and Lady Chapel remain intact. They have been incorporated into the present house, which has a very relaxed family atmosphere. There are many romantic legends associated with the Abbey—even claims that it is haunted!

All our courses (see on) are residential. Students will be accommodated within the historic convent buildings, and the emphasis will be on classic, traditional cooking. Every evening, the family and students will gather for dinner to eat the food prepared during the day. Our aim is to make these occasions happy, relaxed, and convivial.

Good cooking is not about fussy presentation or display: that is the preserve of restaurants. It is about pure and honest ingredients, prepared with loving attention, with rigour, skill, and care. It is that art to which we aspire and that discipline we will endeavour to teach you.

—Stella Mortland, *Introduction to the Prospectus*,
The Abbey School of Cookery, August 1, 1967

Winifride, this is the last letter I shall send you. You will not reply. Even if you did, after these long years of silence, I would not receive your message. I am dying: a tiresome task, but I am nearly done with it.

It tires me to write; I will be brief. I have a final confession to make. I will not seek absolution from the priest who comes to us from Deepden, so this confession must be made to you, my dearest Sister. Long ago, at the time of my novitiate, you told me the love I felt for you was worldly and impure, a delusion of the Devil—and I believed you. You urged me to cast this wicked love from my heart, so I obeyed you, left you, and journeyed here. For years I told myself that your silence and my prayers would quench the flame of that love, given time. They have not done so.

I am old now, and, lying here alone for long days and nights, I have come to believe we were wrong. Is any love truly wicked? My love for you, a mother's for a child, a man's for his friend or country: could not *all* loves be said to light a taper in our hearts, one which can illuminate our lives and guide us towards that eternal beacon of light which is the Love of God, in Heaven?

One summer's day long ago, you kissed me, and I returned that kiss: we were very young and no doubt foolish. When I think of that loving embrace now, I do not repent it. No doubt I shall shortly be called to account for this heresy.

Beyond the walls here lies a small dark wood, Winifride. I think of it as a place of danger, but one where wisdom may be found, if sought for. Walking there, I have soberly considered the nature of love and the unexpected ways in which it may be revealed to us: I fear that when we encounter love, we do not always understand or recognize it. But if I was once blind, I am blind no longer. From first to last, you have brought me untold joy, dearest Sister; and now, at the end of my journey, I bless you for it.

Isabella

—*The Letters of Isabella de Morlaix to Winifride of Ely, 1257–1301*, edited and translated from the Latin, V. B. S. Taylor, 1913

[SIXTEEN]

Waiting for Godard

I T'S THAT LAST DAY. It's August 7, 1967. Bright morning. It hasn't rained for a month; the harvest's under way. Daniel, the Dan I used to be, wakes early in his bedroom at the Abbey. Eyes closed, sitting here at my Highbury desk, I watch him. He can hear the drone of the McIvers' new combine harvester. It must be working near the house, in the fields he used to call Grandage, Pickstone, Nuns', Wellhead, and Holyspring. It's seven o'clock. I watch myself pad across to the window and draw back the curtains. The landscape unscrolls. My eyes rest on the familiar: the cloister, the elms, the wood, the church tower, and the lush green grass in the graveyard. . . . In a few weeks, I'll be leaving for London. I'm on the edge of a new life, and that knowledge makes this panorama sweet. Its power is intense. I can love this place now, without reservation, because I know I'll soon be escaping it.

I'm already seeing this valley with the untruthful eye of nostalgia. I open the window wide and take in a breath of English air. It's like breathing pure optimism.

Anything's possible. I'm twenty-two. I'm in love. I can't wait to see Finn, can't wait to speak to her—that's my only imperative. As I wash, shave, and pull on jeans, I have no Roma sense of foreboding, not the slightest hint that this day will end with a fall. If I've inherited that gift of divination, as Gran still claims, then today it's deserted me.

I'm on my own. No assistance from the supernatural.

I'm on my own and—I must take this into account—that Daniel is someone I scarcely recognize. Who was he? Who was I? That was the summer I was blinded by movies—I do know that. Movies had struck me down, like Paul on the road to Damascus. I was steeped in cinema then, obsessed with the grammar of film. I'd spent so much time at Cambridge watching movies, working my way religiously through Bergman, Vigo, and Kurosawa, through Truffaut, Antonioni, and Godard; so much time chain-smoking in wonderment in dark cinemas, so much time winding celluloid through ancient Film Society projectors, so many hours editing 16-mm student movies, that I saw life through a viewing screen. Time didn't pass, it unreeled. I could wind it back or forward at will, I could shoot and edit it any which way I chose.

I was in control of life's narrative. It was easy to insert a celluloid strip in the editing guillotine. Slice and splice; remove just two frames, one incident, and you alter the sense. You could do it with life as well as film. So yesterday I seemed trapped in some *L'Avventura* nightmare, on an island of entropy, searching for someone who will not be found, whose disappearance will always remain inexplicable? Do an overnight reshoot, and today this story's Technicolor: It's clear to everyone, even me, that Finn still loves Dan. Give it a while, and in this screwball Rock and Doris version there'll be Hollywood wedding bells.

And if I disdain that approach, no problem: I can reshoot the European way. This time, in grainy black and white, with a jazz track, wit, insouciance, and sharp editing, Finn and I will still find each other—it just takes longer, that's all. We have to screw the wrong people first. We have to riff, philosophize, and smoke umpteen packs of Gauloises. There'll be misunderstandings and a brush with tragedy, we'll have to age a bit, sure—this is not some La-la-land candyfloss confection, it's an intelligent, bittersweet film. But it can still end with a kiss. I see it as a *jeu d'esprit*. This is *my* film and *my* future. I'm the director, the *auteur*, and I've decided: It ends with a long, slow beautiful panning shot; then, as I take my Finn in my arms, it's *freeze frame*—the best way to end a love story, much better than a fade-out.

There were so many possibilities here: I used to get drunk on them. I'd dream in long tracking shots, because that's how a day looked, especially when stoned—a journeying, a great stretch of res-onant meaningfulness. I'd think in jump cuts—the kind I learned from watching the films of my new god, Godard. How I worshipped his steely contempt for the steady tramp of traditional narrative progress. Well tutored by the nouvelle vague, how I despised the con-cept of causality. I despised it as much as religion. Watching *Les Cara-biniers* for the fifty-fifth time, I'd sit in the dark and think: Right on, Jean-Luc—tell it like it is. Life is arbitrary; everything is random. There is no God, and there is no plot. Who needs those tired old lies?

Yes, that's how I saw things then. Now, in London, listening to that helicopter, things have changed. For a start, I no longer believe I'm in control of this film, this life of mine. Somehow, with the passing of years, I've been moved in front of the camera—when did *that* happen? I'm now just the poor actor, and the director—call him God, Fate, Allah, Eisenstein, or Clint Eastwood, it doesn't mat-ter—is an unpredictable son of a bitch. He could have *anything* planned for the next day's shoot, and he likes to keep the script se-cret. He has a long memory, too, a nasty memory—nothing gets past this bastard.

Look, I'll say, why am I doing this? How come Dan is behaving this way? It's out of character. These jump cuts make no sense. One minute I'm successful, I'm on top of the world, happy as a lark; the next it's a close-up on Dan's face, and it's a close-up on—*an expression of pure horror.* Why? What's going on? What have I done? What happened? This script is a mess. It's arbitrary. It's random.

Random? But of course, replies the fascist in the director's chair. *On the other hand, remember the thirty-sixth frame of the second reel? Remember what you said then, what you did then? You thought it was unimportant? Wrong, saddo. In this movie, actions have consequences. Or they do sometimes; it depends on my mood. . . .* And he yawns.

Of course, I *don't* remember that thirty-sixth frame. Reel two is one big blur. I'd thought it was safely cut, lying on some celestial editing room floor, about to be consigned to the garbage. Now, I'm going to have to find it again—and the prospect's daunting. I'll have to rewind, I'll have to employ hindsight—and how much do I trust hindsight? About as much as I'd trust a cobra.

All those spools of memory, coiling out of the cans, all that tangled toxic celluloid spillage: How do I decide which frames are missing, which are relevant? Ancient celluloid, like memory, is highly combustible; its chemical composition makes it liable to self-destruct. . . . Even so, I'll try. I have a white sheet of paper. I'm in that white place now; this has to be done.

I'll be methodical, I decide. I'll look at that last day frame by frame. I'll examine who was where, when, and why. I'll replay the dialogue, for which I'll have perfect recall. Who said what to whom? When they said one thing but meant another, a common occurrence, it won't escape my new patient, all-seeing eyes. Then, with this omniscient godlike gaze, maybe at last I'll understand: I'll see through walls, as Bella did. I'll be released. I'll be able to say: *This is why Maisie jumped. This is what went wrong, that summer.*

That helicopter is still circling. I think: *Here goes.* I'm determined, but am I optimistic? Well now, reader—if anyone should ever read this, which won't happen, which is impossible, because when it's finished, I'm going to burn it . . . Well now, *hypocrite lecteur, mon sem-blable, mon frère*: Am I optimistic of success?

Would *you* be?

And *cut*. I've gone downstairs, and I'm in the cool of the Abbey kitchen; there's the appetizing smell of bacon cooking. It's supplied by Colonel Edwardes (Indian army, ret'd.); when his Heavy Hogs go to the abattoir, a flitch is always sent up to the Abbey. As I enter, a dreamy Stella smiles at me. She puts three more rashers in the pan and breaks a guinea-fowl egg into the sizzle of bacon fat. "Another beautiful day, Dan," Gramps says as I join him and Finn at the break-fast table.

I drop a kiss on Finn's hair. It's safe to do so: Stella has her back to us; Maisie, seated at the far end, is reading and doesn't look up. Gramps is preoccupied: I could ravish Finn on the floor, and he'd notice nothing.

Finn makes a wry face and swats at me. I sit opposite her. Finn and I have reached a state of truce. We've agreed that I will stop being suspicious and jealous of Lucas; Finn has sworn there's no need. One Daniel believes her; the other Daniel smells some linguistic trickery. He's waiting for Finn to explain that although she still feels love for him, it's shrunk; the love's now friendly, or sisterly. I keep that darker Daniel, Mr. Hyde to my Dr. Jekyll, well concealed. Finn's face this morning has that expression that so hurts and angers me. She looks saturated, brimming over with sexual secrecy. There's a blurry look to her features, as if she's been dreaming of a lover all night. Her dark blue eyes are as blind as a kitten's. Despite her reassurances, physical and verbal, I cannot believe that I'm the man who blinded her this way.

"This summer will go into the record books," Gramps says, fuss-ing with the stacks of papers and brochures piled next to his plate.

"Now, Dan, I need your opinion. Take a look at this wine list I've drawn up, and tell me what you think. It's pretty comprehensive, at least I hope it is—but we need to cover every eventuality."

Eating bacon and eggs, I inspect the list. My ignorance of wine is impressive, and Gramps knows that, but he enjoys consultation. He likes to feel busy and he likes to feel useful—and this is the first opportunity he's had in years. I hadn't realized that Stella's cookery school would require this kind of male expertise, male input. I thought food would be involved, period. Gramps has other ideas. In his mind, this enterprise is turning into an Edwardian house party. He's reliving his pre–World War I youth. We've already migrated to Elde, and we're still at the planning stage.

I run my eye down lines of bewildering Bordeaux and Burgundies; I glance at the wine merchants' catalogs. These have prices on them; his list does not. He's looking at me so beseechingly that I can't bear to cavil. "Amazing," I say. "Out of sight."

Gramps lights up like a three-thousand-watt bulb. "I'm very glad you think so, Dan," he says. "But what about some pudding wines? When these girls have been slaving away all day, a nice glass of Sauternes might be just the ticket, don't you think? If they've made an apple pie, for instance—Humphrey says apples and Sauternes are a marriage made in heaven."

"Gramps, they won't need Sauternes—really they won't," Finn says firmly. "It's too expensive. They'll be here learning to cook. We mustn't spoil them."

"If children behave badly, we say they are *spoiled*. If food has gone off, we say it's *spoiled*. We say that someone is *spoiling* for a fight. We also speak of the *spoils* of war," Maisie interjects, looking up from her book. "The spoils of war are desirable—men fight to acquire them, anyway. Spoiled food is not desirable. Spoiled children are not desirable. English is a curious language, don't you agree, Dan?"

I agree. I quickly agree. There is a silence. Poor Maisie, she is getting *worse*, I think: The degeneration is becoming more and more noticeable. Four years ago, there were hopes of progress; Stella began speaking of schools again, of the "special" schools that might cope with a child of Maisie's intelligence, needs, and peculiarities. Remembering the earlier fraught and disastrous episodes at such establishments—none of which lasted more than three weeks because Maisie refused to eat, sleep, or speak—it was decided to wait. Now, once again, the topic of education is banned. When the holidays are over, it will be back to the old regime: Stella will teach English and French; various saintly helpers, including Dr. Marlow, Mrs. Marlow (an unused degree), and the rector (a doctorate in philosophy as well as divinity), will be drafted in to assist. History and geography will be dangled, religion, myth, metaphysics, and mathematics will be essayed. Maisie will soak up knowledge if the subject interests her. If it does not, she will ignore it—and when Maisie ignores something, be afraid, be very afraid . . . imagine a granite wall coming toward you at two hundred miles per hour: That's our Maisie.

Maisie has an IQ of 155. She likes *lists*. Sometimes, when I've felt too kind or too weak to escape, she's recited them to me. There are the plant lists, the bird lists, and the mammal lists—with the emphasis on dwarf species. There's the list of everyone executed during the French Revolution and the Reign of Terror, with full names, titles, and dates. There's the list of endangered animals—that gets longer by the day. There's the list of rivers of the world, organized alphabetically or, sometimes, according to length (that one's truly terrifying). There's the list of the body's bones and muscles, all ten million of them. There's the periodic table and the pure horror of prime numbers. There's the list of Greek gods, goddesses, heroes, and prophetesses, with full details as to their countless offspring and complex incestuous connections, and, as of this month—it had to happen— there are the stars. Each star, by name, in each constellation, by name, in an appalling, mind-bending galaxy. You pray to die, listening to that one.

There are also the poems, which break my heart, because they're often bad poems, and they're invariably long ones. There are the stories, which last forever and have a point invisible to everyone except Maisie. And then there are the nuns—I don't even want to think about the nuns. Get Maisie started on that, and you're there for the next century: saints' days, abstruse rituals, niggly degrees of sinfulness, the Office of the Dead, subdivided into 350 million minikin particles, into psalms, nocturns, canticles, and more canticles . . . It's pitiable, yes, but it's also insupportable.

I know how Maisie persuaded rich cousin Edmund to write that £2,000 check, I decide, looking at her bright, tight expression. Everyone else was astonished: *But, Maisie, what did you say to him? How did you persuade him? You mean he handed it over, just like that?* Pretty blind, I feel. I reckon Maisie just launched herself on a few lists. Half an hour of the stars, half an hour of Zeus and Calliope, ten minutes of *Hiawatha* or (her latest) *Samson Agonistes,* and anyone would cave in. Given how loaded Edmund is, and how desperate to escape he must have been, I'm surprised it wasn't more.

I know that Maisie is like a hermit crab, deeply secured inside an alien shell, scuttling about the seabed in frantic search of nutrition. I know she can't help the hellish taxonomy that afflicts her. Classification is the only way she can impose order on a world whose chaos I assume she fears. I know that none of the medication, which keeps changing, ever works. They've now put her on some growth hormone, and that isn't working, either. I know I ought to listen more, help more, simply be available and be kinder. But I can't. I shrink from the task. Her lists inflict boredom so intense, it's homicidal.

There's another problem, too: Sometimes, trying to attend to the strange deadpan linear stories, for example, those stories drenched with finicky details, I've felt my own grasp of the world start to slacken. Listen to Maisie long enough, and everything unravels. You start thinking, Hey, maybe she's on to something; this is starting to add up now, maybe I should look at things the way she does. . . . And then you're in trouble. The doors of perception open, and it's eyeless in Gaza time. You're as blind, as batty, as Maisie, and you can't understand *anything*.

I'm not going to let that happen again. My vision is twenty-twenty, thank you, Maisie: I trust my own eyes and my own viewing-screen way of seeing things. So I'm not going to get drawn into a discussion about the vagaries of English or the number of angels that can polka on a pinhead. I'll help Stella wash up, and then—work to do—I'm out of here. There's no point in remaining since Finn will be leaving shortly. Gramps is in charge of Maisie today. Stella and Finn, armed with lists of kitchen equipment and food supplies, are driving to London and will spend the day there. It's a cookery school shopping spree.

So, *cut* to the rear drive, and—I have to try to track the time sequence—it's maybe half an hour later. "Soho, all those wonderful French and Italian grocers," Stella is saying, approaching the prehistoric Wolseley. It's years since she's been to London, even longer since she had money to spend. She's flushed with nerves, almost trembling with excitement. "Fortnum and Mason," Gramps says wistfully, helping them into the car. "Watch the clutch, Stella dear, it's getting a bit bolshie."

"Bye, Finn, safe journey," I call, and the car jerks forward. In the passenger seat, Finn turns to look at me. Her face is imprinted on my mind, as she looked then, that bright morning. There's no hint of duplicity: Her expression is frank and joyous, lit with anticipation. Her skin glows; her dark blue eyes meet mine; she blows me a kiss and waves her hand. My own *Final Finn*: I'll never see her this care-free again.

Behind us, Maisie stands in the hall doorway. She also waves. Her face wears its habitual fixed, alert expression. Did she know, then, what she intended to do later that day? Had she planned it already, selecting this date because, for once, Stella would be absent? Or was Maisie planning it then, as the car moved off down the driveway?

Adjust focus. She appears to be listening to something I can't hear. I ruffle her hair affectionately, and then, feeling repentant, I go to give her a hug. I draw back just in time: Maisie does not like to be hugged; even Stella is barred from embracing her.

"Are you listening to the nuns, Maisie?" I ask; she probably is. Those nuns of hers are almost certain to be praying. It's bound to be time for matins or whatever.

"Oh no, my nuns have deserted me," she replies. "I don't have time for them anymore. They're sulking. They're angry with me."

"That's not very Christian," I reply. Then I ask the wrong question. Instead of asking why these nonexistent nuns are angry, I say, "Nuns shouldn't sulk, surely, Maisie. Isn't that a sin?" It's my first lost opportunity of the day—and there'll be others.

She considers this, frowning. "If so, only venal," she finally replies. "Not mortal. Ten Hail Marys, I should think." She pauses. "Are you going down to the village today?" I tell her I am. "I hope Bella is feeling much recovered," she says with studied politeness. "Please give her my sympathies."

And taking her grandfather's hand, she trots inside the house to give him a natural history lesson. She's launched on the survival of the fittest before they're past the door. I watch her go through her ritual of crossing the hall. Today, on that chessboard floor, she's a bishop. She swoops across on a black square diagonal and skids to a halt in the far corner. "*Checkmate,*" she cries to her eternal invisible opponent.

.   .   .

Cut, and it's still early, around nine. I'm leaving for the village; my footsteps crunch on the gravel path that leads from the cloister, past the refectory. There are walls of yew either side of me; the trapped heat bakes my skin and blinds my eyes.

"Hi, Dan," calls Lucas several seconds before I'm visible to him. When I round the corner of the refectory, I find him sitting outside on the step, sunning himself like a lizard. Next to him—and this surprises me because she rarely rises before noon—is Julia. They're sharing a cigarette—no, a spliff, I realize as its scent reaches me. Have I interrupted something?

I can't tell. Both are immobile, sun worshipping; there's no sign of furtiveness, yet I sense concealment and secrets—as I always do when I catch them alone. Julia's position suggests abandonment. She is stretched out in a provocative, sun-sated attitude. I look at this miniskirted Danaë, at the lovely, luxuriant lines of her body: bare feet, bare legs, golden throat exposed, eyes closed, Rhinegold hair tousled; an arm weighted with silver bangles. In the distance, the combine drones. Did she spend the night here?

Through the doorway, in the shadows of the refectory, I can just see *The Sisters Mortland,* propped against the wall. Julia's painted double seems to beckon mockingly—I've felt that since the painting was first unveiled a week ago. That illusion—the painted Julia is *not* beckoning—angers me in some obscure way. "Want some?" Lucas inhales and holds the spliff out to me. Julia sits up: I'm inspected by two amused pairs of eyes.

"No thanks, have to work," I say. "It's one of my earn-some-money days."

"I'm impressed," Julia says in a dreamy manner that may or may not mean she's stoned. "Is it straw baling today or mucking out? Barman at the Green Man, doling out money to pensioners at the post office? Mending tractors?" She yawns. "You are just so fucking industrious, Dan."

"And you are just so fucking lazy, Julia," I reply.

And I hate her in that moment; hate her with an intensity that surprises me. I hate her for her unfailing ability to rile me. I hate her because Julia and I are alike in many ways, and we're in the same predicament. We're both eager to escape, both hungry for success; we're both about to go to London, both about to seek work—and neither of us has any money.

I hate her because I know I'm going to struggle while Julia will breeze past these difficulties. There were difficulties when she announced that she was taking that year's postgraduate course at Berkeley. They didn't check her then, and they won't check her now. On that occasion, the airfare was wheedled out of her grandfather's dwindling savings; a friend of a friend found her somewhere to stay. The obliging friend was male and well connected; he was an editor on the *San Francisco Chronicle,* with valuable contacts in the world of journalism and media studies. He provided a rent-free room, gifts, and an entrée. Once she's in London, once she's a journalist, expect more of the same. When a woman is as beautiful as Julia, some obliging man will always help her on her way—and Julia will see nothing wrong in that. "Don't preach at me," she said to me once when I voiced a similar criticism. "Fuck off, Dan. If you think being a woman is an advantage, you're a fool. It isn't. I intend to play by my rules."

I angered her then, and I've angered her now. You'd have to know Julia very well to see that—but I do know her well. "Oh, come on," she says. "You're not that hard up, Dan. I know about your windfall. Have you heard about it, Lucas? Bella told me the other day—how Joe had been saving up all these years in a secret post office account, how he presented it to you last week, Dan, and made a speech wishing you well. I was touched: all those hard-earned shillings, twenty years of putting by. A hundred pounds, Bella said. I call that generous. That could keep one going in London for weeks. A month, if one was stingy. It would buy me at least four dresses. I wish I had a hundred pounds."

"Start charging," I tell her, smiling. I walk on. The combine eats wheat in the distance.

And *cut*, it's around noon, three hours later or so—and I'm still aching with anger. My heart's pumping some thick venom along my arteries. There's a hot mist clouding my vision, and all I can think about is punishing Julia. I will not forgive her for what she said. Joe earns nine pounds seven and sixpence a week, with two pounds coming straight off the top for rent. I can remember how he looked, bashful and excited, when he handed me that post office book. I can remember the halting speech he made—and the guilt it induced. Joe has no concept of how expensive London is, and I'm not about to enlighten him. He doesn't understand how long it may take me to get a job: I've written to thirty-five advertising agencies, and so far—nothing.

To Joe, a hundred pounds is a fortune. To have that mocked by Julia, to have my dad ridiculed by Julia: I can't stand it. I'll make her regret those words, and I've spent three hours, maybe four, thinking how to do it. Meanwhile, wounded and vicious, unable to punish her yet, I've been punishing anyone and anything that comes into range.

I've punished Gran by erupting into the cottage and yelling at her. "Just don't tell Julia anything," I've shouted. "Keep our private life *private*—is that too much to ask? For fuck's sake, Gran, how could you *do* that?"

And Gran, who's just had the last of her teeth out, who's used to men twice her size flailing their arms and yelling—she grew up with it; she married it—Gran doesn't budge from her chair by the stove. The temperature in the kitchen is infernal. The tarot's on the table; her swollen jaw is wrapped up in a white handkerchief. She looks ridiculous—and she's in an evil mood. "Don't you shout at me," she replies with indistinct savagery. "I had enough of that from your granddad. He was a mean bastard when he had the hump—just like you, you ungrateful little sod. I'll say what I like when I like. It's something, one hundred pounds. My gums ache. Bugger off out of here."

Next I punish some windows. That's what I'm doing today, cleaning windows. I wring out the shammy and imagine it's Julia's neck. I rub the glass panes; however hard I rub, Julia's face reappears in them. The sunlight reflects like daggers. I clean the windows at the rector's house, a grim, cost-efficient bungalow built by a failing Church of England on an economy drive. Then I attack the Marlows': I lug a ladder out of the garage and punish it. I punish the bricks of the Old Rectory by slamming the ladder against them. I punish the bucket, the water, the sponge. The windows here are tall Georgian sashes, all with fiddly, stupid astragals. Anyone who admires them should try cleaning them. Twelve panes in every one of those twenty windows, inside and out. It's as endless as Maisie's Office of the Dead: 480 painful panes, and I punish every single one.

I clean the drawing room windows—that graceful, faded room where I was dissuaded from Taboo. I clean the windows of the study, a room where the ghosts of yesteryear's learned clerics still linger. I clean the dining room windows. It was at this oval mahogany table with its linen place mats, its bewildering array of silver cutlery, that I learned not to hold a knife like a pen, that salt belonged on the side of a plate, not sprinkled all over everything with Gran's and Joe's gay abandon. I clean the bedroom windows; I clean Dr. and Mrs. Marlow's room—they sleep in neat twin beds, with no-nonsense candlewick bedspreads and fat cotton eiderdowns. Do they still have sex? Did they ever have sex? It's unimaginable. I clean Nick's room, two windows; it's a corner room, like mine at the Abbey. It's in stasis; there's evidence that a man sleeps here, some of the books, for instance, but it's still a boy's room. Maybe Mrs. Marlow prefers it that

way. It's unnaturally tidy. The bed is freshly made up—and that's because Nick is expected back today. He's been working the night shift
at University College Hospital for three weeks, Mrs. Marlow's already told me. It's the first thing she told me, but then she lives for
Nick's return and dies a little in his absences.

Yes, he's been on the night shift in Casualty, and it seems to spill
over into the day shift, so he's been working a twenty-two-hour day
for three weeks, if you can believe his mother. Now he has two days
off, and although he'd said he'd stay in London and catch up on his
sleep, Nick has changed his plans. He will be on the four p.m. train;
he'll be here in time for tea. When I cleaned the kitchen windows,
his mother was baking fairy cakes.

Stuck in the bloody past, I think, starting to punish Nick's windows
on the inside. When Nick was six or seven, yes, he liked fairy cakes;
so did I, always wolfishly hungry when I came here to tea. But for a
medical student, twenty-five years old, suffering from fatigue, escaping too many close encounters with human misery? But then, who
knows, maybe cakes are just what he wants. Maybe such routines are
soothing. Nick appreciates home comforts; he's good to his mother;
he returns to Wykenfield at every opportunity.

It's three weeks since I've seen him. He went back to London the
day the Mortlands went to Elde, the day Lucas took off for Cambridge. Why did Lucas take off for Cambridge? He said he was there
to rent a room, for when he leaves the Abbey. He said he walked and
thought and saw how to finish the portrait—but do I believe that?
He did return two days later and began painting feverishly, but is that
the whole story? Has he got some woman there? Is he screwing Julia
or Finn or both of them? Why can't I ask him? Because he won't answer, and I'm too proud. I chuck the sponge in the bucket of water
and rest my head against the burning panes. My head aches. My
heart aches. I look at this museum of Nick's past and my own: two
bald teddy bears, annual school photographs, Nick instantly recog-

nizable in even the earliest ones, the village primary ones. Who's that black imp peering over his shoulder? It's me, it's that heathen Gypsy trash Danny—pikey Danny, the Gyppo boy.

A shelf of Meccano models, Airfix and balsa-wood planes suspended from the ceiling—there's a Spitfire, a Hurricane, a Dornier, a Stuka, and a Messerschmitt: I made that one. A bookcase laden with worn Biggles, Kipling, Ransome, Conan Doyle, and *Just William*, more poetry than I'd have expected from Nick and more novels, too. Numerous medical textbooks: I pull one out of the shelf; it's an anatomy textbook. I open it at random. I'm looking at a colored diagram of the female reproductive system, and—what a piece of work is a woman—what a piece of sublime plumbing: scarlet womb, two black-ribbed ovaries joined up like headphones, navy blue vagina . . .

Let's freeze that frame. I can remember staring at that diagram, but what was I feeling? Anger—yes, the anger was still seething away. But there's something else, too, and my retrospective eye can't quite read it. Misery, probably, because optimism had leached out of the day. Maybe bewilderment. Fear of the future, of not finding work, of failing. Confusion, hurt, and jealousy, sexual frustration, the usual rich stew . . . but there might have been something more.

Looking at that explicit diagram, did I see a way to punish Julia? Or did I simply close the book and return to cleaning windows? The windows at the Old Rectory overlook gravestones.

And *cut*, I've finished those 480 panes. Mrs. Marlow is tucking two ten-shilling notes into my shirt pocket; she finds it embarrassing to put money in my hand. "I've made some cakes—I expect you'd like one?" she says. "A sandwich and a glass of something cool, perhaps? I'm so grateful to you. What a splendid job you've done." She hesitates. "You'll be off to London soon. I'm going to miss you, Danny."

I stare at her. In the retrospect viewing screen, she's wearing a tweed suit, because she usually was. But she can't have been, not that day, not that last day—it was far too hot. One of her Horrock's frocks, then: upper-middle-class summer uniform. I redress her in waisted cotton, full skirt, short sleeves, modest neckline, string of pearls, pale pink lipstick, graying hair, style unaltered since 1950. I've just understood something. This woman, this intelligent, mildly snobbish, and well-meaning woman, is lonely. Her family believes she married down and could have done better than a country GP. She's a graduate who's never used her degree. She's aging; despite running the parish, the Women's Institute, and the local Tory Party, she's overqualified and underemployed, and she's missing her son. She'd like to sit with me, in her kitchen, and talk about Nick. Since she can't talk to him, I'm the next best thing. I'm her protégé. Here, as at the Abbey, I'm a surrogate son.

I'm hungry and I'm thirsty. I'd like a cake and a sandwich. I'd give my soul for a cold beer; I'd settle for the barley water or Ribena that will be on offer. But I'm still in that state of churning rage and confusion. I don't want to be anyone's protégé, and I'm sick to death of being a surrogate son. *I have my own mother*, I want to shout. Remember her? She's lying in a white slipper-satin shroud in the churchyard over the wall. There's a nest of worms in her white rib cage. Stop trying to turn me into something I'm not. I don't fucking fit here, and I don't fucking *want* to. I'm—someone else.

And who is that, Dan? Some hick, some obscure son of the soil, some Gyp, some bit of rough, some graduate, some revolutionary cineast, some coming man? I haven't a clue, but whoever I am, I don't want fairy cakes and fucking *Ribena*. Watch out, offering me things like that, because I bite the hand that feeds me. "No thanks," I reply. "No time. I'm late. Colonel Edwardes is expecting me."

I'm not usually so offhand. I've never verged on rude before. Mrs. Marlow colors and manages a few awkward pleasantries. I can see she's hurt, possibly offended. Now she's worrying whether she's paid me enough. Good: I've punished her, too. Serves you right for the book token, I think. She probably doesn't even remember that incident—and I find that unpardonable.

Cut, and we're at the last house of the day. Colonel Edwardes, breeder of Heavy Hogs. Scene: a large Victorian morgue two miles outside the village. I clean fifteen filthy windows and one glass house full of dying tomato plants. It's three p.m. when, sweating and filthy myself, I finally finish them. Now it's back to the Abbey.

Colonel Edwardes comes scurrying out. He's wearing a cravat and a linen jacket; he smells of cologne. I don't trust him and I don't like him. This feeling may or may not be mutual. I'm none too sure he was ever in India, let alone the Indian army. Is he really a colonel? Where it touches his scraggy neck, the edge of the cravat is greasy. When I first started doing these windows, I was twelve and small for my age. Now he has to look up to me.

"I think we said seven and six," he begins.

"Sorry. Ten bob. That's what we agreed. I did the greenhouse."

"Can't we make up the difference next time?"

"No, we can't. And there won't be a next time. I'm starting work in London in a couple of weeks. I'm saving up. So I need the money now."

"Of course you do. Not thinking. . . . Well, you'd better come in and I'll find the rest. Time for a snifter, maybe?"

It's always time for a snifter at the colonel's. His is neat whiskey; mine is beer. We go in through the servants' entrance. I stand by the kitchen sink, drinking the beer down, while he searches through umpteen canisters and boxes until he's made up the ten shillings in change. He counts it out on the table in pennies. The rumors are he's losing a packet on his pig farm, that he's in hock to the bank, and that the house will be on the market sometime soon. The kitchen is

dank and cheerless; no one is certain whether the colonel's a bachelor or a widower, his histories vary according to the number of
snifters, but a bachelor, I'd say: the eternal kind. On the kitchen
table, under a muslin protector, is the colonel's supper in waiting:
two pork chops and some leftover mashed potato. There's a small tin
of peas next to them. A fly buzzes.

"Still breaking hearts in the village?" he asks. "How's the love life,
Daniel?"

He always asks this, and I always give the same answer: "Ticking
over," I say.

He puts the coins in an envelope and licks the seal. He downs the
whiskey in a single swallow. "I hear you spend a lot of time at the
Abbey these days," he continues. He cocks his head to one side and
gives me a roguish look, man to man. He has gleaming false teeth; a
liverish complexion. I do what Joe would do in such a situation:
Stare stolidly; say naught.

"You want to be careful with that family," he continues—he's
quite a gossip, Colonel Edwardes. Not too well informed, since he's
widely disliked, but assiduous. "They're well connected, of course.
And the senior branch, they're wealthy, very wealthy indeed. Live in
some state, I believe. Yes, Elde Hall—quite a palace, I've been told,
not that I've ever been invited there myself, you understand. . . . I
hear they're investing in this cookery school of Stella's, is that right?"

"I wouldn't know."

"Well, someone must be, because they haven't got two brass far-
things to rub together. I wish the project well, naturally—as I'm sure
you do, Daniel—another beer? . . . No? But I can't help thinking it's
misguided. Wykenfield is the back of beyond—and Stella, fond
though I am of her . . . well, she doesn't have any qualifications as
such, does she?"

I find this kind of hypocrisy tiring. Why disguise malice as
friendly concern? It's such a waste of time. Why not come right out

with it and admit schadenfreude? Why not just say, "I can't wait for it to fail"? If Stella's cookery school flops, he'll be the first to cheer.

"She's a very good cook. Maybe that's qualification enough."

"I don't think so, Daniel, not these days. People want Cordon Bleu, that kind of thing." He pronounces "bleu" as "blue." I can't tell whether this is affectation, a joke, or ignorance. "And the Abbey is so run-down. Frankly, I can't see them pulling it off. Though I wish them every success, naturally."

"I'd better go."

"A word to the wise," he says, and winks. "Just a little hint, Daniel, my boy. Be a bit careful: Julia and Finn—delightful, delightful. But poor Maisie . . . well, there's no hiding it, is there? I saw her in the village the other day, walking along, talking to those nuns of hers. The invisible holy sisters—tragic. So sad. And her father was the same, you know—completely off his rocker, or so I hear. It's in the *genes*, you see. Dear old Henry's been dotty as long as I've known him, but his son . . . Terrible. They covered it up, naturally. No one talks about it. Guy Mortland cut his throat, you know, took a razor and sliced his throat from ear to ear. Bled like a stuck pig. Poor Stella found him. Mind you, she must have known it was on the cards. Depression. Mania. He'd had every treatment in the book, drugs, electric shock therapy, private clinics. Cost a packet, and none of it worked. In and out of loony bins for years—"

"Sanatoriums," I say, coming to a halt in the doorway. "Sanatoriums. He had TB."

"Oh, I know *that*. But that was later—he got infected at one of the funny farms. The TB responded to treatment, I hear—and it made a good cover story. But it wasn't why he was invalided out of the RAF, believe you me. No, no—it was psychological problems. It was the war that pushed him over the edge. Battle shock. Happened to a lot of the fighter boys. Your generation—you don't know how lucky you are. . . ." He pauses.

"But my point is—be wary. I hear you and Finn are very thick. People talk. You've been seen, you know. Out in the woods at night, naughty, naughty. And of course she seems normal enough at the moment, can be charming when she wants—a little curt, perhaps, or she is to me, anyway. But you have to look at these things long term, and with a father like that, a sister like that—who knows what the future holds? Want children one day, do you, Daniel? Bound to—handsome young man like you. On your way up, fine strapping fellow, bit of a clever clogs, Cambridge and so on. But you want to pick and choose, that's my advice. Plenty of fish in the sea; play the field and all that. Besides, you and the Mortlands—very different backgrounds, aren't you? Expect you feel like a fish out of water sometimes, eh? I'd be careful if I was you. . . . Daniel? . . . Daniel? What's your hurry? You're forgetting your money. . . ."

I'm outside, in the gloomy backyard. In the warm air, there's a rich smell from the Heavy Hogs, a stink of pig swill and ordure. Colonel Edwardes is in the doorway, waving the envelope. I tell him to keep his ten shillings.

And *cut*, I'm on the road. I'm trudging back to the village. I'm dripping sweat. The sun's merciless and there are no trees, there's no shade. My boots kick up white dust as I walk. The white dusty road runs alongside Black Ditch; both run as straight as a die between the fields, Angus McIver's fields. They were pasture; now he's experimenting with sugar beet. Sugar beet is a thirsty plant; it consumes gallon upon gallon of water. Every twenty yards there are irrigation pipes. The anger's gone. I feel sick. I feel heartsick. Was that true? Does Finn know? If she knows, why has she never told me? One foot in front of the other: Truth or malice, truth or lies?

The white road is a Roman road. Black Ditch is even older. It predates the Romans; it predates the Iceni, and this is Iceni battleground territory. As a small boy, I used to imagine Boadicea here, bowling along in her chariot, murderous knives bound to its wheels. I can hear the rumbling of those wheels now and the tramp of centurion feet: the march of history, the sound of the inevitable; it's marching behind, and it's gaining on me.

Black Ditch, which is Iron Age or older, mirrors the sky in its unmoving, unwinking surface. Yes, this road runs dead straight, and I can feel something die in me as I walk along it. Miles of Roman road behind me, miles ahead of me: This is the road I still walk along in dreams.

I know what lies at the end of that walk. When I reach the village, the church clock will be striking *four*—so I can be exact about the time. Hens will be pecking on the verge. I can just hear the distant combine; I hear the distant report of a shotgun. At our cottage, all the windows will be closed—Gran distrusts fresh air. No doubt she will still be sitting by the stove, nursing her sore gums. Maybe, to keep her hand in, she'll be consulting the tarot. I won't call in to see her. I won't discover what the Rider-Waite deck predicts today. I won't encounter Joe, either; he will be working in the last of the McIvers' hay fields, over a mile away.

By the village green, I'll pause. I'll count the ducks on the duck pond. I'll examine, for the millionth time, the famous pargeting on the pub: a wily fox, a foolish goose. When I was little, I used to stare at them and think, *Which am I?*

Next to the pub is the village shop and post office. This is where, one afternoon a week, I'm temporarily employed in a clerkish capacity. I issue wireless, dog, and TV licenses; I put stamps on parcels and count out money to the numerous village pensioners. In the window there are big plastic-lidded glass jars of sweets: bull's-eyes and gob stoppers, licorice sticks, flying saucer sherbets, bubble gum. I can remember when sweets were rationed. Nick was always forbidden bubble gum. There's a Fox's Glacier Mints display ad in the

window, made of tin. It shows a polar bear, standing on an ice floe—
and when you look at the ice closely, you see it's mint shaped. Why
aren't they called Fox's Iceberg Mints?

I'll take the letter out of my jeans pocket—I've been carrying this
letter around all day. It's the thirty-sixth job application. It's the second I've sent to this particular agency, the first having received no
acknowledgment or reply. This ad agency is the one I most want to
work for—but this letter isn't like the others I've sent. "You're too
formal," ultraformal Maisie said yesterday, scrutinizing the sad carbon
copies of my previous efforts. "I wouldn't give you a job if you wrote
like that to me."

"Thanks, Maisie—but that's the way it's done. There are *conven-
tions* here."

"It doesn't sound like you. It sounds stiff. And it's too long."

Pretty rich, Maisie, I thought, coming from you. "Okay," I said.
"Why not? I'm getting bloody nowhere. You tell me what to write."

"If I do, you swear you'll send it?"

I swore. Maisie dictated. There were two sentences. Lynx eyed, she
watched me while I typed them out on Stella's ancient machine.
And it's this letter—this ridiculous letter—that is in my hand as I
stare at that Fox's Glacier Mints advertisement. And in the end, I'll
post it—because by then I'll be beyond caring.

I'll post the letter, I'll turn into the lane, and I'll trudge up the hill,
past the Doggetts' orchards, where the apples are ripening, and past
Acre Field. By then it's *four-fifteen.*

As I walk, I'll be trying to concentrate on my next task. I've
promised Stella I'll paint one of the cookery school bedrooms. I'm
afraid these rooms will never be used, because Stella isn't going to
have any takers, though I've done my best with the ads that have
been inserted in various small magazines. On the other hand, Lady
Violet, alias the Viper, seems to be being helpful for once. She and
some Veronica woman, her grandson's fiancée, have promised to

spread the word. They're sending out the prospectuses we had printed; they're talking us up in London, in W1, SW7, and SW3. . . . I can't understand why the Viper is doing this, given her past record, given her charity bypass, but doing it she is. So perhaps there will be enrollments. Meanwhile, at the Abbey, brushes, rollers, and gallons of white emulsion are waiting for me.

I'll come to a halt at the top of the hill. I'll pause in the shade of the elms. The McIvers' combine still drones away in the distance. It's reached the last corner, in the field below Nun Wood, the field we called Holyspring. I'll have no desire to slap white paint on bedroom walls. I'll want to see Finn, ache to talk to Finn. But Finn will still be in London, not due back till seven p.m. at the earliest. I'll look at my watch. I can remember looking at my watch. It will tell me it's now *four twenty-five*. I'll look blindly at the valley below. In the distance, a shotgun fires. I scan the fields. No one's out in the fields after rabbits, nor would they be—it's too early. It fires *again* once more; the report is closer this time, though it's always hard to estimate the distance and direction of a gun shot, especially in the echoey bowl of this valley. It sounded as if it came from Nun Wood.

I turn to look at the woods. Their green shade is inviting. I move across to the gate at the head of the lane and peer toward the trees. I see something move—some small, pale, crouching thing. It's there, and then it's vanished. The gun fires again, and this time I'm certain the report comes from the depths of the wood. I hesitate, peering into the shadows. Was it a child I glimpsed or a deer? Was it a trick of the light, or could it have been a woman?

I can hear something moving in the undergrowth ahead of me; the fronds of bracken tremble. I listen intently. *Maisie, is that you?* I call softly. *Maisie, someone's shooting in there, come out.* There's no reply. The bracken shivers. Quietly, I move forward under the trees. At that point, when I decide I'd better investigate this, Maisie has less than four hours of normal life ahead of her. So have we all.

SEVENTEEN

Nun Wood

WHATEVER IT IS that's moving ahead of me, it isn't a man. No man could move through this undergrowth with such delicacy. Could it be a hind? There are deer in the wood, though they're shy and I've rarely encountered them. Could it be Maisie, playing some game with me? The bracken makes an impenetrable screen. Its green fronds, the curled undersides laden with dusty brown spore, twenty million on one tiny leaf, Maisie has told me, are at heart height—and I'm six feet three; they'd easily conceal some-one smaller, a child or a woman. I can see the fronds trembling. I know these woods well: Joe first brought me here to shoot pigeon when I was seven years old. I've shot pheasant here, for Stella. But pigeon and pheasant don't take refuge in bracken, and my voice would have driven a deer away. I move forward silently, placing my feet with care, parting the fronds, watching, and listening.

The wood is more overgrown than it used to be. As I move away from the edges, there's less light and the bracken thins. It's choked out by a tangle of dark undergrowth, stunted holly, hazel, and bram-bles. Peering through the greenish shadows, I glimpse movement again: something white, something fleet—and then it's gone. It's too swift and too silent to be a child, surely? I hesitate, listening. I circle round to my left and find the path I remember. It winds through the trees and ends at the clearing where the ruins of the building the nuns made are still just discernible. It's years since I've been to that part of the wood. I stand on the path, irresolute.

I think of nuns. The nuns here belonged to the Cistercian order; they wore white, not black. I think of three newborn skeletal babies, with rosaries. I still feel connected to them, my ancient unwanted kin. This wood has always been able to make a child of me.

Nick and I used to make dens here. We'd dare each other to build them near the clearing where the babies were found. But we never went too close, for all our bravado. Once, and only once, we camped the night in the wood—and, older then, determined to brave it out, we set up camp in the center of the clearing. We laughed at our former timidity—or we did until dusk fell. With darkness, our nerves failed us. We lay side by side in Nick's Boy Scout tent, two adolescent boys, rigid with terror. Owls hooted, the wind stirred the leaves—but we weren't fearful of such noises, which had a known, natural explanation. Nothing happened—nothing we could name, at least. Yet neither of us slept, and by common consent, that experiment was never repeated.

The wood is silent. The air eddies with a faint breeze. I have the unpleasant sensation that the trees are breathing, that someone unseen is watching me. I begin to move silently along the path: I can see something now, in the distance, something small and pale. It doesn't disappear as I move, but it seems to stir, as if it's caught, as if it's shivering.

I walk toward it stealthily. As I move, I see that this path seems to be in use—and that puzzles me. Nun Wood is private property; it has a reputation for being haunted—no one in the village would trespass. Joe and I are the only people who come here. Has someone been poaching? Does Lucas walk this way? Lucas comes and goes as he pleases, so it's possible. Someone's certainly been using this path.

I come to a halt. The trees are still; not a leaf moves. A jet from

Deepden screams overhead. I peer at the dark undergrowth on all sides: I can see nothing, hear no sound except my own breathing. I can't see the clearing, either; it's farther on, beyond the next winding of the path. But I can see it with my mind's eye: a rough circle of random stones, low broken walls overgrown with ivy, a greenish watery light filtering through. The air there smells of leaf mold, of rich soil; it's spongy underfoot. There's a grassy bank and a circular area of thick moss—moss that's an insistent emerald green. Before those archeologists arrived, I used to think of it as a fairy ring, as a place of enchantment: I don't now.

I've reached that tiny shivering, fluttering thing I glimpsed. I can see that it's real enough. It's a scrap of material, impaled on a broken branch, a scrap of material perhaps three inches square. At first, I don't recognize it. Then I do recognize it, and my world starts to change. I ease it off the branch and hold it in my palm. It's fine white Indian cotton, woven with a faint scarlet pattern of leaves and flowers. So delicate is the pattern that it looks like veins, like capillaries.

I know this material. It's torn from one of Finn's dresses. I bought that dress for her, on impulse, in Cambridge a few months ago; it wasn't expensive, I could just afford it. It came from one of those new shops that have begun to spring up, a shop that sold joss sticks, crystals, and healing stones. A hippie shop, I suppose. Finn had admired it in the window, and I persuaded her to try it on. I stood inside, breathing smoky jasmine and patchouli fumes, while Finn ducked into a dark, curtained corner and then, laughing, emerged transformed, saying, *I'm not sure, Dan, is it me, d'you think?* So I remember the dress—and I remember when she last wore it. She last wore that dress three weeks ago, the night we all had dinner in the cloister, the night before the annual visit to Elde.

Late that night, very late, when the sky was thick with stars, Julia played her records, her California LPs, with their discordant, irresistible, psychedelic wailings. Acid music: Grace Slick as Alice, pursuing a White Rabbit through the mind's underworld. I danced with Finn to those discords; and in the shadows, jealous and afraid, because I'd seen the way Lucas watched her, I kissed her—kissed her in the now forbidden way, more deeply and more longingly than I'd kissed her in months. Breaking away at last, she gave me a searching, pained look, as if she wanted to tell me something or imprint my face on her mind. Then she left me and slipped away to her bed: I couldn't persuade her into mine.

But she couldn't have slipped away to her bed. She must have come here. And if she came here, in darkness, I know with absolute certainty that she would not have been alone. *You've been seen,* Colonel Edwardes said. *Out in the woods at night.* . . . I should have realized then. I've never brought Finn here, but someone else has. I stare at the soft material stupidly; it has meanings, implications, this scrap of cotton. One of the implications is that Finn has looked me in the eyes and lied.

I put the evidence in my pocket: I will show this to Finn later, when she returns, when I accuse her, I decide—not that I'm capable of thinking, let alone deciding anything. I gave Finn that dress. I gave Finn my heart. I walk back down the path, trying to reread my own past. When she said that to me, can she really have meant its opposite? When we did this, did it mean one thing to me and another to her? Can it amount to *nothing,* all these years?

I stumble back down the path. I go through the gate. I'm staring at a view I've never seen before, at an alien valley. It's silent. In the distance, a combine disappears down a road to some barns. I turn and encounter Maisie for the second, and final, time that day.

Maisie is not alone. She's walking toward me, holding a bottle of milk and a bunch of flowers. On one side of her is Lucas; on the other, her grandfather. I look at Lucas, my friend: He's slighter in build than I am and not as tall; his hair is shorter than mine and dark brown, not black; but we usually wear similar clothes, and I can see that he could be mistaken for me in poor light by village spies. Most villagers are unaware of his existence, whereas they'd expect to see me with Finn; they've been watching us for years. I can't bring myself to speak. Lucas, bizarrely, is carrying a spade and a scythe. Seeing me, he stops and smiles. I stare at this apparition, and eventually the air calms. I begin to understand that these three people actually are there. Maisie asks her grandfather the time, and he tells her it's *a quarter to five*.

Maisie frowns. I see that Lucas looks comparatively fresh. Gramps, in charge since eight-thirty, is showing acute strain; he's white with exhaustion. I know where they're going, because I've been on these expeditions with Maisie before. They're going to visit the dogs' burial ground. When they reach it—it's farther on, at the north edge of the wood—the weeds will be scythed back, and the little stone memorials to generations of Mortland dogs will be scraped clean of lichen. They'll be decorated with funeral flowers. A libation of milk will be poured on the ground. Then Maisie will recite the list of dogs. There are at least twelve generations of dead pets here, and that list takes a while. It's not as fearsome as Cassandra's links to Apollo, and his to every other Greek deity you've ever heard of, but it's quite fearsome enough; last time I submitted, I timed it at an hour.

Maisie comes to a halt when she sees me. She begins speaking, and—this can be a worrying sign, though not always—she speaks fast. The speech is addressed to the air over my left shoulder; Maisie rarely looks you in the eyes.

"Dan!" she cries. "I hoped we'd see you. Gramps and I have had an excellent day. We read about bivalves and mollusks all morning. Then Gramps made me a sandwich for lunch—Gramps makes very good sandwiches. I ate nearly all of mine. We made a start on my pergola— you remember I told you about my pergola? We've begun to dig the holes for the posts. It's difficult, because the ground is baked hard, but we made progress. After that, Gramps said we'd earned a bit of a rest, so we walked down to the refectory to see Lucas. He made us a most refreshing cup of tea. Now we're going to visit the dogs' graves, which are badly neglected. Daddy isn't pleased about that. We shouldn't forget the dead, he says. We should honor and appease them." She draws a quick breath. "If we don't, they become restless. Daddy says they get lonely and hungry—down there in the ground."

She pauses. There is a silence. I feel a shaft of pity for her, deep and immediate, like a blow to the solar plexus. Mentioning her father in this way is a new development. So now he too has joined the ranks of the invisible, with whom Maisie converses much of the time. Her grandfather's gaze meets mine; the pain in his eyes is raw. He worshipped his only son, and he worships Maisie. Lucas gives a sigh. I haven't greeted Lucas, I haven't looked at him. If I look at him, I might punch him or kill him or break down and cry.

"Maisie," Lucas says, more gently than I'd have expected, "stop this. You know it upsets your grandfather." He crouches down so their faces are on a level; Maisie's has become a mask of obstinacy. "You remember what we said before? No heaven, no hell, no angels, and no ghosts. The dead don't talk to us, Maisie. You know that perfectly well."

"I remember that discussion," she replies, her voice sharp with scorn. "But you're an unbeliever, Lucas—much you know. You're wrong: The dead are everywhere. You could see them, too, if you weren't half-blinded, if you'd only learn to use your eyes. That's what's wrong with your portrait—you left them out. You hadn't realized that, had you? Well, look at it again. And the dead do talk to me, because they know I can interpret them and understand them— I can, I can. Can't I, Dan?"

Her face is red with anger. She's quivering with indignation. "Of course you can, Maisie," I reply soothingly. When these outbursts occur, it's as well not to cross her; so that's what I say. For the best of motives I give a placatory answer, and, glancing over my shoulder at the wood, I think maybe it's true, maybe she can. I don't feel sane, I don't even know what the word *sane* means anymore—so why assume this little girl is unbalanced, or abnormal, or mad? What are ghosts? What does it mean to be haunted? I can see a phantom now: a shadowy Finn, who stands next to Lucas and embraces him; I never knew my mother, and she haunts me still.

The reply seems to calm Maisie. "Come on now, darling," her grandfather says, and I admire him more than I've ever done in that moment, because he's old, and I can see he's at the end of his rope. Maisie can be tyrannical; but I've never known him to lose patience with her, and he doesn't lose patience now. "Come on, Maisie. Give your old Gramps your hand. We've got a job to do, remember?"

And she trots off with him, apparently consoled. Lucas, to my surprise, does not duck out of this task; he goes with them. Maybe he's avoiding me.

"When Gramps first came here in 1919," Maisie begins, her voice receding into the distance, "he owned a Clumber spaniel. He named her Isabella, after our ancestor, who founded the Abbey here. She was generally called Issy. She had numerous progeny and lived to be thirteen. . . ."

I turn back to the house. That was the last sentence of Maisie's I ever heard. Then it was without significance. Now it echoes and re-echoes through my mind. As I cross the cloister, I see that numerous small scrapes have been made in the grassed areas. They're about one inch deep; a blackbird is already using one as a dust bath. At first they puzzle me, then I realize that these must be the post holes for Maisie's pergola-to-be. There are at least forty of them. They are scattered at random all over the lawn.

I glance up at the library windows; the middle one is closed, the others open. I cross the flagstones by the house, enter the hall, and walk across the chessboard squares. It's *five-fifteen*. The long-case clock strikes the quarter as I pass.

EIGHTEEN

What a Piece of Work . . .

FIVE MINUTES LATER I'm in the attics, and as promised I'm painting walls. White, everything has to be white. It's a tabula rasa. Erase the past: Begin again.

I've opened all the windows, but here, directly under the roof, the heat is stifling; no air seems to be getting in. I've stripped off my shirt, and I'm dripping sweat, glistening with sweat. I've finished half of one small chimney wall, and the roller isn't working properly. It's spitting white paint all over the floor. I switch to the brush, paint two stripes—it's going to take at least two coats to cover years of neglect and grime—and then I stop. I can see it's a hopeless task, for a hopeless person, in a hopeless world.

I've lost Finn. Finn has been lying to me. When she's said, *Give me time, Dan,* and, *Nothing's changed,* she's been lying. She's been thinking about Lucas and when she can next meet him in Nun Wood. He's my *friend,* how could he do that to me? How could she? But I can see all too plainly how she could do it and why she would do it. Lucas has gifts—gifts she admires. I've seen the way she's pored over his work, bending over him when he's drawing. There's a ruthless impatience to Lucas that I could never achieve. If she prevaricated with him, if she started in on all those ifs and buts and maybes that drive me insane, Lucas would simply walk away. *You're boring me,*

Finn, he'd say, and that would whip her into line. Boring Lucas is something we all fear.

Lucas is going to be famous, he's going to achieve something. He's never said so—he doesn't need to—but he doesn't doubt it for one second: Lucas has more self-belief than anyone I've ever met. He's an artist, and for bookish Finn that's appealing. If he were a poet or a novelist, I'd have known I hadn't a prayer. But a painter will do—it certainly has more appeal than someone on the dole queue.

I'm never going to get a job. I'm never going to escape this damned place—I'm genetically programmed to stay here. I'm going to end up a laborer, Dan the obscure, a plowman with "BA (Cantab)" after his name. *That's artistry, that is*, I think, slumping against the wall, thinking of Joe and his skill. Up the field, down the field, perfect lines, perfect turns: king of the Massey Ferguson tractor and the Ransome's of Ipswich plow; one of the few men left who worked with horses as a boy, one of that dwindling number who still knows how to handle horses, the Suffolk Punch horses that are trotted out and tarted up once a year, for the valedictory plowing competitions at the agricultural show. Yes, those horses are magnificent beasts, huge, intelligent, docile, and powerful. Yes, it's hard to guide a tractor and plow with Joe's precision. Yes, it *is* artistry—but not to me.

"It's not for the likes of us," Joe said when I won a place at the grammar school. "At your age I'd been bringing home a wage four years," Joe said when I explained I wasn't leaving school, I wanted to take A levels. When I told him about my Cambridge place, he was proud, but bewildered and afraid. "Where'd this boy get all his cleverness from, Bella?" he asked—and as usual, no answer came. "All this book learning—I was never one for books. But you'll have letters after your name, Danny—think of that. Bachelor of arts. No one can put you down, I reckon, not once you've got those letters. And if they try—they might try, Danny, you best be ready for that—you mind you fight your corner, boy."

Joe has faith in those letters. I don't. Those pathetic letters mean sod-all to thirty-five advertising agencies. And where did this cleverness come from? I don't know. I wish I hadn't had it inflicted on me; it's like a disease. All it does is make me a misfit—born a little Martian, still an alien. That long line of my obscure ancestors: I'm terrified of being like them, but it's a no-win situation, this. If I'm not like them, then I'm betraying them, I'm a traitor to my family, a traitor to my class.

I paint another stripe on the hopeless wall. Why am I even doing this? Why am I up here, under the roof, suffocating, dying of heat stroke, when there are umpteen rooms on the next floor down that would be far more suitable? These attics were once the nuns' dormitories. When Gramps converted the house, they became servants' rooms. "Are you sure you want the students to be up there, Stella?" I said when she explained her plan.

"Oh yes," she replied, bright-eyed. "Once they're painted and spruced up a bit, they'll be lovely. We'll put down rugs, and move some of the good furniture up there, find some paintings. The rooms are large, and the views are wonderful. Besides, it will give the students a degree of privacy. They won't want to feel on top of us all the time."

Well, yes. Except in winter it's freezing up here and there's no heating. There's one bathroom, with a vast claw-footed bath, heavily stained with rust, and a geyser for hot water, last used circa 1932. It's probably defunct. No one's thought to check it. I know why Stella decided on this plan, and I should have realized before: In these rooms, the students will be well away from Maisie. With luck, they'll remain ignorant of the journeyings Maisie makes once everyone's asleep, once it's dark.

Maisie sleepwalks. She sleepwalks all over the house; she sleepwalked into my bedroom once. I woke to find her standing by my bed, plucking and scratching at my hand, a small ghost, a miniature

Mrs. Rochester, a little demon in a white cotton nightdress. "Where's Dan?" she demanded. "Where's Dan gone?" I had to fetch Finn, and we carried her back to bed, along miles of corridors, moonlight striping the walls, Maisie's eyes wide and glittering. So, yes, Maisie sleepwalks. As far as I know, she's never sleepwalked here in the attics, but who knows where she journeys, what she discovers, on those nightly expeditions of hers?

I think of the prospectus Stella wrote, which even now is being handed out in W1, SW7, and SW3 by an abnormally helpful Violet. I tried to help with that prospectus, but when I read what Stella had written, all that guff about the "family" and the Abbey's "relaxed and convivial atmosphere," my heart failed. I couldn't bring myself to object, and there was no way of persuading Stella to alter it. That's what she saw in her mind's eye. What *I* saw was that cold, ugly dining room, with Maisie at the table, taking an hour to chew a lettuce leaf; Maisie, with that heartbreaking air of bright attention, starting in on her lists, asking one of her peculiar and unsettling questions, launching herself on one of the stories. . . . Is this cookery school going to work? Is it hell.

On the other hand, I want it to work. I passionately want it to work. It has to. The money's running out, and Maisie will always need care; there are no alternatives. I want it to work, because if life were fair, it would. And because I love this family. *Give them a fucking break for once*, I think, and start slapping paint on twice as fast.

I've reached the dormer window section, when I hear footsteps— no, not footsteps: What I hear is the soft slip-slap of thonged sandals against a woman's heel. *They flee from me, that sometime did me seek / With naked foot, stalking in my chamber* . . . I know at once who is coming along the corridor.

It's Julia. I turn my back on the door. Through the window, in the far distance, I can see Maisie, her grandfather, and Lucas walking back toward the refectory. The ceremony of the dogs—shorter than

usual—must be over. Maisie must have decided the dead are pla-
cated, for the time being, anyway.

I look at my watch. As Julia enters, it's *a quarter to six*. Or there-
abouts.

She barely greets me. I think she says, "Hi, Dan," or, "I wondered if
you'd be here." Something offhand. Beyond that, she seems to feel
no need to explain her presence, but Julia is like that. She always as-
sumes her presence is desired.

I continue painting; she begins to move around the room. I can
smell the scent she's wearing; it has a cool, blue fragrance. I wonder
if I smell of sweat—then know I do. Too bad: I didn't invite her up
here, and—unlike her—I've been working all day. She circles the
space, inspecting the sections I've already painted, peeling little bits
of paper off the walls that remain to be done.

"Don't do that, Julia," I say, with irritation. "You'll just make it
worse."

"Sorry," she says absently. "Though it would be hard to make it
much worse. God, it's so dingy up here."

"Yes, well, that's why I'm painting it white. Two coats and it'll
look completely different."

"If you say so." She frowns. "I tried to talk Stella out of this, you
know. She wouldn't listen. She has a thing about these attics. She
claims they have good vibes—because the nuns slept here, I guess.
This is where she stayed when we first came back to the Abbey, did
you know? I think it was this very room—though it's hard to tell,
they all look the same. She locked the door and stayed here for a
whole week. We used to come and tap on the panels and leave little
presents outside."

"What kind of presents?"

"Offerings. We wanted to tempt her out. Her favorite things—

flowers, fiction, and food—that was my idea." She makes a wry face. "So Finn brought books, and Maisie brought bluebells—and I brought food. I laid a tray with a lace cloth. I made tiny sandwiches, with the crusts cut off—Stella liked that sort of thing then; she lived on sandwiches. Oh, and a tot of whiskey—American whiskey. Jack Daniel's, I think it was."

"Stella doesn't drink whiskey—of any kind."

"I know. But my father did. I thought that might help. Something must have worked. She came out eventually."

"Why did she do that? Why lock herself away?" I turn to look at Julia. I think of Colonel Edwardes, and a fly buzzing. "Was it grief?"

"Maybe. It's hard to tell, with Stella. It might have been fear—she could see the way the future was shaping up, I suppose. Maybe she read it in one of her books—maybe that's what someone did in one of her books. It's more than possible. Who knows why anyone does anything? I hate explanations, don't you? They're such a drag."

She moves off to explore a built-in cupboard under the eaves; she opens the door, closes it again. She's taken some trouble with her appearance, I notice, glancing at her covertly. Julia looks beautiful whatever she's wearing, but when she makes an effort, as she has now, the effect is bewildering; you can't believe she's real. Sometimes I think beauty's like a deformity: It can be hard to see beyond it to the person inside. Her abundant tumbled hair is washed and fragrant. It lies across her smooth golden shoulders in ripe, wheat-colored coils. She's wearing a long, loose, pale blue dress with thin straps, one of her Haight-Ashbury flower-child dresses; its color intensifies the bluebell darkness of her eyes. All three sisters have eyes this color. The dress is almost, not quite, transparent. It suggests the body beneath it. I look away.

Why does she wear so many bracelets? I think. She's wearing four, five, on each slender golden arm. They're Navajo silver and turquoise, with strange, indecipherable runic signs cut into the metal. They were a gift from that useful friend of a friend at Berkeley, the friend whose letters she now ignores. Every time she moves, these squaw bracelets slide against her wrists; they chink and clink against one another. Even when I'm not looking at her, I can track her movements: There's a faint tintinnabulation, like very distant, or imagined, bells.

"So, tell me what you've been doing today," she says, and she's closer than I'd realized.

"Stop creeping up behind me, I'm trying to fucking paint, Julia."

"I can see that. Sorry." She brushes her hand across my bare back. I flinch away. "You're doing well. Only two more walls, another coat, and three more rooms. Why, you'll be finished in no time. Would you like me to help you?"

"In that dress? I don't think so, do you?"

"I could always take it off." She touches my back again. She runs one cool finger across my shoulder muscles. "How brown you are," she says.

"Cut it out, Julia. I'm not in the mood. I'm hot, I'm tired, I stink of sweat—"

"I like that. It smells fresh and manly. It gleams. You look like a gladiator."

Now I *know* she's taking the piss. I say: "Julia, give it a rest, okay? I've got a splitting headache, and I've had a fucking shitty day. I've cleaned about fifteen million windows, and I'm two pounds richer. According to your calculations, that should last me about five seconds in London. Now go away."

"Ah yes, London. What I said this morning. That's one of the reasons I came up here. I'm contrite. I actually am sorry. I've been regretting it all day. It was wrong of me, I shouldn't have said it—and I don't know why I did. Except . . ."

"Except what?" I turn to look at her. I can't read her expression. I seldom can.

"Oh, you know." She shrugs. "I was annoyed with Lucas. That annoyance spilled over onto you. Also . . ." She pauses. "You said I was lazy. That made me angry. Because I'm not. We just go about things differently, you and I. I've been working on my escape plan for over a year. Now everything's in place, and there's nothing more I can do till I get to London. I'm just resting before the final push. Amn't I allowed a holiday?"

"I guess so."

"Besides, I can see you don't like me—so sometimes I think, Let's see what reaction this gets. Forget it, it's not important." She holds out her hand to me; the bracelets shiver down her arm with a tiny jangling sound. "Apology accepted? Friends, Dan?"

"Well, let's not go too far," I answer, but I shake her hand anyway. Her grip is cool and firm; she laughs. I don't trust her, but the hate, all that hate, it's suddenly evaporated. "I should apologize, too," I begin, and then hesitate. There are some things that, oddly, it's easier to ask Julia than it would be Finn. Finn is deeply reticent; she shies away from questions of any kind. *Do you love me?* for instance—that's a question she resists, especially now. Whereas with Julia you can ask anything, and the answer's usually truthful—direct, anyway.

"I was told something about your father today," I say. "Something I never knew. Something Finn's never told me, something I'm not even sure she knows. . . ."

Julia has become very still. All expression has been wiped from her eyes. "About how he died?" she says. "It's bound to be. You'd better tell me."

And so I do. I tell her about the windows, and Colonel Edwardes, and that dank house that stinks of loneliness and something worse. I tell her how I couldn't stand to take his money, how I stood outside, how I walked back along that endless dusty road.

As I speak, Julia's dark blue eyes never leave my face. I think now—looking back now—that it's then Julia makes up her mind. I think she came up to these attics with a plan, and—during my halting speech—she decides to go through with it. All my instincts tell me that, but I can't understand why, and—I don't trust hindsight— I can't be sure.

"I wonder where Edwardes got his information," she says in her cool way when I'm finally silent. "It upset you, I can see that. You shouldn't let him get to you, Dan. He's a disgusting, malicious man. You should just grind people like that under your heel and walk on by. That's what I do."

She pauses. For one moment there's a shadow in her eyes, then she's back in control. I think, Does she ever lose control, Julia?

"His version isn't accurate, anyway," she continues. "But it's not entirely wrong, either. It wasn't a razor. My father wouldn't have done that to Stella, even when he was at his lowest point. No, he drove the car out to some quiet place in the mountains and attached a hose to the exhaust pipe. The cops found him. Gramps identified him."

"Does Finn know?"

"Yes. But she can't remember it as clearly as I do. She hardly remembers New Mexico. Just isolated incidents—she remembers Stella crying, and Maisie's being born. She remembers going to see Daddy at that last clinic, but not much more. She was barely nine. I'm two years older than she is. That makes a difference, I suppose." She pauses. Those dark blue eyes rest on my face, assessing me. "I wouldn't raise this with Finn, if I were you," she continues. "In fact, if you'll take my advice, I wouldn't press Finn about anything, not at the moment. Whatever you think—or feel, Dan—bide your time."

"I don't need your advice about Finn," I reply stiffly, though I know she's right. You cannot push Finn; you have to wait—and wait—until she comes to you.

"Have it your own way," she says without rancor. "And say nothing to Maisie. Be very careful about that. She believes the TB story. She doesn't—and she mustn't—know."

"I wouldn't dream of it. I'd never say anything that would hurt or damage her. I like Maisie. I'm fond of her. I always have been. You know that."

"I do know that," she replies, and to my astonishment, she leans forward, raises herself on her toes, and kisses my cheek. That blue scent . . . it's like diving into water. "Such muscles," she says, resting her cool hand on my arm, smiling, drawing away. "So strong." She frowns. "You look magnificent, Dan, you know that?"

"Yeah, sure."

"No. I mean it. Leave this, put that brush down, will you? There's something I want to show you. That's the main reason I came up here, and I'd nearly forgotten. A secret. You're not going to believe this. Come with me."

I look at her uncertainly. I watch her silver bracelets slide along her arm as she raises it. She backs away a few steps and turns; her thonged sandals slap against her heels. "Come on," she says. "It's exciting. Really. You need to see this."

And she beckons to me.

I put down the brush. I wipe my paint-stained hands on my jeans. I pull on the discarded shirt, and I'm buttoning it up as I follow her along the corridor and through an anteroom. We pass the door to the Squint and descend some stairs. As we enter the library, with two of its tall windows wide open and those motherly stone angels looking down at us, one of the many clocks chimes. It's *six p.m.* Soon Finn will be home.

Julia has darted ahead of me. I follow more slowly. I pass the cobra table and the lionskin. I glance out of the windows. Maisie and her grandfather are in the cloister below; he's slumped in a deck chair; Maisie, trowel in hand, is scraping more random post holes in the grass. I see her sit back on her heels, look up, and gaze intently at the air. Her lips move; she addresses the invisible; she smiles, then bends again to her task.

The light is softening; a swallow passes overhead. I turn away from the window, to find that Julia is now in the far corner of the room; she's fumbling with the paneling to the side of the fireplace wall. She's looking for the panel that slides back, the one where stairs lead down to an ancient blank wall.

"Goddammit, how do you open this thing?" she says. "It seems to have stuck."

"No, it hasn't. Let me do it. What is this, anyway? What do you want to show me? There's nothing down there, you know that—just stairs that don't lead anywhere." I cross to her side and press the hidden catch. With a creaking sound, the panel slides back. There's a waft of stale, damp air from the shadowed space beyond.

"Come on—you have to see this."

"See what? I don't understand. This had better not be some stupid trick. . . ."

Julia glances over her shoulder and smiles. She steps through into the small, dark landing space at the head of the ancient hidden stairs. I hesitate and then follow her. When we're both inside, Julia touches something on the wall. The panel slides back into place, and we're on the other side of it, in absolute darkness, our bodies pressed together in a space the size of a grave. There's a silence. I feel an instant shaming fear—Gran used to threaten to lock me up here as a child. It was the punishment I feared most of all. She'd drag me, whimpering and pleading, to this panel, and she'd whisper tales of nuns, of errant nuns who were walled up at the foot of these stairs and left to die in the dark. How did they die? How long did it take?

Was it a slow suffocation, or did they cry out for weeks while they starved? *Listen: Hear that scratching sound? That's them, scratching and tearing at the stones. They're after you, Danny. Their fingers are bleeding. They've ripped their nails. Think of that! Nothing but bones now, and still trying to get out after five hundred years.*

I draw in a breath of musty air. I can smell Julia's blue scent. I feel slightly dizzy. I still don't understand why I'm there. Peering into blackness, disconcerted and unsure, I'm expecting Julia to produce a torch from nowhere. I'm expecting the unlikely: Julia is about to show me a marvel, a loose stone with a religious treasure behind it, a pectoral cross, some tiny relic, or some scratched ancient inscription she's found. She moves slightly. I hear her bracelets chime as she raises her arm; my body reacts a second before my brain does—and *then* I understand.

"Don't move," Julia says in a low, unsteady voice. "Don't move suddenly, Dan. There's just room for two people here. I don't want to lose my balance. If I do, I'll fall down the stairs and break my neck—and that's not my intention."

"I hope you know how to open that panel again," I say—and my own voice sounds unsteady, too, and strange to me. "I hope you know, Julia, because I don't."

"I do know. I've been practicing all afternoon."

"Have you now?" I say, and I think it's that word *practicing* that's fatal. It's so shameless. It's said with such cool amusement. It's filled with suggestions and possibilities, and my mind takes five dizzying seconds to explore them all. That's when time stops. That's when I start wanting her, and wanting her urgently, when I didn't want her five seconds before.

I lean my weight slowly and deliberately against her, so she's pressed between my body and the wall. I have her trapped. She's six inches shorter than I am, she's slender; I'm far stronger than she is: I could do anything—she's powerless now. My cock stiffens against her, and a shudder goes through her. I feel for her throat and tilt her head back; I rub my thumb across her lips. She gives a small moan.

"You said you had something to show me," I say, still in that voice that isn't mine. "Well, I have to tell you, Julia, I can't see a fucking thing in here. I can't see the stairs or the wall or you. You could be anybody."

"Not anybody." I feel her lips curve in a smile. "I'm not a man. I'm female. And I can tell you've noticed that. Give me your hand. There are other ways of seeing, and this is the best one. I'm blind, you're blind. Touch me, Dan."

She guides my hand between her legs. She's wearing nothing under the dress. She's wet, wonderfully wet. I think, *This isn't happening*, then suddenly she's scrabbling at my shirt buttons, fumbling at my jeans, and I want that cool hand of hers around my cock, want it so much, want it so urgently, that I can't think, hear, *or* see. I feel for her dress, and then her breast is under my hand. I cup it in my hand. I put my mouth to it.

"This is what I was thinking about upstairs," Julia says.

"Was it? Was it?" I say, kissing her mouth, and then my fingers slip inside her cunt.

She gasps and moves against my hand. "Today, yesterday, all summer. You've been thinking about it, too, don't deny it," she replies.

She makes a sighing sound and shudders. She slips her fingers inside my jeans. I feel the cool clench of her hand as it closes around my cock. "No, Julia," says the man I've turned into, as her touch flashes from groin to mind. "I've never given you a second thought."

"You will after this," she murmurs, and I feel her soft, wet mouth open under mine. Then she makes a sliding movement, so for a lurching second I think she's fallen, and next she's on her knees, with her soft mouth around my cock, and—no one's ever done that to me before. I've read about it, I've heard about it, I've imagined it, but it's the dark ages in rural England, and as far as I know, only tarts do that kind of thing; it's so forbidden, so transgressive, the only way you're ever going to experience it is to pay for it. I hear myself groan. I can't believe the urgency of the pleasure. I'm going to come, feeling for her breasts in the dark, stroking her nipples hard, her lips and her tongue giving me all that illicit pleasure. But just when I'm at the edge, and she judges it well—when did she learn that, Christ, who taught her that?—she draws back and stands, so my body's rubbing against hers and her mouth that smells of me is on mine. "Fuck me, Dan," she says. "I'm on the pill. It's safe. Welcome to paradise. Pretend I'm Finn if you must. I don't care."

And I do fuck her. I fuck her standing up against that wall in the dark, my jeans half-on, half-off, my shirt buttons ripped, her dress rucked up round her waist, those silver bracelets of hers cutting into the skin of my buttocks as she guides me into her and shudders and cries. I fuck her against a wall, a knee trembler, the boys at school used to call it, and I've never done that before, either. Always it's been lying down, missionary position finally achieved after hours of persuasion and pleading, weeks of lead-up, a fortnight just to get as far as undoing the brassiere, two weeks more to touch the underpants—outside only; give it six weeks and with luck, with the generous girls from the village, you might get a hand job. At Cambridge, forget it. There has to be an engagement ring on the finger before they'll show you their stocking tops. The best I've known is intercourse, a snatched act accompanied by guilt, fear, falsity, and condoms. I think, *So this is the Californian way, is it? This is what they mean by free love?* And, Oh my America, do I feel free. Free of frustration, of confusion, of conflict and consequences; free for the very first time. I think: *We're up against the altar wall.* I think: *Is this what she does with Lucas?* I think: *At last.* I think nothing, nothing, nothing. I slam her up against the stones, and I fuck her hard in a way I've never fucked before, or knew you could, and—I never knew this was possible, either—Julia fucks me back, we're both fucking. This isn't a favor that's being granted, and there's no price on this act. Julia is as frantic as I am. This is something we both need, both crave.

I don't think of Finn once. Not once. It's Julia's breasts, cunt, mouth—and it's Julia's name I cry out when I come.

Then there's a winged silence, broken only by our breathing, by her small, half-stifled moans, and by the noises of our bodies, wet, pressed together, both of us shaking, my semen running down Julia's thighs as I withdraw. I kiss her open mouth. I trace her face in the dark. It's wet, I can't tell if it's sweat or tears. In the dark, invisible to each other, we find each other's hands.

"Oh God," Julia says as my fingers close around hers. Her voice sounds different; it sounds broken. "Oh Christ, what's happened? Dan, what have we done?"

NINETEEN

Fall

WHEN JULIA presses the hidden mechanism and the panel slides back, and we step out into the room, the light is blinding. My eyes take a moment to adjust to that light. One of the many clocks strikes, delicate chimes. It's *six-thirty*. Was that clock accurate?

We stand by the windows, facing each other. Julia's eyes are averted; so are mine. I haven't answered her last question: I can't. I also know something has happened, but I don't know what it is. It's come at me out of the long accumulation of the day, or it's come from some lair in the left field of nowhere; it's sprung out at us from the air.

In a very short time, another minute or so, an inevitable shame, a predictable guilt, will occlude my vision even further. I'll realize that, very soon, Finn will return, and I'll have to face her. But before that happens—sitting here at a London desk, sleepless in Highbury—I have to look closely at Julia and me, at the room in which we were standing, at the exact circumstances then—because I have to be sure, totally sure, that this act could not have been a factor in Maisie's fall. Is it possible that this act could have influenced an event that's ticking toward us, only ninety minutes away?

Julia and I are standing by the windows. Two of them are open, but the middle one is closed. Am I certain of that? Yes, I am. We're three feet apart. We've adjusted our clothing before we reentered the room, and even if someone had walked in then, we might have looked innocent—at a distance, anyway. And no one did walk in. I look out of the window. I've been condemned to look out of that window ever since, and whenever I do, I still see the same view, frame frozen, unchanged in over twenty years: I see Gramps, slumped in that deck chair in the cloister below. Maisie is not there. I can see the trowel she'd been using earlier; it lies abandoned on the grass, its metal glinting in the sun. The cloister is quiet; we're on the edge of a summer's evening. The birds are beginning to sing as the heat of the day diminishes; the shadows are lengthening; swifts and swallows hunt the upper sky.

But there's a hidden possibility. I can look at it now. Is it possible that someone unseen is watching the two of us, standing there?

It *is* possible, I know that. It didn't occur to me then: I had other things on my mind. If someone had been looking down at us from the Squint, we'd have been unaware of a hidden presence. But even if someone was there—and there are only two candidates for spy, Maisie or Lucas—why would it matter? Nothing incriminating was said or done; the exchange between Julia and me was in the eyes.

"Stella and Finn will be home soon," Julia says after an interval. She turns to me and meets my gaze, a long, measuring stare. I hear the chime of her bracelets. We look at each other in silence; the minutes tick by. Then Julia stretches and smiles. "God, it's so hot—I think I might have a bath before the others get back," she says, and her tone is so ordinary, so unexceptional, that reality splinters, and I think, *Did I imagine that, did that panel ever open, did it close?* She leaves the room. I hear the slap of her sandals on the stairs, and then—very distantly—the slam of a door. I walk back to my own room at the opposite side of the house, listening to the antique mechanisms of the Abbey as they stir and come to life. The water pipes begin to vibrate; there's the familiar whispering, wheezing, and breathing that means a bath is being run. I think: Is it this ordinary sound that Maisie interprets as nuns at prayer?

I also want a bath, and I take one. I kneel in two inches of rusty lukewarm water and wash the day off me. A mirror tells me I did not imagine that encounter in the dark. Julia has left her mark on me. I can conceal the scratches, but I can't seem to alter my eyes. I try smiling at the liar in the mirror. I know what's going to happen: Finn will smell my guilt, and when she looks me in the eyes, that guilt will be confirmed.

I go back downstairs. As I reach the hall, I find Julia, changed, scented, and tense. She's pacing that chessboard floor. "Have you seen Maisie?" she asks.

I was expecting questions. Women always ask questions after sex—or the women in this village do. But not that question. I look at her, confused. Do I feel alarm? I don't think so. "Maisie? No, why? She was in the cloisters earlier. Maybe she wandered down to the refectory. She's probably talking to Lucas—maybe he's drawing her again."

"No, she isn't there. Gramps fell asleep, and when he woke, she'd disappeared. He's been calling and calling—and she's not answering him. He's already been down to the refectory. Lucas is there, fiddling around with that damn portrait; he's redoing part of it, some quarter inch he's decided he has to change. He hasn't seen Maisie."

"Then she'll be in the orchard—feeding the chickens, perhaps. Or in her bedroom—maybe she's gone up there and she's reading. Writing those lists of hers."

"I've looked. She isn't there. I've been running all round the house—every single damn room. Gramps is getting desperate—we can't find her anywhere."

"She'll be fine. She won't have gone far. She takes off sometimes—why the alarm?"

"Because she's *worse*—she's been talking about Daddy all day. Gramps made her promise not to leave his side—and Maisie always keeps her promises, you know that."

"It's because Stella isn't here," I say. "Maisie doesn't like change. I expect it's unsettled her, that's all. All right, all right—I'll go and look. You check the back. I'll check the front—she won't have gone far." There's a pause; we've been careful not to look at each other, and now we do.

"Julia—," I begin, but before I can say anything else, before I can make a start on the thousand justifications and accusations I've already dreamed up, Julia forestalls me.

She says: "Do you want Finn to know?"

I give her a surly, mutinous look. "What do you think? Of course I bloody don't," I answer, moving away.

"Not the most gallant of replies."

"Sorry, but it happens to be true. Listen, Julia—"

"No need. I can script what you're going to say. That's fine." She gives me a cool glance. "It didn't happen. I'm sworn to silence. Can you be silent, too?"

I hesitate. I don't want to lie, especially to Finn—and silence will involve lying. But does a large lie matter when I lie in small ways every day? Why shouldn't I lie about my actions, when I lie about who I am half the time? I touch the scrap of material that's still in my pocket and feel anger. Why shouldn't I lie to Finn? She's lied to me.

"I can hold my tongue. I've had plenty of practice," I reply.

"So I've heard." Not a flicker of expression passes across her face. "That's agreed, then. Now go and look for Maisie." She turns away.

"Julia, for fuck's sake, it isn't as simple as that. Don't go. Look, you started this. This is your fault. I have to know why—" I've reached for her arm. She shakes me off.

"No questions, Dan. And if you ask them, you certainly won't get answers—not from me. I told you: I hate explanations. I hate justifications even more. Now go away and do something useful. Maisie's very devoted to you. If you call for her, she'll probably come out from wherever she's hiding. Hurry up. We have to find her before Stella gets back."

She walks away toward the back of the house. I watch her traverse that chessboard floor. I listen to the slap of her sandals against her naked heels. She disappears from sight; a door slams. Trappist Julia: As far as I know, she was true to her word. She never told anyone what had happened, and neither did I. Events later that day distanced it anyway, until it became, for me, a ghost of an encounter, an experience that was shadowy and elusive, like a half-remembered dream. Even so, all these years afterward, the questions I never asked, the ones she refused to answer, remain.

I'll be on a plane or waiting for a phone call, and I'll suddenly find I'm back at the Abbey that last day. I'll watch my younger self, walking out to the cloister to search for Maisie. It's a still summer's evening; my world is about to change. I begin calling Maisie's name. But I'm not yet alarmed, and it's not Maisie's predicament I'm concerned with, it's my own. I'm replaying darkness and heat, a cool hand, amusement, and ambivalence. I'm feeling the heat of sex that burned my mind.

I'm already trying to extricate myself morally. I'm already thinking up a score of excuses for what I've done. It helps to shift the blame on to Julia. *Bitch*, I'm thinking, *slut, whore*. I want to follow after her, seek her out, fuck her again—and show her who's master. Julia used sex, but what she wanted was power—and two could play at that game. I envisioned a different Julia, a submissive double, a Julia who begged me not to leave her, a Julia begging me for more.

I stood there, looking at the patterns the cloister arches made on the grass. I knew I'd betrayed Finn. I knew I'd betrayed myself. If my love for Finn didn't define me, what did? There was nothing else left. But if I loved Finn, how could I have done what I'd done? Who am I? I thought. Where am I? I don't know who I am.

Then I walked on, shouting Maisie's name, in search of an invisible girl. I walked along the drive. I went down to the old tennis court, through the shrubbery, round the lake that had once been the nunnery fishponds. I searched everywhere I could think of, all the old hiding places I'd used as a child. First irritably, then with growing anger, I called again and again.

I tried to recall what Maisie had been wearing that day and then remembered it was her blue dress, the one with the smocking: her Liberty dress, given to her by her grandfather several years before. It was her "best" dress—and it's the one Maisie wears in Lucas's portrait of the sisters: a sky blue, old-fashioned little girl's frock of a kind you scarcely see now. Maisie will wear that blue dress for an eternity now.

I'd completed a circuit and reached the cloister again. They were silent. *Where are you?* I shouted. A bird sang; no reply.

A few minutes later, over twenty years later, and I'm still walking around the cloister calling Maisie's name. I'm on my second circuit, peering into the tangle of shrubs and roses by the walls, when Julia reappears. She and her grandfather come round the corner of the house together: I can feel their fear from ten feet away. Julia's face is white; Gramps is having difficulty breathing. He stops and leans against a bench. He presses his hand against his heart. He sits down.

"Any sign of her?" Julia calls, running toward me.

"Nothing. I've been right round the front of the house—"

"Did you go down to the lake?" She's reached my side. She lowers her voice so her grandfather cannot hear.

"Yes. I did. Julia, I promise you, she wasn't there."

"She can't swim. Oh Christ."

"Julia, she won't *be* there—"

"She could be. She could be anywhere. Anything could have happened. Gramps and I have been right round the vegetable garden, into the fruit cage, the orchard. We've looked and looked—we've tried the house again. There's not a sign of her. She never does this. She must have had an accident. If she could hear us, she'd come when we called."

"Could she have gone back to the refectory?"

"No. She'd have heard your voice. I could, and I was miles away. Lucas would throw her out anyway. Gramps says he's repainting like a madman—that damned sky in the background, some stupid detail he wants to change. If he's doing that, Maisie could bleed to death in the doorway and he wouldn't care. Don't expect any help from that quarter."

"Could she have gone down to the village?"

"I doubt it. The shop's closed. Why would she go there? They just stare at her and whisper behind their hands. Stupid ignorant peasants—I hate their guts."

Her eyes have brimmed with tears. I'm one of those peasants, I think. "Don't cry, Julia," I say. "Stay calm. Let's think this through. She hasn't been gone that long. When I last saw her—"

"When? When did you last see her?"

"When we went into the library. The clock was striking six. I looked out of the window, and she was here, on the grass." I stop. We both look away.

"And when we came out?" she says finally.

"I didn't see her then. Gramps was still there, but she wasn't."

"That's an hour ago. More. . . . I'm going back down to the lake."

"Julia, she isn't *there*. I told you. I walked right round it—"

"Can you see under the water?" Her face contracts. "You may have second sight, Dan—but is it that good? I don't think so. And you know something's wrong—I can see it in your eyes."

And by then—alarm and fear are catching—I do fear something is wrong: I can feel it, the way a swimmer feels an undertow pulling him out into deep water, away from the safety of the beach.

"Fuck it—I'll go and get Lucas," I say. "He can help us look." But Julia is already running off. I hear her say: "Gramps, darling, you stay here. I'm just going to check the gardens again. No, please don't come with me—you look ill. Why don't you stay here, in case Maisie comes back?"

"This is all my fault," I hear him say as I approach. "I should never have sat down. As soon as I did—it hadn't been an easy day, she does talk so, I just dropped off. You go on, Julia. I'll catch you up. What are we going to do? Where can she have got to, Dan? I promised Stella I wouldn't let her out of my sight. I gave her my solemn word. If anything's happened, I'll never forgive myself."

That makes three of us, I think. I watch Julia set off at a run and an old man with a weak heart rise from a bench. Something he's just said alerts me. I know Maisie, and I know she's capable of cunning. "Gramps," I say, "wait. Did Maisie say anything—when you sat down in the cloisters? Before you dozed off?"

"No. I don't think so. I was so tired, Dan. I could scarcely think straight. She wanted to finish that pergola of hers: 'I must get it done today.' I think she said that. She was very sweet. Thoughtful. 'You look tired. Why don't I fetch a deck chair for you, Gramps?' she said. 'Then you can sit down and watch me dig some more holes for those posts.' "

"Where did she put the deck chair? In the shade?"

"No. I suggested that. But she wouldn't have it. She said I'd get chilled. I do, you know—the circulation isn't what it was. So she put it in the sun—I was basking in the evening sun. It was very warm and comfortable. Then she was as quiet as a lamb, bless her, and before I knew what was happening, I was drifting off."

I say nothing. At a slow, faltering pace, he sets off after Julia. He doesn't seem to realize the import of what he's just said—and I'm hoping it does not cross his trusting mind how deliberate this act of Maisie's was. But I can see that Maisie wanted to escape her benevolent jailer and, with some guile, ensured she did so. But why would she want to be alone? Where has she been for the past hour? What can she be doing? I raise my eyes to the twenty-one eyes on the Abbey's south face.

Minutes later, I'm outside the refectory. Its windows are wide open; its door is padlocked. Pinned to the door is a note that reads, "Gone swimming." So the touchings-up, the alterations to the portrait, must be finished. It's unlike Lucas to explain his absences, and I wonder to whom that incommunicative message is addressed. Then I know. To Finn, of course.

I feel jealousy and anger rise like bile at the back of my throat. I walk across to the archway in the ruined curtain wall that once marked the confines of the nunnery. I stand there, in the warm, slanting evening light, scanning the fields for a blue dress. In the stubble left by the combine, larks are feeding; it's the evening for bell practice at the church, and as I stand there the first peal begins. Church and convent are contemporaneous, so Maisie's nuns, her eternally watchful, indestructible sisters, might once have stood here; and if they did so, this is what they would have heard. A six-bell peal to the glory of God; to a God I don't believe in, and they did.

In the far distance, I see a pale, naked figure by Black Ditch. I think: *So it's true, Lucas has gone swimming.* The figure raises its arms, dives, and disappears. Could Maisie have gone back to Nun Wood, returned for some reason to the dogs' burial ground? I scan the lane and the bracken at the edge of the trees, where I walked this afternoon. I see that someone, a man, is leaning against the gate.

He moves, and I realize it's Nick. He'll be on his way to the Abbey. I shout his name; he swings round, sees me, and raises his hand in a salute. He's too far away to hear any shouted explanation or request for help, but I make urgent beckoning gestures. He straightens, semaphores, and makes for the path. I don't wait for him. I don't wait because something is happening to the air: The air is altering in a way I recognize and fear. It's infinitesimal, the disturbance of a wing, of a pinion. It's no more than the brush of a feather, this brief bending of time, but I've known it from my earliest childhood, and for want of a better name, I've adopted Bella's term for it. This, such as it is, is my Gift.

It brings with it an adrenaline surge. In an instant, I'm tense as a wire: I'm a string that's ready to be plucked. I'm back in the court-yard. I'm staring at a locked door, a brief note, and six windows: I'm willing them to speak. I run across to those windows and lean into the shadows beyond. There's a stink of oils and turpentine—on a large canvas, leaning against the wall opposite, are *The Sisters Mort-land*. Julia, Finn, and a small girl in a blue dress. Maisie stares me in the eyes: The fear I feel then is intense.

I start running back to the house, and although I'm a fast runner, today I can't run fast enough. I can't see anything beyond those black yew walls either side of the path. I burst out into the silence of the cloisters. They are bleached of all color and etched with threat. I see the random pattern of shallow scrapings in the soil, the glint of a dis-carded trowel. I turn my eyes to the Abbey windows, the twenty-one eyes on the south face, and there, at the central window of the Lady Chapel, something moves, the faintest shape—and I know at once that it's my mother; she's come back.

I cover my face with my hands. When I next look, my mother's fig-ure has gone; all I can see is glass and the sun's glint. I look away. My camera eye pans that courtyard, one last long, slow pan, searching for the unseeable, for the something I know is wrong. I scan the patched and altered walls of the Abbey, rose brick, stone, and knapped flint; I scan the creepers clinging to those walls and the shrubs crouching at their feet. The bells are still pealing in the valley; I can hear Julia's calls and her grandfather's shouts. Beneath the arches of the cloister where I'm standing the shadows are deep, and they're beginning to speak. The arch nearest me is pitted and worn; lichens bloom on its stone. Tucked away at its apex, where the pillar meets the vaulted cloister roof, there's a swallow's nest, mud, and, just visible, a tiny gaping beak.

I've never felt such desolation, before or since. How many seconds have passed? One, two? It's very brief.

I back away, onto the grass. And then, in the very corner of my eye, at the far periphery of my vision, something moves. It's like Icarus in that Brueghel painting, a tiny inverted detail, an error in the far corner of the world. To my left, a nestling. To my right, something small, something silent, something terrible, begins its fall.

Maisie doesn't cry out, and neither do I. Shock slows her fall, so to my eyes there's a moment when she's still cradled by air, when I can believe the air will hold her up. Even when I see her land on stone, at that hideous angle, and her arms and legs fly up, and the ground tosses her, twists her, and throws her down again, I still hear nothing, and I can't seem to understand: There are so many voices in my head. My Gift has tricked me. I was expecting pain, fearing death, but I'd thought Finn was at risk. Running across the grass, I still believe that, though I know it cannot be: Finn isn't here; Finn wasn't wearing a blue dress. I reach Maisie's side. I still can't understand, but I can see at once how terribly broken she is. I think I give a cry. I kneel down. Maisie has come to rest on her back, with her arms and her legs flung out and her eyes shut.

She makes a strange, low, mewing sound, and then there's silence. Pinkish bubbles have appeared at her lips. I see that a glistening patch is spreading out like a cloak beneath her shoulders. I lift one of her hands and chafe it. I start saying her name. Her hand feels warm; she must be alive—but that warmth is ebbing. There's blood trickling from her ears and her eyelids—and something else, too, from her nostrils: a leaking colorless fluid. I don't know the name of this substance, but I fear it: I know what it is.

I bend over her, my one instinct to protect her, to cover her, and I have nothing to cover her with. I've started unbuttoning my shirt when I hear footsteps running across the cloister. I hear Julia's scream and a broken cry from an old man, but it's Nick who reaches my side first.

"Don't touch her—don't move her, you mustn't move her," he says.

Then he's down on his knees beside me, and I can see him resting his doctor's fingers against her throat. I know what he's about to say, but the rules are being broken here, just as they were at my birth, so instead he tells me she's alive, that she's still breathing. "Call an ambulance, Dan," he says. He pulls off his jacket. "Now. *Now*. Do it quickly. *Move*."

As I stumble toward the hall, I look up at the Lady Chapel windows. The middle one, closed before, stands wide open. I pick up the telephone. I can hear the sound of a car on the drive at the back of the house. Stella and Finn have returned—returned to this.

As I'm dialing the third nine, the long-case clock whirs, hesitates, and strikes eight.

PART VII

Ten of Swords

Mine own sweet dear heart, I write in stealth and at speed <for I am always watched>. It is VIII of the clock. The field boy swears he will carry this message to you. I promised him a kiss, and two coins, since the coins alone would not content him.

Oh my love, what a place this Abbey is! You would not think my eyes so pretty now, for I can scarce open them for lack of sleep. No sooner do I lie down to think of you, than I must <up again to> pray in the dark and the cold—my knees are worn out with this praying. For all that, it is not as dolorous a place as I feared, this labyrinth. I may keep my orange silk kirtle and my bracelets and the dear little dog you gave me <and do not have to sleep with the old nuns in their dormitories. . . .> Sister Maria Agnes said that for a trifling sum, I might have mine own room, as she does, with a fire on cold nights, and fine linen sheets, too, for I could not sleep in their hempen ones, which scratched me half to death. This Sister and I are become great allies, our predicament is alike: what a curse it is, to be the youngest of six, with a dowry so small it is of no interest to a sweet young man, and of less interest to that young man's noble father. Still, I find my poor dowry serves me well here; it swells <the nunnery coffers nicely. . . .>

Dear heart, mark me well: this prison has doors that unlock; there is a place nearby where true lovers may meet for an hour in safety—will an hour in the woods content you, my sweet?

I shall not be the first to make such an escape, nor the last, I warrant you. <Sister Maria will make these secrets known to me next week> and I shall write again; <so be prepared, for> believe me I cannot live until I am clasped in your arms again. So I say as always: Come, come, come, mine own darling. But be warned: I grow stern and chaste since last you saw me: you will need all your dear arts, and hard application of them, too, my love, to overcome my novice modesty. <Ah, I forgot.> They have made me cut my lovely hair, so prepare yourself for the boy who will greet you. In the dark <and at night>

Will you recognize me?

—MS SFC Bel 209/83.5 [?circa 1450] writer and recipient unknown; Belcamp collection, Suffolk County Archive, Ipswich [MS damaged and indecipherable in places; marginal annotation in a second hand also indecipherable]

TWENTY

Corporal Body

I'VE RETURNED to my Highbury bed. I lie there listening to that striking clock at the Abbey. It's dark and cold, and the helicopter's gone. In this world, I have no idea what time it is. I close my eyes at last, I slip into sleep—and it's a deeper sleep than I've had for months.

I dream. In my dream I have a long conversation with a woman, an interchange that leaves me healed and refreshed. I feel that I know her, but I'm not sure who this woman is. When she finally leaves me, she leaves regretfully, with many a backward glance. Just as she's about to disappear, I see that she's an empress, a Mozart queen of the night. She's carrying a crystal ball and an ivory scepter, and she's clad in a white slipper-satin dress. *Ten thousand coupons, Danny*, she whispers. I reach out my hand to detain her, to call her back, and I wake up. I think: *Today is the first day of my new life.*

Well, all right, I've thought that before. I've said that before, and once, when I was at the lowest of low ebbs, I even wrote it down. I later tore it up. But this time it's different. This time I feel confident of success.

I don't have a hangover, for one thing—and I've had a hangover for the last six weeks. I feel oddly purposeful. Last night's retrospective has been of use. I know what I need to do today, I have a very exact program, and I'm going to start on it at once. *Mens sana in corpore sano,* I tell myself as I turn on the shower. That's the first item on the agenda: no mind-altering substances—no alcohol, no coke, speed, blues, or reds. My brain is clear on this point, but my body is recidivist—it starts to voice a few doubts. I blast it with very hot water, then with very cold—and that shocks it into silence, that shuts it up. By the time I'm showered and shaved and into clean clothes, the body's taking a humbler line; it's prepared to negotiate. How about black coffee, how about a cigarette, how about a triple vodka or some cough mixture? it's saying. What's so wrong with the gradual approach?

I march the body downstairs. In the hall, both mind and body, ego and stroppy id, remember for the first time that on the other side of my sitting room door there's a young woman, asleep on my Milanese sofa. An awkward and manipulative young woman. At this, the body's pleas for booze or something stronger rise in pitch. I march it downstairs to the basement kitchen, and when it sees *that,* the body has a major relapse. It looks at the overflowing bins, the un-washed plates, the dishwasher that had a seizure weeks ago, and it feels desperately faint. It feels it needs to be taken back to bed and covered up again. *It's not five yet,* it says. *What the hell's going on?* Welcome to the new regime, I tell it. This is the second item on the agenda. Now: Get this place cleaned up.

Mirabile dictu, the body obeys. It actually does what it's told to do. It starts finding plastic bags and stuffing things into them. It deals with the green Eternaloaf and the one-month-old Christmas Day's uneaten chili-sauce kebabs. It doesn't balk at the fridge—or the smell in the fridge. It whisks through that lot, and before you can say "Highly unlikely," it's emptied the fridge and washed it out with some piney disinfectant stuff. Then it moves on to the cupboards, and it's out with the Nicey-Spicey sauces, out with the prehistoric

Herby Toppings that have been our loyal companions for umpteen years in umpteen bachelor flats. It's got the bit between its teeth now, my body: *Abracadabra*, it says, dunking dishes in a fine sudsy froth in the sink. *Takes no time at all*, it remarks cheerily as it yanks out the sick dishwasher, dekinks its hose, shoves it back, and *voilà*—it's cured and ready for the next blitz.

It's alarming, this manic burst of energy. *Let's not go mad here*, I tell the body as it starts running up and down stairs, dumping eight trillion sacks in the garbage cans. *No problem, mate*, it says. *How about I wash the floor? Wipe down those dodgy worktops? Clean the windows, maybe? Give me five minutes, and you won't know this place. . . .*

Well, I need to rein it in, but I have to say that this unlikely work-man, this NCO from some bad Brit war movie, makes a good job of it. This billet gets *clean*. It's ready for inspection. It's so orderly, it's alarming. The cupboards are empty. The fridge is empty. The last packet of Marlboro is empty, too—but even this catastrophe doesn't faze Corporal Body. He takes ten minutes to nip down to Mr. Patel at the open-at-dawn corner shop—he actually runs there—and he returns with a sackful of booty. There are eggs from unhappy hens and bacon from Danish pigs. I have supplies of Nescafé, Eternaloaf, and "I Can't Believe It's Not Axle Grease." I have a notebook and pen, cornflakes, milk, sugar, and marmalade; there's a five-pack carton of cigarettes.

We sit down at the table, my body and I, safe in the knowledge that its surface has been cleaned with a lemony vitriol fatal to every known bacterium in the universe. We share some cereal, some Nescafé, and a Marlboro. We congratulate ourselves on the fact that we now have the means to get Miss Amyl Nitrate out of our life. Po-litely. She will be given breakfast and then dispatched. She'll be gone by eight-thirty at the latest, and then we can get on with our new life. We'll be leaving for Wykenfield, obviously; but before we do

that, we need to talk to Nick, and we need to see Lucas. I look at
the pages I wrote last night. There are questions to ask Lucas, as became very evident during my Abbey retrospect.

What's more, he's going to answer them. We feel confident of that.
By now—we're on the second cigarette—we're in complete accord,
the body and I. We're at one again. Time to make a list. I draw out
the pristine notebook, flick it open, and pick up the Biro. I write:
Today I will . . . Then stop.

Maisie wrote lists. Not just recited them, also wrote them down. We
knew this, but even Finn and Julia hadn't realized how many lists
there were and how meticulously they'd been organized. We discovered how many she wrote, after that sad leap into the unknown by
then officially designated as "Maisie's accident."

We found this library of lists three days after her fall, when she'd
been moved from the first hospital, the former cottage hospital at
Deepden, and was beginning a medical odyssey that finally ended in
London, in a specialist ward for coma victims. But that event was still
in the future. In those first frantic three days, I'd embarked on a
quest. I was convinced that Maisie's fall was no accident. For three
days, I'd been replaying the sequence of events that led up to her fall,
and I was certain that, if this action of Maisie's was willed, she would
have left behind some explanation. There had to be a note, a letter,
something. After three days of argument, I persuaded Finn and Julia
to help me look for it.

Stella and Gramps were at Maisie's hospital bedside all day, every
day—at that point she was in intensive care in Ipswich, and the number of her visitors was strictly limited. A search in their presence was
out of the question. Both clung obstinately to the accident theory, and
to query it caused distress. Now was the perfect opportunity, I argued.
If we could understand Maisie's reasoning, we'd know what to say to

her now—and that was vital. There were numerous cases of coma victims returning to consciousness when the right words had been spoken to them or the right music had been played or the right memory triggered. Nick reluctantly confirmed this, while pointing out gently that Maisie's injuries were extensive and she might not live. I could see that privately he thought this a waste of time, of therapeutic use to us, perhaps, but not to Maisie. That made me all the more desperate. I was drowning in guilt; I was a man possessed.

So Finn and Julia, persuaded by me, helped me search. We searched that large house, with its million hiding places; we searched it from attics to cellars. All we found—and we found them immediately— were Maisie's notebooks. They could hardly escape our notice. Some were lying open on her writing table; the others had been labeled, indexed, color-coded, numbered, and arranged by subject matter on the shelves by her bed. Mammals and birds, gods and goddesses, verbs and adverbs, stars in their spheres, victims of the guillotine, wartime airfields, etymology, and entomology, the Abbey dogs, the Office of the Dead, each office with its designated psalms, nocturns, and canticles. There were two hundred notebooks, at least—maybe more. We read them in silence. This was a language none of us spoke.

When we found nothing—no hidden envelope, no letter disguised as an entry and tacked on to a list—we went through her books. Maybe the missing note that made all clear had been tucked inside the pages of Darwin or Enid Blyton. It had not.

"We've missed it," I said. "I know it's here. Maisie's secretive; she's clever and she's cunning. Something's hidden here—and the hiding place won't be obvious. We have to try to think the way she did. Imagine you're Maisie. Now—where would you put it?"

"I'm not sure she'd write anything," Julia replied. "At first, I thought it was possible, but now I look at this . . ." She hesitated. A sea of troubles, a sea of notebooks, lay on the floor all around us. "It could have been a spur-of-the-moment decision. She was hiding in the house somewhere. She went into the library, looked at the windows—and then she jumped. She was unhappier than any of us had realized—and beyond that we'll never know why she did it. Maybe there is no why. Let's stop this."

"I don't agree," Finn said in an obstinate way. "I think Dan's right. I think she planned it. It was eight o'clock when she did it—and you say she'd been missing for an hour and a half, at least. She could have done it at seven-thirty, or seven, or even earlier—so why didn't she?"

"Maybe she was afraid," Julia said. I knew she had no wish to discuss the timing here. Neither had I. "Maybe she couldn't summon the nerve. I don't want to talk about this."

I said nothing. I was thinking of the many occasions when Maisie had explained her nuns' Liturgy of the Hours to me; the many occasions when I'd cut her short. "Eight o'clock is the time the nuns retire to their cells," I began slowly. "Immediately before they retire, they observe Compline. It's the last prayer period of the day, and it begins at seven-thirty. The term *Compline* comes from the Latin *Completorium*. It marks the ending of the day and the prayers for the night. Roughly translated, the word means—"

"A state of completion. The completing of things," Julia said.

"And the prayers for Compline would be said in the Lady Chapel," Finn continued after a silence. "She chose the day, the time, and the place. We should have known that at once. Maisie never acted on impulse. She was disciplined. And if she decided to leave a message, it wouldn't have been a general one, it would have been specific. She'd have decided to whom it was addressed, and she'd have left it in a place where that person would find it. That person and no one else."

There's another pained silence. I'm looking at Finn: I'm wondering if she's realized she's just used the past tense. I want to take her in my arms. I've been wanting to take her in my arms for three days and three nights. I want to show her that torn scrap of dress material—

and I can't do that, either. I want to talk to her. Somehow, I can't. I've lost the right, I've thrown away the right—and besides, Finn bars me. She bars everyone. Finn walks around now as if she's shell-shocked; the message "Noli me tangere" is stamped on her face. I can see the effort it costs her to function at all, to speak, or lift her hand, or turn her head. She looks the way Maisie looked when she sleepwalked. Her eyes are open, but their sense is shut. She's looked that way since she returned from London. She looked that way when I intercepted her and her mother in the hall—and that was before I'd had the task, the appalling task, of telling them what had happened.

I can't understand why that should be. But I know Finn is closer to Maisie than anyone else, far closer, for instance, than Stella or Gramps. I trust Finn's instincts more than Julia's rationality—and what she's said strikes me as astute. "If that's the case," I say, "who would that person be? Would it be you, Finn?"

"I don't think so." She looks away. "It might have been once. But not recently. I'd failed Maisie. She never forgave that kind of failure."

"Why do you say that?" Julia asks. I also want to know, but I know what kind of answer she'll receive—and I'm right.

"It doesn't matter. I had, that's all. There was a moment a few weeks ago when Maisie needed my help, and I failed to see it. Leave it at that."

"If it's not you, then there aren't many candidates," Julia says. "Not Stella. Maisie could be cruel to Stella, and she never confided in her—not that she confided in anyone. Certainly not Gramps. Maisie wouldn't waste time on him—she'd know he'd never look for any last message, and if he found one, he wouldn't understand it. He'd cling to the obvious and the false. Gramps always wants the soft answer."

"That's unkind, Julia," I say.

"The truth often is."

"He loves her. You know that. This is crucifying him."

"I do know that. But love doesn't preclude stupidity. Alas."

Her tone is cold. Is that remark, accurate and unpleasant, directed at me? I feel that it is. I meet the flick of Julia's glance at me with a banked hostility. *Why did I ever touch this woman, how could I bear to touch her?* I think.

"Who, then?" Julia continues, turning away to Finn. "Lucas? She spent enough time talking to him when he was drawing her. . . . No. Not Lucas. Not once she'd seen the portrait. She'd never forgive him that. It must be Dan. She adored Dan—she always did, from the moment we first came to the Abbey."

"No," Finn says in a bitter way before I can speak. She gives a gesture of impatience. "Not Dan. Think a little. Who did Maisie talk to most of the time—because none of us had the stamina or kindness of heart to listen to her long enough? Because we'd all interrupt, or slink off, or refuse to understand, or pretend we were busy doing something else? The dead. She spent most of her time talking to the dead. And if she's left a message behind, she'll have left it where they can find it. So think about it, because it narrows the field. . . ." She pauses and looks at us sadly. "If Maisie decided to explain herself, if she decided to leave one last message, there are only two possible recipients. Either she wrote to her nuns, to her Sisters—or to Daddy. Can't you see that?"

I look down at my task list. I've written six tasks:

1. Nick
2. Lucas
3. Abbey
4. Finn
5. Ashes
6. Afterwards

I've no recollection of writing this list; it's been written on autopilot. I've been watching that scene, listening to that conversation in Maisie's bedroom. It ends abruptly. Finn speaks that last sentence, then suddenly scrapes back her chair and stands up. I see her sway and think she's about to faint. "I'm going to be sick," she says. "I'm sorry. Excuse me." Then she leaves the room. I hear her footsteps in the corridor and the sound of retching. Julia and I look at each other in silence. She's wearing a tawny, deep orange dress; no bracelets. I can't bring myself to speak to her—the detestation I feel is too great. When Finn returns and says that she'll understand if we wish to pursue this but that she does not, I think I know why she's come to that decision. I can see the strain she's under. I can see this is making her ill. I curse my own stupidity in making it worse.

I say nothing of that to her or to Julia. From that point onward, both sisters close ranks. They refuse to make further searches of any kind. I continue, intermittently, without great hope, and whenever I have the opportunity. I find nothing—and I fail to see that there is another mystery, a mystery that involves Finn, not Maisie. It takes me months to discover what Julia knew long before: Finn is also facing a sea of troubles—and she'd known that these troubles would have to be resolved before she left with Stella for the day in London.

So much for my own *Final Finn*: for that expression of frank, unclouded happiness I saw on her face when I waved her off in the car that bright morning. I'd misread that expression, just as I'd misread so much else. Just as, in all probability, I'm still misreading, I expect.

Why am I recording this? I ask myself. Why try to make sense of the past or impose a shape on it? I look at the stack of A4 pages on the table. Why bother with these misreadings, guesses, and approximations that I'm going to burn or feed through a shredder? I'd thought I was writing to myself. Now I doubt that.

I think I'm writing to the dead, too. To all those I've loved: to Joe; to Bella, who was kind as well as unkind toward me. To Dorrie, whom I never knew. To Maisie, who is as good as dead; Maisie, who cannot (or will not) speak or communicate. And to Finn, above all to Finn, who is alive but lost to me. Finn, who is never going to journey down here to this place I'm in; Finn, who is never going to play Orpheus to my Eurydice; Finn, who is going to leave me to extricate, to rescue, myself. Notes from the underworld, love letters to the dead, that's what this is, I tell myself, resisting the urge to tear it all up, resisting the urge to check whether, earlier this morning, I really did make Corporal Body tip all the vodka supplies down the sink.

At which point, just when I'm on the most dangerous edge of all, that cliff face famous throughout the mountaineering world as the Self-Pity Drop (watch it: One false step there and you're falling six thousand feet straight down onto rocks), I notice something that should have been obvious some moments before: The front-door bell is ringing. Loud and long and shrill. Someone's got an index finger on the bell push, and he or she is not removing it.

Interesting, at a quarter to six in the morning. Now, who could that be? I wonder, making for the stairs fast before he or she wakes the amyl-nitrate girl on my Milanese sofa. Maybe it's a deus ex machina—Finn, for instance. Chance'd be a fine thing. Maybe it's Nick. Or the milkman. Or the bailiffs. Maybe it's Malc.

I open the front door. Parked by my gate, in the ill light of a London January dawn, is a large black limousine pumping exhaust fumes.

Standing on the doorstep is Julia. She is holding my long-lost briefcase.

TWENTY-ONE

Double Trouble

JULIA GIVES ME a smile like frostbite. "This is yours, I think?"
She hands me the briefcase. "Now, may I have the photograph of
my sister, please? The one you removed from my notice board last
night?"

"It's upstairs," I say—and I say it bravely.

"Then go upstairs and get it."

I go upstairs. I retrieve the photograph from yesterday's suit
pocket. I return. This doesn't take very long, a minute at most, but
in that minute I've convinced myself, *convinced* myself, that all will
yet be well. True, this isn't a good beginning, but I can deal with it.
Now is my chance to show Julia how much I've changed, how far
I've moved on. It's my chance to make amends, set things straight.
It's a God-given, early morning opportunity—exactly the kind I
need on this first day of my new life.

This optimistic mistake, and it is a mistake, is one I've made
before—in fact, I've been making it since birth, so you'd think I
might have learned. But no: As I run up and down stairs, I'm thinking of Julia as she appeared to me last night. That Julia is before my
eyes with a visionary clarity. There she stands, a young, beautiful, and
ambivalent woman. We're in that attic at the Abbey. I can smell her

blue scent and hear the chime of her bracelets. As I extract Finn's photograph, that Julia is beckoning to me.

Blessed by hindsight, I can see, now, where I went wrong then. It's so obvious—why was I blind to it? I should never have blamed Julia for what happened that day in the dark. We were equally to blame—and why use the word *blame,* anyway? Let's reexamine our act: Let's scrape away the poisonous Pauline guilt that's attached itself to such acts over the centuries; off it comes, all that phony crypto-Christian sexual revulsion and fear that too many generations have accepted as the diktats of God. Let's remove the other accretions, too, several millennia of misogyny, sexual stereotyping, and gender bias, for instance; we certainly don't need them—all they're doing is impeding our view, so *they* can come off. Let's get rid of scummy linguistic concretions, too, words like "fornication," for example: Out with it. Let's scrape off all that sorry obscurantist accumulation of pseudo-morality and consign it to the eternal garbage can where it so rightly belongs. Let's toss the complete works of Sigmund Freud in after it, and what are you left with? An unmarried young man and an unmarried young woman experiencing intercourse. In short, a fuck.

A fuck we both wanted; a fuck that gave both of us deep physical pleasure. Is that so evil? What's so wrong with that? Nothing. Nothing. Nothing. Twenty-plus years on, in a more enlightened era, I can look at that incident with new eyes. Apart from anything else, I can see how rare it was.

I'm back in the hall, photograph of Finn clutched in my hand. I know why the man I was reacted to Julia as he did, I know why he felt that anger and revulsion. But I am no longer that sad man. I am a new man. I am a liberal and a leftist; I'm a paid-up, card-carrying, evangelical, moral, sexual, and political radical. I'm not that dark, archaic thing I used to be, that creature who teemed with demons. And this new man, this new Adam, owes Julia and her sex an apology. Urgently.

Does it occur to me as I stand in the hall that while my mind has been following this pleasing trajectory, Julia's could have followed a different one? No, it does not. But then I never do see, until too late, that half the time I'm on the wrong wavelength, out of radio contact with the rest of the world and waving wildly at it from a different galaxy. "Julia," I say, coming to a halt in the doorway. "Julia, I'm sorry."

I hand her the photograph. I'm sure it will be clear to Julia that I'm not apologizing just for myself here: I'm apologizing on behalf of the male sex for the last two millennia. "Listen, Julia," I continue, "I'm sorry I came to your house last night when I know you don't want me there. I'm sorry I fucked up that espresso machine—I'll get you a new one. I'm sorry about those 'That Way/This Way' ads. I'm sorry we ever fell out. I'm sorry for all the times when I've said the wrong thing and thought the wrong thing and done the wrong thing. There was a moment—I think there was a moment, when you and I might have taken a different route. And then we didn't. I don't suppose you regret that—I mean, look at me. But I'm trying to reform, I'm trying to change. Do you remember that time at the Abbey, in the attics, when I was painting the walls? Apology accepted? Friends? I'd like us to be friends again, Julia."

I'm waiting for her to take the hand I'm holding out to her. She doesn't. This message clearly didn't compute. She looks at me as if I'm certifiable. She takes the photograph, puts it in her bag, and takes something out of that bag—but I can't see what it is.

I look at her uncertainly. She isn't looking her best—in fact, she looks as if she hasn't slept. She looks pale and tired, and her hair is a mess, but even so, with no makeup and shadows under her eyes, she still looks beautiful. I say: "Julia, you look beautiful."

"Please," she says, snapping back to life. "Spare me the charm. I'm not a complete fool. Why did you take that photograph?"

"I don't know. Truly, I don't. Finn doesn't answer my letters. I miss her badly. It was an impulse."

This reply, honest as it is, doesn't seem to compute, either. Her mouth tightens. She says: "I see. Was this an impulse, too? Or did this require more thought?"

And she holds out the small object she took from her bag. I see that it's a Post-it note that has been scrunched up and smoothed out. On this Post-it, in my hand, is a message. It says: "Julia, beware! Your husband's thinking of leaving you."

It gets worse. "You see," Julia continues in a calm voice, "after you left, Dan, there was quite a lot of clearing up to do. As you obviously know, you'd sabotaged my espresso machine, and once you'd made good your escape, it blew up—I'm sure you'll find that gratifying. Coffee grounds everywhere—on the ceiling, on the walls, on the floor. And when I'd finished sweeping all that up, and washing the entire kitchen, I put all the mess—all the mess *you'd* caused—in the rubbish bin. And there, mixed up with some eggshells—because my stupid husband actually made you scrambled eggs and God knows what else—I found this. So I thought I'd come round and ask how you got that information. It's going to make me late for location, and I'm inconveniencing an entire production team—but I'd like to get this settled. I'm intrigued, Dan. You seem to have some insider knowledge here. Why would you believe my husband is about to leave me? What did Nick say to you?"

"Nothing. He didn't say anything. Really, Julia—we didn't talk about you at all."

"Then you have some other source, perhaps?"

"No, I don't. Look, I don't *know* why I wrote it—it doesn't mean anything. I was a bit high, and—it was just a stupid joke, it was a reaction to those notes you'd left for Juanita or whatever her name is. I wrote it, then I saw how dumb it was, so I chucked the damn thing. I didn't mean you to find it." I pause. I can hear myself floundering. "Listen, Julia," I say, "trust me. This is the truth. I've been thinking about you half the night."

"How odd. I was thinking about you half the night as well. I was thinking what a troublemaker you are, and how, no matter what happens, I am never, never, going to let you back into my life. I was thinking how I can't stand you, because you're a liar and a fool and a woman chaser, and you always think you can turn on the famous charm, and whatever you've done you'll wriggle out of it. Well, you're not wriggling out of this. So just don't lie to me. Nick said something to you, didn't he? I know he must have said something—so you can stop protecting him. Who is he seeing? How long has this been going on? Who is she? Christ, we've been married twenty *years*. We have two children. Tom's only nine. Now tell me."

Something terrible is happening. Julia's voice is unsteady. Under her words there's a current of emotion, and it's powerful. "Julia, don't," I begin. "*Shit*. Julia, don't cry, please. Look, please don't cry. I promise you, I give you my word, Nick didn't say *anything*."

"I don't care anyway," Julia says, making a choking sound in her throat. "Living with that man is like living with a public monument. Sod him."

I'm shocked into silence. When I get over the shock, I say firmly: "You don't mean that, Julia. Believe me, you do not mean that."

And in an awkward, tentative way, not knowing what else to do, I put my arms around her. Julia stiffens, and for a moment I think she's going to slap my face. Then tears spill from her eyes; she gives a sigh, she swears, makes another choked sound, and steps blindly into my embrace. She buries her face against my shoulder and weeps bitterly. Those tears affect me: Latterly, I've found it hard to believe that alpha Julia, empress of trend, could weep—other than crocodile tears. I'd convinced myself she was a coldhearted alpha bitch. That was wrong of me. After all, I've seen Julia weep before. I saw her weep bitterly for Maisie, and for her grandfather, when the stroke finally took him, which—a few months after Maisie's fall—it did.

I'm not good with women's tears. In the past they used to anger me; now they remind me that, as a consoler, I'm inadequate. But I do my best. I make soothing noises. I utter the gentle platitudes we all need at such moments—and I've discovered what they are, because I've longed for them a few times recently, and I had to learn them in the long months when I sat by Joe's sickbed. I stroke Julia's cashmere-coated back and her hair—her beautiful hair, which she, like Finn, has cut boyishly short. Its gold is shot through with the finest silver. I stare over her head at the black limousine, with its invisible driver. He's running the engine; the sickly smell of diesel washes across the weeds in my front garden. It's barely light. It's cold. In the distance, I can hear the rumble of traffic, the sound of the city, of the great beast of the city; of the kraken, as it wakes.

It feels strange, almost tranquil, standing there on my doorstep, consoling Julia. I tell myself I'm being useful, at least. *Women like a shoulder to cry on*, Joe used to say. It was one of his core beliefs—not that Joe, a chaste widower for five decades, knew much about women, I suspect. Still, my consolations seem to be effective: I'm looking at this event distantly, through a pane of thick glass, a sensation probably due to an absence of stimulants; but Julia does seem to be growing calmer—and I feel calm, too, almost contented, which is *progress*, I tell myself. This isn't how I'd planned this first day of my new life, but I'm dealing with it. In a minute Julia will pull herself together, and I'll walk her to the car, and that will be that. And if Nick has been deceiving her, he can make that confession: I'm staying out of it. If I get involved—Julia is right about that—I'll make the situation worse. Another lesson I've learned. Though I don't understand why this curious malfunction happens; why is it that my interventions always provoke some catastrophic short circuit? It's been happening since birth.

Julia's sobs have stopped. "You're thin, Dan," she says in a muffled voice against my shoulder. "You're painfully thin, and you used to be so strong. What's happened to you?"

"Oh, you know, life. Age. A few things like that. Drugs don't help."

"Are you off them?" She draws back, lifts her face, and looks at me steadily.

"I wasn't yesterday. I am today. But it is only six o'clock."

"That's something. I'm glad about that." She hesitates and then steps away from me. She pushes back her hair; she is wearing one narrow silver bracelet on her slender wrist. She glances along the street. "Rather a public place," she says. "The last time you put your arms around me, we were less conspicuous. A long time ago, of course. Your apology is accepted. And I apologize, too. I shouldn't have inflicted this on you first thing in the morning. I've been working very hard, long hours—you know what it's like. I wish . . ." She hesitates. "I'd better go, Dan."

"Do you have to?" I hear myself say. "Must you? Can't you keep that production team waiting a bit longer? I could make you coffee, Julia. I could even make you breakfast. We could make our peace with each other over bacon and eggs. I'd like to do that. I feel we—"

I don't complete that sentence. Julia had been looking at me in a quiet, thoughtful way; she'd been about to accept, I felt. Now something behind me has caught her eye. An expression of horror and disbelief comes upon her face. She appears to have seen a ghost.

I glance round and discover that Frankie, my amyl-nitrate nymph, has chosen this worst of all possible moments to manifest. I'd forgotten her existence, but now she's wandered out into the hall, and she's rubbing her eyes sleepily. She's barefoot, and the spray-on jeans have been removed. She's wearing that black lace corselet thing and a pair of lacy briefs. She looks like most men's erotic teen dream, but not mine. Ill timing. Can mortification be fatal? I feel it could.

Frankie curls her toes and exclaims at the cold tile floor. She stretches luxuriantly and skips toward me girlishly. I turn and give her a look that would annihilate most women at forty yards. Frankie is made of sterner stuff. "I feel great, Dan," she says. "What I really need now is a shower? After that, let's fall into bed and screw for England, right?"

Then she sees Julia. They stare at each other. All color has drained from Julia's face. She says: "*Fanny?* I don't believe—Christ in heaven. Fanny, what are you doing here?"

"Well, it's pretty obvious what I'm doing," Frankie replies smartly. "I just spent the night here. And I didn't expect to find my mother on the doorstep when I woke up."

There is a difficult silence. A very long silence. I say: "I think there's been some mistake." I say it once. I say it twice.

Some while later, I say a few other wise things, such as "Hang on a minute" and "Just a second" and "Let's all stay calm." Such as "Frankie, why don't you get dressed?" and "Julia, trust me, you're jumping to conclusions here." No one's listening. They probably can't hear anyway: By that time, they're too busy yelling and screaming . . . you know what women are like.

A scene ensues. It's loud. It's epic. It's Sophocles, soap opera, and Wagner. As far as the neighborhood's concerned, it's the best, the most sublime thing that's happened in Highbury Fields since 1308. It stops the early morning dog walkers dead in their tracks. The elderly couple next door emerge in dressing gowns and watch in wonderment. Julia's chauffeur gets out of the car, approaches, thinks better of it, and retreats. Malc and his merry men appear from some alleyway, take up position, and stare, shouting vile encouragement. *Oh look, it's that pretty woman on the telly*, remarks the old biddy next door, over the garden wall, and Frankie—aka Frances, aka Fanny Marlow—loses it.

"Piss off, you nosy old cow!" she yells at the top of her voice, emerging into full view on the steps and eliciting a chorus of catcalls and foul abuse from Messrs. Malc & Co. "Fuck off, assholes!"

she shouts at them. "Swivel on it, motherfuckers!" she yells, making a gesture of such naked aggression and obscenity that it shocks even me. . . . My, my, the things you learn when you're a junior PR to a rap group. And white-faced Julia, who has already told Fanny fifteen times to put her clothes on and get out of this house *right now*, says, "That's it. I'm calling your father. He can deal with this."

From her bag, she produces one of those yuppie banker bricks. It's even bigger than Malc's brick. She pulls out the antenna and starts punching numbers.

"Oh, that's great, that's just fucking great," Fanny shouts. "You are such a bitch. You are ruining my life, always interfering, where am I staying, who am I seeing, why can't I just go back to uni and get a fucking stupid useless degree like everyone else? I can't breathe. I *hate* you. Why shouldn't I sleep with Dan? So he's old enough to be my father? So what? I'm nineteen, for fuck's sake. What am I supposed to be, a *virgin*? What's your problem? I know what your problem is—you want him yourself—you want every man you see, you can't wait for them all to lie down and worship you. Well, I've found the one man who doesn't worship you. He hates you—he always did. He doesn't want you, he wants *me*—and you can tell Daddy that while you're about it."

"Could I put in a word here?" I say. "Can I just clarify something?"

"No, you bloody can't," Electra yells as Julia begins speaking into the brick. "Just stay out of it, tosser. I'm out of here. I've had enough of this."

She storms off. The sitting room door slams. Two seconds later, Electra emerges fully dressed. With a jangling of bracelets, she pushes past me, blanks Julia, and stalks off down the street. Julia continues to speak into the phone. I can't hear what she's saying. I can't hear the traffic; I can't hear the shouts and jeers from Malc and crew. I can't hear anything. I'm in a white distant desert place, thinking, *So much for the first day of my new life; this really is the end of my friendship with Nick.*

Julia terminates her call. She retracts the antenna, paces the path, then returns to my front steps. She gives me a long, glittering-eyed look. "I can't believe that you—even you—would stoop to this," she says in a dangerous voice. "You've hurt me in the past. But Fanny? She's a child. She's always adored you. How could you do this?"

"Julia, can I just explain? Can I just get one fucking word in edgeways, please?" I begin. "I didn't know it *was* Fanny. She told me her name was Frankie. How was I supposed to recognize her? I haven't seen her for nine years—she was a *child* when I last saw her. And if she's a child now, I'm the pope. Will you listen to me for a second?"

"Oh, please. I've never heard anything so lame and ridiculous. You're telling me my daughter pretended to be someone else?"

"Yes, yes! That's exactly what she did. Because she knew damn well that if I'd realized who she was, I'd have called Nick two seconds later. Julia, listen, I *swear* to you, she spent the night on my sofa—alone, I'd like to stress. I'd met her once before, at some party—*once*, Julia. And that was months ago. Then, last night, she just turned up on my doorstep, out of the blue—and proceeded to give what I now see was an Academy Award performance. She spun me a line. . . ." I pause. I remember all those questions about Finn. "Damn it, she spun me a whole lot of lines. But the important one is—she said her boyfriend had just chucked her out. She said that if I didn't take her in and let her stay the night, she'd be walking the streets—"

"I'm not listening to this," Julia snaps. "Come on, Dan, you can do better than that. She didn't just *turn up* on your doorstep. Fanny was at home last night for once—and you spoke to her, didn't you? The minute Nick went upstairs to Tom, the minute he left you alone, you saw your opportunity. You moved in on Fanny. You chatted Fanny up, turned on the well-known charm—and you persuaded her to come here. It's bloody *obvious*."

"What? *What?* I do not believe I'm hearing this. Julia, listen. I didn't even know Fanny was there, for God's sake. Can we just recap? I arrive at your house. Tom's upstairs with the nanny. Nick makes me supper. We sit down in the kitchen and talk. Just the two of us. Then, about half-past nine, the unseen nanny calls down from the hall and says—"

"What nanny? It was her night off last night. Fanny was looking after Tom."

"Julia, I didn't *know* that. Believe me, I never saw Fanny, I never spoke to Fanny—"

"Oh, come on, Dan. It would have been easy to persuade her to meet you—she's always had a crush on you, don't pretend you didn't know that. And you didn't waste much time, I'll give you that. Fanny was leaving the house by the time I got home, I saw her sneaking out when my taxi drew up. She lied to me, of course. She said she was going to some club. I knew better than to argue. And you couldn't wait to follow her, could you? No wonder you shot out the door so fast. So much for Nick's help and trust—the second he's out of the room, you're making an assignation with his daughter."

"An *assignation*? What language are we talking here? Read my lips, Julia: I didn't speak to Fanny at your house, I didn't invite her here, and when she turned up out of the blue, I didn't recognize her, and she knew that. She was upset . . . well, she seemed upset, and— and I just tried to be *kind*. For fuck's sake, I tried to be helpful. I didn't do anything. I didn't touch her. I made her coffee and biscuits. End of story. That's it."

"I see. So you're saying my daughter is a liar and a fantasist, are you? Put the blame on her. What a coward you are, Dan. For Christ's sake—I've known you since I was eleven years old. You've been a skirt chaser all your life—you screwed every stupid obliging girl from Wykenfield to Ipswich; there wasn't *one* who wasn't panting after you. Why do you think Finn broke with you? She knew what you were like, and she couldn't bear it. Who could? You'll never change, you're going to be a cut-price Casanova for the rest of your sad life. Women talk, you know. I don't want to think how many hearts you've broken and lives you've wrecked with your vanity and your eternal quest for a quick, cheap fuck. You make me sick. I loathe and despise men like you. And don't imagine for one second that I don't know why you did this. It's only too damn obvious: This is *my* daughter you're talking about. How dare you stand there and tell me these contemptible lies? I heard what she said to you." Julia approaches closer. She's now on the next step.

These grotesque and hurtful untruths are more than I can tolerate. "Right, I've had enough," I say. "Let's be clear, shall we? For once in my life, this isn't my fault. Fanny is . . . well, she's troubled, to put it mildly—"

"Excuse me?"

"She's troubled, Julia. Mixed up. Confused—"

"Are you suggesting my daughter's unbalanced?"

Resisting the urge to point out that Fanny is a demented hellcat, the most toxic teen-type it's ever been my misfortune to meet, I say: "Look, Julia—she has *problems*, that's obvious enough. People do, at that age. You ought to know that. This has nothing to do with me, I've got caught up in some strife I don't begin to understand, because your daughter inveigled her way in here and lied through her teeth. So, yes, I think we can say she's just a bit mixed up and rebellious, and, let's call a spade a spade, untruthful and manipulative. This has everything to do with your relationship with Fanny and nothing to do with me, and you might have thought about that before dragging Nick into this—"

"Are you saying this isn't my husband's concern? Nick's best friend is fucking our daughter, and I'm not supposed to involve him?"

"For Christ's sake, Julia, I haven't damn well *touched* her. I don't want Nick hurt. I value his friendship more than you'll ever understand—"

"You despicable liar. You don't know what friendship is—"

"—so I'm not too anxious to explain to him that his daughter is a promiscuous lying little bitch, who turned up here hell-bent on sex. That she's exactly but *exactly* like her damn mother, in other words—"

Mistake. Julia gives me the thousand-yard stare. Before I can do or say anything more, she raises her telephone arm and hits me hard, full in the face, with the brick.

TWENTY-TWO

What's God *On?*

NOT LONG AFTER this episode, I rise from my semirecumbent posture. I pick myself up, dust myself down, and start all over again. Before you can say "Pack of lies" or "Come clean" or "Verily this is bullshit," I'm on my way out of my house, en route to Wykenfield.

All right, I'm writing the truth here, and that isn't what happened. What happened was a gap. I don't know how long that gap lasted: ten minutes, fifteen, perhaps? When it was over and I came round, I discovered that only one of my eyes was working, that I was in an advanced state of hypothermia, and that my clean shirt was spattered with blood. With care, I sat up. I observed the wet world. I observed that I was still in my open doorway. Julia and her limousine had vanished. Malc and his merry men had vanished. Across the road was a police car, and standing with their backs to me, scratching their heads, were two police officers. One was a twelve-year-old boy, and the other, the fairy-frail Woman Police Constable, was either a person of restricted growth or a primary school pixie. I knew at once what had happened. Predictably, someone had called the cops— around here, that's a reflex. Predictably, these cops had been given, or had gone to, the wrong address. Now, the law was baffled. It climbed back into its kiddie car, cruised up and down the street, and then drove off. Should have called for help and didn't—story of my life, I guess.

If I had been the old me, that tall, strapping Dan of my youth, this would never have happened. But running very hard in circles for two decades has told on me—and, as Julia had observed, I'm a shadow of my former self. Julia, meanwhile, is strong, she almost certainly works out; she's always been superfit. That phone brick packed a punch. I was still processing the accusations she'd made; that "cut-price Casanova" remark, a vicious untruth, had me reeling. The blow caught me off balance; I wasn't expecting it, and down I went like a ninepin. In the process, something caused ancillary damage to the skull: maybe the large iron doorknob or the hard tile floor, perhaps. The malignancy of inanimate objects, not to mention murderous, ir-rational, and vengeful women, is fucking *unreal*. Hell hath few Furies like a woman scorned, I tell myself.

Some while later, I stand up. In no particular order, I then make a few further discoveries. I discover that I don't have any painkillers, because they all went down the sink with the vodka. I discover that the left side of my face is the color of a Fauvist sunset and is swelling up like a yeasty, glossy brioche. There's a gash that's missed my left eye by half an inch, and that eye can't open because it's too puffed up. I discover that while I've been lying in my open doorway expe-riencing that *gap*, Nick has called and the answering machine's picked up because I forgot to switch it off. He has left a message. It informs me that he has two emergency patients and will be at the hospital until midday. At which point he will come straight here. He will then require an immediate explanation for my conduct.

One further thing, the final blow: During that gap, I've had visi-tors. There's not a great deal of damage these visitors could do—they can't have had much time, and there's nothing to nick anyway—but I'm a Londoner now, and I know that only gets them irritated. Sure enough, when I finally drag myself into my sitting room, I find that they've slashed and disemboweled the white Milanese sofa, sprayed the word *wankah* on my walls, pissed in the fireplace, and torn Finn's book token to shreds. A confetti trail leads to the mantelpiece; my ivory sphere has gone. . . .

I inspect its absence; inspect it for a long, long time. I stand in the wreckage of my room, in the wreckage of my life. In each case, I know who's to blame, who's responsible for this.

Later, when I'm calmer, resolution comes. I leave the house, carrying two letters and a small bag of clothes. I'll need some clothes in Wykenfield, several sweaters at a time, probably, because the Nunn family's ancient tip of an estate cottage has no heating. I jog blindly down the road and, as hoped, encounter huge Malc and Malc's five huge monks. They're back on the usual corner, and—I don't intend to waste time—I stop. *Sod the street cred, sod the argot.* I'd like to beat Malc to a pulp, but since that's out of the question—work to do, can't afford to die just yet—I'll have to employ guile instead.

I wish Malc good morning. "*Respect,* man," he replies. At this witticism and right on cue, the five sycophants grin horribly and move in. Malc then launches on a vile description of Fanny and Julia. Why do I have this perverse need to make light of things, why did I ever pretend Malc was laughable? He's not. Close up, Malc is sixteen stone of serious urban threat. Eyeing me with crazed hatred and contempt, both of which I reciprocate in full, he suggests that Fanny, Julia, all women, and possibly my facial injuries could do with a seeing-to. I'm watching Malc's boiling eyes: full-blown psychosis, I'd guess; advanced paranoia and chronic life rage. My diagnosis is crack. The hoodies are doing that looming thing they do; they're starting to crowd me. I interrupt.

"Malc," I say, "some anus has just played me a low cur's trick. While I was lying nigh unto death in my vestibule, this mongrel cutpurse climbed over my recumbent form, entered my abode, sprayed pigment on my walls, and used my chimneypiece to demonstrate the territorial imperative. What's more, he nicked a carved white plastic ball thing—about the size of a tennis ball, right? My poor old mum bequeathed me this worthless ball shortly before she died a lingering and tragic death. When this thick-witted clown, this numbskull, this Oedipal son of a harlot strumpet, tries to flog that ball, you know what he'll get for it? About fifty pee. And fifty pee ain't going to buy him too many wraps. So what I want you to do, Malc me old mucker, is this: Should you run into this scumbag, tell him he can flog it back to me, twenty quid, cash in hand, no questions asked, you know what I'm sayin', man, and I can't say fairer than that."

I zip through this very fast. I'm feeling brave and fucking angry, but I'm not *totally* stupid. The remarks take a while to get processed, but the sound economic argument, as hoped, wins out. *Miraculo:* One of the hoodies has just found something remarkably like a ball of that description under this very privet hedge. The hoodie hands it over. I shove it in the bag, hand over the twenty, and prepare to scoot. I suspect Malc's enmity for me, always atavistically deep, is getting deeper. There is a perplexed scowl on his face. This will take some time, but each bead on the rusty mental abacus is slowly clicking into place. Should Malc realize that I've dissed him, I'll be in serious trouble. I don't care. Where I'm going, I'll be way beyond the reach of Malc and his ilk.

Next item on the agenda: I'm off to visit Lucas in Ladbroke Grove's hinterland; once there, an incisive interrogation will take place. Before that, a brief detour is necessary. I zip along Upper Street at speed, and after two blocks I'm out of breath—I think the Marlboro intake explains this, though pain, deep emotion, and a near death experience may also have had an effect. *No hay problema.* I limp into the nearest chemist's and explain my predicament. The two pretty and charming girls behind the counter take a sympathetic interest. "Ladies," I say, throwing myself on their mercies, "I need your help." They sell me eight packs of Nico-Nix patches and eight packs of Nico-Nix gum. With much giggling and many flirtatious glances, they agree to show me how these patches are best applied. One rolls up my shirtsleeve; the other applies the patch, taking far longer to do so than is strictly necessary. Considering the state of my face, I'm encouraged. Maybe I haven't entirely lost my touch. *Pace* Julia, and her allegations, is that so very wrong? They were pretty. It cheered me up—for a bit.

Outside, one Nico-Nix patch proves inadequate, so I apply a few more and try the gum. This tastes so poisonous that it *must* do some good. I walk on. I reach Nick's house shortly after nine—pretty good going, considering the complications that fascist in the director's chair has thrown my way this morning. I mount the steps.

The nanny answers the door: I'd been counting on that. The nanny is young; she proves not to be Juanita or Perpetua (all right, I'll confess: I invented Perpetua). Her name is Ingrid, she's from Stockholm, and we . . . get on. It's evident that Ingrid knows who I am, and I suspect she's been warned off me. Does this influence her? No. This is an independent-minded woman, and she's going to make her own assessment of my character. We have a pleasant discussion about Sweden and that Bergman movie where a man plays chess with Death. This takes about three minutes. Ingrid says I don't look well. She says that she's about to have a cup of coffee, and I might benefit from one. I'm a man of honor, and I don't want to compound my felonies, so I decline, with thanks.

I hand her the two envelopes. Each contains a letter, and each letter is brief. The one to Fanny says: "Dear Fanny, I know I can trust you to tell Nick and Julia the truth. I think you should, don't you? No hard feelings, and good luck, Dan."

The one to Nick says: "Dear Nick, There's been a misunderstanding. Fanny will explain. I'm leaving the country today—that seems the best course of action. I may be away some time. My love to you and to Julia, Dan."

Considering these were written when I was concussed, blinded, and bleeding, I feel they cover all necessary ground. They're pithy and to the point: Maisie would approve. I regret the lie to Nick about leaving the country, but it's unavoidable. I don't want him pursuing me to Wykenfield. The tasks I have to face there need to be faced alone.

So: I hand these letters to Ingrid, and just as I'm about to leave, the one thing I hadn't foreseen happens. From behind her skirts, a small voice says, "Hello, Dan."

It's Tom. It's my godson, Tom. It's four long years since I've seen my godson, who's now peeping out at me, and I was always devoted to him, and—I wasn't prepared for this. I don't deal with it too well. In fact, I don't deal with it at all. What happens, and I can't prevent it, is that my eyes fill with tears. I want to sit on the doorstep and howl. Howl for all the things I've lost and thrown away, howl for friendship, love, marriage, the children I'll now never have, and the affection of this small, melancholy child from whom I'm barred, this little boy who's the nearest I'll ever have to a son.

I can see that Tom has been warned off me, too—either that or, as children do, he's overheard fraught marital discussions on my failings, and he's learned I'm taboo. His face lit up when he first greeted me, but it's now clouding over and he's hesitating. Ingrid's realized her job could be on the line, and she's trying to usher him away. I never knew what it meant to feel like a pariah until this moment, and the pain is acute. Someone's just jabbed a great jagged dagger of misery right through my heart.

I look at my godson. He's small for his age, and the resemblance to Nick is strong. He has the same dark coloring, the same prep school haircut, the same solemn, trusting air that Nick had as a child. His eyes are Julia's. He's resisting Ingrid's embarrassed efforts to persuade him away from the leper on the step. Tom stands his ground.

He says: "You've hurt your face, Dan."

"I know. I walked into a door. Stupid of me. I wasn't looking where I was going."

"It needs a bandage. You should put a bandage on that cut. Ingrid will get you an Elastoplast."

A doctor's son, I'm thinking. Most hurts can be cured. What bandage would bind up a broken heart? Can you mend a mind? "It's fine, Tom, really," I begin. "Can't stay, have to be going—"

"No," says Ingrid, surprising me. "Tom is right. I will fetch first aid. We do not want that cut getting infected. And your poor eye is all swelling up. One minute, please."

Ingrid leaves Tom standing in the doorway, at risk of infection from me. She disappears downstairs to the basement. After a lengthy pause, Tom says in a small voice: "I still have that triceratops you gave me. I keep him by my bed. But I'm more into computers now."

"Of course you are," I reply unsteadily. "Everyone has to move on, Tom."

"Why are you crying?"

"I'm not. It's just this cut—and the bruising around the eye. It sort of makes it weep."

"You shouldn't be ashamed of crying, Dan," Tom says earnestly, his brow creasing into a frown. "At school, they say boys shouldn't cry—that's for girls. But Daddy says that's wrong. He says men can cry, too, when something really bad happens." He pauses and looks anxiously at me. "Like if someone dies, for instance. A man might cry then. And Daddy often cries—I've seen him. He was talking on the telephone last night, late last night, after you'd gone, Dan—and he was crying badly then. I couldn't sleep, and I went in, and I said I'd fetch Mummy for him, because she was downstairs in the kitchen, cleaning up all that coffee stuff. But Daddy hung up the phone very quickly and said, No, not to bother Mummy now, because it was only hay fever. He never used to have hay fever. But there's a lot of it around."

"There certainly is," I say quickly. "Every second person seems to have it. It's not serious, you don't need to worry, Tom. It's caused by—pollution and . . ." I stop. I can't go on.

"Pollen," Tom says, fixing me with melancholy eyes. "Pollen is the main cause, Dan."

"Right," I say. I can follow his line of thought. "Absolutely. Pollen is the culprit. And you can get a high pollen count in London even at this time of year. Even in January, Tom. The plants don't die back, you see—it's climate change. And pollen gets in everywhere, through the smallest crack, round the edge of windows, under the doors . . ." I pause. I'm not convincing him. Inspiration comes. I say: "Look, Tom, there's some right here. . . ."

I hold out my empty palm. Tom inspects it. He frowns. He remembers. His face brightens. He looks at me hopefully. He says, "I can't see anything, Dan."

"Watch," I reply. And—I can still palm cards, I can still palm coins, these are arts I inherited, arts Bella honed, and I've never lost them— I perform the requisite hand movement that tricks the eye. One second later, and Tom is clutching a fifty-pence piece conjured from air; he's been distracted, and Ingrid has returned. She opens a large red first-aid box with a white cross on it and, watched closely by Tom, applies some soothing unguent to the gash on my temple. She applies a pink, shiny Elastoplast. Great. No doubt I look even more foolish than before.

But these ministrations seem to have done some good. Something has done me some *good*, I realize. A great wash of emotions flows through my heart. Love for Tom, whose sleeplessness is not caused by anxiety over school, as I've just learned. Pity for Nick, whose situation is graver than I'd understood. Gratitude to Ingrid, for simple kindness to a stranger. A sense that blessings can be bestowed when you're most aware they are fleeting. *Lacrimae rerum,* yes, that. The tears of things, I suppose.

I thank Ingrid. I drop a kiss on Tom's forehead. As I do so, I make a silent wish, or—who knows—a prayer, that the way will be made easy for him, that he will flourish and not be exposed too young to damage or pain. All the good that a godfather might wish a godson at the font, I wish him now.

It feels powerful, that wish. How strange. I turn to leave and then turn back. "Have a good day, Tom," I say, wondering if he'll remember this, too.

"Have a better one, Dan," he replies promptly, and grins.

That was the form of farewell Ocean taught me, a thousand years ago. She claimed it was a traditional Roma response, as taught her by her great-grandmother—which may or may not have been true. I can still remember the words in her language, in the old language. I say them under my breath. I know I won't see Tom again; I know this will be our last meeting, so I add a rider: "Good-bye, Tom," I say, and leave him, waving after me, as I walk off down the road.

I go to the Angel. The Angel is my favorite of London's tube stations. When I first came here from Wykenfield and took up the advertising job that Maisie's letter of application had secured for me—yes, that ridiculous letter did the trick—this was my local station. Nick and I were sharing that shabby flat just around the corner. I'd leave from here every morning, and every evening, when I returned, I'd think: *I'm home.*

It's dangerous, the Angel, of course—and famous for it. In the majority of underground stations, there's a wall and a concourse between the up and down lines: not here. Here, they run either side of the platform, and that platform is straight. When you stand there, especially at rush hour, it's perilous. You could get elbowed off the edge in front of you or behind. Standing there, you can feel the doubled deadly suck of air as the trains approach, the thunder that rolls down the tunnels ahead of them and booms its warning from the dark tunnel mouths. It's four feet from the edges of the platform to the rails that are live. A child could easily fall across them. It's one easy step for a man, for mankind.

By the time I get there, the rush hour is past and the platform's deserted. Out of habit, I judge the posters. They include one of mine, part of the "Handful of Dust" TV, poster, and print campaign we did. At the time, I said: *Look, you may not like it, but people get compassion fatigue. The first time they see a starving child, it hits them in the guts. Then they see it again and again, every time they switch on the TV, every time they open a newspaper—and the effect wears off. They go blind to suffering, so if you want them to get out their checkbooks, we're going to have to do something else.*

I got my way; I usually did. So there were no shots of starving children, no harrowing footage from the field hospitals, and no information as to where this was. We just filmed some of the many, many funerals: the small graves, the tiny coffins, and the mothers' hands, with their last sprinklings of ritualistic dust. Handheld camera, black-and-white footage, very fast images; jump cuts. There were no words—I was losing faith in words. We used the sounds of grief, that truly international language that everyone speaks. You heard the sounds of the spades, of the actual business of death. Over the intercut images, we ran the terrible statistics, and then: *Shall I show you fear in a handful of dust?* Presumably we showed them something, because the contributions flowed in. But then they will, if you prompt correctly. People have hearts, and those hearts can be touched.

My train has arrived. I get on it and then forget to get off. The journey takes forever. At one of the stations, I'm not sure which, I see Finn—and I see her just as the doors are about to close. I leap up, jam my foot in them, and hurl myself onto the platform. I land at Finn's feet and then discover it isn't Finn at all; it's a young, blond-haired Australian backpacker. Close up, she doesn't resemble the Finn of twenty-three years ago very much, and she certainly doesn't resemble the woman Finn is now "You all right, mate?" she asks, helping me to my feet. I tell her I am. I can see she doesn't believe me, and I don't blame her. I am fine, obviously—but with a shiny pink Elastoplast and all this Fauvist sunset swelling, what can you expect?

I finally reach the station that is only an eighty-mile walk from Lucas's house. I trudge the eighty miles and come to a halt at the famous wall that abuts his gate. Lucas, like me, lives in an area on the cusp between desperation and chic. Occasionally, there'll be excitable articles in newspapers predicting that this neighborhood is next on the remorseless gentrification list. Any minute now, they say, the money's going to start spilling over here from the adjacent citadels. Any second, there'll be skips outside every house, the merry whistle of workmen, and those bloody four-wheel-drive tanks, bane of my life—they'll be parked on the pavements, waiting to pick up the kiddies for the off-road trek to the private nursery two hundred yards down the street.

Well, it hasn't happened in Highbury Fields—not yet. And it hasn't happened here, either. Lucas lives too close to what's known locally as bandit country. He's lived here twenty years, only two hundred yards from the overpass that marks the divide, and that's too close to the border. Besides, the recession is gripping, and the bankers are running for shelter—they're liquidizing assets, they're in retreat.

By now, it's pouring with rain and threatening sleet. It's cold. The sky is black. January in London: High noon, and any minute it will be dark on the streets. I stop to inspect the famous wall. I always do this. I find it comforting. In the past, this was a wall of history, of wit. This is where I first saw, in huge crude letters, the slogan NIGGAHS OUT. Hours later, the reply, *But he'll be back tonight,* appeared underneath in perfect, corrective, cursive script. That made my month. I also enjoyed NO MORE WAR, a perennial favorite, that, and HO CHI MINH RULES and VIVA CASTRO, later emended to VIVA CASTROL—who was the petrol freak? I enjoyed WOMEN NEED MEN THE WAY A FISH NEED A BICYCLE and WHAT WE BOTH NEED IS A FERRARI, which swiftly appeared under it. I enjoyed the CAMPAIGN FOR NUCLEAR DISARMAMENT badges, and the RELEASE THE BIRMINGHAM 3, 500, or 8. I enjoyed CLASS WAR and SUPPORT THE MINERS and LIFE SUCKS and IF YOU THINK THAT YOU WANT TO TRY THE ALTERNATIVE.

I liked WHERE IS THE FALKLANDS ANYWAY and the answering GO TO ANTARCTICA DUMMY & TURN RIGHT. I liked IF THEY CAN PUT ONE MAN ON THE MOON, WHY DON'T THEY PUT THEM ALL THERE? In that instance, I was touched by the comma and the question mark; it's nice when people bother to punctuate. I'd look at this wall and I'd think, *Talking 'bout my g-g-generation:* This is my life.

Once upon a time, it did the heart good to see all those little Margaret Thatchers and Ronald Reagans dangling from gibbets, the iron ladies so well depicted that I suspected Lucas had a hand in it. I suspected Lucas was responsible for many of the surreal, heretical artworks and imprecations that appeared from time to time, and I'd imagine he crept out, after dark, with his skilled brush and pots of paint.

He always denied this. And if he ever did indulge in this pastime, he's obviously given it up. What's happened to culture? To history? To politics? This country is going to the dogs. The wall's now a

sludgy, ugly mess of tags, not one of which displays the least origi-
nality, let alone wit. There are many tedious obscenities, cocks and
balls and swastikas, that kind of stuff. There's only one slogan left, and
that's been here as long as I can remember, though if I had a spray
can right now, it's the first one I'd paint out.

GOD IS WATCHING, it says under a huge eye. Who is this
voyeur, and what's his problem? Why can't he stop watching, and intervene occasionally, the way Zeus did? Nothing too extreme, just a
few well-aimed thunderbolts, I'm not asking for much. *Zap*, there
goes world poverty. *Zap*, say good-bye to war, famine, disease, and
pestilence. *Zap*, farewell to the four horsemen of the Apocalypse.
Zap, I can relive my past, and this time around, Finn and Dan will
marry and Maisie will never jump. The eye has a black pupil and a
chalky white surround. This large pupil is unnaturally dilated, I note,
inspecting it. What's God on? Whatever it is, I could do with some
of it.

I lean up against the wall. My clothes are getting soaked. My face
hurts. That Nico-Nix is a total rip-off, because never, in my whole
sorry life, have I experienced such intense longing for a cigarette.
Just to the left of this famous wall is the narrow arched gateway that
leads into Lucas's hidden, invisible from the road, house. That narrow gate, secured and protected by technology's cutting edge, is
made of steel plate, painted black. You can't see through it, or under
it, or over it, or around its edge.

The other side of that gate is a small courtyard. On one side of
that is Lucas's studio building, with a huge north-facing window and
a door that is never left unlocked. On the other side is Lucas's calm,
civilized, and welcoming house. When you visit Lucas, it's the house
you must go to, not the studio. Even if you know Lucas is in there
painting, even if you can see him, you have to pretend he's invisible.
You walk up to the front door of the house and knock. Eventually
Lucas will emerge from the studio, wearing one of the many iden-

tical boiler suits in which he works. You'll enter the house—and you will enjoy yourself.

Lucas is an excellent host. He's amusing, he's erudite. I've even known him to be kind—up to a point. He will provide excellent wine or excellent malt whiskey—whatever your weakness, Lucas will have it on tap. His food is somewhat peculiar, because on the whole Lucas forgets to eat, and food does not interest him. So it tends to be whatever involves the fewest number of man-minutes. For some years, this was a strange *mittel*-European soup (Lucas's ancestry is *mittel*-European, I think; I wouldn't know, he never discusses it). Then he discovered macrobiotics, which pleased him; all he had to do was cook up one huge pot of brown rice a week. Recently, he's discovered sushi, which he can now buy from a new shop nearby called PURE—he approves of sushi, as it's nutritious, quick to eat, and doesn't involve heating up. Purity matters to Lucas; it always has.

So I could go and signal through that gate. I have, after all, come a long way, a spiritual marathon. If I do, Lucas will emerge, feed, and water me. He'll give me raw fish to eat. And I could ask him all those questions that, last night and first thing this morning, seemed so urgent. Rest assured, those questions weren't vulgar—I'm not a fool, and I've had time to think. So I wasn't going to ask Lucas whether, twenty-plus years ago, he was Julia's lover as well as Finn's. I think I know the answer, in any case. I wasn't going to ask him whether, by any remote chance, he had watched Julia and me that last evening, when we emerged from our medieval hiding place. I know he didn't. He was in the refectory. He was reworking a good painting and was making it great.

I know what prompted those alterations. He had listened to Maisie, who told him, in front of me, what was wrong with his version of *The Sisters Mortland*. Maisie said the dead were missing from his portrait. Lucas was inserting them—honoring them, perhaps.

That was what I saw, what I finally understood, when I stood looking at the painting in the gallery yesterday: the three sisters, and all those dead, all those generations of the dead, who were both with them, and inside them; who are beside, and inside, all of us. Who are in and with me, and whose ancestral voices now speak with eloquence and understanding and warning inside my genes, blood, heart, and head.

I slump against the wall. That fatigue's hit again, that peculiar fatigue that's been affecting me of late. I'm tired. I've come all this way, and I now understand that I'm in the wrong place. I shouldn't take the Jonathan Aske route, that cul-de-sac. It isn't Lucas I need to question. Everything Lucas has to say on the subject of the Abbey, and the sisters, and Maisie, of that particular summer and all it stood for—it's in his portrait. *The Sisters Mortland* is his last word on the subject—and quite right. What I should do is concentrate on my last tasks—and for those, I need to be in Wykenfield, not London.

I push myself off the wall, take one last look at Lucas's locked gate, and walk away from it. I start trekking back the way I've come, the rain pelting down, a cold wind blowing, the London air so thick with water vapor that it's like walking through sea fog. I've gone about fifty yards when a black cab passes me at speed, spraying me with filth. It stops farther up the road behind me, and when I hear the squeal of brakes, my sad, small, and unreliable Gift flickers back to life.

I stop dead and turn round just as the gate into Lucas's lair swings open. I know it's Finn, know it one second, maybe two, before I actually see her. She comes out of the gate, clangs it shut behind her, and runs across to the waiting cab. She's wearing a mackintosh, the belt knotted. Her hair, bleached by the African sun, is as short as a boy's, just as it was in that photograph. It falls over her forehead. As she bends forward to speak to the cabdriver, she pushes it back from her face. I know that gesture. Forget the rain, the failing light: I'd recognize Finn, my Finn, across a thousand years. I'd know her from outer space.

I shout her name and start running toward her, but the taxi's engine drowns out my voice. Finn climbs inside, and the cab pulls away fast. It accelerates into the distance, out of my life.

I run across to Lucas's gate. I hammer on it hard. I shake it and rattle it. After an interval, that bloody intercom thing he insists on using crackles to life and Lucas's voice says, "Yes? What is it?"

"Lucas," I say, frantic now. "It's me. It's Dan. Let me in, let me in."

"No," Lucas says. "Sorry, but I'm working."

"Lucas, fuck it, fuck you—open this gate."

There is a lengthy pause, then Lucas's crackly, distorted voice says: "You saw Finn?"

"Lucas, I thought she was in Africa. I thought she was in Mozambique—Lucas, I have to see her. Where is she going? How long is she here? Why hasn't she called me?"

"I can't answer the final question," Lucas replies, a slight tetchiness creeping into his voice. "As to how long she's here, about another hour. She's late for her flight. As to destination, I believe she mentioned Cairo."

"Holy Mary Mother of God. Which airport? Which *airport*, Lucas?"

"Heathrow, I think." And the intercom clicks off.

We'll pass over the subsequent debacle. Forty-five minutes of running in the rain, semaphoring, before I found the one taxi in London that wasn't occupied. Gridlock trying to get to Heathrow. Two hours circuiting Heathrow's hells, making sure that there were no later planes to Cairo, two hours checking whether Finn had decided to miss her flight and by some divine chance sit in one of four terminals, in one of six thousand cafés, drinking coffee, a Francesca waiting patiently for me, her Paulo, to turn up.

This odyssey nearly finished me off. I made it back to Liverpool Street station, finally. I got on one train and then a second. After that, I think there was a bus, maybe a taxi. Half a day later, and close on midnight, there I was, cold as charity, back in Wykenfield, trying to light the kitchen range, in the house of my ancestors.

I got it going eventually. I lit the candles under the pictures of Ocean, my ancestress. I put the eight-inch-square box with my father's ashes in the funereal front parlor, where Dorrie was laid out. Then—it seemed so cheerless and lonely there—I brought Joe back to the kitchen and put him close by, on the table, with the crystal ball and the tarot. I put the ivory sphere I'd rescued next to the Rider-Waite deck. Once these powerful objects were in place, I sat down, picked up a pen, and began writing to the dead, the loved, and the lost again.

I wrote for hours, Joe. I got this far, Maisie. I got as far as *this page*, Finn. Then I fell asleep, with my head on the table. The sky wept rain all night.

I'd survived Saturday or—as Julia so accurately used to call it, Shatterday. She was quoting someone. Today, it's a new morn. It's Sunday—or, as I'm going to call it, Son's day. The sky's still weeping; the world's awash.

My dearest Finn, my beloved Finn, I'll wait until it eases, and then I'll walk up to the Abbey. I'll be reunited with you there, in one sense, at least.

TWENTY-THREE

Netherland

URING THE MORNING—I'm not sure of the time, and time
doesn't matter, in any case—I set off from our cottage. I'm carrying a spade and a Sainsbury's plastic bag, inside which is the box
with Joe in it. My penultimate task, and I can't shirk it. This is what
sons do. They determine a parent's final resting place. If they want
to involve religion, some guru or priest, fair enough. If not, and I
don't—Joe was not religious in that sense, though he was in many
others—then some alternative ceremony is needed. Maisie favored
libations. I'm thinking more along the lines of a handful of dust and
some words of mine, together with powerful words from the King
James version of the Bible, for which—unlike the modern abomi-
nations that have superseded it—I have the deepest respect.

I'm no sooner out on the road than I'm lost. Another of those
Hamlet moments, but this time I'm on some misty Elsinore battle-
ment, waiting for my father's ghost. He will tell me where to go
next. I stare at the familiar village street and discover it's become un-
familiar overnight. Of the old landmarks, only the pub, with its wily
fox and foolish goose, remains. The duck pond is long gone—filled
in when they installed mains drainage. The shop and the post office
have gone; the school has gone. Each of these, as Realtors would say,
is now a *desirable residence*. But these changes haven't happened in the

last six weeks: I had plenty of time to discover them, and rage over them, last summer, when I was here with Joe. So what's now making this street so alien? I think it's the behavior of the road, which is undulating. I don't like it, this switchback road; I don't like this ride. I want to get off.

I frown at the road, sway a bit, and wait for it to stabilize, which—eventually—it does. I inch toward the lane that leads up past Acre Field to the Abbey. The long line of elms has gone, killed by a Dutch disease some years ago. The roof of the Abbey is just visible, and peering at the chimneys, I can see hallucinatory smoke. Up there, on the higher ground, a thick, heavy rain is falling; it doesn't appear to be falling here in the lane where I'm standing. I raise a dry hand to my wet face.

It looks impossibly far to the Abbey. I'm no longer sure that Joe will want to lie in the haunted environs of Nun Wood or in a garden he once tended that will be knee-high in dead docks. Maybe I should choose some other place? I begin walking toward the fields—those fields he loved, those fields he and his father and his grandfather worked—and I can't *locate* them anymore. I can't find any hedgerows or gates, and they're impassable, these dark prairies, newly plowed, the sticky boulder clay instantly adhering to the feet. It's making my feet leaden. I can scarcely move. I find I've somehow got myself into a vast Somme of mud, a terrible no-man's-land saturated with pesticides, pumped full of high-yield profit, unprotected from the wind, featureless and bleak.

I don't know this England. I don't know where I am. Is this the field where my grandfather, aged six, was paid a penny to stand for eight hours, on just such a day as this, scaring birds off the newly seeded wheat? Or am I in Pickstone, so called because its ground sprouted flints and the village women and their children were paid to pick up the stones at a rate of tuppence a bushel? I bend and pick up a stone. I can't remember what a bushel is, but it's a lot, especially for a child, and especially when engaged in such a miserable task as that. I don't know when that happened and when that ancient practice was finally discontinued: back in the dark ages, I think—that is, within living memory; in my father's boyhood, about 1928. Am I there, in that world of rural penury, where Joe's parents couldn't afford to buy him boots? Or am I in that hay field where I lay with Finn, the sweet grasses making us a fragrant hiding place? That field where we pledged adolescent hearts, and I said, *Will it be for always, Finn?* And she said, *Yes*.

Whichever field it is, I find I'm in it one minute and in the graveyard the next. I have no recollection of moving from one to the other. The morning service must be over: I'm alone. I wander between the gravestones, trying to find the fifteen Nunns here, the Nunns to whom I spoke as a child, a very small child. They would always listen patiently and wisely and—unlike Bella—couldn't lose their tempers and pinch me or smack my head. I find five of them or six, but I can't find my mother. And then I'm inside the church, inspecting Guy Mortland's neat, rectangular final resting place, and that of Gramps, which is next to it. I inspect the Tudor wife's brass memorial, the wife whose head has been almost erased by polishing. I inspect the grinning devils with their sharp pitchforks in the Day of Judgment fresco. They're enjoying their work. One of them, he's obviously a senior devil, bears a strong resemblance to Malc.

When the church floor begins to move, to snake and switchback, I slump in the pews and sit there for a while, head bowed. I discover this church is hellishly hot, and I'm freezing to death. I stagger outside—I really can't walk at all well at this point, and whatever's wrong, my body's definitely refusing to deal with it. I make it past the Old Rectory and the almshouses and the former school that's now such a desirable residence.

I can see our cottage up ahead of me: Bella and Joe are standing at the gate. *Supper's on the table*, Bella says. *Come on, lad,* Joe calls. And pain shoots through my lungs and heart, because I know they're there, and I also know they're dead. I'll never hear these voices again. That world's gone, they've gone, and, Christ, it's ten feet, ten miles, to that gate.

I increase my pace—or I try to do so, but it's hard, there's such a weight of mud on my boots, such a weight around my neck—and then that treacherous road rises up to cushion me—and I don't remember much after that. There's another of those *gaps*.

During that gap—it was the first of several—I was rescued. I now know that. I was rescued by Hector McIver, a man as strong, brave, and heroic as his Trojan namesake; by Hector, the son my father should have had. Hector's mother, Flora, had seen me tottering around the village like a ghost, and when she saw me pass by for the third time and—this time—saw my face, she realized something was wrong. So Hector, as tall and muscular as I once was, girded up and came out to rescue me. The ignominious truth is that, with ease, he lifted me over his shoulder, carried me into our cottage, and—with assistance from various McIver womenfolk—got me into bed.

That bed has, has always had, a feather mattress. Old feather mattresses are uncomfortable at the best of times: I sank into its scratchy lumpy billowing folds, and—it was an inferno down there. I was suffocating; I was burning up. I started yelling for Joe, who ought to have been beside me, a reassuring presence throughout my childhood nights. I started yelling for Bella, and the M&B tablets they gave me when I had whooping cough, back in prepenicillin prehistory; they always did the trick. I yelled for those horse pills. I croaked for water; I cried out to the queen of the night, that empress in a white slipper-satin dress who was standing by my bed. She didn't reply, and after a few more gaps I heard that most feared, most terrible, of all sounds: the voice of a woman doctor. When I heard *that*, I started fighting for my life.

This fiend stuck something invasive in my ear. She was now putting something cold and deadly on my chest. "Thirty-nine point five," she said. "I don't need to ask if he's a smoker. Why is he wearing *three* patches? Why is he so thin? What's happened to his face? Turn him over, will you, Hector, and hold him down. I need to get at his nether regions. I'd better give him a shot. Severe bronchial infection, possibly pneumonia. We'll have to take him in, I think. He can't stay here—I mean, *look* at this place."

That needle was eight inches long—minimum. It was the kind of needle you'd use on a rhino, an elephant. I don't like needles; in fact, I fear them, as do many of the wise male sex. I don't like needles when they're stuck in my arse for an eternity, either. The instant it was extracted, I rose up like God from the bed. "No, you don't," I cried out in a voice of wrath. "My gran died in this house. My dad died in this house. I'm not going to some fucking hospital. I know you. I remember you. I'm going to die here. Let me die *here*. Get your hands off me, you bitch."

Well, I did have a high fever—normally I would, of course, show a woman, and the medical profession, more respect. After that, I calmed down. The temperature stayed at Fahrenheit 451 for a bit; no doubt I babbled o' green fields, the full Falstaff deathbed riff. But that shot—that shot was a miracle; God knows what was in it, but whatever it was, it was extraordinary in its effect. It was liquid gold, fluent insight. De Quincey, Coleridge, all those illustrious morphine junkies—they'd have envied me this. It shot me straight to Xanadu and back.

That substance gives me seven days and seven nights of time traveling. On the seventh day, I'll surface, but meanwhile, down there in netherland, I've been gifted with new eyes. I see Maisie clear. I see Finn clear. I also see myself.

I watch the curious circumstances of Maisie's partial recovery; I watch me make the only proposal of marriage I've ever made or am likely to make. And this time, thanks to the Xanadu effect, I've lost the power to edit, soften the focus, or adapt. Reel two starts to loop through the viewing screen. I watch the past's jerky footage: I watch the events after Maisie's fall; I watch what I inexorably became and what I did.

The loop begins in that hospital in London, in that ward where Maisie rose from the dead.

TWENTY-FOUR

PVS

PATIENTS DESTINED TO EMERGE unscathed from a coma usually return to consciousness in the first two to four weeks. Maisie did not do so. "Is that a bad sign? What does that *mean*?" I asked Nick—he and I were sharing that Islington flat by then; he was working at University College Hospital, the same hospital where Maisie was being treated, though not on the ward where she lay, hitched up to monitors, silent and unresponsive.

Nick explained again. He'd already done so many times; he'd drawn me diagrams; he'd explained there was almost certainly irreversible damage to the cerebral cortex, that part of the brain used for higher cognitive functioning. Although Maisie could now breathe without assistance, and although there appeared to be a sleep/waking cycle, and although she would sometimes smile, and sometimes weep, and sometimes make strange mewing sounds, this did not mean that Maisie's brain could function normally or ever would.

She was unresponsive to sound, touch, and light. The smiles and the tears and the grimaces, the occasional moments when she gripped Stella's hand, as if in response to something Stella had said, meant nothing. I had to think of them as random, a random muscular reflex. Maisie was being kept alive by a gastrostomy tube; she was incapable of swallowing. If that tube was removed—and unless she improved, a decision as to whether or not it should be removed would have to be made eventually—then Maisie would die of starvation or, more accurately, of thirst. Dehydration would bring her story to an end, but her passing would be eased, obviously, with the very latest and kindest medication.

Maisie had drifted away into what we would now call PVS, or persistent vegetative state. That term had yet to be coined; "deep coma" was the phrase Nick used then. The condition remained mysterious, he said. The diagnosis was reached by clinical means—and there were instances when patients in deep coma did surface to consciousness. He then cited the various percentages. The first year, especially the first three months, was critical. In that time 52 percent of patients made a recovery; in 18 percent of those cases, that recovery was classed as "good"; in 33 percent of those cases, patients were left with disabilities, which could range from severe to slight. I would always stop him at that point. I kept thinking about that other 48 percent, the ones who were left awake but not aware, alive but dead, the ones who *never* surfaced.

Stella refused to accept such explanations, but then Stella was in denial—a state I'm familiar with. "The doctors don't know Maisie," she'd say to me again and again. "This abnormality, that abnormality—they first told me Maisie was abnormal when she was three years old, and they've said it ever since. She isn't abnormal, she's just *different.*"

"Stella," I'd say as gently as I could, "this isn't quite the same. You know that."

"I can get her back," she said fiercely to me once. It was at night, and I'd come to visit after work. "I can get her back. I know it. I just have to find the right words, the right book—something that reaches her. . . ." I glanced at the book Stella had been reading to Maisie when I entered. It was *Jane Eyre,* a novel Maisie disliked. She disliked all novels. What Maisie liked was scripture. And poetry. And facts.

"Maybe if you tried the Bible, Stella," I suggested, pretending not to see the tears that fell regardless down her cheeks. "Or *Palgrave's Golden Treasury,* or some history, or Darwin. *On the Origin of Species, Voyage of the Beagle* . . ."

"Of course," Stella said, embracing me. "How stupid I am, Dan. I'm not thinking properly. That's what I'll do. I'll get Gramps to send them. . . ."

When I next visited, Stella was there, with the Bible on her lap and a history of the French Revolution on the bedside locker. She wasn't reading to Maisie from either. Set-faced, she was telling Maisie the story of how she, Stella, had first met her husband, Guy, encountering him one wartime evening outside the refectory, by the old nunnery gates.

On various visits, I came to hear that unlikely romance often repeated. I'd listen to the details of some equally unlikely literary pilgrimage that preceded it. This pilgrimage was punctuated by, and packed with, maiden aunts—their number seemed to me remarkable. But who was I to question these maidens? Stella's story, word perfect, never deviated from by so much as a phrase, became a daily occurrence. And one day—it would have been late in September, I think, Maisie did respond. I was there, and I saw it. We'd reached the point when Stella, standing by Jane Austen's grave in Winchester Cathedral, holding a copy of *Mansfield Park,* had heard the whispers in the nave that presaged war. At the word *war,* Maisie made one of her strange and frightening grimaces, a rictus of the lips. Tears leaked from her opened eyes, and her hand, clasped in Stella's, jerked.

"She *reacted*, Nick," I said later that night. "I saw it. Something happened."

"Dan, it's possible," he said wearily and a little irritably—he'd just worked an eighteen-hour day on a cancer ward. "It probably means nothing. I told you: Maisie is subject to involuntary spasms. You see her move, and you think the movement's been prompted by a word or a touch. It hasn't. It isn't a case of cause and effect. It's arbitrary. I advise you to remember that. Guard against imagination and sentimentality, Dan. They won't help."

I've always had a problem linking cause and effect. I'm not going over that again. And although I didn't confess it to Nick, I couldn't accept his diagnosis. There was a primitive part of me, an instinctive part—the Roma part, I used to think—that clung to a different belief. I'd known Maisie since her earliest childhood. I'd witnessed her peculiar ways of thinking and her intractable will for a decade. When I was sitting by Maisie's hospital bed, I'd think of Maisie's loyal companions, her invisible nuns, and of the disciplines they'd observed. I'd remember Maisie explaining how a day was divided: Vigils, Lauds, Eucharist, Terce, and so on. I'd think of the time she chose to jump, and the implications of Compline, and I'd feel convinced the doctors were wrong. I felt that Maisie was capable of speech but chose not to speak. Balked of death, she'd taken a vow of silence. This wasn't damaged circuitry of the cortex: It was a discipline, of sorts.

Late one evening in September, I found myself alone with Maisie for once. Stella had gone to fetch some tea; the nurses were at the other end of the ward. Taking her small hand in my mine, I leaned over the bed. Maisie smelled of hospital soap and rubbing alcohol. Her appearance made my heart ache. I spoke quietly and directly to her. "Maisie, I know you can hear me," I said. "I know you wanted to die. But you *haven't* died, and this silence of yours—it's terrible. It's breaking Stella's heart, and your grandfather's. The whole family—everything's disintegrating, Maisie, since you did this. You're intensely loved. You're intensely missed. Now come back from wherever you've locked yourself, come back, and speak. I know you can. Please, Maisie. For the love of God, Maisie, *speak*."

I waited. There wasn't the smallest flicker of movement. Her eyes, which were open, remained fixed on space. That failure left me hurt, miserable, and angry—and my miserable vanity was wounded, too. For a moment I'd believed, I'd actually believed, that I could be the one to effect the miracle. I feel now that Maisie may have sensed that vanity and ego were involved, that this plea wasn't as pure as I'd have liked. With her obsession for niggly but accurate degrees of sinfulness, I wouldn't put it past her.

I visited less frequently after that.

A month later, and it's early October; the second monthly anniversary of Maisie's fall. In the hospital, the situation is unchanged; there's been no improvement. Meanwhile, the fallout from that fall is only too evident. Gramps has had the first of his two strokes; Finn has been looking after him at the Abbey, which he's too weak to leave, but the Michaelmas term has just begun, so Finn has had to return to Cambridge, to Girton College. A nurse has had to be hired, as Gramps can't cope on his own. No one knows how this nurse will be paid for; it's one of many spiraling expenses.

Stella has refused the Viper's offer to put the Viper's Eaton Square house entirely at her disposal; the Viper is displeased. Stella, who can be obstinate, has chosen instead to stay in some room at a friend's house, a shabby bohemian house off Tottenham Court Road, close to the hospital. This friend, a man of literature, edits a vituperative literary magazine; the magazine is small, as is its circulation. Stella has known him "forever"; she has "kept in touch over the years," and he's now kindly letting her pay seven pounds ten shillings a week for a miserable room in which you can't swing a cat. This is one pound more than Nick and I are currently paying for two rooms in Islington. I suspect that this man may be one of the maiden aunts from Stella's premarital literary pilgrimage year. I do not say so.

Julia, whom I rarely see and sedulously avoid, has begun work on

The Observer, been poached by the Sunday *Times*, and is already earning a certain réclame. To my rage, I've discovered that Julia can actually write. She wields a poisonous stiletto of a pen. Point her in the direction of some famous man (and her editors are smart enough to do just that), and lovely Julia will fix this man with her bluebell eyes and bewitch him. When he's sufficiently disarmed, blinded, and convinced of her luscious stupidity, Julia gets the quotes that will damn him. I have to admit that, in the process, she's lethally funny. I cannot forgive this. My loathing for her deepens once I learn that Julia is living virtually rent-free in a desirable flat off Portobello Road. Two outrageous queens own this flat, and—according to her—the deal is Julia irons their shirts, or possibly their dresses. I don't believe in this deal or the sexual orientation of this flat's owners. I do not say so.

And I? Well, I haven't actually made the commercial that's going to wing me to Hollywood yet—it's early days. I'm at my agency of choice. My job involves making tea and coffee, sorting the post, and being humble. As of this week, I have my first trial assignment: writing copy for a mail-order catalog. This catalog, aimed at the larger lady, features a thousand variations on the Crimplene tent dress. I've already learned that a maximum of fifteen words per sentence is standard for this kind of copy. Any sentence longer than twenty-five words is unacceptably Dickensian. Paragraphs longer than fifteen lines are offputting to larger ladies and everyone else, so I eschew them. I'm keen: I've been out on the streets doing my own market research. I stop larger ladies outside shops and ask them what they want from their clothes. These larger ladies are good fun. One suggests I come home with her and she'll show me. As a result of this research, my intro copy reads: "Ladies, want to feel comfy *and* look like a million dollars? Want to make men's pulses race? Also want a nice sensible flexi-waistband? Here's the answer. . . ."

I write to Finn once a week, and I telephone frequently, though it's difficult to call Finn. First, Nick and I still haven't acquired a tele-phone, a process that seems to take about three years and involves negotiations of labyrinthine complexity. Second, at Girton there's only one phone, near the porter's desk. So I have to call from a box, and it takes a pound of penny coins before Finn's fetched and can answer. The corridors at Girton are religiously long; Finn's answers are sibylline.

Meanwhile, working in the ad agency has taught me that it's not just larger ladies whose image needs an overhaul. Mine does, too. This image of mine has already gone through more adjustments than I care to remember. It's been Elvis; it's been Borstal escapee (blame the grammar school); it's been James Dean, complete with cigarette pack tucked into the rolled-up shirtsleeve—the acme of cool. It's been rocker and Jagger, it's been borderline hippie, or hip—I was never sure which. Now, given my salary, I'm aiming at eclectic, via Oxfam shops. Oxfam, I say, is where it's at.

When Stella calls me at work early in October and asks me to come to the hospital the next day as backup, I agree at once. Next I start planning what I'll wear. Yes, I know, I know, but youth can be trivia obsessed. Besides, this visit is key: Finn will be there, and I haven't seen her for weeks. And the Viper, who has been interfering and pulling strings and humiliating Stella from day one, is also going to be there. Stella fears what Violet calls a "conference" and she calls a "showdown." I can't wait to encounter Lady Violet, a woman I've detested at long range for years. I plan to slay this dragon in front of Finn, thus earning Finn's undying admiration. I plan what I'll say—and I dress accordingly. Do I look like St. George? Do I look chival-ric? Not exactly.

I turn up in a long Oxfam tweed overcoat made by a superior tailor. Under it, I'm wearing an Ossie Clark velvet jacket bought in King's Road, a jacket that cost two weeks' wages. The outfit's com-pleted by ripped jeans, an antique shirt, an embroidered waistcoat, and no tie. My hair, disheveled in a way that takes hours to achieve, brushes my collar.

I enter the hush of the coma ward. One glance at Maisie, and I'm ashamed of myself. The curtain that separates Maisie's bed from the other occupants is drawn. Finn is not there. Julia is. Stella is also there and is in a state of obvious distress. A woman who can only be the Viper is standing at the end of Maisie's bed. She's wearing a mink coat. And pearls. And impeccable tweeds. And shoes that whisper handmade. Her presence is formidable, and so is her voice. This accent—I thought it had died a righteous death.

Wrong. That accent and the attitude that goes with it are alive and well. For the first time in my sheltered life, I truly understand the meaning of the term *ruling class*. I'm ready to hate—and so is the Viper. As I make my appearance, she pauses and turns. Her ice blue gaze rests on me. It takes her one second to sweep that gaze over me from head to foot and less than one second for her to write me off. I don't think she knew who I was at that point—Stella, in her usual muddled way, hadn't warned her that Danny the Gypsy lad would be joining this conference. But Violet doesn't need to be told who I am; she can smell me out at a hundred yards, just as I can smell her. We are mortal enemies before a single word's been spoken. I see Violet register the fact that I've strayed in from the wrong side of the tracks, the wrong side of an eternal divide. This upstart shouldn't be here in her presence, but—since I am, since she's going to have to endure my weirdness and working-classness for a short while—it remains only to put me in my place.

The English upper classes are rude and insensitive—at least, that's been my experience. And Violet's rudeness is way up there on the winner's podium. As Stella begins on awkward, muddling introductions and explanations, all of which are resolutely ignored, Violet turns to me, inserts the tips of her still-gloved fingers very briefly between mine, removes them before any soiling can take place, averts her ice blue gaze, and, having cast me into the outer limits of invisibility, turns back to Stella, interrupts her, and says: "Stella, do let's get on. Pull yourself together. I've already spoken to Maisie's consultant. I'm not impressed. You should have brought my man in, but of course you wouldn't listen. Even so, the situation is clear. The prognosis is very poor. Now, Stella, are you going to accept that?"

You cunt, I think. You rich, mink-coated, unfeeling, unmitigated *cunt.* Stella's face is a mask of misery; she's flushed crimson, and her eyes have filled with tears. Julia, to her credit, I have to admit, intervenes fast, before I have a chance to do so. "Stella is in a rather better position to judge Maisie's situation than you are, Violet," she says. "Remind me, how many visits have you made?"

"I have made two. And two were sufficient."

"Please feel no obligation to make a third," Julia replies—and it's only then, it truly is only then, that I realize there's another woman present, a young woman, who was sitting down, invisible behind the Viper's sweeping mink, a young woman to whom Violet saw no need to introduce the peasant.

This young woman now rises to her feet. I see she's about nineteen or twenty. She has shoulder-length dark hair, held back by a velvet Alice band. She's wearing one of those piecrust-collared blouses that Julia scorns and a pink cardigan. She has a sweet, entirely unremarkable face and a gentle demeanor. Let's cut to the chase: virgin and 1950s-style debutante. "Violet," she says in a gentle voice, laying her hand on the mink, "please, we mustn't upset Stella. This is so frightfully hard for everyone."

And, astonishingly, this girl's intervention is far more successful in its effect than Julia's full-frontal attack. Violet pauses, then pats the gentle hand. "Yes, well, Veronica dear," she says, "you may be right. We should discuss this quietly, and this is not the place in which to do so. Forgive me, Stella. I always speak my mind, as you know. And the past two months haven't been easy for any of us."

There's then a flurry of activity, during which Violet persuades Stella to accompany her to a quiet room where the two of them can talk this through in private; during which Julia insists that she will accompany her mother—and overrides the Viper. Violet extracts me from the proceedings expertly; it's happened before I'm even aware of it.

The sweet-faced girl and I are left standing at the end of silent Maisie's bed. Maisie's eyes are closed; she may, or may not, be sleeping. The sweet-faced girl, coloring, holds out her hand and explains who she is. She is Veronica, bride-to-be of Edmund Mortland, Violet's grandson and heir. This gentle girl is staring at me, I realize, staring in a dazed, hypnotized way I've come to recognize and find tedious. Eventually, in an apologetic tone, she suggests that while the others talk we go downstairs and have a cup of tea in the hospital's singularly unpleasant and depressing cafeteria.

We navigate our way downstairs, through a hospital maze, to this cafeteria. "So what exactly is this conference about?" I ask Veronica as we sit down. "Why is it necessary?"

"Violet thinks—she feels the moment's approaching when—when a decision will have to be made." She hesitates. "Whether treatment should be withdrawn, in other words. I've tried to argue with her. I still hope Maisie will recover—it's terrible to see her like this. But Violet is so decisive. She sort of sweeps all before her."

I pass the sugar bowl to the child, who blushes again and refuses, and all the time I'm wondering why Violet should do this. This kind of intervention seems unwarranted, even for someone so viperous.

I offer Veronica a cigarette. She accepts one, and I light it for her. She's not a smoker; her nervous, inexperienced puffs betray that. She's accepted the cigarette, though, and I think I know why. *Silly little thing*, I think, and for no very good reason beyond boredom, and a lazy curiosity as to whether or not it will work, I switch on the charm. I've learned how to do that. Within five minutes, less, and in that unpropitious place, too, with its clatter of cups and smell of fatty food and stale cakes, I can see that the charm is working. Veronica is chattering away, her remarks punctuated by small darting glances in my direction, as if I were some exotic creature behind bars in a cage at a zoo, a creature that might prove charming and diverting or might prove stealthy and deadly.

She tells me that her marriage is to be moved forward; they had been going to wait until the spring, and a much bigger affair had originally been planned, but in the circumstances that seems inappropriate. The wedding will now take place quietly, in November.

I'm not interested in wedding plans. I'm miserable. I'm thinking about Finn and wondering why, having promised to attend this conference, she's not done so.

"I was disappointed at first," Veronica is saying. "But I can see Violet's right, of course. And, in a way, it's nicer for Edmund and me. We're going to Paris for our honeymoon, then Rome. I'm madly excited. I've never been to Rome."

"Have you known Edmund long?" I ask, surfacing.

"Forever. Edmund's older than I am . . . well, eight years, which is nothing, really. Violet and my grandmother are like that." She holds up two crossed fingers. "So I've always known him. But he's frightfully shy, and I am, too, so it took us a while to understand how we felt. Then Edmund had to get up the nerve to propose, of course. . . ."

This child's ingenuousness has a fascination of a kind. I can't believe this shining naïveté. "And how long did that take, Veronica?" I ask dryly.

"*Years.*" She blushes deeply. "I thought he might propose when I left boarding school, because he'd been so sweet to me when I first went there. It was such a ghastly dump, like a prison camp. Edmund knew how miserable I was, and he wrote and used to come down and take me out to lunch . . . and Granny said she was sure he was mad keen, and he was just waiting till I was older. But my birthdays came and went. When I was sixteen they whisked me off for two whole years to this horrible finishing school in Switzerland—and Edmund hardly ever wrote then, so I gave up hope. In fact, I'd met someone in Switzerland. I was quite fond of him, actually. . . ." She glances at me. "But nothing came of that in the end. When I came home, Granny said she and Violet were going to have a council of war. . . ."

My silence and inattention have finally registered. Veronica's story dwindles and stammers to a halt. She apologizes. She says she's sorry, she can see she's boring me. Only fifteen minutes have passed, but I can't take much more of this vacuity. The thought of Violet brow-beating Stella, even with Julia by her side, is making me uneasy. "Maybe I should go back upstairs," I say. "They must have finished this conference by now."

"Oh no, don't go yet," she says eagerly. "They won't have finished—you have no idea how Violet *talks*. Stella will be fine, Stella's actually quite tough, don't you think? She has Julia there, and Julia's super, isn't she? She's so beautiful. And clever. She makes me feel frightfully stupid and frumpy. . . ." She pauses. I say nothing. "Besides," she continues, blushing again, "it's not fair. I've told you all about myself—and I don't know anything about you. How do you know the Mortlands?" She hesitates. "Are you Julia's friend? I did wonder—I thought maybe—"

"Julia's friend? No. Not in any sense of the word. Rather the reverse."

"Do you live near Wykenfield? You sound . . . I wasn't sure. I thought you might be Irish."

"No. Born and bred in the village. My father's a farm laborer there. My grandmother is the cleaner at the Abbey. I've known Julia and Finn since we were children."

I'm wondering what the reaction will be, and it doesn't disappoint me. She takes several seconds to recover. "I'm sorry," she manages finally. "I didn't realize. I thought—you look, you sound . . . Your eyes are so dark, and your hair, too."

"I have Gypsy blood. My grandmother brought me up, and she's pure Romany. So you can cross my palm with silver, Veronica, and if you do, I'll read your fortune."

"Heavens—are you teasing me? I can't tell whether you are or not. Romany—are you truly? I don't believe you can tell fortunes. I don't believe in that kind of thing . . . not really. On the other hand, sometimes I do get a strange premonition about something. Or someone. . . . That can feel so unsettling." She darts a glance at me. "Has that ever happened to you, Dan?"

"Yes, it has happened to me," I reply solemnly. It's hard to keep a straight face, and I know I should stop it right there—she can't help her manner of speech; I bear her no particular ill will. Yet somehow the temptation to push it further, to see whether the laborer's son can overcome two years at a Swiss finishing school and an upbringing that will have taught her to distance herself from someone like me—the temptation's too strong. And the possibilities are too amusing. "You choose, Veronica," I continue. "I'll tell your fortune for you, but which method? Tarot, tea leaves, or palmistry?"

"Well, the tea's made with bags," she replies, smiling. "And I can't believe you carry a tarot pack round with you. Besides, those tarot cards are frightening. A girl at school got hold of some, and I *hated* them. So I suppose it will have to be the palm." And she holds out her sweet pink hand, with its large diamond-and-sapphire engagement ring.

"Will it take long?" she asks breathlessly.

"I very much doubt it," I answer.

And I make her change hands, because she's right-handed and that's the palm I need. I glance down at it. The *mons veneris* is soft and plump; the lifeline is long. I've read Veronica, and there's little this palm can tell me that I don't already know. I turn her hand sideways and examine its edge. I have scant faith in palmistry, but according to the marks below her little finger, Veronica will marry only once and have only one child.

"Well, well, well," I say, sighing. "Veronica, you have hidden depths. You surprise me."

I'm well tutored by Bella, and I know this approach is tried, tested, and virtually infallible. As a child, Bella watched Ocean employ it to great effect everywhere from Yorkshire to the racecourse at Epsom. With a woman, I've never known it to fail. I accompany the remark with a dark-eyed glance—a technique I've added to the repertoire.

I speak for some while. By the time I've finished, Veronica is pale and seems stricken. "I can't believe this," she says uncertainly. "I can't believe that you can know me so well. We've only just met, but it's as if you've known me for years. It's uncanny. I've never met anyone like you in my life. You're—extraordinary, Dan. Truly extraordinary."

"I'm working class," I reply. I'm irritated. "That may be extraordinary to you. To most people, it's only too workaday ordinary." This is too easy, I think; it's tiresome.

"That's not what I meant at all," she says with a quick flash of anger in her eyes that makes me like her marginally better. "Don't say that—it's horrid. I'm not a snob. I couldn't care less about class. Those days are over."

"You think so, do you, Veronica?"

"Yes, I do." She takes a deep breath. "I'd like us to be friends. You already know me better than most of my friends do, anyway. Here . . ." She takes a card from her handbag and scribbles on it. "That's my telephone number. I'm sharing with two girls from school, Victoria and Virginia—people call us the Three Vs! We have this adorable little cottage in Chelsea, just off the King's Road. I'd love you to come and have dinner with us. Say you will, Dan—it would be such fun.

You could bring your tarot cards—I wouldn't mind if you read them for me. I wouldn't feel frightened then, and . . ." She stops. She's seen the expression on my face.

"I don't do party tricks," I answer. "I'm not for hire. Sorry."

"I didn't mean it like that—why are you so touchy? Please, just take it. It can't do any harm. Look, just *take* it. You don't have to call if you don't want to."

I take the card from her. Her tone was insistent; her expression is offended, possibly sulky. I glance at the card, then tear it into small pieces and toss them into the ashtray. "Bad idea," I say. "Bad idea, Veronica. Trust me."

And that is the truth. She does not, of course, believe me.

Without further remark, she follows me out of the cafeteria and back through that hospital labyrinth. We return to Maisie's ward without a single word being exchanged. In the ward, we find Violet, and Stella, and a tight-faced, angry Julia.

"*There* you are, Veronica," Violet says as we enter. "I was wondering where on earth you were. In the *cafeteria*? Well, I hope you haven't been chattering away. I'm sure Mr., Mr.—I'm so sorry, I've forgotten your name—but I'm sure we're keeping you—"

"Daniel Nunn," I reply. "And on the contrary, I'm in no hurry to be anywhere."

Violet's ice blue gaze sweeps across my face once more. It's a brief scan, but I sense I'm now being committed to memory. She turns back to the bed, on which a silent Maisie is still lying, in the same position as before, eyes closed, and unmoving. Attached tubes pulse with nutrients and waste. A monitor is flickering.

"Stella, I will say this one last time," Violet begins. "Ask yourself: Do you wish to prolong this suffering? It's not only Maisie we have to consider. This whole affair has made Henry desperately ill. You're worn out, Stella—and if you continue like this, you'll have a breakdown. It's terrible for Julia and Finn. So a decision is going to have to be made, and by the end of the year at the latest, if not sooner, in my opinion. I know your inclination is always to put things off, but in this case, you can't. This situation is not going to improve. Maisie's condition is *degenerating*—and that is evident to all the doctors and nurses. It's painfully evident to everyone, Stella."

Maisie's eyes fly open. They open wide at exactly the moment Violet pronounces the word *degenerating*. They fix themselves upon Violet at the end of her bed. And that gaze, alert, fixed, and baleful, carries a strong charge—just as it does in Lucas's painting. It's this once familiar expression of Maisie's that Lucas caught in his portrait—I'd never realized that before. Even Violet, armored as she is in virtually impregnable self-esteem, is unequal to it. She steps back with a small nervous exclamation.

Slowly, and with great difficulty, Maisie turns her head on the pillow and looks directly at Stella. Her lips move. No sound emerges, but her lips do move. And then, in a way that makes my skin go cold, Maisie begins to move her right hand. She moves it jerkily, and she is impeded by the intravenous drip in her arm, but this movement could not possibly be dismissed as involuntary. She moves her hand, which is white skinned, bruised, and thin, across the white cotton bedspread, moves it an inch at a time. Her hand seems possessed of its own creeping volition, though an expression of intense concentration is visible in her face. Stella, leaning over the bed, appears transfixed. Maisie's hand inches crabwise toward her mother's, stops, inches again. With one last effort, Maisie manages to lift her fingers; they make a spidery progress across the back of her mother's hand and scrabble at it. Stella turns her palm upward, and Maisie's grip tightens. She makes a low growling sound in her throat. I could not have said with any certainty what that growl signified, but Stella was in no doubt as to its meaning.

"I'm here," she says. "Maisie, I'm *here*, darling. Oh, I knew you could hear us. I *knew* you'd recover. . . ." She gathers Maisie awkwardly in her arms, tears spilling down her face. "Julia," she says, "Dan. You saw that. You witnessed it. Quickly, go and fetch Sister, get the doctors, *now*—I want them to see this. . . ."

The nurses and various ranks of doctors duly arrive. During the ensuing melee, Violet departs, accompanied by a wordless Veronica. I move across to the bed, to kiss Maisie's forehead and wish her good-bye. I feel this moment is for Julia and Stella, not me—and, warned by Nick, I know such apparent progress does not rule out a relapse. I don't want to witness that or betray my fear of it to Stella.

As I bend over her, Maisie's eyes meet mine. She looks at me directly, a steely look, as if we were greeting each other for the first time, as if in my eyes Maisie saw someone she recognized as her co-conspirator or her familiar or her confederate. Something implacable in Maisie's expression shocks me. I realize I must be imagining it; even so, I step back sharply.

I walk out into the hospital corridor. Julia, to my surprise, follows me. "You don't learn, do you?" she says without preamble. "Thanks for all the help, Dan. Tea in the cafeteria—that poor girl looked as if she'd been struck by lightning. Leave Veronica alone. She's a sweet-natured child. She's an uneducated innocent. Tell yourself, just for once, that you have nothing to prove. You could break her with your little finger, and we both know it."

"For God's sake, what are you talking about?" I answer. "I was having a cup of tea—end of story. And dying of boredom, I might add. She's about to get married. She's been in a Swiss finishing school for two years—and she took two years to tell me about it. If you think that girl's remotely my type, you *really* don't know me. The sweetness alone would asphyxiate me."

"Good. She's been very kind to Stella, and I don't want to see her hurt. And I *do* know you, Dan. I see right through you. You can't resist conquests."

"No, you *don't* know me, Julia. You don't know the first fucking thing about me. I'm not thinking about Veronica. I'm thinking about Maisie. What's the matter with you? Not jealous, by any chance?"

"Get lost," she replies, and slams back into the ward. The doors swing shut behind her.

I start walking through that endless hushed maze of hospital corridors. Within minutes I've forgotten Julia's accusations: I'm thinking about Maisie, and the moment when her hand began to move, and how strange, how disconcerting, that moment was. It made Stella joyful; it should have made me joyful—and yet it didn't. There was something stealthy about that hand, moving so purposefully across the bedclothes. For no reason I could define, I was mesmerized by that hand, and I found it disturbing.

I finally find my way back to the hospital's main entrance and go outside; it's dusk. I can hear the rumble of London's traffic, the sound of sirens; an ambulance is pulling in, blue light flashing. From a wall, a shadow detaches itself, approaches, and tugs at my sleeve. I turn and, to my astonishment, find this shadow is Finn—a Finn I scarcely recognize.

"Dan?" she says. "I've been waiting and waiting. Where can we go? I must talk to you."

TWENTY-FIVE

Fin

I CAN'T SEE FINN PROPERLY—I realize that now, lying here featherbedded, not sure whether night's day, or tomorrow's yesterday. Time is displacing, and although that loop—Finn and I, standing there in the dusk, a blue light shining and flickering—is running and rerunning, I see her only in snatches. I see her pale face lifted to mine, her gloved hand on my sleeve, and the expression in her eyes, which is agitated, opaque, and distracted. I'm trying to understand how a few weeks, four (or is it five?) since I last saw her, could effect such a transformation. Finn has put on weight; her face looks swollen and pale, and I can see she's been crying. She's bundled into layers of drab woolly garments: a thick skirt to the ankles, a sweater that envelops her from neck to thighs, a loose woolly cardigan over that, and over everything else, a huge baggy tweed coat that she's hugging around herself; she's shivering violently.

I can't hear myself as I watch that loop, and I'm not sure what I was saying. I was trying to ask Finn what was wrong, I suppose. I was probably trying to understand why she hadn't come up to the ward, why she should wait for me here; and at some point, I think I must have tried to tell her about Maisie.

"No, no, no," she says, backing away. "I'm not going up there now. I can't face it. I can't bear to see it—all that hope on Stella's face.

Maisie isn't coming back, Dan—she's not coming back. You know that as well as I do."

"I promise you, Finn—this was different. There is a change. I saw it."

"How much of a change, Dan?" Her face flared at me, blue lit, out of the dusk. "Is Maisie going to walk again, talk again? You know she isn't. The damage is irreparable. Nick explained that to me—at the Abbey. I've been in the library, the university library—I've been there for days, reading all these medical textbooks, and—and some things are irreversible. That's what they are, *irreversible*. There's no changing them, there's no going back, or undoing or rewriting, Dan. That's it, forever and ever."

And she begins to cry. I can see those tears spilling from her eyes, blue tears in a blue light, and then her face is in shadow. She's plucking at my arm again. "Look, where can we go?" she's saying. "Somewhere we can talk. There must be somewhere—some little café, there's hundreds of cafés round here. You must know one."

I don't know one. I suggest we could go back into the hospital and talk in the cafeteria, but Finn shies away again when I suggest that. "No, no—not in there. I hate hospitals. All that hush, and death behind every door. And we might see Stella or Julia—was Julia there? I don't want to see either of them, not just now, not yet. Let's just walk, Dan—please, just walk with me. We'll find somewhere."

And we do find somewhere, in the maze of narrow adjacent streets: a Greek-Cypriot coffee bar. After the dusk outside, its fluorescent lights are dazzling. They throw blue skull shadows under Finn's eyes and drain her face of all color. We are the only customers. We sit at the back, in a warm fug of cooking smells and steam from the coffee machine. The noise of this machine, the clatter of cups and plates in some dishwasher, the soft conversations in a foreign tongue between the owner and his assistant: Well, for mine own part it was all Greek to me, and Finn and I were islanded. It was intimacy of a sort, the two of us, facing each other across a speckled red Formica-topped table. There was sugar in a dispenser and paper napkins; Finn began to fiddle with these objects, first the dispenser, then the scarlet napkins. She pleated them between her black-gloved fingers, scarlet and black, and when I couldn't bear to watch her do that anymore, I put my hand over hers and said, "Finn, tell me."

"I've done a terrible thing," she said. More tears spilled. "You'll never forgive me."

"Finn, there's nothing you could do that I wouldn't forgive. And forgiveness doesn't enter into it, you know that. Not for us. Now tell me."

"Do I look different?" She raises her eyes to my face. "Tell me what you see, Dan."

I hesitate. I can feel the premonition then, and it scares me so much that it's hard to speak. "You don't look well," I begin slowly. "You look desperately upset, Finn, and tired and pale—"

"Do I look stupid?" she asks, cutting me off. "Do I look stupid to you? Because that's what I am, Dan. Stupid, stupid, stupid. I thought I was clever once. Intelligent, anyway. That's what people told me. I had a brain, a good brain, and I was going to go to Cambridge, and they'd teach me how to use it. And I was so happy about that—it's the only thing I've ever wanted to do. Go there—and read, learn to *read* for three whole years. Imagine the luxury of that. Imagine the joy of that. Well, I've thrown that away—along with a few other things, my self-respect, not that that matters much, I can do without that. My sense of who I am—yes, that's gone, that's definitely got lost by the wayside. I don't know who I am, and . . . Dan, I'm sorry. I can't talk anymore. I can't think anymore, not the way I used to. My brain isn't working. It just goes round and round, like a rat in a trap. And it's making me selfish. I can't think about Maisie, not properly, or Stella, or Gramps. And I haven't been able to think about you, either, not the way I want to think—and that makes me feel so wicked and guilty—"

All of this spills from her very fast, and I'm trying to follow it and make sense of it, and trying to put her words and the expression in her eyes together, and I'm still sick with apprehension. There's one part of my mind that blocks all the others. It's thinking, *No, it can't be, she's not going to say that.* And then, awkwardly, struggling with the table, Finn stands up. She parts the folds of her coat. She lifts those layers of jumpers, and I see the thickened waistline, the curve of the stomach they've been hiding.

Do I say anything? I don't know. I think I bowed my head, because I can see red-speckled Formica, and I think I'm counting the speckles in it, seeing their patterns. A hand places two see-through plastic coffee cups in front of us, the coffee black, with an inch of brownish froth on it. Then Finn says, "Four months."

I can hear myself echoing that number, saying something like, *Four? No, it can't be four.* And then I'm trying to count back stupidly, and the number won't compute. All the months muddle, then settle, and I hear myself say: "Four—but that would mean . . . Finn? That's not possible. Early June? We were still in Cambridge then. It was before we came to the Abbey. How can that be? We were—I thought we were, I thought you were—"

"I know what you thought," she says quietly. "Dear Dan, my dearest Dan—I know what you thought, and I know how I've lied. I'm so sorry. Believe me, I'm so terribly sorry."

I look at her face, which I can't see properly, because the café is now blurred, indistinct, and muddly. I can feel that I'm trapped, and Finn's trapped. This encounter, this conversation has been scripted a million times. I know all the lines she could say, and I could say. I don't want to say any of them, though I can feel them rising to my lips. I don't want to storm out of that place, or interrogate her, or insult her, or plead, or weep, but I can see all those well-scripted routes, a great fistful of them. Which to go down? They're all pointless, humiliating, obvious, and inadequate.

"Does Lucas know?" I say finally. I can scarcely speak.

"Yes. He does."

"How long has he known? When did you tell him?"

"Two months ago. About two months ago. I had some tests—you know, they do these tests. And the results came back the day before Stella and I went to London. I told him after that—I can't remember when, not exactly, because of Maisie . . . you know."

"Who did the tests? You can't have had them done in Wykenfield. You didn't go to Dr. Marlow—not Nick's father, surely?"

"No. Obviously not. Lucas borrowed Gramps' car. He drove me over to Deepden. I had them done there. I made up some stupid story, gave them a false name, said I was just staying in the neighborhood, something like that. They didn't believe me, of course. But then they see it all the time. It's so predictable—that's one of the things I hate the most, how sordid and predictable it seems to other people. Dan, it was awful, they made me feel so dirty. I've never been so humiliated. . . . Well, I hadn't then. I have now. I'm getting used to humiliation now. Which is just as well, I suppose, because there'll be plenty more of it."

She gives a wry smile, her eyes still brimming with tears. She picks up the sugar dispenser and looks as if she can't imagine what it is, then shakes it, tips it, adds three doses of sugar to her cup. Finn doesn't take sugar in coffee, or didn't. Where was I that day? I'm thinking. The day Lucas drove her to a doctor at a discreet distance, where was I? Cleaning windows? Mending tractors? Counting out money to pensioners at the post office? How many hours Finn had in which to deceive me.

And then I ask the question. I have to ask it, no matter how stale and predictable it is, no matter how many other men in this situation have asked it before me. I'm trying to control my voice. I say: "Finn, just answer me this. I won't ask you again. Did you love me? Did you ever love me?"

"You know that I did." Fat tears spill down her cheeks, and her voice breaks. "Oh, Dan, you know that I did. In some ways, you're closer to me than anyone else, and you always will be. And I used to think—you know what I used to think. I couldn't imagine a time without you. You were my all-in-all, my everything." She hesitates. "Sun, moon, and stars, Dan. But, we *were* very young. And then— this happened."

"It's the women, isn't it," I say before I can stop myself. "Christ, Finn—you know very well that if you'd let me—just *once*, Finn. Just once, and I'd never have looked at a single one of them. I wouldn't have touched them. There weren't that many anyway, and none of them matters. I can hardly remember their names, or what they look like. I wanted them for half an hour, because I couldn't have you— and you know that." I stop. I've thought of Julia. Was that true of Julia?

"Maybe I do." She lowers her gaze. *She doesn't know*, I think—and I hate myself. "That's what I used to tell myself, anyway. Though that's what men always say—or so I hear. It was nothing to do with them, those girls, anyway. I woke up one day, and five and five made ten—and then the next day, they didn't. Sometimes they made nine, or a hundred. And I realized that's what people meant by falling in love. Not being able to add up, or think, or see. . . . What a pre- dictable conversation we're having. I hate it."

"Marry me, Finn," I say. And I lean across the table and take her gloved hands in mine, and force her to look at me, and I launch myself on that one and only proposal of my life. A hideous, inco- herent mess I make of it. All I could hear was Finn confirming she had loved me, and that was enough: I could rewrite this script, alter it the way I wanted. And it made such sense. If four months had gone by, Lucas must have left her in the lurch—and I couldn't imagine his doing otherwise. Lucas, and the pram in the hall? Lucas, trying to paint with a squalling infant? No, I couldn't imagine that, and I knew Finn wouldn't imagine it, either. She'd have no illusions about Lucas, even if she loved him: Finn, my Finn, was too clear-sighted.

I knew what Finn was facing as an unmarried mother. They didn't want *them* at Cambridge. A woman was sent down merely for having a man in her room overnight, whereas a man caught with a woman was gated for a few weeks. A double standard operated and always had. So Finn was facing certain expulsion and an uncertain, unsupported, unthinkable future. "*Marry me*, Finn," I say. I see myself moving to Cambridge, finding some kind of work there—who cares what, I'll clean windows if need be. Once married, Finn will be allowed to continue her degree course. Somehow, between the two of us, we'll manage to look after the baby. And I will love it, this child, this child of another man; I'll love him and rear him; I'll love and protect him and Finn. I know I can do it. Simple. Inevitable. Then I hesitate.

"Is it too late, Finn?" I say. I'm ashamed, but I do say it. "Four months is too late, isn't it."

"I think so," she replies, looking away. "It's illegal at any point. Though that doesn't matter. There are always kindly doctors who will help you out. I don't mean back street: I mean the works, a private clinic, everything. It costs one hundred and fifty pounds, I hear. You can be in and out in a day. So they'd probably do it at four months. I expect they'd do it at eight months, if you paid enough. But that's irrelevant. I don't want this baby killed or harmed. I love this baby, Dan. I want my baby."

She rests her hands across her stomach in a protective way, and I watch her face change: a dreamy determination in the eyes, a calm, female inwardness, a strange, fierce joy and concentration. It kills me, that look. I'd give anything to see that expression and to know it was my child she was carrying. Then I wonder who gave her this detailed information—and I know at once: Lucas, who found himself staring down a cul-de-sac and went for the cheapest, most obvious route—backing out of it.

I see my way clear then. "Marry me, Finn," I say. The love I feel for her is so deep, I feel it must speak to her. I talk on and on, convincing her, convincing myself, and it takes a long time for me to see that Finn has become quiet and still, that her pale face, blotched with tears, is set in an expression I know well, one of sadness and unshakable obstinacy.

"Finn, trust me, believe me. I *know* we could do this. It's all I want in the world."

"That's not true," Finn says quietly. "It *isn't* all you want in the world, Dan. Of course it isn't. And why should it be?"

"Finn, darling Finn, listen to me. I love you. I know I could do this."

"But I couldn't. Not to you, Dan. And anyway, it's impossible."

"Don't say that. It isn't. Finn, it *isn't.*"

"It is. I'm already married."

I stare at her. "I married Lucas yesterday," she continues in a flat voice. "In the register office at Cambridge." She frowns. "It wasn't much of a ceremony. There were plastic flowers—I minded about them. They were hideous. There were hundreds of stupid forms to fill in—who your father was, what he did. When I said mine was dead, the registrar, he was this small fat man, with glasses, in a suit that was too tight for him—he said, I'm sincerely sorry to hear that. And I thought, What a stupid thing to say. Why would he care? Why even pretend to care? But there you are, we had to go through all the formalities, and I suppose that was just part of them. It took twenty minutes. I timed it. Anyway, it's done now. Look."

She removes her gloves. And there on the third finger of her left hand is a wedding ring of sorts. It looks dull and brassy. It's too large for her. It looks like a curtain ring. Knowing Lucas, it probably *is* a curtain ring.

I'd have sold my soul to buy Finn gold, diamonds, rubies, whatever she wanted. If she'd wanted St. Paul's Cathedral for her wedding, I'd have moved heaven and earth to get it for her. But Lucas, of course, would have viewed the matter very differently. Lucas had always been contemptuous of ceremonies and traditions and bourgeois tokens—wedding rings, marriage, till death do us part, for instance.

It was called Georgio's, that café. It's still there. I pass it from time to time. I never enter it. I never look in the window to see if there's another couple in there, this afternoon, this morning, having a similar, or happier, conversation. I cross the street and avert my eyes. I'm good at that. I've perfected the art of ignoring the painful.

But lying here, in this place where two decades are two seconds, and ten years ago is yesterday, the painful won't drift away as it usually does; it comes looping around with an insistence I can't control. And it makes me watch what I did next, after I'd taken Finn back to King's Cross and watched the lights of her Cambridge train disappear into darkness. Lucas would meet her at the other end, she'd said. When he left the Abbey, Lucas had taken rooms in Green Street, not far from our old college. I imagined them going to those rooms. I envisaged them there, together.

Then I walk; that's what I do. I don't know where I walk, or for how long, but miles and for a long time; it's late when, on some street corner, I finally stop outside a telephone box. I can palm coins; I can read palms; I have a facility for such tricks—and for remembering numbers also. So I step into the box and dial the number of a little cottage off King's Road in Chelsea. I'm hurting: I want to punish Finn and the world and Lucas and myself. Meanwhile, I'll punish anything and anyone else that comes within range, especially when Julia has put the idea into my head, and especially when Julia, of all women, has warned me against precisely this course of action.

I hear the lift in sweet Veronica's voice when she realizes who's telephoning; then I hear the hesitation. All alone on a Saturday night; that trinity of Vs has split up. The two schoolfriends have gone home to their country-living parents for the weekend; all alone, and it is late. Why, she was about to go to bed; it's eleven-thirty.

"Now or not at all," I hear myself say. "You've got one minute to make your mind up."

It takes her thirty seconds. Half an hour later, I'm in Chelsea, outside a former laborer's cottage; it's been prettified. Inside—not that I really see the inside, I'm blind to it—inside, I'm vaguely aware of girlish chintzes, and silver photograph frames, and tapestry cushions; too many tapestry cushions, cushions with trite little sayings embroidered on them. A bottle of Blue Nun wine has been opened in my honor; candles have been lit; Veronica's used that half hour to put on a pretty pink dress, to apply pink lipstick, to brush her shining hair, and to spray scent on her pulse points.

It's October, and the room reeks of spring flowers; it's choking, that scent. One hour later we're in bed. Half an hour later and Veronica's lost her virginity.

A simple seduction, like taking candy from a baby. There's a certain savage pleasure in that, I discover—and I discover, too, that there's a new Dan inside me, one whose heart is easily hardened. He can ignore female tears, jealousy, and reproaches, though they anger him; he learns that the more women like Veronica are ignored or slighted, the more eager they are for similar punishment. *Where have you been, Dan? Why didn't you call? Who were you with? There's someone else, isn't there? Tell me you love me—why won't you ever say it?* I detest this weakness and masochism, but I'm prepared to exploit it.

The affair continues, messily and intermittently, for another six weeks. I break with her, finally, two days before her wedding that November. It's easy to forget her; there are plenty of women eager enough to take her place. Besides, I'm busy. I'm busy forgetting Finn; busy climbing the success ladder; I'm busy at work; I'm busy running all over London, engaged in that quintessential late sixties task: finding out where it's at and making sure I'm there at the heart of it.

Where it's at: That's the phrase we all use. A restaurant, a street, a person, a shop, a party—they can all be where it's at, and the weird thing is, you're no sooner there, right at the epicenter, than, hey presto, where it's at has moved on. It's someplace else, and you have to run hard to keep up with it or—secret ambition of everyone—be ahead of it. Christ, you'd think—what's happened? Where it's at was here yesterday, it was here this morning—but it can't be here now, not at this party, surely, not when these same where-it's-at people are driving me crazy, so I can't wait to escape and just walk home and be silent and breathe air again. Where it's at has moved on—that's what it always does. Where's it gone *now*, I'd think, and how do I get there quickly? On the q.v. twenty-four hours a day, seven days a week. It's exhausting. And numbing.

And then, one summer's day, I'm walking down King's Road after a celebratory lunch at a where-it's-at Italian restaurant. I think it's the following summer. Yes, it must be then, because by then, and somewhere in the haze that's now my daily existence, Gramps has died, and Finn's baby has been stillborn at seven months, and the rumor is that she and Lucas are unhappy, though still living together. I don't know if the rumors are true: Finn won't see me or answer my letters. Yes, it must be then, because Maisie has finally been moved to that care home where she remains to this day, that care home where nuns look after her with quiet fortitude and patience. Maisie's condition has improved—to an extent. She can now feed herself, with assistance. She can walk a little, with assistance, but spends most of her days in a wheelchair. She cannot speak or communicate in any way—and it's now clear that, barring a true miracle, she will never do so.

Yes, it's the following August, the dog days of summer, about ten months later, and I've just clinched my first major campaign, I've been celebrating at a client lunch: I've drunk two cocktails and half a bottle of Soave. There's a spring in my step: I'm in that kindest of all states, neither drunk nor sober, and I'm on my way back to work when, in Sloane Square, outside Peter Jones department store—where else; I imagine her haunting it—I bump into a young matron who says: *Dan, don't you recognize me, it's Veronica.*

"That's wonderful news, Dan," she says warmly when I tell her about the major campaign—which I do at once. "I'm so pleased for you. I'm up from Elde for a day or two to do some shopping." She pauses. "I'm staying at Violet's place. It's just around the corner. Why don't we go there and have a drink and celebrate?"

I find myself in Violet's Eaton Square outpost. Its drinks cupboard contains excellent brandy. There's chintz in the drawing room and chintz in Veronica's bedroom.

What happened to that sweet-faced girl? I wonder as I go through the preliminaries. This young matron is too brisk, too knowing, and too insistent. I can't bear the dress she's wearing or her scent. I can't bear the tension in her body. "Look, sorry," I say, rolling off her. "I must have drunk too much at lunch. Let's forget it, shall we?"

Then she does an appalling thing. She stands up and smooths down her skirt. "Shall I tell you what I'm wearing?" she says, smiling at me in a knowing way. "White knickers. Clean ones. Clean white panties. I put them on this morning. You're not allowed to touch, but I'll let you look, if you like. If you're good. If you're very, very good. Watch, Dan. Look closely."

Before I can stop her, she lifts the hem of her dress in a coy peek-aboo way that makes my skin crawl with embarrassment. And there are the white panties, with a revealing panel of lace; they do nothing for me. I can see she's shaved off her pubic hair; that does nothing for me, either.

"Veronica," I say, "this really isn't my thing. I'm not into games or role-play or whatever the hell this is. . . . Can you stop this?"

"Oh, all right," she replies. She looks at me in a curious blank-faced way. "What *do* you like, Dan? Ah, I remember now. . . ."

And then she begins to touch me and to do things to me that indeed I do like, and I find that if I lie back and close my eyes, I can wipe her, wipe her completely. I can smell the cool blue scent and hear the chime of bracelets that always makes me hard. It's easy then. I fuck her, and it's okay—average, but okay—and when I come, I think *at last*. Then I wait. The postcoital wash of distaste never takes long to arrive, and this time it's immediate. I look at a blank-faced Veronica lying back on the bed, and I can't see that sweet-faced girl at all. I think, Did marriage do this to her? Or am I responsible?

The nostalgia fuck: They're the worst; they're to be avoided. The fuck for old times' sake—there's nothing as bad or sad. Never again, I tell myself. All I can think about is the minimum number of lies that will ensure a fast exit.

To my surprise, it's easy. No reproaches this time, no pleas to call her: Veronica has achieved her objective, it seems. She's as anxious to get me out of the house as I am to leave it.

I never see her again or hear from her. I erase both her and the incident from my mind. My memory's already learning how to be forgiving. I haven't thought of her, or that last brief encounter, in years—twenty years, probably. But I'm not going to be spared shames down here in this netherworld. Next up, it's Bella, dwindling away on a tide of Alzheimer ramblings; it's Bella and all the excuses I make not to come here to visit her. It's me on the phone to Joe, spilling poison into his ear, taking a high-handed line, and saying: Look, Dad, I'm sorry, but I can't just drop everything. Gran doesn't even know who I am—what difference can it possibly make? . . . I know. I know. . . . Look, Dad, I *know*, all right? It's hard for you, and I'll get down as soon as I can, but it won't be this month. . . . What? . . . Well, I can't help that: I'm in Milan tomorrow and New York next week, and when I get back I've got meetings wall-to-wall. . . . What? . . . What? . . . Oh, very well, I'll try to get down in a couple of weeks, but I've got a big client meeting coming up, and umpteen presentations, so I can't promise anything. . . .

Next up: Family Christmas, the family Christmas I couldn't avoid, because Gran's dead, and Joe's alone, and so I agree to come and arrive late, and *shit*, I've only been in the house ten seconds and I can see all the trouble he's gone to. There are paper chains hanging from the kitchen beams and fake snow on the windows and a clean cloth on the table and a Christmas tree in the corner with a pile of ill-wrapped bulgy presents under it. And there's a huge turkey—there's only the two of us, and it would feed twenty without difficulty—crammed in the oven, and Joe's telling me that he's getting on quite well with the cooking now, and Flora McIver's told him how to cope with the festive bird, and—look—he's got it all written down. Four and a half hours on a medium setting.

And it takes about ten hours for the blasted bird to cook, and Joe won't sit still and keeps jumping up and down, tipping more coke in the stove, and consulting his notes, and saying, *I don't understand this, Danny, that bugger should be done by now.*

And I'm sitting there, staring at the presents I brought, now under the tree, in all their Bond Street elegance. Who applied this expensive paper, these bows, these ribbons? Not me. Some girl in a store did it—and I never went near that store. Me, troll around the shops in December? I don't think so. I sent out the junior PA with a list, and she took care of it. What's in those parcels? Things Joe doesn't want or need: Jermyn Street shirts, cashmere socks, a calendar, a book of *Giles* cartoons, a silk tie, a soft leather wallet, and one of those male toys, an upmarket adult version of a boy's Swiss Army knife—a neat, ingenious tool that will open bottles, undo screws, cut wire, and God knows what else. Why did I get these things? Why did I get the car, which is garaged in one of the McIver barns and which I suspect has never been driven, though Joe loyally sings her praises and says she's a right little beauty. Why did I get any of these things? Because I'm guilty, so guilty that I'm already on my third Scotch, and these are my guilt offerings. Sorry, Joe, for letting you down, for never being here, for not knowing how to talk to you when I am here. Sorry for the boasting, and the lies, sorry I'm not the son you should have had. *Sorry, Joe—here's a handmade shirt. Does that make up for things?*

And then, finally, close on nine p.m. and only five hours late, we can sit down and eat that turkey. It's tough. It's dry. I force it down. I eat the turkey and the wet sprouts and the soggy spuds and the Bisto gravy, then we pull the crackers and put on the party hats, and Joe takes ten minutes to read the jokes, which are crap jokes anyway. And then we light the brandy and admire the Christmas pudding, and then Joe pours out a glass of something unbearably sweet and lifts a glass, and I know what's coming. "Absent friends, Danny," he says. Absent friends, I croak, and I can see the tears he's blinking back, and *I hate to see a grown man cry*, I can't stand it, I can't *deal* with it.

Then it's the presents, and Joe will say something like, *That's a fine shirt, Danny, and no mistake. I'll be keeping that for best, don't you worry.* And I know it'll go straight in a drawer, with mothballs, and never be seen again, until I next visit, when Joe will loyally take it out and wear it. And I, meanwhile, I'll be opening my lumpy parcels, wrapped with love, bought with love, after hours of fretting and list making and window-shopping. And I can act as well as Joe, so I'll say, *Hey, these gloves are great, Dad—where did you find them? How did you guess? They're just what I need.* When I never wear gloves and I've got five unused pairs already.

Oh, the pain of it all, the love and the guilt inextricably entwined. And the worst moment of all, when, paper hatted, we sit having what Joe calls a quiet smoke and a wind-down before we tackle a mountain of plates and pans that will take three hours to wash, because there's no hot water, so it all has to be boiled, kettle after kettle, and Joe won't let me buy him a nice cottage, with hot water on tap and these things, Dad, that are called radiators. Yes, we're having that quiet smoke and wind-down, and then Joe says, in a gentle, anxious way: *It'll be a fine day, tomorrow, Danny. Dry and sunny. I thought we might go for a walk, maybe? The McIvers would like to see you, I know. Then a nice bit of lunch . . .* And I'm half-tanked, my eyes slide away, and I'm saying, *Dad, didn't I explain? I can't stay. I have to get back, I really have to get back to London. . . .*

And Joe won't reproach me. He'll sit there opposite me, his huge, capable hands clasped in his lap and that expression on his face, slightly bewildered, as if something's happening here, something wrong and unnatural that he can't understand. I can see the wound in his steady gaze, and I know what he's thinking. He's thinking that *he* failed *me*—when this man has never failed anyone in his entire life, least of all that prize shit of a son of his, Danny.

Dad, I love you, all right, I say. But I don't think I said that then. I think I'm saying it now, too late as usual, too little and too late as usual, lying here in that bed we once shared and in which I now lie alone, loneliness eating up my heart, a black crow of misery eating up my heart, because you can't go back, you can't alter it. *Forgive me, Father, for I have sinned.*

Only one life, and some things in that life, as Finn said, are *irreversible.*

Yes: It all floats up out of this Xanadu dream, which has become—
as I should have foreseen, why can't I foresee anything; so much for
my Gift—a Xanadu nightmare.

It loops and reloops, Joe wearing a paper crown; a blank-faced
Veronica; their ghosts are here to reproach me, along with Finn in
her drab black clothes, in a café with red Formica tables; and Maisie
in her hospital bed, her thin hand snaking across the bedspread. All
those hands: Joe's strong, square ones, hardened and callused from
decades of physical work; Maisie's bruised hand; Veronica's soft palm,
with its faint marriage line; Finn's thin hand, emerging from a
shabby glove, and her wedding finger with Lucas's brassy curtain
ring on it.

I've had enough of Xanadu. Christ, let me get out of this place.
Then a cool hand touches my temple, and a voice, it's that woman
doctor's voice, says, *I think we've turned the corner. Pulse rate back to normal. And the temperature's dropping.*

PART VIII

Nine of Wands

I was once told by a relative of mine, that having in her childhood fallen into a river, and being on the very verge of death but for the critical assistance which reached her, she saw in a moment her whole life, in its minutest incidents, arrayed before her simultaneously as in a mirror; and she had a faculty developed . . . for understanding and comprehending the whole and every part. This, from some opium experiences of mine, I can believe; I have, indeed, seen the same thing asserted twice in modern books, and accompanied by a remark which I am convinced is true; viz. that the dread book of account, which the Scriptures speak of, is, in fact, the mind itself of each individual.

Of this, at least, I feel assured, that there is no such thing as *forgetting* possible to the mind; a thousand accidents may, and will, interpose a veil between our present consciousness and the secret inscriptions on the mind; accidents of the same sort will also rend away this veil; but alike, whether veiled or unveiled, the inscription remains forever. . . .

—Thomas De Quincey, *Confessions of an English Opium Eater*, 1822

The last of the Sisters were reluctant to leave the Abbey, I am told; it was so remote a place that they obstinately believed they might continue here, unobserved and unregarded. . . . But news reaching them, first, of the departure of the monks from Deepden, and then of the failure of the Pilgrimage of Grace, so many executed and that man of peace, Robert Aske, hung in chains from a church tower until he died of thirst and starvation . . . they made the decision to leave. And a sad departure it was, I am earnestly informed, many of the nuns having lived here sixty years or more, and all of them in as frail and fearful a state as may be imagined. These events are described to me with the utmost vividness as if they happened but yesterday; my witnesses wink at the fact that it was their great-great-grandsires that demolished much of the Abbey, using its stones to prop up their byres and repair their humble cotts: an admirable husbandry. . . . Venturing that way, this evening, I encountered an irreligious pig: he was disporting himself in the nuns' former chapter house. But he was a fine pig for all that, and I look forward to sampling his rashers.

—William Naismith, *Recollections of a Suffolk Rectory*, 1818

TWENTY-SIX

Honest Ghosts

I'M SHARING THIS COTTAGE.

I discover this when I start surfacing from Xanadu and find myself on that road the McIvers call the "road to recovery." I already know that, I think: I'm sharing this cottage with my ghosts, with Joe and Bella, with that long line of my ancestors—but these aren't the companions Flora McIver is referring to when, three times a day, she brings over the food that is going to "set me on my feet again." No, it's rodents who are sharing this house. What I have, it seems, is an infestation of wee mousies.

Whenever she comes over with Scotch broth, or porridge, which you can't beat for setting a man up, or a hot pot so good that I eat all of it (*Now that'll make a new man of you*), Flora checks on these insolent, shameless creatures. At first, she thinks they're confined to the kitchen, where they've eaten a pot of raspberry jam she made for Joe, chewing through its waxed-paper cover, consuming the raspberries, and spitting out the seeds on the larder shelves: the cheek of it. Then, no, they've invaded the bedrooms, too, and they've had a good gnaw at Joe's slippers, the ones I gave him last Christmas, his last Christmas—*and such a fine pair of slippers, too, Danny.*

Day six of Xanadu, and Flora takes action. She comes armed with traps, which she baits with cheese and chocolate. In her experience, which is considerable, mice prefer Cadbury's Dairy Milk to Cheddar. They also have a weakness for Wunderbar.

I don't want these small companions put paid to. Call me sentimental, but I feel for these mice. Joe must have tolerated them. I don't want their necks broken.

I wait until Flora's departed, then ease myself off the feather mattress and slip my feet into Joe's nibbled slippers. A perfect fit, which surprises me. What's more, a combination of those shots and Flora's broth has done some good. Six days have passed, and I can now stand—even walk, I discover, walk well enough to totter round the cottage and spring all the traps. I hide the chocolate and cheese, evidence of my perfidy.

Returning, unsteady but determined, in the dead of night to my bedroom, I meet one of the intrepid mice. It's sitting on the end of my bed, grooming its whiskers. It's a wood mouse—*Apodemus sylvaticus,* I hear Maisie whisper: smaller than the house mouse, browner in color. *Wee, sleekit, cow'rin', tim'rous beastie, / O, what a panic's in thy breastie!* It has a sensitive pointed snout, pink-palmed paws, large, darkly bright eyes, and quivering, silky whiskers. My heart goes out to this mouse. We inspect each other. It whisks off the bed and disappears beneath the gappy floorboards—indestructible elm boards, as also used for coffins once upon a time, worn and ancient.

I kneel down and feel around for the loose board under which my childhood treasure trove was hidden. I find the board, lever it up—and the hoard's still there, I discover. I adjust the dim bedside lamp and explore the dark cavity. The wee mousies have had a fine time. They've been nesting down here; they've been *breeding* down here. Fourteen-year-old Finn's letters to me—they've made a good nest. The photographs, too, those small Box Brownie pictures Finn took one year, they've lined the nest softly. Even the picture, the only picture, I had of

Dorrie—a blurry sepia smile in a prewar summer—that's been munched, too. I find I can accept this. Torn, chewed, and pulped, they've served a useful purpose. I can let them go now, and do so without regret, even—how curious this is—without heartache.

I feel around in the dark, pungent space. I can feel something hard, which proves to be a hazelnut. Finally, my searching fingers close over the one object of no use to nesting mice. I draw it out and inspect it. It's a small, tinny charm, pressed into my four-year-old palm by my dying great-grandmother Ocean. It's old and worn; its talismanic signs, guaranteed to protect against evil, are indecipherable. I put it in the pocket of Joe's pajamas. I don't possess pajamas, but in this cold house you need them. Joe and I were the same height, so these fit, though I'm still anorexic thin and they're loose on me. *Let's get you decent,* Flora said, handing them to me.

I climb back into bed. I've left the curtains open. There's a moon, a bright moon, shining. There are icicles hanging from the guttering; they glitter like a promise. I lie back and begin on an ancient task, one familiar from my earliest childhood: extracting the feathers from this mattress, the feathers that poke out through the worn cover and scratch at you. Here's a duck's feather, here's a swan's, here's swansdown. I'm asleep in moments.

When I wake to the new day, I don't have to piss in the chamber pot, thank God. I'm strong enough, and steady enough, to make it outside to the privy in the garden. There's a hoar frost; each plant, each bush, each branch, each tree, is etched white against a clear, cold blue sky. The world, new made overnight, is both beautiful and silent.

I feel an absolute calm. Returning to the house, standing in the kitchen doorway, my breath visible, I watch a sparrow pecking at the frosted cabbages and sprout stalks, vegetables Joe planted his last summer, a few weeks before his disease truly took hold and set upon its slow and remorseless process of destruction.

I close the door. The readiness is all. My way is now clear: I'll go to the Abbey as soon as I'm strong enough.

The woman doctor gives me the thumbs-up two days later. There's no surgery in Wykenfield now, so she's had to drive all the way from the group practice in Deepden. A kind action—but then, she is kind, this woman. She and her partners were good to Joe, last year; good to me, too. Today, she gives me one last shot—in the arm. She listens to my chest, checks my pulse and temperature.

Right, she says. *You'll do. You won't be needing me anymore.*

There's then a pause. She replaces her stethoscope in her bag. She looks at me. She's about thirty-five, I'd say: an attractive and unmarried professional. There are certain occasions when she's looked at me in a speculative way that I find familiar. I'm her patient, however; there is the question of ethics—apart from other questions such as: What woman needs a walking, talking liability? Today, I sense she might feel I'm less of a liability than I was. She considers this, and I watch her doing so. Then she picks up her bag and briskly bids me good-bye. When she's halfway down the path, I call after her.

What was in those shots? I ask.

"An antibiotic," she replies, briskly again. "Latterly, some vitamins: high-dosage vitamin C and B$_{12}$. I swear by it."

I set off for the Abbey on my interrupted task. I'm carrying a spade and a Sainsbury's plastic bag inside which is the box with Joe in it. I know where he wants to lie now.

It's one of those winter days that Joe used to call "soft." It's not cold, there's no wind, and in a high, pale sky a blurred sun is shining. The ground is damp underfoot, the night frost on the grass is melting; as I walk up Acre Lane, I see a rivulet of white in the ditches either side. The snowdrops are out; in another few weeks, unless the weather turns cold again, the primroses will be blooming.

I go through the gate at the top of the lane and turn toward the bare trees of Nun Wood. Here, on the edge of the wood, where the bracken grows tall in summer, is a clearing where Joe wooed my mother. "Courted" was the word Joe used. I like that term, antique, long discontinued. I prefer it to its modern equivalents, to the language used now in this modern porno world. Courtship: nothing blatant or coarse. It's gentle; it implies quest and dedication.

The spade slices into the soft soil. It slices through the rhizomes of the bracken. My strength is returning. I bury Joe's box one foot down and say the words I've planned. It's quiet here: no ghosts. It's peaceful. There's a thin, whitish vapor rising from the frosted grass where the sun warms it. Through this mist, and at the edge of the trees, I can glimpse a still, watchful shape; when the shape moves, I realize it's a deer. It steals silently away, there and then vanished. I know he will rest well here, my father.

I pick up the Sainsbury's plastic bag and take from it the other object I've brought with me, my Chinese ivory sphere. I leave the spade by the gate for collection on my return and begin walking up the gravel path, now narrowed and overgrown, that leads past the refectory.

I stop and look down across the valley. The village has grown: ribbon development. These ribbons, composed of new houses, most of them bungalows for retirees or starter homes for young families, now stretch along all the approaching roads to Wykenfield. The largest development, at Orchard Close, has been built where the Doggett brothers once cherished their apple trees. That name is their only memorial. None of the occupants of these new houses works in the village; there *is* no work in the village. The McIver farm, once four hundred acres, employed twenty men in Joe's youth. The farm's now grown to one thousand acres, and it employs two. Students, paid punitive wages, supplement them at harvest time, picking the summer vegetable crops that Hector, under punitive contract, grows for one of the big supermarkets.

When Angus McIver first came south, in the depths of the agricultural depression, escaping the land starvation in Scotland, where twenty-thousand-acre shooting estates owned by English grandees were commonplace and it was impossible for a small farmer to increase his holding or make a living, he looked at the potential richness of these then neglected fields in disbelief. The old boys down at the pub, satiric yokels who included my grandfather, were waiting for him to fail. They'd buy him a pint, make a few sly jokes about the invasion of Scotsmen here in Suffolk, then they'd tell him just how killing, how man-breaking, this land was: the heaviness of the boulder clay, the droughts in summer, the flints that blunted the plow, the need for costly drainage schemes. Meeting their mocking gaze with his steady blue Presbyterian eye, Angus informed them that he could deal with flints and heavy soil: Where he came from they plowed up boulders of granite.

Now, Hector tells me, a farm of one thousand acres is scarcely viable. It's too small; the overheads are too high; the grants, involving night after night of paperwork, are insufficient. He's thinking of following the latest trend: selling out entirely or renting the land to a management syndicate. There's a new syndicate that now manages all the land from here to Deepden except his, and a good four thousand acres beyond that. They understand concepts foreign to him, such as taking productive land, high-yield land, and using it for set-aside. There's going to be big grant money in letting fields lie idle.

A policy reverse. Change of faith. A reformation. Having laid out trillions to subsidize unnecessary food mountains, they're now to be abandoned. I look toward Deepden; it's somewhere over there, beyond the blue, bowled, pale horizon. At night you can see the lights from the American air base staining the sky. *Could you do that?* I'd asked Hector. *Maybe so, maybe so,* he answered.

Father and son; dark prairies; five decades of toil, of stubborn faith in yields and chemicals. Where there were once cattle, sheep, and pigs, there's now not an animal in sight. Fewer birds sing. I turn away from the valley of my childhood and begin walking toward the Abbey.

I cross the old moat ditch on a plank that looks as if it's been recently replaced, go through the archway, and pause in the courtyard. The refectory is padlocked and shuttered, but sound. The roof is intact; the guttering looks well maintained—and that surprises me. Hadn't Joe said this place was going to rack and ruin? Then I smell woodsmoke. I look up, and once again I see hallucinatory smoke coming from the Abbey chimneys.

I pass my hand over my eyes. I thought I was healed, over the illness—yet I'm seeing the invisible, conjuring the nonexistent. I look again. The smoke is still there, curling up into the pale sky—I haven't imagined it.

I'm cautious in my approach then. Someone—Julia, perhaps, since she's the only candidate with enough money—must have decided to take this place in hand. Maybe repairs are being done, with a view to selling the Abbey. It's been empty and unused for so long. Maybe Julia has decided, and Finn agreed, that it's a liability. Maybe there are workmen here, though if so, it seems odd that neither Flora nor Hector McIver mentioned it. Maybe a replacement for Bella has been found, and the Abbey has a new guardian who goes in from time to time to warm the place and air it; to dust the tables and shake out the covers on the fat armchairs; to polish the silver photograph frames, as Bella did, and wax those hulking "good pieces" of furniture that came from Elde Hall, those relics of Gramps's privileged childhood.

I make my way between the yew hedges—they haven't been cut back. There's no evidence of any work here, and the path is so narrow that it's almost impassable. I push my way between the yews and find myself on the edge of the cloister. I can see that the door into the chessboard hall is wide open. I can't hear any voices, though; there's no evidence of men at work. I make my way quietly round the east end of the house, keeping close to the walls and out of sight of the windows. I intend to replace the ivory sphere in the Lady Chapel, in its rightful position alongside its fellows. I feel I should do this now; this will be my last visit to the Abbey. In the old pantry off the scullery, there was one window that never latched properly, and I feel certain I'll get in easily enough by this means or some other. But when I reach the back of the house, looking out over the wilderness of weeds that was once Joe's orderly and prolific kitchen garden—I'm glad I didn't take him there—I find that subterfuge is unnecessary. I try the back door. I turn the handle of the back door. The back door opens immediately and silently.

I stand there, listening. I can hear no voices, no footfalls, no sounds of human presence.

But in the stillness of the house, I can hear that multitude of other sounds, the shifting and creaking of old timbers, the scurrying of mice behind wainscot, the breathing and movement of an aged building. Listening carefully, I find I can hear the sighs of those inhabitants Maisie befriended, those men and women who will never leave here.

It's an illusion: I know that. Even so, as I stand there, I feel the rush of the past, of prayers repeated and repeated, day after day, century after century; I can half hear, almost hear, the whispers of those families who lived here after the nuns left, the whispering tides of their births, deaths, and marriages. I can hear Stella, at the piano, faltering her way through *Für Elise,* the sad cadence drifting down the stairs to me. I can hear Gramps saying to me, *Look at this wine I've found, Dan. I thought this had all been finished up years ago, but there's one bottle left, hiding away for an evening like this. A fine vintage, a historic vintage, let's take it up and we'll all drink it tonight, shall we?*

I can hear myself, standing at the kitchen door, saying, *Please, ma'am, Joe says would I bring you these?* And Stella, exclaiming in delight at the new potatoes, saying, *How lovely—aren't they beautiful? You must be Danny. Come in, Danny, we're just about to have tea; you must have tea with us. Now, let me introduce you. This is my daughter Julia, and this is Finn, and this is the baby of the family, Maisie.*

I can feel the force of my stare, over thirty years later. No one had ever told me that potatoes could be beautiful. It had never occurred to me that these three girls, whom I've already pursued for months, alive with curiosity, peeping out at them from trees and hedges, spying on them in the church, even in the house, wondering if they will be my friends, as I'd so often imagined—it's never occurred to me how powerful they might be: not until I'm face-to-face with the sisters in triplicate, three identical blue stares meeting mine. Are they assessing me, dismissing me, accepting or judging me? I cannot tell.

I can't read them. Can they read me? I wonder.

I pass my hand over my face. The boy vanishes. The sisters vanish. The past is making me dizzy.

Which of seven staircases to take? One for each day of the week. I start climbing the main staircase, the one that will lead me directly upstairs to the library, the Lady Chapel. I stop dead halfway up, and my skin goes cold. I am not alone in the house. I am not alone in this house. I can hear footsteps in the library; I can hear footsteps, pacing back and forth, light footsteps, like those of a woman or a child—and for one cold moment, I think, *It's Maisie.*

I hesitate, then, calming myself, telling myself it's more likely to be a visiting housekeeper than a visiting ghost, I turn onto a side land-ing. Silently, I begin to climb the stairs that branch off it. I climb them stealthily and turn into the corridor on the floor above the Lady Chapel. I've always felt an interloper here: so many doors on this corridor where the sisters slept. As a small boy, I used to feel that an enchantment might lie behind them; later, that a Lucrece might lie there—all I had to do was open an illicit door, to look down at her, defenseless and sleeping.

I find myself outside a smaller door. It looks like a cupboard, but it isn't. I open it carefully—it always creaked if pulled back too hard—and I'm in a familiar dark place. In front of me, now directly at eye height, is a small, square aperture. It is surrounded by stone and crumbling mortar. No doubt spiders lurk in its crevices—but insects no longer have the power to scare me, though those pacing footsteps do. I can hear them clearly now; I can hear some other sighing sound in the room below me. Now I can sense who's there, pacing back and forth. I know whom I'll finally see: my mother, Dorrie. I close my eyes and then open them. I lean forward, careful to make no noise; I lean toward the Squint, Bella's marvel.

Not my mother, not Maisie, not one of the sisters, either. It's Finn. It is Finn—and it cannot be Finn. Finn cannot be here. She caught a plane; she's somewhere in another world, doing all those things she does that I don't comprehend, in parts of the world I've never vis-ited. I shouldn't have come here.

I watch a Finn who cannot be there, and my vision is misting; there are cobwebs in this tunnel; I can't see properly, but I'm begin-ning to see that she is insubstantial, this pacing figure by the win-dows. She's a shadow of her former self; she's a phantom, conjured by need. Such a frail ghost. If it weren't for the brightness of her hair, I'd scarcely recognize her.

I'll go down to her, I think sadly. I'll go down to her now, and when I do, I'll be cheated again. She'll vanish into the air, as she always does. And I'm about to do that, I'm just about to draw away from this aperture, when I hear a sound—and the ghost woman below responds; her whole demeanor alters. I see her stop pacing; her body tenses. She moves to the middle window and looks out and then, fumbling with the catch in her eagerness, begins to open the casement. I hear footsteps below in the hall, the sound of a man running and a man's voice, calling, *Finn, Finn? Where are you?*

She turns away from the window, she swings round, and her face lights with joy and anticipation. I can't move. I'm transfixed. I'm waiting to watch me walk into the room below. I'm going to stand here forever. I hear the man's footsteps cross the landing to the door of the Lady Chapel, and then I see Finn move forward swiftly; she gives a spring, and his arms close around her. He's wearing a black overcoat. Finn buries her face against his shoulder. I see his hands come up to cradle her head. He lifts her face to his and kisses her mouth. Then, drawing back but still holding her tight, rocking her, pressing her against him, he half turns, so I can see the anguish on his face. It's my friend, my oldest friend, Nicholas Marlow.

I hear him say in a low voice, a voice that is broken with emotion, *Finn, my darling, my dearest love. Don't cry, I'm here now. And I won't leave you.*

I draw back at once, deeply ashamed. I have no right to spy on this. I walk away half-blinded. I descend the stairs quietly. I leave the Chinese ivory sphere on the kitchen table and quietly return to my cottage.

There, I find I'm now able to face the task of packing up all Joe's and Bella's belongings. It doesn't take as long as I'd feared, and I can now undertake this task—with regrets, and sadly, but efficiently. I work away at it like an automaton.

Flora and Hector have already provided me with boxes. Within two or three hours, those boxes are filled and the cottage is naked. All the monarchical china and knickknacks packed away; the bright ribbons on the dresser hooks undone and discarded. Sixty years, more; all the memories and residues sorted. This box for Oxfam, these for the rubbish bin. When I come to examine them, the objects here, though so powerful to me, are small in number: Joe, Bella, and I had few possessions.

I want very few things: I want Joe's plowing certificates, the photographs of Ocean, and that tinny charm she once gave me. I'll keep one of the nine surviving crystal balls and Bella's greasy, much-used pack of tarot cards. I'll keep Joe's shotgun, which he trained me to use. I'll keep the shotgun—and one box of ammunition.

It's dusk by the time the job is complete. I know now that I'm not going to stay here, that I'll return to London. My last task is best achieved there. I lay out the Rider-Waite deck, using the Celtic Cross spread, and—the cards can sometimes be very clear—they confirm the correctness of this decision. How strange these cards are. Many people find them frightening and are perhaps right to do so. They track a fool's journey through the world, a journey that may lead him toward wisdom and insight—or divert him to other, less pleasant regions. I look at the Major Arcana, at the Empress, the Hanged Man, the Lovers, and the Emperor—a good card that, signifying fatherly influence and authority.

I spread the four suits: Wands, the suit of creativity; Cups, the suit of feelings and spiritual experience; Swords, the suit of intellect, thought, and reason; and finally, my weakest suit, Pentacles, which signifies the forces of practicality. The difficulty with these cards—aside from the obvious possibility that they may signify nothing at all and are mere toys and superstition—the difficulty with these cards lies in the reading of them. Each numbered card carries a particular resonance, which may contradict the overall force of the suit to which it belongs. Each card qualifies the others; the placing—and the interpretation of the placing—is all. Each card in this pack signifies one thing but contains and can also signify its opposite.

I've drawn the Three of Swords, a card that indicates heartbreak and betrayal, and the Five of Cups, which indicates loss and the abandoning of hope. I have the Tower, the card of sudden change, of a fortress that is also a prison. These cards might imply the very opposite, of course; but I doubt it. I've rarely seen a less auspicious spread. There's one sole card of comfort: the Chariot, signifying assertion and resolution. I slip the cards back inside their worn case. I believe in them. I do not believe in them.

The part of me that will always be Roma, the part of me that will always belong to Ocean and Bella, says: *Read wisely and you will understand*. The part of me that Cambridge forged, that twin who used to dismiss these cards, now says: *What does it matter? It's no worse a way of imposing a shape on the world than any other. It's like religion and philosophy: fake, in other words.*

I put the cards in my bag. If I leave now, if I call a local cab, I'll be at Deepden station in time for the last connection to London. Back to Highbury Fields and Heartbreak Hotel. That's fine for my purposes; that's fine. In London, there's anonymity.

I don't want to perform any act here that would leave shadows behind it or cause distress to those who, like the McIvers, have shown me kindness. *Put out the light*, I remind myself. Then I hear footsteps outside, and Nick enters the denuded kitchen. I'd wondered if he would seek me out, my honorable friend. I'd wondered if my honorable friend might feel that, this time, it was he who owed me an explanation for past conduct.

TWENTY-SEVEN

Nick

WAS IT ALWAYS YOU, Nick?" I say.
"Yes, always," he answers.

He's sitting at the table by then. I've found a bottle of whiskey bought for Joe before the illness took hold, and I've poured Nick a glass of neat Scotch: I can see he needs it. I'm drinking water; I can't risk alcohol—one sip and I'll be right back where I started. On the table in front of him is that ivory sphere, which he's returning to me at Finn's request. They'd seen me leaving, crossing the cloister. When they found this, in the kitchen where I'd left it, they had understood. Finn would like me to keep it. I sit opposite him. Seeing the pain in his face, I feel no anger or bitterness. I've been deceived for over twenty years, for most of my adult life, more mistaken in my readings than I could ever have imagined. I don't blame Nick or Finn; I don't even blame myself. It happens.

"Not Lucas?" I hear myself say. "I was so sure it was Lucas. How stupid of me."

"Not necessarily stupid—after all, she married him."

"Was it your child, Nick?"

"Yes." He covers his face with his hands. There is a long silence, then he says: "I nearly told you the other night, when you came back to my house. I wanted to tell you. Finn is dying, Dan. She has another two months, maybe less. She wanted to spend them here, and I've promised to spend them with her."

"*Dying?* Finn is dying?" I look down at the table and trace its lines, the waves and islands of its grain. It's a long while before I'm able to speak. "So that's why you were in the gallery," I say finally. "That's why you were there, looking at the portrait. I should have known from your face. You knew then, didn't you?"

"Yes, I did. I'd just come from the hospital. I'd had to give her the results of the tests. We both knew what they were likely to tell us. She had an operation last year in South Africa. It's cancer of the breast. She had chemo out there; I've been supervising her treatment in London for the last eight weeks. But she'd left it too late. It had spread to the lymph glands. Now there are secondaries."

"There's no chance that—"

"None whatsoever."

"Nick, why didn't you tell me? If I'd known—oh Christ. Finn doesn't want to see me, then? Not once, just to say good-bye? I'd like to have seen her. She's said her good-byes to Lucas, hasn't she? I saw her leaving his house." And there is bitterness in my voice now: I can't hide it.

"Yes, she has. But it's easier for her to see Lucas than it would be you, Dan."

"Oh? And why is that?"

"She'd prefer you to remember her as she was, I think. You knew her in ways Lucas never did. And you'll mourn her more. You know what Lucas is like. We all do."

"For Christ's sake, I loved her," I hear myself say. "I *loved* her. My whole life . . . And I loved you—my closest, oldest friend. The one person I trusted always to tell me the truth. You lied, Finn lied, Lucas lied—*everyone's* lied to me. Why did you lie to me, Nick?"

"Because Finn asked me to," he replies, looking away. "That was the first reason. And then, because I was ashamed. Once you begin lying, it's easier—and it can seem kinder—to go on doing so. That's what I told myself, anyway. One can lie to oneself as well, Dan— don't you know that?"

"I don't believe that. I don't damn well *believe* it. We shared a flat for nearly three *years*. I saw you daily. I thought we had no secrets from each other. Did it never cross your mind to tell me the truth? You knew what I thought. Did you lie to Julia as well—or was she in on the secret? I'm sure she was. So she lied to me, too. A clean sweep—all my friends. That takes care of fucking everyone."

"No, you're wrong. I lied to Julia, too. She knew nothing about this—and I don't think she even suspected, not once in a twenty-year marriage—well, maybe once or twice, maybe latterly." He pauses. "I finally told her this week. And it took me a week to work up the courage to do that. Finn's been here for a week on her own—I'd promised to be here with her, and I still prevaricated. I couldn't face Julia, I couldn't face my children—that's the kind of man I am. Now do you understand why I could never explain this to you?"

"No, I don't. I don't understand. I don't *want* to understand. What does it matter now? Nothing matters. Finn's dying."

"Dan, I'd like you to know. I'd like to tell someone—I've had it on my conscience long enough."

"I don't want to be your father confessor. Find someone else," I reply angrily, rising and moving away from him. So much for all those resolutions of mine, I think an instant later. There's a silence.

"There isn't anyone else I could tell," Nick says eventually in a quiet voice. "I've made a complete mess of my life. I couldn't begin to discuss that with anyone else. You're the only confessor candidate, Dan. . . . I'm sorry. I shouldn't have come here."

I look at my friend, at Nick, who has never found it easy to speak about himself, at Nick, who is reticent, as expert at concealment as

I am. I return to the table and sit opposite him. "Forgive me," I say. "Tell me. I'm listening."

He begins to explain, and I watch the past alter. I see all the events that were invisible to me before, hidden behind lies—and behind my own self-absorption. Nick opens a door: I step into the sunlight of the Abbey cloister, but everything's changed. The shadows are deeper; they're not in the same, the expected, places.

"It was when Finn told me about the baby," Nick is saying. "You remember what you wrote in your letter to me? 'The summer it all went wrong'? For me, it went wrong when Finn came to me and told me she thought she might be pregnant.

"Can you imagine how I felt? We'd been so happy, so . . . I loved her so much, Dan. It began the previous Easter—suddenly I saw her differently, and I couldn't . . . I just wanted to be with her, every moment of every day, and—after that, I used to visit her at Girton whenever I could. We were secretive, because Finn was so afraid of hurting you. We were always careful, but there was one occasion towards the end of the summer term, when . . . well, I won't talk about that. I knew we shouldn't have taken that risk—I was worrying about the consequences for weeks. Every time I came home, every time I came to the Abbey—it was so difficult for us to be alone, I hated all the lies and the subterfuge. Finn seemed unconcerned, she kept saying it would be all right—and then . . . Do you remember the night before their visit to Elde—that evening, when we ate outside, in the cloisters? We all stayed up very late, and we danced—and then later, Finn and I went to Nun Wood. We used to go there sometimes—it was one of the few places where we felt safe, where we knew no one could find us or surprise us. That night—it was such a beautiful night—we made love and—something, I don't know what it was, the wine we'd drunk, or that music Julia played, or just the place, the silence of it, and the moonlight—I felt healed somehow, confident again, free of all anxiety. I thought: It's going to be all right, I needn't have worried. . . . And then Finn told me. It was two months, and she was certain—as certain as she could be—that she was carrying our baby.

"She seemed overjoyed, Dan. But I couldn't—my whole world began to fall apart, from that moment. That made me feel guilty. I was shocked—and I was terrified. I was still training. Finn hadn't completed her degree. We had no money and nowhere to live. My parents had never liked Finn, I don't know why—and I knew how they'd react. . . ."

He hesitates. Had his parents heard rumors about Finn's father? Did that explain their antipathy? I stare at those whorls in the wood of the table. I see myself plucking a scrap of Indian cotton off a broken branch in Nun Wood. I say nothing.

"I couldn't believe I'd let this happen, Dan. I didn't know what to do—so I tried to look at it rationally. You know what I'm like—I like to plan things. I don't like to ricochet around and make stupid decisions in a moment of panic. It seemed to me that these weren't the best possible circumstances to bring a child into the world. I was working eighteen-hour days in London. Even if we married, and they let Finn stay at Girton, there was no way she could look after a baby on her own and complete a degree. I didn't say that then. Finn might have been wrong; it could have been a false alarm—so I persuaded her to get some pregnancy tests done. Finn agreed to meet so I could give her the results. It was the day she came up to London. She left Stella wandering round shops and came to the hospital. The tests had come back positive."

"*You* arranged the tests?" I say.

"Well, of course. I wasn't going to let someone else do them. Why should that matter?"

"Nothing. No reason. That's not what Finn told me, that's all."

How well Finn lied to me, I think. How expertly she had lied in that red-tabled café. It had never occurred to me that Finn could be so duplicitous. I can see that she wanted to shield me. I can also see that she must have known her lies altered my whole perspective. I could believe in Lucas as some cardboard seducer, but if I'd known Nick was her child's father, my reaction would have been very different. Finn would have known that. I look at the grain on the table and think: *Who is the woman I've loved?*

"When I saw Finn at the hospital—it was terrible, Dan. I'd had time to consider by then, and I'd planned what to say—but I'd been working impossible hours for a three-week stretch, and I'd scarcely slept. . . . Everything I tried to say—somehow I put it badly and clumsily. I just wanted to make Finn see that we had a choice. Of course, if she wanted to keep the baby, then I'd marry her—we'd always planned to marry. We'd been going to wait a year, until she'd completed her degree and I was fully qualified. I told her, if that was what she wanted, I'd do it, of course, and we'd manage—somehow we'd manage. But there was an alternative. I knew people who would help. Doctors. Good doctors. At ten weeks, there would have been no risk involved. I could easily have made the arrangements."

He passes his hand across his face. "I don't know, Dan, what I truly felt. I was twenty-five. I was afraid—and I was angry, too, perhaps there was a part of me that blamed her. Christ alone knows . . . all I know is that I couldn't find the right words, and whatever I said seemed to make the situation worse. I went on and on talking, trying to be sensible—and Finn said nothing. Not one word. She—her face changed, Dan. She didn't cry or argue. She heard me out, and then she just stood up and told me not to trouble myself, she'd make her own *arrangements*. And then she walked out."

I look at the day of that London visit. I watch myself, cleaning windows, and Mrs. Marlow telling me Nick has changed his plans, that he'll be back on the afternoon train. I watch myself, later that day, searching for Maisie in the cool evening air. I'm standing by the old nunnery gates, scanning the fields for a blue dress. Then, at the top of Acre Lane, by Nun Wood, someone moves, and I realize it's a man, that it's Nick. I gesture toward him. . . . "I see," I say finally. "I see now. So that's why you came back to Wykenfield?"

"Of course. I was frantic—I had to see her. I had to talk to her."

"And then Maisie jumped."

"And then Maisie jumped." He looks away, his voice breaking. "And after that—it was hopeless, it was so utterly hopeless, Dan. I was in a state of desperation—Maisie was in a coma, I had to go back to London and work, Finn would scarcely speak to me. When her grandfather had a stroke—I thought she must see then how impossible this was. I kept pleading with her, to make up her mind, to decide what we should do, because we were running out of time. But she wouldn't listen. What I still couldn't see was that she'd made her decision. She'd made it in the hospital in London. I'd failed her; and Finn is ruthless—she doesn't forgive failure. I was phoning her every day, pleading, writing, trying to persuade her to talk to me—and then I found out: She'd married Lucas."

"She didn't warn you what she was going to do?"

"No. You know what she's like. She just did it. She said it was a business arrangement. Lucas was perfectly amenable. It meant she could continue with her degree. . . . Maybe she wanted to punish me. I still don't know. She looked so ill, Dan. She was under terrible strain. She blamed herself for what had happened to Maisie. She said Maisie knew just how faithless she'd been, how she lied to you. . . . She wasn't capable of thinking rationally, Dan, any more than I was. So I'll never know for sure why she married him. . . . I suppose it doesn't matter now, anyway."

"She could have married me. I asked her, Nick."

"I know you did. But Finn wouldn't hurt you. She knew there was no possibility of hurting Lucas. He didn't love her. I'm not even sure he was ever very interested in her."

"He drew her often enough."

"That's different."

I stand up. I start walking around in this cold, now emptied room. So Finn had told him about my sad and inept proposal. Nick knew everything, all my secrets—and I knew nothing. I'd spent over twenty years walking around a maze of ignorance. All this had been happening to Nick when I was sharing a flat with him, and I'd never once guessed. If he was on edge, miserable, incommunicative, or irritable, I'd blamed the hours he worked and the nature of that work. A crisis in my friend's life, and I'd seen nothing. Not that my blindness matters now, I think; it's too late to alter anything. Finn is dying. It's over.

"And later," I say, returning to the table. "I still don't understand, Nick. Tell me what happened later."

"What is there to say? Finn wrote me out of her life. Once she'd married Lucas, she wouldn't meet me or answer my phone calls or my letters. Even when the baby died . . ." He covers his face with his hands. "Nothing, Dan. She wouldn't let me anywhere near her. She behaved as if it weren't my child, as if I had no right to feel anything. . . . I went to see her once, one last time—she'd forbidden me to go, but I went anyway. I drove to Cambridge, and I went to that horrible flat Lucas had taken in Green Street. He wasn't there—I think he very rarely was, by that time. Finn was alone—and I scarcely recognized her, Dan. The flat was filthy, and she'd let herself go—and I could see she was ill, that she needed help. She had that same expression on her face that Maisie used to have, do you remember? Blank—as if she were listening to someone else, as if she couldn't hear you. And I tried—I tried, Dan, to talk to her, to ask her about the baby, it was a little boy, that's all I knew, and—I broke down. I started weeping . . . and she just stared at me, and then she said: 'Why are you crying? He's dead. That's what you wanted, isn't it?'

"Something happened then, Dan. I couldn't forgive her for saying that. She told me to go, and I left, and—I hardened my heart, per-haps. I learned to harden my heart. I felt she was treating me unjustly. I resolved to put all of this behind me, to move on, remake my life. . . . And three years later, I married her sister. I'd always liked Julia. I'd always admired Julia—she's a considerable woman. Once I was married to Julia, Finn forgave me. Make what you like of that."

"Forgave you when you married Julia? I don't understand."

"Neither do I. But that's what happened. Finn wrote to me for the first time in three years within one month of my marriage. We met again, in secret. I didn't tell Julia, and—I won't say any more. Within hours—*hours*, Dan—I was right back where I started. I can't—somehow I can't—if Finn beckons, I go. That's just the way it is. I've despised myself and hated myself, I've tried to change, but I can't, somehow I can't break with her."

"Finn knows that?"

"Of course. She's always known it. We've both always known it." He hesitates. "So don't ask me about my marriage, Dan. Don't ask me about Julia. I've lied to her and deceived her, and I've done it for twenty years—on and off, throughout our marriage. Large lies and cheap ones, all the rubbish bin of adultery—alibis, hotel rooms, se-cret letters, and phone calls. I've lied to Finn, too. I've been faithless to everyone—to my wife, to Finn, to my children, and to myself. I can't undo any of it. All I know, the one thing I know, is that I'm here now, and I'll stay at the Abbey for as long as Finn needs me. I'll stay for the end. I've loved Finn for most of my life. And it's the last thing I can do for her."

There is a silence. I think of Julia, standing on my doorstep, de-manding to know the truth, weeping in my arms. I think of Tom, troubled with nightmares, anxious and afraid, trying to believe the protective lies his father had told him. I look at my friend, the man I always thought of as disciplined, judicious, principled, as everything

I was not. "Christ, Nick," I say before I can stop myself. "What a mess. What a fucking awful mess."

"I know. My fault. I got myself there."

"I wouldn't say that. I'd say you had some assistance."

"Don't blame Finn. Don't do that, Dan."

I'm not blaming Finn. I'm not blaming anyone. I've loved someone I didn't begin to know, a creature of my own stubborn invention. I can see now how lost to me Finn is, how finally and irretrievably lost. I think: *I never knew her. I've loved a woman who never existed.*

I look at Nick, who presumably *does* know her. I'm numb with pain and disbelief. I can't bear to look at the past anymore. I'm trying to make my mind function, to see beyond the present, to imagine what will happen to Nick when Finn is gone. I want to ask him: *What will you do—afterward? Will you go back to Julia? Will she take you back? What will happen to your children, to my godson?* I can't ask him questions like that, not now. My heart goes out to Nick—not that my heart, sympathy, or concern is of much use to anyone.

There is a long silence then. I'm still listening to it. Nick, his head bent in his hands, has begun to weep. Tears are catching. *I hate to see a grown man weep.* I put my arms around his shoulders awkwardly. I say some of those inadequate things I'd learned at Joe's bedside, those platitudes we all know to be meaningless but which give comfort anyway. When Nick is calmer, I reach my hand across the table to him. I can see my hand held out and his hand grasping it.

"Listen, Nick," I say finally. "You're a fine doctor. You saved Maisie's life—if it hadn't been for you, she'd have died at the Abbey long before that ambulance got there. You've saved many people's lives; that's what you do, that's what you've devoted your life to doing—and you shouldn't forget that. You've always been a loyal friend to me, the one person I could turn to. You're a good friend, a good doctor, a good man, and a good father. . . . Maybe you haven't been such a good husband. . . ." Nick raises his head, meets my eyes, smiles wanly. "But you're not the first unfaithful husband in human history, you're not some stupid Lothario, some Casanova—and your marriage can't have been that bad, or Julia wouldn't have put up with it for a day, let alone twenty years. It is possible to love two women at a time—at least I think it is, I think it is; I can see it might be . . . and of all the women I know, Julia's one of the few who might actually understand that. That's for the two of you to resolve. Meanwhile, you shouldn't be here, talking to me. So I'll just say this: You're not alone. Been there, done that, got every single one of the fucking T-shirts. However guilty you feel, or ashamed, you don't need to say anything or explain anything to me. I know all about infidelity. And guilt. Betraying yourself, betraying others—you're talking to a master, Nick, a fucking PhD. Now drink that whiskey. Then go back to Finn. You shouldn't be here."

Nick did drink it. He grasped my offered hand. We talked quietly for a short while, and then, not long afterward, he left. We embraced in the doorway. Odd, how weakness brings people closer, how it knocks the barriers down. I'd known Nick all my life, and I'd never felt closer to him, more assured of our friendship, than I did at that moment. I was glad of that. Our final parting was a good one. Something's salvaged from the wreckage.

TWENTY-EIGHT

Shredder

I MISSED THAT LAST TRAIN. I took the first train the next
morning. After Nick left, I didn't want to think, so I turned on the
television I'd given Joe. I channel-hopped. My fingers danced on the
remote buttons. I watched armies gathering in a desert, and night
strikes, and laser-guided smart weapons that could travel three million miles and enter a building through the smallest of windows. I'd
known a war was imminent, forgotten it for six weeks; now I
watched its commencement. I watched bits of old movies; *Casablanca*
was on. I watched them prepare to round up all the usual suspects. I
watched game shows and quizzes and ads and interviews with ad-
dicts; I watched dancers and comedians and endangered species and
polar bears giving birth and sitcoms and aliens star-trekking. Then I
went and lay down on Joe's stripped bed and watched the moon rise
and decline. I listened to the mice inside and the owls outside, the
owls waiting to hunt them.

In London, on my way from the station to Heartbreak Hotel, which
I've decided to rechristen Hotel Resolution, I called in at an office
supply shop.

Result: one brand-new megafast heavy-duty shredder. It is called, inevitably, the Supa-Shredda. So much easier than the bonfire I'd originally planned for these pages. Won't cause a back-garden forest fire, won't attract attention, won't offend the neighbors. It can slice through forty pages of A4 at a time, this baby. Made in Taiwan. CIA approved. It has a hungry look, steel teeth. I'm already fond of it. *Not long to wait now*, I tell it.

The house is in an orderly state. Everything's prepared. I've chucked the rope and the razor blades—won't need those particular weapons. I've told the importunate milkman, who's been pressing for payment for weeks, that I'll pay him tomorrow and if by any chance I don't answer the door, he should just keep ringing. As a fail-safe, I've just posted a brief note to Julia. I couldn't think of any-one else, and with luck, if she gets it on return from location or wherever she is, she'll come here and ensure that the police come with her. The cops in their kiddie cars, I'm sure they'll cope. And if they don't, too bad. Sorry, lads—it comes with the territory.

Now I'm just sitting here, with the beloved Nescafé and a Marl-boro, thinking about long words that begin with C. Such as Con-summation, as in —— *devoutly to be wished*. Such as Completorium.

I'm at the window, with a good view over the Fields. There are four illegal skateboarders, two illegal cyclists, and several furtive dog walkers. Malc and crew are back on the corner. But if I look hard enough, I can't see any of them—not Malc and his myrmidons, not the walkers, skateboarders, cyclists; not even these sad onetime pas-tures. Instead, I can see the people I've loved, and the places I've loved, the fields of my childhood, where I walked, played—and learned to use a shotgun.

Hamlet couldn't do it, he couldn't top himself, not at the "To be or not to be" point, anyway. Why not? I'd think every time I read or saw the play. *Why not?* I'd think that time at Cambridge when I directed it. Why not? Because Hamlet claims not to know what's on the other side of death and to fear what might be awaiting him. *That undiscover'd country from whose bourn / No traveller returns*, he calls it—yet he knows that statement's untrue. The dead do return: Hamlet's already spoken to his father's ghost; he's already received his dead father's instructions.

At the end of the last act, Hamlet will meet death unsuspecting, flicked with a poisoned rapier, at a point in his life when he's ready to die anyway. . . . But earlier in the play, that unknown afterdeath region puzzles his will and stays his dagger: *For in that sleep of death what dreams may come / When we have shuffled off this mortal coil, / Must give us pause* . . .

I'm obedient. I pause.

What do I see on the other side, in that undiscover'd country? Not the heaven or hell of Joe's Bible, that one book in our cottage—though I could believe in Dante's subtle divine comedy, his vision of paradise and inferno. Maybe I see a territory that mirrors the one we come from, the prebirth nothingness—and I don't fear that. Should you fear nonbeing's emptiness, the prewomb nonexperience? I don't think so. . . . Maybe it will be like the underworld of the Greeks—now that I can half believe, that I would welcome. A Styx to cross, Charon at the helm and shades lifting their hands in greeting from the far side of a dark river. The other side of Black Ditch . . . maybe I'll see Joe and Bella and my lost mother; maybe Ocean is waiting to greet me. . . . Or maybe Shakespeare, using Hamlet as his mouthpiece, was right as always: What awaits me will be a region of dream—and it will be as unpredictable, as repetitive, as resonant yet enigmatic, as benign and terrible, as dreams are. Yes, I can believe that also.

An eternity dreaming. I've spent nearly forty-six years in such shadows, so no doubt I'll cope with more. By the time I find out, there'll be no choice in the matter.

I just hope you don't have to *watch*. Because if you're damned with

angelic eyes and condemned to spend an eternity viewing the proceedings down here on earth; if the final twist is that you're fated to be
a celestial voyeur, fated never to intervene . . . that *truly* would be a hell.
Think, look, look; *look closely* at the mess, the diurnal evil and bloody
horror we make of it now. Would anyone want to watch its continua-
tion? Watch their children die, watch those they love suffer? Will I want
to watch an eternal sequel, know what terrors await Maisie, or Nick,
or Julia, or Fanny, or my godson, Tom? No, I would not want that. No,
I do not want that. Christ. Spare me that possibility.

Barring some last days' cataclysm, it's going to get worse slowly: the
hole in the heavens widening; the seas and rivers poisoned; the land
sick; Europe become a Sahara; more wars; more widespread famine;
new diseases and new pestilence . . . Think of the tools we have now,
our stupidity, our arrogance, our blindness, our cruelty—all those lethal
weapons in the human arsenal: Can anyone see life on earth improving? I certainly can't. *What's God on*, indeed. He must be on something,
on some ultimate acid; he's got to be celestially spaced out, because
otherwise even he might notice his creation's unbearable. Or maybe
he's just had enough; maybe God, in his many guises and aliases, has finally given up on this evil narrative and *lost the plot*. Given man's millennial inhumanity to man, and not forgetting man's millennial
inhumanity to woman—who could blame him?

On the other hand, maybe the Buddhists are right—in which
case, I'll be coming back again, coming back as some lowlife no
doubt, like a worm or a caterpillar. Given my performance this time
around, I'll probably come back as something truly obscene, an epiphyte, for example, or an oncosphere . . . *shit*.

I've just tested the shredder. Its appetite's keen. The light's poor outside, and it's starting to rain. Only two skateboarders now and one

last dog walker pacing the Fields. I never thought this would be easy, but it's hard in ways I hadn't foreseen. I wonder if Maisie felt that.

Maybe I was wrong, maybe all my theorizing was wrong, and the timing of Maisie's fall had nothing to do with Compline. Maybe she was somewhere hidden away, listening to us calling for her, trying to summon the nerve to act—just as I am. Or perhaps she wanted a stretch of silence in which to let the world go. I could understand that. I can understand that.

I'll never know why she jumped, I see that now—I never could have known, I realize. Even if I had found that imagined letter, that last explicatory document I'd been so sure she'd left behind—what would it have told me? Would Maisie have said that she couldn't bear her outsider status any longer, that she could no longer endure being a curiosity, a child who could not fit people's expectations of children? Would she have explained the loneliness and isolation I think she must have felt?

Or would she have said that she felt herself a burden to her family—a burden she had the power to remove? Would she have accused us of being blind to her distress, of turning away, impatient and bored, when she tried to communicate with us? Would she have said that we had turned away from her once too often? We were all certainly guilty of that. Blind to suffering. Misreading. No answer to that accusation.

How they weigh on me now, the sins of omission. Maybe Maisie would have been more specific, have given us some reassuring instance of cause and effect? Revealed, perhaps, that she had somehow learned the truth about her father's illness—and that that had tipped her over the edge? I suppose that might have been possible, given the gossip in the village. Or would she have claimed that art had done the damage; that she could not live with the Maisie she saw in Lucas's portrait? When she jumped, it was only a week after seeing that painting for the first time. . . . Perhaps there was some hidden factor she'd reveal in this convenient document, some incident or influence that none of us had had the wit to suspect. . . . Or would she simply have said that, on a fine summer's evening, aged thirteen, she'd decided she had had enough of this world and wished to join her father and her many friends among the dead?

Any of these things, I think now. She might have written *any* of these things—and no matter how specific, how clear or how detailed her words, the information would still have been approximate. We look aslant at our own lives. I doubt Maisie would ultimately have known why she did what she did. I don't know why, or how, I myself got to this point—sitting at this table, writing a last page, looking at a gun and a shredder, and switching on the desk lamp in the failing January light.

I can see some of the stages on my journey and some of the forking paths I didn't take, and I'm beyond the point where they matter. But I also see the final comfort of suicide. At last, I'm in the right place. Like Maisie, I won't be subject to circumstance anymore, and no outside factor will determine how I end. Load the gun. Open the window. Step through it: our choice. It feels pure, doesn't it, Maisie, strangely pure, this state.

I mustn't hesitate. If Maisie, a child, had the courage to do this, surely I—my hands are steady enough, and that's important—I don't want to botch this. But there are voices—I can hear voices, calling my name, tempting me back. This action grieves my father, I can sense that. Christ, they're all so clear and so close: I didn't expect that. Here's Joe, lifting me onto the tractor seat that first time, and I'm plowing my first furrow, and I haven't got the art, the knack, and it's crooked; here's Bella, reading my fortune in the cards and then sliding them quickly into their case and saying, *Life's what you make of it,*

Danny, you know that. And here's Finn, taking my hand as we walk up Acre Field and saying to me, to the summer evening, *It isn't possible, is it, Danny, to be happier than this*? And here's my blood brother, Nick, helping me bait a hook for the sharks I know lurk in the Abbey lake. And here is Maisie, five years old, weeping over the rabbits I've just shot, saying, *Why aren't they breathing? What have you done? Make them come back to life, Danny. Make them come back to life for me*. . . .

No more listening to those voices. No more looking back—those fields, that sunlight, those voices, that England: They break my heart. They're too dear to me, I can't risk it.

It's coming up to three—it's nearly three o'clock. I am dealing with this. It should take fifteen minutes at most to feed these pages through the shredder. Then I will _____

PART IX

Queen of Cups

TWENTY-NINE

The Way He Did It

I'M LOOKING at what Dan wrote: I have that last page in front of me. At the end of the final sentence there's a mark, which perhaps began as a dash but became a long jagged line that trails off the edge of the paper. Dan was sitting by the window as he wrote this page—I could see him sitting there as I approached his house. I think he looked out of the window as he wrote that sentence. When he saw what was happening in the street, I think he rose to his feet, knocked the desk, perhaps—and his pen made that mark. I cannot be sure of this, obviously, but the timing would fit.

I will tell you what he saw. I will tell you what he then did. I want *someone* to know. I want you to know, Nick. And you, Fanny. And when you are older, Tom, I want you to understand. You, Tom, witnessed some of it, but not all. I saw everything.

I am Julia. Wife and mother and—according to Dan, a few other things besides, such as empress of trend, alpha bitch, et cetera, et cetera. Let's put those comments on one side. I'll come to them later. I am Julia. I am the eyewitness. Let's forget what I told the police, inventive though that was. This is what happened.

·   ·   ·

Earlier that same day, you, Nick, had called me from the Abbey. You'd promised to do so. I won't say that your departure had been without acrimony—a little acrimony is perhaps to be expected when a wife discovers that before and during a twenty-year marriage, her husband has been conducting a tangled and passionate affair with her sister. But my sister was dying, and although Finn maddens me with her obduracy and blind selfishness, I love her, so the acrimony was not as deep as it might have been. When he telephoned, I was hoping Nick might tell me that Finn was now ready to see me: I wanted to see her one last time; but I knew I would have to wait. You cannot push Finn. You have to wait and wait until she comes to you—even Dan knew that.

That moment still hadn't been reached, Nick told me. I could tell from his voice that Finn's condition was worsening. He did not give details, and I did not press him. He told me that he had gone to Dan's cottage and finally told him the truth. Dan had packed up all the family belongings, was preparing to leave Wykenfield for good, and was returning to London. I tried to envisage this scene and couldn't. "That must have been difficult for you both," I said awkwardly.

"Of course it was difficult," Nick replied with faint irritation: I'm not supposed to trespass on the secret territory of male friendship. "But Dan was very good, very understanding. It wasn't as bad as I'd feared. He was far calmer than I was."

I made no comment. I doubted this.

Nick can be very blind—for a doctor, astonishingly so. His diagnostic skills, so acute when assessing disease, are less accurate when assessing people's feelings. That he should be blind at this particular moment, I could understand; he could not really see beyond Finn. But I also knew how deeply Dan must have been affected—Dan, who has always been adept at concealment. Concealing his feelings is his religion. It is also mine.

"Did Dan try to pass it off with a joke? Did he make jokes at any point?" I asked. I think that question puzzled my husband.

"I can't really remember," he replied. "At the end, when I was leaving, maybe. He said something about T-shirts, I think—he was just Dan. You know what he's like."

I do. Nick wasn't alarmed by Dan's apparent calm. I was. I started to feel guilty, too. After all, I had hit Dan in the face with a heavy cell phone, and even if that blow was glancing, I shouldn't have then left him, and swanned off in my car in a rage, and spent the next five days on location nursing more resentment and fury. And on my return, when Fanny finally came to me contrite and confessed the truth, I should have written to Dan, telephoned, done something.

I found I was in a strange state. I had recipes to test, but I was pacing my kitchen, and fiddling with things, and spilling them, and I couldn't understand where I was or what I was doing. Eventually— it was about two by then—I found I couldn't bear the indecision and inertia any longer. I phoned the PA and told her to cancel the afternoon's appointments, and I put on my coat—it was a filthy day, gray and raining—and set off along the terrace. I'd gone about a hundred yards when I changed my mind and went back to the house. I'd take Tom with me, I decided. I'd kept Tom home from school that day, because he'd scarcely slept the previous night, and although there didn't seem to be anything physically wrong, he hadn't a cold or a temperature, I knew he wasn't well. He was ill with unhappiness and with fear. He couldn't understand where Nick was and why he'd gone, and he couldn't believe that he'd ever be coming back, though I kept telling him and telling him that Nick would come back. In due course. Eventually. Maybe I couldn't lie very well anymore. That might have been the reason. Anyway, I felt I shouldn't leave Tom with Ingrid—and then I thought, Why not take him with me?

And that seems a perfect solution. It will be so much easier to make it clear to Dan that I'm sorry, that the ban is over. I've never doubted how much he loves Tom, how much it matters to Dan to have Tom as a godson. Dan is childless, but if he had had a child, I believe he would have made a good and loving father. Besides, visiting Dan alone might be misinterpreted—especially now my husband's walked out. If I take Tom with me, it will be obvious at once that I come as a friend. There's no possible ambiguity.

So I wrap Tom up in coats and scarves, and he's pleased and excited to be doing this, and at the last moment, he runs back upstairs to fetch that triceratops plastic dinosaur thing that Dan bought him, and off we go. We walk along Upper Street, and we're both in a much happier state by then, laughing and talking—and I stop and think, Maybe I should buy Dan something, a kind of peace offering. I almost buy a bottle of wine and then realize that, for Dan, that's probably the worst gift I could get. I haver about and can't think of anything suitable, because I've passed all the bookshops by then. In the end, I buy the first thing I see that's beautiful, which happens to be oranges, a great pyramid of oranges, Seville oranges, just in, the perfect season for them. And I don't know what Dan will do with them, because he can't cook and never could, but I think, He could make marmalade. I'll show him how to make marmalade. I can see now, I was in a nervous jittery state and not—as I usually am—rational.

I buy a kilo of these oranges, and Tom and I swing along the street. He's waving the triceratops, and I'm swinging the bag of oranges. Then, on one of the corners, the worst corner, just by the Highbury and Islington roundabout, I stop. I stare at all the lorries, and a wave of sadness crashes over me, such a huge wave that for a moment I can't move. It hits me without warning: fears for the future, fears for my son. I just stand there, despairing and paralyzed.

It passes eventually. Tom clutches my hand, and we navigate the crossings. We start the trek Dan describes, across Highbury Fields, a miserable, godforsaken place—I hate it. We navigate the ugly erupt-

ing tarmac paths and nearly get knocked down by two skateboarders, and one of them shouts, *Awesome turn*, and then we come out of
the park, such as it is, and I can see Dan's house up ahead of us on
the left—and I can see him, too, see his bent head, at an upstairs window. There's a faint light in the room, perhaps a desk lamp, but it's
visible because out here in the drizzle, the light is already poor—
we're walking in that perpetual January London twilight.

I take Tom's hand again: I've realized that we can't reach Dan's
house without passing those youths who were here the last time I
came—the ones who shouted all those obscenities at Fanny and me.
My daughter isn't afraid to shout obscenities back. I'd like to shout
them, too. But I know that would be deeply unwise; besides, Tom's
with me, and I'm afraid of them. So I grip Tom's hand and try not
to look at them, with their faces hidden under those hoods. I go into
urban threat mode; never meet their eyes and pretend they're invisible. *If they say anything, Tom, ignore them. Don't reply.*

I'm wishing I'd covered my head—I don't want them to recognize me. Tom and I keep on walking, as if they aren't there—and
then, just as we're about to pass them, they move, move in that fluid
way they somehow contrive, as if they're part of one organism, all
five of them. They don't say anything or signal to one another; they
just move. We can't pass them, because they're blocking the pavement, and when we step into the road and try to walk round them,
they move again. They block us off. Tom and I come to a halt. Two
of them peel off from the others and move behind us. It was a mistake to have stepped into the road. Now we're being edged toward
the gate in the railings around the Fields, toward the gathering dark
beyond them. The largest of the five—the one I now know is called
Malc—steps forward and says, *Goin' somewhere?*

The skateboarders have gone. I peer toward the railed-off grass
area to our right. I can't see any walkers or cyclists. The street is deserted. The street lighting is poor. I mutter something about a friend

who's expecting me. And they laugh—they crack up, they do that threatening thing they do, slapping one another's palms, and laughing, when you know they're not really laughing, and what this means is trouble. They know where I'm going, anyway, and my destination, I think, is compounding this trouble. The two behind us move closer. "Look," I say, "I'm in a hurry. May I get past, please?"

They don't like that remark. They don't like my voice or my clothes; they don't like my son or me. They hate us—and I can feel the heat of that hatred. I try to see past them. I'm thirty feet from Dan's house, less. I can still see the light in his window and his bent head. I'm willing him to look up, but he doesn't. I know I mustn't let them sense that I'm afraid of them. That will make the situation worse—and immediately. I look carefully at the three who are in front of us. Are they on drugs? The threat they give off is powerful, but only three of the five are physically large; the two behind us are strong, lanky boys of about fourteen. Even the ringleader, Malc, and the two huge grinning henchmen either side of him—they're young. Not one of them looks more than sixteen or seventeen.

It angers me, it enrages me, to be afraid of mere boys, of stupid grinning teenage bullies. So I say, "Let me pass, please," and Tom and I take a step forward. With one accord, they move; they all move, all five of them. One grabs Tom, and one grabs me, and they start pulling us toward the park railings. I scream, and Malc punches me in the face. The blow sends me sprawling. I drop my bag, with the cell phone in it. I drop the oranges, which spill everywhere, and I can hear them saying, *What's that you got, boy?* And I hear Tom make this little sound, this small gasping sound, and I start getting up and scrabbling for my phone, and everything's slowing. I see them snatch Tom's plastic dinosaur out of his hand; a white trainer comes down on it and kicks it in the gutter.

Then they start tossing my son, my small son, from one of them to another, lifting him off his feet and just bundling him between them. With each pass they're getting him closer to the railings and the Fields. I run at them then, holding my phone, trying to hit them, but the blows just glance off them, and I can't reach Tom. One of them says, *Get the phone, man, she got a phone, get the fuckin' phone*, but I can't hear properly, I've gone deaf, and I know I've screamed again, but I can't hear it.

"Let him go," I say. "He's only a little boy—let him go." I'm sure I was saying that, and I think I said, "Look, just let him go. I'll come with you if you let him go." Something like that, because the biggest one, Malc, came at me then, laughing, thrusting out his hips, and waving his hands, and saying, *What I tell you, man? You hear? She's ready for it, she's beggin', fuckin' cunt is beggin'*.

But they don't let Tom go; they've got his wrist twisted up behind his back now. He's crying out in pain. One of them has his arm locked around my neck; they're dragging both of us into the park, into the dark, and I can see Tom trying to squirm free and hold on to the railings, and then a voice behind me, a voice I don't recognize, says: "Put him down now. Put him down now, or I'll fucking kill you."

All five of them freeze. They stand very still, unnaturally still. They let go of me and of Tom, and he stumbles across to me. I put my arms around him and start backing away, and that voice says: "Go into the house, Julia. Take Tom into the house, the door's open." And I turn around, and I see Dan—a Dan I scarcely recognize, and I can see he's holding something, and then I run to his house with Tom, push Tom inside, give him my phone, and tell him to call the police and to bolt the door and not let anyone in. *Now, now, quickly*, I say, and the door slams, and I start running back to the street because I've understood, now, what Dan was holding.

Those five men are still huddled together, backed up against the railings. Dan is standing in front of them, about six feet away. He's holding his father's shotgun, holding it the way I've seen him hold it a hundred times, easily, familiarly: out in the fields, looking for rabbits, looking for pigeon. Dan was once a very good shot, the best in the village. He's looking at them intently, his finger on the trigger. He's done something to his hair—he's cut his hair, cropped it close to his scalp. There's something black and something glittering tied around his neck. His face is white and concentrated. He's not wearing a jacket, just a white shirt; it's cold, but he isn't shivering.

I hear him say in an easy, conversational tone: "Let's have a spelling lesson, shall we? Malc, you can start. Spell 'wanker' for me."

"Man like, shit—cool it, just fuckin' don't—"

"Spell it, Malc. Here's a clue. It doesn't end in 'ah.' It ends in 'er.' Like cocksucker. Like motherfucker. Like sinner. You want to try spelling those, Malc?"

Malc makes a sound in his throat, risks a glance to the side. "You goin' to stand there and do nothin'?" No one moves. "You just goin' to stand there and let him do this, *fuck*—look, man, no hassle, yeah? Jesus, shit, man—"

"You know how far I can see today?" Dan says. "The other side of eternity, that's how far I can see." The gun moves again, and one of them makes a retching sound. It's the smallest of them. He bends forward and vomits on the pavement. "It's a quote, Malc," Dan continues. "You know about quotes? Shall we try a few? How about, *You talkin' to me? You talkin' to* me? How about, *You feelin' lucky today, punk?*" He pauses, and I see him frown. "You know what this can do at this range, Malc? It can blow a hole in your chest so big you won't have a chest—or a heart or lungs or a rib cage. It can blow your fucking head off. So how d'you feel about dying today, Malc? You ready to die in the next ten seconds?"

And I watch all the color draining out of Malc's face. I hear: "Man, like cool it, okay? Like don't do it. *Fuck*—I didn't mean nothin'. Just havin' a laugh, just—like you dissed me, man—fuck. Jesus—sweet Jesus, like don't do it, man, you crazy or what?"

There's a moment of silence then. Traffic in the distance. Dan moves the gun. One of the others says, "Fuck, man." I see the stain in Malc's crotch and the agony in his face, and he slumps to his knees and starts saying, "Shit, man, don't do it, like just don't do it, I got kids, man, I got two fuckin' kids, man, okay?" And I'm thinking, That can't be true, he doesn't look old enough. But it goes on and on, that gabbled animal pleading, and sometime during that pleading, Dan's stance suddenly alters.

"You stupid fat fuck," he says. "You coward. You dumb assholes— it's not even loaded."

He throws the gun down on the ground. It clatters and slithers into the far gutter. Dan just stands there, waiting. I can see him now, standing there, waiting—his head slightly bowed, his arms by his side, an attitude of resignation. I don't think he knew I was there. If he had known, he wouldn't have cared. He knew what was coming—I'm sure he knew what was coming. And it came at him fast. There was a brief moment of disbelief, then all five of them moved. One of them bent, picked up the shotgun, held it by the barrel, and swung it. It hit Dan on the side of the skull. Then they closed in on him, swarmed over him, and I couldn't see him, they swallowed him up. It was very swift. I saw arms raised, a glint like glass or metal. I could hear the blows, under the wail of sirens, and I could hear a voice crying out, and I could see myself, running forward, grasping at shadows. One of the shadows knocked me flying. The pavement scraped my face, and when I could see again, there was something on the ground, which they took it in turns to kick. The smallest boy was the last to kick, aiming at the throat. Red on a new white Nike trainer.

Then the lights of the police cars came, yellow and blue up the street, and I could hear running feet, and they were all gone, melted into the dark. I crawled across to Dan, who was lying on his back with his eyes open. There was so much blood. Blood on the stock of the gun beside him, blood on his shirt, his white shirt, now red, and his face utterly altered. I lifted his head and cradled it in my lap. I think he knew I was there—or that someone was there. He focused his eyes on mine, and I could see recognition in them. His lips moved. He was trying to say a word that began with "d."

It might have been "Dad"—he might have seen Joe at that moment. It might have been "deal"—he might have been trying to tell me that he would deal with this, even with this—I can imagine that. I suppose it might have been anything, any word that begins with a "d," and he never completed the word anyway. He coughed, just a small clearing-the-throat cough, the kind of cough you might give if you were about to make an after-dinner speech. The little cough brought up a gush, a spew of bright arterial blood. And that was the end. There were no more words, or attempts at words, but he continued to look at me, and I continued to cradle his head, until one of the policemen came, made the usual checks, signaled to a policewoman, and said, "He's gone, love. Leave him to us. We'll take care of him."

Tom let me back into Dan's house, and we waited for the police there. I didn't want to wait in that downstairs room, which had been trashed, with the sofa slit to ribbons. So we came upstairs, to the room where I'd seen Dan sitting. The light was still on. There were shotgun cartridges scattered all over the desk, and—I don't know why—I put them back in their box and saw that two of them were missing.

That shotgun *was* loaded. The police would later confirm that. Why would he have a loaded shotgun in London? they'd ask. I knew by then: I'd guessed. And that wasn't difficult. There was a pile of objects on the desk—all Dan's family memorabilia, the photographs of Ocean, and so on. And a small note next to them saying he would like Tom to have them.

I took that note, before the police arrived. There was a holdall on the floor next to the desk, and it was easy enough to pretend it was mine. I took the note, the box of ammunition, the gifts for Tom, and the manuscript, those pages Dan had decided to put through his shredder. I believe he did mean to do that and would have done so. The shredder was there on the desk, plugged in and ready to use. The pages were stacked next to it, except for the last page, the one he'd reached when life interrupted him. He had looked out of the window, out through the glass; his pen made that jagged mark as he rose to his feet. He saw then that there was another way, a better way, of dying. And, being ready to do so, he took it.

THIRTY

Dosta

THE POLICE INTERVIEWED me three times. They had tried, and failed, to trace the shotgun. That didn't surprise me. That gun had originally belonged to Joe's father. I doubt Joe had used it recently or had ever bothered to license it. The gun had been cleaned and oiled: I knew Dan must have done that. I told the police, three times, that the gun was not Dan's. I told them three times that Malc had produced this weapon. That statement didn't accord with my son's, they informed me. My son is just nine, I replied. He was terrified. He can't remember the details. Malc produced the gun, then there was a struggle, and Dan got hold of it. If he hadn't, I would not be here for you to interview.

Then how did your assailants get it back from him? the police wanted to know. I said: Dan wasn't a vigilante; once Tom and I were safe, he wasn't prepared to use the gun or harm anyone . . . he knew the police were on their way; we could hear sirens; he was trying to defuse the situation, to take the cartridges out, when they rushed him. I had to say that. They'd have found traces of ammunition on Dan's hands. When lying to the police, who have the advantage of modern technology, one has to lie carefully.

I said: I can't remember the exact details, it happened too fast. I said: I've told you what happened three times. I had to watch them

do that to an unarmed man. It was five against one. He was my husband's oldest friend. He's my son's godfather. He had a brilliant career, he had everything to live for. My son and I owe our lives to
Dan. I find this deeply upsetting. If you want to pursue this, and if
you continue to question and harass me like this, I'll call my solicitor.

They'd caught Malc by then. They subsequently caught two of
the others. I identified them in the lineup. All three contradicted one
another, accused one another, and invented a farrago of lies. There
were wildly inaccurate witness statements from the various neighbors who had called the police and watched this event from behind
their net curtains. The number of assailants varied from five to fifteen. No one could agree as to their age, build, height, skin, or hair
color; no one could agree as to what they'd been wearing. Every
witness to and participant in this event had a different version of it.

I perjured myself well. When, finally, a year later, I was called to
the witness box, my story proved unshakable. I was a clear, unemo-
tional, model witness—and commended as such by the judge. I was
determined that there would be no mitigating pleas, and if illegal
possession of a firearm could be added to the assault and murder
charges, that seemed to me a bonus. Besides, I did not want the issue
to be clouded by suggestions of self-defense, deliberate provocation,
or suicide.

Malc, who proved to be nineteen, was sent down for life; with good
behavior he'd be out in fifteen years or less, my solicitor informed me.
I did not think good behavior was too likely, in Malc's case. His two
co-defendants, aged sixteen and seventeen, went down for four and five
years, respectively; the sentences would have been more severe had it
been possible to prove who had struck the blows to the skull, who had
stabbed Dan in the throat, and whether all five assailants were equally
responsible. The other two, those lanky boys—both juveniles in any
case, I think—were never caught or identified.

·　　·　　·

Fame can on occasion be useful. I have a certain degree of fame; Dan was well known, or had been. Those facts ensured that this became a cause célèbre immediately. Once the trial was over, I set about my task: to tell Dan's story. I gave interviews. I gave them to everyone who requested them, from national newspapers to the *West Suffolk Gazette*; from ITN to the smallest local TV stations. I am a professional: I gave them the sound bites they needed. I used the term *hero* lavishly, and they lavishly repeated it.

I know the power of photographs, too, so I made sure they all had a photograph of Dan as he used to be, Dan in his youth, at the height of his extreme beauty. It was taken at the Abbey, by me, that last summer. I've always kept it. Dan is standing barefoot, in the cloister, head thrown back, dark hair falling across his forehead, dark eyes flashing. He looks about to conquer the world. That is how I wanted people to remember him—and, now, that *is* how they will remember him. People remember physical beauty and courage—they're rare enough, in all conscience.

The true story is better and more truly courageous, of course. But the truth was too complicated to risk. The media is not good with complicated stories. I hope Dan would approve of all this—I did it for him; it was the last service I could perform for him.

It would amuse him, I was sure of that. Besides, Dan was subtle: By indirection, find direction out. He'd have known that this was my way of saluting him.

I still think about that final word he was trying to say when I held him. That word that began with a "d." Was it "deal," as in "deal with"—a term I found he used again and again? Had Dan, dying, made one last wry joke? Perhaps it was "Dorrie." I'd have liked to ask Nick, or Finn, or someone. But I couldn't ask them, because Finn was dying, Fanny had flounced off somewhere again—and I was alone, except for Tom, for several weeks after it happened. It was Tom, finally, who suggested alternatives—he and Dan, I was discovering, had been closer than I'd realized. Tom thought it might be a Romany word. Dan had taught him some of those secret words, those Ocean remnants. There was *dya,* for instance, which meant "mother." And there was *dosta.*

I looked at Tom. We were sitting at our kitchen table. It was scattered with Dan objects, Dan talismans—the ones he'd wanted Tom to have. There was that crystal ball of Bella's, the tarot cards, the photographs, and the plowing certificates; and Ocean's strange tinny little charm that Dan had been wearing around his neck when he came out of his house with that shotgun. I'd asked the police for it. I'd washed the blood off it. Tom loved these things and examined them endlessly. "What does *dosta* mean?" I asked.

"It means *enough,*" Tom replied. "*Dosta*—he often said it."

Dosta, I said some weeks later, standing at the edge of Nun Wood. The first primroses were out. I'd never heard Dan use that expression, but I trusted my son. Helped by Hector McIver and my husband, I'd just buried Dan's ashes in the clearing he'd described. I wanted him near Joe: I didn't intend him to be scattered in some London crematorium garden. I'd asked Lucas to come, but he wouldn't.

Dosta, I said, and then left Hector, who was returning to the village. He had a buyer for the Nunns' cottage, apparently. He had a meeting with that syndicate, too: time to sign on the dotted line. *Where will you go, Hector?* I asked him. He looked down at the valley and frowned. They hadn't decided, he replied. Perhaps Scotland. His mother had always missed her homeland.

Nick and I returned to the Abbey. Finn had been refusing to lie in bed, and Nick, slave to her every wish, had made the Lady Chapel into her sickroom. She was lying there on the sofa when we entered, next to the cobra table where Gramps always put his evening glass of whiskey. Now that table was piled high with books—though Finn's sight was failing, and I think she could not have read them.

We'd been out of the house for fifteen minutes, no more. But in that short time there had been a change; we could both see that change in her face as we entered. Her eyes were turned to the windows. Outside, it was a warm spring day; the sunlight, entering the glass at a slant, shone across the floor and struck her bright hair. She had turned her eyes, her near sightless eyes, to that light; on her face was an expression of longing.

I knew she didn't want to die, my sister. She wasn't resigned to death. Until this morning, she'd been fighting it with all the strength she possessed—and Finn's strength, her obduracy, had always been considerable. "Ah, dear God," Nick said in a low voice when he saw her face. He crossed to her side. He knelt beside her and took her hand in his. He buried his face against her neck, and I saw Finn move a little, just a little. He was speaking to her, some last words, some outpouring of guilt and anguish and pleading meant for her ears only.

At that point, neither of them was aware I was there. I knew that. Even so, it seemed right to leave them alone. So I left my husband and my sister, went downstairs, and walked in the cloister.

I wasn't an empress of trend that day, Dan. I wasn't an alpha female. I am not, and never have been, the woman you saw—but that doesn't matter now. You had your version, I have mine. I won't argue with you.

Some while later, Nick came down to me—and I knew from his face that Finn had gone. I'd never had any final reunion with her. I took him in my arms and let him weep. I thought: Now I'm alone, I'm the last of the sisters. *You'll get everything your heart desires*, Bella had predicted for me on my sixteenth birthday. She had not, of course, predicted that I would keep it. *Here's a husband and a half, Miss*

Julia. Ah, well. Bella always disliked me, and I'd always suspected her predictions were designed to trick or mislead. Most assertions Bella made were doubled: *Roses all the way for you, my darling*, she'd said to Maisie that day, pointing out the lucky cross on her palm. And in some doubled sense, that is true. There is little evidence, the doctors maintain and the nuns who now look after her insist, that Maisie is anything other than content. In silence, the nuns say, she has found happiness.

Finn had wanted a quiet funeral, and we gave her that. Her ashes were put next to Gramps's and our father's in the church at Wyken-field. Stella came to the funeral, along with that artist friend of hers with whom she now lives in Cornwall. He paints badly and rarely speaks, but he is devoted to Stella—so I'm grateful to him.

My mother wept—but she took refuge from grief with plans and schemes, just as she always did. What was going to happen to the Abbey now? What could we do with it now? Maybe Nick and I thought of moving there, perhaps? Yes, it had sad memories, of course—but so many happy ones, too. And Stella was off and away, remaking the past: Did I remember this event, that picnic, that birth-day; the time Gramps did this or Maisie said that? Did I remember the summers, those glorious, endless summers?

I'd seen the expression on Nick's face when she made these remarks. "Don't worry," I told him when Stella finally left. "I'm not planning on living anywhere with you. And certainly not here. If you want to come back to me and the children, that's a decision only you can make. When you've made it, by all means let's discuss it. Meanwhile, I know what I'm going to do with the Abbey. I've been planning it for some time. Someone in this family has to be practical."

"You're so hard, Julia," Nick said. I could see the distaste on his face. "Were you always like that? When did that happen to you?"

I could have come back at him. I could have said, Shortly after I married you, Nick. Around the same time I realized my high-minded husband didn't actually love me. Around the same time I realized he wanted me and was deeply ashamed of wanting me. When I realized he neither respected me nor knew me. Or recently, perhaps, when I found out that I was a substitute for my sister and had been for over twenty years . . . that seems like a pretty good moment to harden the heart, Nick.

But I wasn't sure that was true. Maybe he's right, and I *am* hard, always have been. So what would my answer be then? Who could I blame if I didn't blame him? My father, for dying? My mother, who was always so painfully impractical; my mother, who needed someone to stand between her and the world—a lesson I learned long before we came to the Abbey? My sisters? Should I blame Maisie, who through no fault of hers disrupted our family and smashed it? Or Finn, who retreated to a far continent, worked hard, and did unimaginable good: tenacious, obstinate Finn, who would never relinquish the hold she had on my husband?

Maybe I should blame my genes—there's a healthy dose of the selfishness gene in my family. But I don't want to blame anyone, other than myself. I am Julia. I am what circumstances and my own will have made me.

So I made no reply to Nick's accusation. I stood there thinking of my past: I married Nick for his rectitude—and that rectitude had always blinded me. I thought of the many occasions when Nick had worked half the night, and I had never doubted that he was with his patients, the patients to whom he was so devoted. I thought of the many occasions when he'd insisted he had to go abroad to some conference, and how it had never occurred to me that such absences gave him a pretext to meet Finn and stay with her for the two or three intense, secret days that fired his obsession and ensured its long duration. I thought of the crisis in their affair, which had come when

I was pregnant with Tom and, in all innocence, telephoned Finn to ask her to be my baby's godmother.

"You're pregnant again?" Finn said after a long silence. I'd heard the sharp intake of breath. I can understand her shock now: I wonder what Nick had told her. Did he lie to Finn, too, and pretend he didn't sleep with me? I think he must have done. That was never true. Whatever it is I provide in bed, Nick has always wanted it. But Finn punished him then. She went abroad, and I think it must have been some while, two or three years, before she relented. I can compute the time: For the first two years of Tom's childhood, Nick and I were closer than we had ever been.

I cannot read my sister. I do not know how pure or impure her motives were. She spared Dan, but she didn't spare me. And eventually—it would have been when Tom was about three—she must have made contact with Nick again. Finn relented, and my husband went running. After that, even I began to see that my marriage was troubled; even I began to suspect that my husband's rectitude might not preclude an affair. Even I began to wonder if his absences and evasions and impatience and irritation might be caused by entanglement with some woman. "Are you involved with some woman, Nick?" I asked him once. He stared at me in that mute, judging way I'd come to detest.

"No, Julia," he replied. "I am not, and never have been, involved with 'some woman.'"

A nice distinction.

I looked at him now: white-faced, scarcely sane with grief, unable to see beyond Finn, unable to see me, because for him I've always been obscured behind the image of my sister. He is not alone in that. I found I had no inclination to argue or accuse. If he believes me hard, so be it.

He left shortly after, returning to our London house; our future remained undiscussed. We agreed that he would spend a week there with Fanny and Tom, and I would stay here. Separated, we would try to decide what to do next. I watched him drive away. For the first time in many years, I was alone at the Abbey.

Unseasonably warm weather for days. For the first time in twenty years I could go to bed when I wanted, get up when I wanted, eat or not eat—as I wanted. There was no husband, no children, to fret over; there were no appointments to keep. There was no TV crew standing by; no interviews or photographs were imminent. I did not need to wear the mask I daily assume. There was no television at the Abbey; there never had been. The ancient wireless set, I discovered, no longer functioned. No one apart from my family knew I was here; no newspapers were delivered. I was cut off from the outside world and all news of a distant war. I was free to think. I had all day and all night to think. And I was free to reread Dan's account of our last summer here, free to consider his interpretation of events— events that I view very differently.

I went up to the attics, where he'd been painting the walls that day, and looked at our ghosts: I could still sense the power of his sexuality. Dan never realized how powerful a force this was, and he never understood its effect on women. He never finished painting these walls. I could see the exact white point Dan had reached: This was where he put down his brush and followed me to the Lady Chapel. This was the window from which he watched Maisie returning from the dogs' burial ground. The penultimate sighting: Then she went to the cloister, and then she disappeared for an hour and a half. I'll never know, now, where she went or why. There are a thousand hiding places in the Abbey—and, as I know, a thousand and one places in which to conceal oneself.

I walked down to the refectory, unlocked it, and went in. I counted the times I'd slept here with Lucas. Five, six? Lucas preferred to come up to the house. He liked to creep into my room in the early morning when the rest of the family was downstairs. He never stayed long—Lucas was a peremptory, unskilled lover. He needed some subsidiary boost, the threat of being caught in the act, to make it exciting for him. Sex did not really interest him, I always felt. It was a means to an end. Lucas needed to see the three sisters; that was necessary for his portrait. So he approached us artfully: Maisie through her stories and me through lovemaking; Finn he simply watched—until, not long after their marriage, he found he had watched and seen enough, and she was no longer material for him. He has a short attention span, Lucas. His gaze is so intent, so all-seeing, but once he has seen what he needs, he loses interest immediately. It didn't surprise me that he'd agreed to marry Finn. Marriage means nothing to him, but it gave him the opportunity to watch her a while longer.

All those drawings he did of her: Like Dan, I'd never realized there were so many. But Dan was wrong about *Final Finn*. It wasn't drawn after their wedding. It was drawn at Addenbrookes Hospital in Cambridge, shortly after her baby son was stillborn. I was with Finn then; I remember that covering of the eyes. I remember the depth of her grief. It didn't occur to me that Lucas was recording it when he retreated to the waiting room with his sketchpad.

In the refectory, there's still a faint sickly irremovable odor of turpentine. Standing there, remembering the unveiling of Lucas's portrait, I felt Dan had been wrong about *The Sisters Mortland*, too. I don't believe Lucas's portrait of us incorporates the dead or that his changes were prompted by anything Maisie said. Lucas was interested not in the dead, but in us—in three girls, three almost-women. He painted us as archetypes: Martha and Mary, temptress and virgin, with Maisie the female child, eternally trapped between two female polarities. It was our physical likeness that most drew him, I think. Finn and I were so alike then that we could have been twins; Maisie resembled both of us, but in miniature. This likeness ensures that, in Lucas's portrait, Finn and I can be ourselves—and our opposites, and each other. We are female, and interchangeable, that's the point: We offer the conventional female gifts—love, sex, nurture, and threat; but beyond that, we have no identity. The power of his painting—and it is very powerful, I would never deny that—derives from the fact that it's reductive.

I returned to the Abbey and went upstairs to the Lady Chapel; I stood there at the middle window. A still evening: a soft evening. You could feel the earth stirring. After a long time spent resisting the temptation, I went across to the panel.

I slid it back, smelled the stale, damp air, and looked into the darkness. I wanted Dan then. That fuck in the dark was the fuck of my life—every woman experiences one true fuck, if she's fortunate. Sometimes she will confess that to another woman—though not, I think, to a man. Since I dislike the confessional mode, I confess to no one. But, Dan being dead, I can admit now what I could never admit to him alive. Most fucking is so impure, Dan, so shot through with trivial concerns, spoiled by irrelevances, or habit, or evasions, or ineptitudes, or uncertainties—*is this love*, for example. But that wasn't impure. Something happened—and remembering it, here where I could feel your presence and your absence, I wept for you.

When I was at my lowest point, I was interrupted by a telephone call from a nun, the Reverend Mother of Maisie's care home.

I'd written to this Mother Superior some weeks earlier; I wrote to her before Finn died, before I came back here. Two days after her phone call, toward the end of my week of seclusion, she drove across Suffolk in her small, smart, nippy Nissan to meet me. I was calmer by then and ready for the encounter.

I have money as well as fame—it doesn't greatly interest me, but I have it. I'm good at generating money, and those I employ—accountants, brokers, and so on—are good at growing it. A use for some of this money now seemed obvious. For over a year, Maisie's nuns had been looking for a new building to replace their present one, which they long ago outgrew. Finn had always resisted any sale of the Abbey; she had wanted it kept as some kind of memorial or museum. The fact that it was crumbling away never concerned her—but it concerned me. Now I felt that the Abbey, with a donation to sweeten the deal, could be useful at last. I knew that the Reverend Mother, a formidable woman of Irish extraction, would know very quickly whether the Abbey would be suitable.

I gave her lunch, a good lunch. Then we walked round the grounds and the cloister. The Reverend Mother had done her research—she knew more about the history of the Abbey than I did. That did not surprise me. She is a small woman in her early sixties, fast-moving and fast-thinking. She is without sentiment, and her acuity delights me. I pointed out to her the improvements I'd initiated this last year: the repairs to the roof, the windows, guttering, and so on. She was alert to other concerns; I suspect these repairs did not interest her.

The attics seemed to meet with her approval, as did the kitchen. In the dining room, she glared at the ceiling and said that it would have to come out. I took her upstairs to the former Lady Chapel; I explained that the altar wall had been there, where the fireplace had been inserted. I showed her the secret panel, from which she drew back sharply, telling me to close it at once. I mentioned the Squint. She glanced up to the high, dark corner where the aperture was concealed—it is virtually invisible from below—and said, yes, she had already noticed it; and had in any case read about it. It clearly did not interest her.

Then she moved across to the windows. Her concentration became intense. She stood in front of first one, then another. She returned to the middle window, opened the casement, and looked out. In the distance was Nun Wood, the village, and the valley.

"Ah, I *see*," she said. She crossed herself. She turned back to me and told me with a smile that, if the terms were correct—and I must remember that her order was poor, dependent on the generosity of others more fortunate—then this building was right, entirely and absolutely *right*, for her purposes.

We went outside again, and I gave her tea in the cloister. She haggled unashamedly—she'd do well in a bazaar or in the City, this Mother Superior. When she had wrung a promised donation twice the size I'd intended, with the land and Abbey thrown in gratis, of course, she departed, well pleased, in her nippy Nissan.

I waved her off down the drive. During her visit, when she'd been standing at that window and I had been thinking of Dan, who had been born by it, whose mother had died by it, an idea had come to me.

I returned to the library. I examined the bookshelves. I took out the musty boxes in which Gramps had stored a mass of memorabilia relating to my father. I found my father's medals and the RAF wings he'd once worn on his uniform. I found his letters to Gramps, newspaper cuttings, war reports, and details about his squadron. I found his medical records—they made sad reading and reawoke old fears. But I found nothing else. I had not found what I was seeking.

I sat there on the floor, the evening light softly declining, thinking of what Finn had said, as recorded by Dan—a conversation I'd long forgotten. I could hear the voices of the dead very clearly. I thought of Dan, who misread me that day; my remark about the stupidity of those who love was not directed at him or my sister. I thought of Finn's claim that Maisie would have written her last message, if she wrote one at all, to the dead, to her invisible nuns—or to my father. Love letters to the dead, Dan called the process: I understand what he meant now.

Behind me, on the lower shelves of the bookcases, were the family photograph albums. They included the expensive leather albums, with gilding, that Maisie had made Gramps purchase when she was about eight or nine. That summer, they'd become her obsession. Inside them, she pasted all the old photographs of Daddy and even the letters he'd written Stella, letters that Maisie—always a little spy—had found in, and stolen from, Stella's underwear drawer.

There were four albums in all. I found Maisie's hidden diary in the third of them.

THIRTY-ONE

Reading Silence

I READ THIS DIARY, this journal, with care—Maisie had written it with scrupulous care, I could see that. I placed her account
of that last summer alongside Dan's. I saw the places where their
two stories intersected. They were immediately, and troublingly,
apparent.

I was not sure if this was the last message, the suicide note, that
Dan had been seeking—there was no indication that it was intended
in that way. Nor was I ready to take it at face value, as I suspect my
little sister might have wished. I knew Maisie's controlling tenden-
cies: I also knew her opinions about storytelling—indeed, Maisie
herself used this tale of hers to emphasize them.

I watched that last visit we all made to Elde, watched that lunch,
watched Maisie walk out of the French windows with Edmund, her
departure at that point a well-established ritual. Now I saw with new
eyes—and a part of me, shocked, sickened, and angered, succumbed
to Maisie's narrative temptations. Easy enough to blame Edmund for
everything that subsequently happened. Easy enough to say: Of
course, that is why she jumped; she could no longer live with this
terrible secret. . . . But was that the case? I was by no means sure—
not when I was calmer. Maisie's tone did not encourage that view;
she was describing an event that took place over two weeks before

she went up to the Lady Chapel that evening and opened the window. It was not the first time it had happened, either—she made that clear. So, was there indubitable, direct cause and effect? Did this story of hers, at last, answer all those questions Dan had asked, that we had all asked? This is why Maisie jumped? *That* is what went wrong, that summer?

I could see only too clearly the damage Edmund might have done, by his actions and by his words. We'd all tried so hard to protect Maisie, to shield her from any knowledge of our father's illness, to pretend to her that although she could not go to school, was constantly having to see doctors, was always being appraised, tested, and medicated—to pretend that, even so, she was not abnormal in any way, she was just, as Stella liked to say, "special" and "different." To have those reassurances ripped away—yes, I could see what damage that might have done to her. Edmund had shown her a Maisie that would have hurt her very deeply. But then Lucas had done so, too, shortly afterward, when we trooped down to the refectory for the unveiling of the portrait. I can still remember the expression on my sister's face as she looked at herself on the canvas, looked at a Maisie made unnaturally small, pinned between her two elder sisters, a tiny pair of scissors clasped in her hand like an instrument of self-harm, or a weapon.

That episode, she did not describe. It lay in the silent period, in the gap between the visit to Elde and her attempted suicide—in those two weeks and five days Maisie chose not to document. I reread what she had written, and any certainty I'd felt slipped away. Where I had seen causal links before, her story unraveled. Why had she chosen to begin it *here* and to end it *there*? Why begin with her storytelling to Lucas and end with a dream, a dream about our father? I looked and I looked, *words, words, words,* and I began to feel that—as with Dan's account of his last twelve days—I needed to read silence rather than words, and how do you read silence?

My secret shall remain inviolable, Maisie had written—and told the truth. I could not know why she jumped, any more than I could know, or guess, what she believed she had seen in the crystal that day at Bella's. What had I myself seen that day? Nothing I can remember clearly, just a haze, glints on glass, reflections—a sense of oddness in an ordinary room, of dislocation. *The second shall be first*, Bella had said to Finn—and of course, Finn, the second sister, was the first of us to fall in love, the first of us to fall pregnant, and the first of us to die—but I refused to be influenced by such coincidences. Bella was canny, as fortune-tellers always are. She made sure her so-called predictions were vague enough to fit all possible futures. If you're going to make a living predicting outcomes, it pays to be dramatic and elastic.

I see a sacrifice. . . . Bella had said that, too. I'd forgotten that particular prediction, until Maisie's account reminded me of it, brought it rushing back, along with that hot, cramped cottage room, that appalling tea; reminding me of Dan's awkwardness and shame and Bella's malice. Did that particular prediction have any significance? None that I could see. No doubt it was shop soiled, a regular part of Bella's patter, of her repertoire.

Maisie had written in a blue notebook. I weighed it in my hand. I moved across to the Lady Chapel windows and looked out. I fitted my fingers into those bullet grooves Dan describes. I opened the middle window, as Maisie had done, and breathed in a sweet evening's air. Something plucked at my heart then: all those unknowns, all those Dans I never knew, all those Maisies I never suspected. Out of the silence in the room, they spoke to me, and out of the silence, the deep silence, I answered.

One question only remained—and I considered it carefully later that night, a night I passed in a state of anxiety and sleeplessness. Should I take action now, as a result of what I'd learned from Maisie's story and from Dan's? And if so, what action could I, should I, take?

Over twenty years had passed since that last visit to Elde. Maisie was a strange child, and she was not always a truthful one. Perhaps it was better, and more merciful, to do nothing.

The very next day, I received a telephone call from Elde, from my cousin-by-marriage, Veronica Mortland. I had been debating whether or not to contact Veronica.

She was calling, she said, to ask my advice. She'd decided that one bedroom wing at Elde needed a complete overhaul, redecorating from top to bottom. She wasn't sure if it was the kind of project my company would undertake and wondered if I might look at it and advise. Besides, it was some time—two years, at least—since we'd met for that pleasant lunch in London. It would be so nice to see me. Translation: Veronica wanted to talk about Dan, she wanted to ask me about Dan and the circumstances of his death. I knew that immediately.

I agreed to meet her. I had planned to visit Maisie before returning to London—I visit her regularly; and Maisie's care home is not far from Elde—indeed, it was Violet who knew of the care home and first suggested it. I can see now why Violet might have involved herself in Maisie's predicament as she did—something that had always puzzled me. I can see too why Violet might have wished Maisie to be near Elde—where she could keep an eye on her. If I'm right, Violet need not have worried: Maisie is permanently silenced.

Veronica said she would make lunch. I said I would go on from Elde to the care home.

That Sunday, that Son's day, Dan, I set off. It was always a long, slow drive to Elde, made worse by our cramped ancient Wolseley and by Gramps's erratic driving. Twenty years had done little to alter these cross-country roads. I am a fast driver, and I was in a fast car—but on this narrow, winding route, speed is impossible.

As I drove, I was replaying the telephone conversation I had had with my daughter, Fanny, the previous night and considering the conversation I was about to have with Veronica. How truthful should I be? It's never easy to judge whether truth will be helpful or irreparably damaging. I'd told Fanny the truth last night—and I was by no means sure that had been a wise decision.

I'd been calling home every night to speak to my children. Last night, Fanny snatched the telephone from Tom. Within seconds, I was immersed in the ten-act ongoing melodrama that is my daughter's life; within seconds, the happiness and reassurance I felt when speaking to my son had fled. Fanny specializes in wreckage. Out flowed the grievances, in one unstoppable torrent: how she'd never get over what had happened to Dan; how his death was completely, entirely, from beginning to end, her fault. How her life was one hideous mess. How she'd chucked in the PR job with that rap group, who were a bunch of sexist losers anyway. How she now couldn't decide: Should she plead to get her place at Durham University back, or wait and reapply to Oxford; should she go to Patagonia or Paraguay, or maybe enroll with Médecins sans Frontières or something—because she couldn't get over Finn's death, either, and she felt, she really, really felt, that she just had to get out there and do some good somewhere.

While this lengthy, extravagant, and foolish speech continued, I thought of my daughter and her thanklessness: of the difficult hours I'd lavished on her and the scorn and hostility that had resulted. I thought of the business meetings I'd canceled or cut short, the long holidays that conflicted with work—holidays that became a daily torture once Fanny reached her teens—holidays in Italy, France, Greece, holidays that were punctuated by a daily lament, a litany of frustration: *This place is so bo-oring, why can't I go home?* I thought of the cost of her privileged schooling and the exhausting energy that had gone into it—all the attempts to help Fanny with this subject or that one; to advise when some teacher or friend had a down on her;

to find activities, drama, music, sport, ballet, horses, anything that might divert Fanny for more than ten minutes.

I thought of Fanny's intelligence, which is considerable, and her self-destructiveness, which is also considerable—as mine was at her age. I thought of my constant fear, never admitted even to Nick, that Fanny might have inherited some defect, passed down through me from my father, a family fault line that might also have accounted for Maisie's abnormalities. I thought of defending my daughter to Dan. I thought of the accusations I'd made against him, which proved false. Those accusations constituted the last conversation I would ever have with him. Had Fanny not appeared when she had, what might have happened? I thought of this, and a door closed in me.

"Fanny," I said, cutting her short, "I'm not going to advise you. Whatever I advise, you will do the opposite. You're nearly twenty. You decide where to go and what to do. If you want to go to Paraguay, earn the money for a ticket. If you imagine you could be any possible use to Médecins sans Frontières, when you have no nursing skills whatsoever and little intention of acquiring them, by all means contact them. Go to Durham, go to Oxford, go wherever you choose. But don't blame other people for problems of your own making. Stand on your own two feet. And stop this sick-making vanity and hypocrisy. Don't you dare to mention Dan to me ever again—ever, do you understand me?"

There was a long silence. "*What* did you say?" Fanny said in a tone of disbelief.

"I said: Grow up, Fanny," I replied. "Just damn well grow up." I replaced the receiver.

Was that wise? It was the truth—and probably long overdue; my daughter is spoiled. But was it too harsh? I'd exhausted every other approach. I found I was now beyond caring.

I'd reached Elde village. I drove past the neat estate cottages and turned in through the iron gates to that three-mile-long drive. Should I be equally truthful to Veronica? Her husband, my cousin Edmund, died about eighteen years ago. He was killed in a car crash some six years after their wedding, killed when returning to Elde from a school reunion dinner in London; he was driving, and he was not sober. Humphrey is also dead, though he lived to be nearly ninety. And Violet too has gone; she died of a stroke about seven years ago. Veronica and her only child, her son, Edgar, named for his Mortland great-grandfather, are left. At Elde, there was no physical evidence of these changes. The park was as perfectly maintained as it had always been. A landscape laid out in the eighteenth century: a great avenue of oaks; and—in the distance—a small temple to Artemis, with a lake in the shallow bowl of rough pasture known as the Wilderness.

As I reached the steps below that great pomposity of a portico at the front of the house, Veronica emerged. I looked at Dan's sweet-faced girl; I saw the debutante he'd met that day in the hospital ward and the sad young matron he'd encountered outside a Sloane Square department store in the dog days of a long-ago August. She had aged, as I have. She was waving at me.

THIRTY-TWO

Circles

I<small>T's</small> <small>A</small> J<small>ULIA</small> <small>LUNCH</small>," Veronica said, kissing my cheek. "I thought we'd eat in the kitchen—I can't bear that stuffy dining room. Look, Julia, I had this room redone about three years ago. I hope you approve—it's pretty, isn't it?"

It *was* pretty. A huge, cool, stone-flagged kitchen; an Aga, inevitably. One of my paints—yes, Dan, I think it was Skylark—on the walls, and another, Tern, on the dressers.

"Very you," Veronica said, coloring. "And the lunch is, too. It's from your latest book—I adore that book. Your recipes are so clever and chic and delicious, and they never let one down."

"They're designed to be foolproof," I replied. Veronica's color deepened. I hadn't meant to imply that she was a fool. It's remarks like that, said without thought, that have contributed to my reputation. I am sharp-tongued. I hope I am not malicious.

"It's a perfect room, Veronica," I said quickly, trying to make amends. "You've done it brilliantly—and thank God not to be in that dining room. I always hated it."

"I hoped Eddie would be here," Veronica went on, chopping basil, ladling soup. "He's down from Oxford for the weekend, but he's gone off with some friends. He said he'd try to get back before you leave—it's such ages since you've seen him; he must have been at prep school. I hope this lunch will be up to standard, it's so intimidating, cooking for you— Damn, is that too much basil, do you think?"

"Perfect amount," I said absently, watching her. She'd changed, Veronica. She must now be forty-three or -four. She'd never lost her girlish prettiness. She was a little overweight—there'd been a thickening around the waist since I last saw her—but her dark shining hair, now short, was well cut and sleek; and she still retained her gentleness of manner. But being widowed in her twenties put steel in Veronica. These days, she sits on committees, oversees the estate, works for numerous charities, upholds the sanctity of the Tory Party, and campaigns on behalf of the local hunt. She is mistress of all she surveys and seems content to be so. She thinks conservatively and dresses conservatively, as she was always destined by her upbringing to do. I thought of Dan's description of their affair. I thought: *Veronica and I have nothing in common whatsoever.*

As I was about to discover, I was misreading Veronica—and had done so for many years. I was making the very same mistake that Dan made: a failure of vision and imagination—that solipsism most of us are cursed with. Blind to distress—a myopia that afflicts many. I ate an excellent Julia cold soup, a Julia game pie (pie included pheasant, not in season, so must be frozen: I forgive you, Veronica). She'd made a good salad with Julia dressing, and the pudding was a gin-and-lime-juice Julia jelly, one I'd invented in a moment of inspiration-deprivation. It was not perfect in its consistency (two gelatin leaves too many, Veronica), but it was good even so. I resolved never to write another cookery book, not if I live to be a hundred. I waited; she would bring up the subject of Dan over coffee, I knew. She did so.

"Will you tell me what happened, Julia?" she said, sitting opposite me. "I've read the newspapers obviously—"

"They can't report that much. It's sub judice," I replied—the trial was still months away when Veronica and I had this conversation.

"I want to hear it from you. It's made me terribly sad. It knocked me for six, actually. Dan was such an extraordinary man. . . . He read my palm for me once, did I ever tell you?"

"No, I don't think you did," I replied with care, and truthfully.

"It was at the hospital that time, with Maisie, do you remember, Julia? Dan persuaded me to go and have tea with him in the cafeteria. I was so young and inexperienced then; it sounds silly, perhaps, to say this, but I could tell at once that he was attracted to me. Edmund and I were about to get married, of course—the wedding was only weeks away, because Violet insisted on bringing it forward—I think she was terrified Edmund would get cold feet. . . ." She frowned. "It never occurred to her that *I* might get cold feet, that little Veronica might realize Edmund wasn't such a great catch after all. But that's exactly what happened. I came as near as dammit to calling off the wedding. Dan was begging me to do that. Do you know what he told me when he read my palm, Julia?"

"I can't imagine." It was becoming clear that it wasn't Dan's death Veronica wished to discuss. His death seemed not to concern her.

"Dan told me all about the fears and uncertainties I felt," she continued, wide-eyed. "He saw them *all*, Julia. And he told me that I mustn't be afraid or timid—I was frightfully timid then—because inside I had all this strength. I had a great *well* of strength, he said. One day I'd learn how to use it, but I must be careful to use it wisely."

I inspected the table. A familiar patter: I'd heard Bella use one very similar. So you were kind, Dan, I thought. Kind on that occasion, anyway.

"I've never forgotten that. Never. I still remind myself of it every day. If I'm ever in trouble, I think of it. I think of Dan, too—I've thought of Dan every day for twenty-three years. I expect I'll think of him for the next twenty-three. I just wish . . ." I heard her voice falter. I saw that her eyes had filled with tears. I looked away. Tears are catching.

"I *loved* him. I loved him so much. I'm going to tell you something, Julia. I probably shouldn't tell anyone this, especially you, and I hope you won't mind—but I had an affair with Dan. Before I married." She hesitated, giving me a small, darting glance. "A very passionate affair. He . . . well, the truth is, Dan was desperate to marry me. But I just didn't have the strength to break my engagement. I was too frightened of what people would think, and too frightened of Violet. That was devastating for Dan. And that makes me feel so guilty now, Julia. . . . I keep thinking, if only he'd known how much I loved him."

"I wouldn't agonize over it too much, Veronica," I replied. I was wondering if she really believed this and how long ago she'd invented it. "No doubt he recovered from the disappointment. People do. You know: 'Men have died from time to time, and worms have eaten them—but not for love. . . .'"

"I'm sorry?" She was looking at me blankly. I could sense hostility.

"Just a quote. Dan was very young then—not that much older than you were. At that age, the heart's resilient."

"Yes, well, I was never much good with quotes. That stupid school I went to. Unlike you, I'm not bookish. Of course, Dan never stopped telling me how clever you were, how the two of you liked the same books, the same poetry—"

"That was Finn, not me. You're confusing me with my sister."

"Really? I don't think so. Never mind—I'm glad you see it like that, Julia. I was worried you might be upset."

"Upset that you had an affair with Dan? No. Why should I be?"

"Well, I always felt there was something between you two. It was obvious. I could see it in that hospital ward. I could see the way he looked at you. Dan always denied it, of course—though I asked him and asked him. I can't bear not knowing the truth, I've always hated it. It's not that I'm jealous—I'm not remotely jealous, and never have been. I just like people to be straight with me—"

"Then I'll be straight," I replied, rising. "There was no love affair between Dan and me. On the whole, Dan disliked me—as many people do."

I hesitated; I could still sense hostility. I said, "I'm pushed for time. Shall we go and look at those rooms now?"

Veronica led the way upstairs, along great processional corridors, under the gaze of ancestors. Her pace was brisk. I followed more slowly. I was thinking about evidence: how you assemble it, how you compare it, how you weigh the statements of the various witnesses. The subject was on my mind anyway: I was still planning what I'd say when the trial took place and how I could ensure that my version of a crime came to be the accepted one.

I was also thinking of the evidence Dan had given me and the new evidence gleaned from reading Maisie's diary, or journal, or last communication—I wasn't sure, really, how to classify it. Now I was confronted with another version of past events. I didn't believe Veronica, but I was saddened that, with Dan so recently dead, she should tell me this now. If I could have believed her motive was purely self-protective, that she wanted to share with me a fabrication she found comforting, I could have accepted it. But that wasn't entirely the case. Veronica, I sensed, harbored a grudge; she had hoped her revelation might hurt me. Not the first time that's happened. Many women dislike me.

"These rooms . . . ," Veronica said, coming to a halt at the far end of the west wing. "All these bedrooms and dressing rooms. Look at them, Julia. Aren't they hideous?" She flung open a door. "This used to be Edmund's. The 'master bedroom,' as ghastly estate agents like to say. Except a house like Elde doesn't have such a thing. They're all master bedrooms. And there are at least thirty-five of them, maybe more. Perhaps one day I should count them."

I went into dead Edmund's bedroom. Veronica's manner was making me uneasy, and this room deepened that unease. I couldn't see why she should describe it as hideous; it was certainly not that. Well proportioned and light; paneled walls, graceful windows. The room seemed pleasant enough to me. I could see no evidence of Edmund here; this space had the anonymity of a guest room. A four-poster bed with old silk hangings—rather dark, perhaps, a dark green silk brocade. Two chests, one of them almost certainly Chippendale. I couldn't see anything wrong here.

"Tweeds," Veronica said in an angry way, throwing open a cupboard door and then slamming it. "He wore tweeds winter and summer. They're all still here. I must be mad—why didn't I sort this out? I'm going to pack them up and send them to Oxfam."

"I don't see that this room needs touching," I said. "It's a conventional room—but you'd expect that at Elde. It's quite beautiful in its way, Veronica. I can't see why you'd want to alter it. Rooms like this are best left alone."

"You think so? What about this?" And, after opening a communicating door that led through an anteroom, she took me into another bedroom, with a more delicate four-poster. "This was mine. Not any more. But when I was married, when Edmund was alive, this was mine. What do you think of this, Julia?"

"Veronica, I don't understand," I began. "This is a fine room. You can't possibly want to alter this. . . ." I looked around me: eighteenth-century hand-painted Chinese wallpaper, now faded, still exquisite. A deep bay window overlooking the park and the lake, a bay with a window seat. Fine furniture, fine rugs . . . I made a slow circuit of the room. I could see nothing wrong. I looked at the hangings on the bed, which were perhaps too dark a red, a gloomy crimson. I looked at the window, the walls. Veronica was watching me. I was beginning to understand that decor was not what she wanted to show me, when, as I turned, I saw the back of the door through which we had entered. That door communicated with her husband's room: It had five bolts on it.

I crossed back into Edmund's bedroom and came to a halt. I saw what I should have seen at once but had missed among the welter of architectural and decorative detail. On the table on the far side of the bed was a small photograph, black and white, in a silver frame. I went across and picked it up. It was a photograph of Maisie, aged about nine, taken here at Elde. She was standing in the long walk, between Violet's celebrated herbaceous borders, those borders where Maisie had identified ten plants by their Latin names and been rewarded with a ten-shilling note by Edmund. "Right, Maisie, where now?" "We could go to the Wilderness again," she had replied to him.

"He was obsessed with her," Veronica said. She had entered the room behind me. "Completely obsessed. He wanted me to *be* her."

There was a silence. The room felt hot and close. On the picture, my sister had written: "To Edmund from Maisie." The handwriting, round and firm, was unmistakable. "Is this what you wanted to show me, Veronica?" I asked. I felt sick and uncertain. "Is this what I'm supposed to change? Beyond my powers—and it's a little late, don't you think?"

"I suppose it is." She gave a shrug. "I don't really know why I brought you up here—not now. It was stupid. You're right. These rooms should be left as they are. I shouldn't change anything. Leave them to the moths—this damn house is infested with moths; they eat their way through everything. Moths and grubs and eggs, eat, breed, eat—look." She slapped her hand down on the dark green silk bedcover. She shook the curtains at the head of the bed. Five or six tiny clothes moths flew out, fluttered in the stripes of sunlight from the windows, spiraled, alighted, and crawled into the dark canopy over the bed. Clothes moths: *Tineola bisselliella,* I heard Maisie whisper.

"Violet knew what Edmund was like," Veronica said. "She thought I was so stupid and innocent, I'd think nothing was wrong. A grown man worshipping a little girl—and not even a *normal* girl. I can't forgive Violet for that, Julia. I always promised myself that I'd pay her back—but she's dead now." She gave the curtain one final, violent shake. One last silvery moth fluttered into the sunlight. Veronica attempted to catch it and failed. She clapped her hands on air.

She drew in a deep breath and seemed to calm herself. "You're right," she went on in a flat voice, "I should leave everything exactly as it is. Let's go downstairs. It's such a lovely day. We could have tea outside."

"I don't think so." I replaced the photograph. "I told you, I'm going to see Maisie, and I don't want to be late."

"I can't imagine it would make much difference," she replied, and I could hear the gibe in her voice—it was now obvious. "Does time make any difference to Maisie? Does she know if it's afternoon or morning? She can't even recognize you."

"The nuns will expect me, even if Maisie doesn't. I'll go now, Veronica."

I turned out of the room and walked back down the corridors. I was walking rapidly. Veronica caught up with me on the main stairs and took me by the arm. "You can't go yet," she said. "You haven't told me about Dan. You promised to tell me what happened."

"Veronica, must I? My son and I were outside Dan's house, and—"

"Why were you there?"

"We were on our way to visit Dan. He was my son's godfather. He lived quite close to us in London. . . ." I walked on down the stairs. I walked fast, Veronica following.

"Your son's godfather? I didn't know that. Did you visit Dan often?"

"No, I didn't. Veronica, I really must go—"

"I used to write to him, you know." She came to a halt at the foot of the stairs. "I never sent the letters, but I wrote to him for years. I had to tell someone what it was like, living here, being married to Edmund. I still have the letters. I could show them to you."

"Veronica, what would that achieve?" I hesitated. I was longing to leave, wishing I'd never come. But I could see she was close to tears. "You'd only regret it afterwards," I went on more gently. "They're private letters, and they should stay private, don't you think?"

"Be discreet, you mean?"

"That's one way of putting it, yes." I turned away.

"How certain you sound. You're always certain about everything, aren't you, Julia? So certain, so superior, and so cold. You don't know what unhappiness is, do you?"

"If I did, I wouldn't advertise that fact. Look, Veronica, I'm sorry, but I'm going to be late. I really have to leave now." I pushed her aside and crossed to the front door.

"I want you to meet Eddie. I told him you'd be here. Julia, don't go. . . ." She ran after me and caught up with me on the steps outside. I tried to turn away, but before I could do so, she saw my face and she saw my tears.

"I knew it," she said, catching hold of my arm. "You *were* lying to me earlier. Dan would never tell me, and now you won't. I have to understand. You can't hide it from me—it's written all over your face. There *was* something between you and Dan, wasn't there?"

"Very well; yes, there was," I replied. "We made love once. That's it. That's all. Once. One fuck, Veronica. End of story."

I shook her off and walked away fast. I scrambled into my car and drove fast, down that three-mile avenue. I kept expecting the gates, and then they weren't there. When I finally reached them, I nearly collided with another car, also driving at speed, which had just entered them. I slammed on the brakes and slewed to a halt in spitting gravel.

I wasn't wearing my seat belt, and I was thrown forward hard. My face slammed against the arm I'd thrown up to protect myself. My arm smashed against the steering wheel. I straightened up slowly. Where were the gates? I was now facing in the opposite direction. I looked at this wrong direction in a dazed way. My car must have spun right round. My face hurt, but there didn't seem to be any serious damage. Just bruising, I thought. Just bruising. Then an angry voice said, "What the fuck were you doing—you nearly killed us both," and I looked up and saw Dan walking toward me.

I managed to open the door and climb out. I couldn't stand very well. The sky was dizzying. I was watching Dan walk toward me; he was wearing old blue jeans and a white shirt, and he was painfully young. I watched him walking toward me, that Dan of our last summer at the Abbey. His face came alive with concern as he recognized me. I took a step toward him and stumbled. He caught me. As his arms came around me, I heard him say my name; he said, "Julia."

He said, "Julia? It is you, isn't it? Christ, I'm so sorry. That was a near thing. Can you walk? Lean on me—let me help you."

So I leaned on him, and he helped me across to his car and helped me to sit on its leather seat, with my feet still on the drive. "Lean forward," he said. "You're as white as a sheet. You're not going to faint, are you?"

I bent forward obediently. I could see Dan's shoes, and they puzzled me. I'd never seen Dan wear loafers like these. I looked at his shoes and the narrow cuffs of his faded jeans. I straightened up; the sky was normalizing. The right height, the same build, the exact same hair and eyes. "I think I'd better take you back to the house," he said. He crouched down so our faces were on a level. "Julia? . . . Mrs. Marlow? You look—did you hit your head? You're not concussed? I think you're in shock. Please, don't cry. I've got a phone somewhere. Let me call the house. Christ—this was my fault, too. We were both driving too fast. But I was late, and I promised to get back in time to see you—"

"We've seen each other now." I took his hand. "Don't call. Give me one minute."

Well, I have my religion, the same religion as yours, Dan—and in a minute or so I did recover. I looked at your son—and I knew that he was your son at once. He was like your twin, Dan. I could do the calculation now: This young man, in his last year at Oxford, reading Politics, Philosophy, and Economics, as Veronica had informed me over lunch, this young man would be twenty-three this coming June. Conceived in the dog days of August, at Violet's Eaton Square outpost, by an insistent Veronica. No wonder she'd been so anxious for me to stay and meet her son—she had wanted me to see this proof of her lasting bond with Dan. She'd have known I could be in no possible doubt as to who fathered him.

I remembered what you wrote, Dan. August in London: a blue scent and a chime of bracelets. I looked at this boy. I wished he could know who his father was. I wished he could know about you, about Wykenfield, Joe and Bella, and Ocean. I would have liked to give him those stories—but I knew I had no right to do so. Revelations like that can harm—and I wanted no harm here. Everything you, Dan, once wished my son, I wished yours. I wished him all the impossibilities: With all my heart, I wished him lasting happiness, absence of damage and pain, and true fulfillment.

It felt powerful, that wish, intensely powerful. How strange. I stood up, thanked him, and told him this near collision was my fault; that I'd be able to drive in a moment or so, and I had to go shortly— I was visiting my sister.

We stood by my car, looking across the park, on a still spring evening. In the distance, I could see the lake and the small temple to

Artemis. The young man by my side, hands thrust into the pockets of his jeans, looked at this idyll in a frowning way. It did not appear to lift his heart; he showed no sign of pleasure in its ownership. Her firebrand son, Veronica had said, would inherit at twenty-five.

"What are you going to do with it all?" I said as we stood there. I watched a swan move across the mirror of the lake. "All of this, what will you do with it?"

"Christ knows." He gave an impatient gesture. "Christ alone knows. Give it to the National Trust is my latest idea. I don't want this around my neck." He gave me a sidelong glance and smiled as his father once did. "Keep that under your hat. It's just a thought— but for God's sake, don't tell my mother."

"Could you do that?" I asked. He was very young, I told myself.

"I think so," he replied. "Maybe. I've seen what it does to people."

"And I've seen what a lack of money can do to people."

"Oh, money." He smiled. "I'm not worried about that. I've got brains. I can always earn money. As you've done, Julia."

I could hear Dan saying that—and he'd have given me the same sharp glance that his son did. I said: "I'd better go, Eddie. I'm going to be late."

I wished him good-bye. I turned away to my car. I drove out of the gates and concentrated on the road ahead of me. I didn't look back; I knew what I'd see if I did. My life, in the rearview mirror: I had no wish to examine that route or to consider its missed turnings. I had to be calm when I saw Maisie. If you are not calm, she seems to sense it, and it can cause difficulties. I drove the fifteen miles to the care home without incident, arriving there later than planned, on the edge of a spring evening.

The nuns had just finished celebrating Vespers when I arrived. I waited in the hall by the BVM statue. I rested my hand on her blue plaster dress. The nuns told me that Maisie was outside in the gardens. She was at work on her latest obsession, they said. I knew these obsessions of Maisie's. For several years, she had been obsessed with the color red and would spend hour upon hour, red crayon in hand, coloring sheets of paper. The color had to be even; it had to extend to every edge of the paper. If she was interrupted when there were still gaps in her coloring, there were tantrums.

After the red period, there had been a blue period, then a black. Then it was parallel lines, then grids. The obsession with grids lasted a long time, almost five years. All the red, blue, and black works, all the parallels and grids, were kept in careful folders in Maisie's bedroom. Now, the nuns told me, pointing me in the direction of the terrace, now it was circles. And what a splendid thing that was, they said; it kept her contented for hours at a time. Maisie's muscular control had become better with the passing of years, and she could now draw very good circles freehand. They weren't as perfect as those you would achieve with a compass, of course, but they were grand things. Did I know, one of them said, that the Japanese masters used to begin learning to draw in precisely this way? That was their apprenticeship. Only when they had mastered this technique were they considered sufficiently skilled to move on to more complex drawing. It might be years before they drew objects, let alone human beings.

Maisie will never move on to more complex drawing. I walked across the terrace and onto the lawns. This building, now outgrown by the order, is a pleasant place. It could only be England. It is reminiscent of the Abbey. The lawns overlook green fields, a narrow valley, and the river that runs through it. So still was the evening that I could hear the sound of the river as I walked. I came to a halt beside Maisie, who was seated in her wheelchair at a small table. It had been placed so it caught the evening sun and was sheltered by budding rosebushes. She was bending over her work, a pencil in her hand. A stack of pages, each with one near perfect circle, lay next to her hand. Pages of circles, of naughts, of nothings. I wondered how many hours had passed while she did this.

I took the chair opposite hers and sat down. Maisie did not acknowledge my presence; this is usually the case. I waited, listening to the river. I thought of my own future and what Nick and I might decide when I returned to London. I thought of my children. I thought of what Veronica had shown me in those upstairs bedrooms and what it might mean. I thought of Dan's son. I missed Dan, my lost Dan, missed him acutely.

I was not calm, despite my efforts, and I think my lack of calm communicated itself to Maisie eventually. She looked up. Her dark blue eyes rested on my face without sign of recognition, as always. I looked at my sister, who has never grown since her fall, my sister who is now a child of thirty-six. She cannot speak or communicate. She is incontinent. She is four feet nine inches tall. Her left leg, the worse fractured of the two, is in calipers. Her left hand has developed arthritis and is badly swollen and twisted. Her fair hair is graying a little at the brow. Her face is unmarked by lines, and serene; her gaze can seem untroubled; at other times, as Dan saw and Lucas captured in paint, it seems baleful. Her responses are unpredictable, and her moods are inexplicable. They pass across her face like clouds across the sky. At the moment, that sky seems gentle.

"Dan has died," I say. The words aren't planned. I speak them without premeditation. It's Dan I'm thinking about and his name that comes to my lips. Maisie doesn't react. Her serene gaze has moved—it's now resting on space, somewhere to the left, over my shoulder.

"I thought I should tell you," I continue, compounding my own stupidity. What was I going to do next? Tell Maisie about Finn's death? Tell her about my own life, ask Maisie's advice as to whether I should divorce or try again? Should I tell her about deception and a maze of lost opportunities? Ask her to explain bolts on a door and an old photograph? Ask her why Dan decided to die before I intervened—always supposing that I could have intervened, anyway? Beg Maisie, at last, to unravel the past, tell me what happened, why she jumped, why that summer went wrong, plead with her to make sense of everything? I might as well talk to a stone, to the air.

"The nuns tell me you draw circles now," I say. "They tell me you're good at it, Maisie."

I hate the patronage and desperation I can hear in my voice. I think Maisie dislikes it, too, though I'm probably imagining that. Her face takes on that expression of scorn I remember so well. She continues to stare over my shoulder.

So I revert: I do what I usually do when I come here on these monthly visits. I start to speak about the past. I conjure up memories to a woman-child who is without memory. I say: Do you remember that time, Maisie, when we had a picnic by the lake at the Abbey? Do you remember Daddy's memorial service, and all the fuss Stella made about the stone, and the carving on it? Do you remember how Stella locked herself away, and we took up those offerings to tempt her? Flowers, fiction, and food—do you remember that, Maisie? Do you remember how you saw Dan first, before anyone else did, that wild boy, looking through the glass pane in the church window?

Do you remember walking through the woods on my sixteenth birthday—and I had a new white dress, with stiff petticoats and *broderie anglaise*. Do you remember Bella and the cottage and the pink blancmange and the photographs of Ocean? Do you remember the tarot, the crystal ball, the chickens and guinea fowl, and how Finn gave them their names? Do you remember watching Joe plow, and counting the gulls and the furrows?

Do you remember your nuns and our first bicycles, and Dan teaching us to ride down Acre Lane, and how fast we went; do you remember the books, and the dogs and the scents, and the meals and the talks and the plans and the hopes and the fears. Can you remember Wellhead? Can you remember Holyspring? Can you remember the fields and the elms and the skylarks?

Do you remember it, Maisie, all the love and the pain and the loss of it, do you remember how it twists in the heart? Please remember it, Maisie, because if you don't, I'm the only one of us left who does, and when I'm gone there'll be nothing left, it will vanish like a dream, and no one will care. It won't matter, and why should it, to anyone?

Maisie, answer me, I say; please, just this once, answer me, because for once in my life, I don't know where to go or what to be or who I am. I am alone. Speak to me, Maisie.

I hear these words. I hear silence, the sound of the river and birdsong. After the warmth of the day, the air is cooling. I look at my sister.

Her attention has been withdrawn. She is no longer staring at the space over my shoulder. Her head is bent to the paper; her thick leaded pencil is clasped tightly in her fist. Her tongue is clenched between her teeth in concentration. With a firm, steady hand, she draws a perfect unwavering circle on the clean piece of paper in front of her.